S X

FRUITS
OF THE
POISONOUS
TREE

Other Books by Archer Mayor

OPEN SEASON
BORDERLINES
SCENT OF EVIL
THE SKELETON'S KNEE

FRUITS
OF THE
POISONOUS
TREE

ARCHER MAYOR

THE MYSTERIOUS PRESS

Published by Warner Books

A Time Warner Company

Mysterious Press books are published by Warner Books, Inc.,
1271 Avenue of the Americas, New York, NY 10020.

W A Time Warner Company

The Mysterious Press name and logo are registered trademarks of Warner Books, Inc.

Printed in the United States of America
First printing: December 1994

10 9 8 7 6 5 4 3 2 1

Library of Congress Cataloging-in-Publication Data

Mayor, Archer.
Fruits of the poisonous tree / Archer Mayor.
        p.   cm.
ISBN 0-89296-557-6
1. Gunther, Joe (Fictitious character)—Fiction.
2. Police—Vermont—Brattleboro—Fiction.
3. Brattleboro (Vt.)—Fiction.   I. Title.
PS3563.A965F78   1994
813'.54—dc20   94-15163
                                              CIP

To Jonathon and Elizabeth—
whose natural knack
for living joyously
makes me
happy, proud, and hopeful.

FRUITS
OF THE
POISONOUS
TREE

Chapter One

I woke with a start, muscles tense, my eyes darting around the darkened, familiar room. There was no sound, nothing amiss, no obvious cause for alarm. I was alone, in bed, in my apartment—as usual.

I pushed back the covers and swung my feet to the floor, wincing slightly as the cold hit my body. It was early fall, not even foliage season, but the nights were already yielding to occasional temperature drops, warning shots from an approaching winter.

I pulled on my pants and a flannel shirt and went into the living room, awash in the colorless half-light from the street lamps below. It was a large room, book lined, indifferently decorated, with a few pieces of comfortable furniture that would have been Salvation Army–bound a long time ago in a conventional home, but which my bachelor's habits had retained for decades, icons to their owner's flair for fashion.

I settled into a patched leather armchair by the dimly glowing bow window, wondering what had woken me up. It hadn't been a dream; my pager hadn't gone off, nor the phone. I cupped my chin in my hand and stared down at the vacant street.

Whatever it was, it had blown me out of my sleep like a grenade.

The twin beams from a pair of approaching headlights slid along the sides of the empty cars lining the street. I instinctively checked my watch—four-ten in the morning. The car slowed before my building and stopped, not bothering to park.

Tony Brandt—the police chief, my boss, and my best friend in the department—got out, glanced up at my dark windows, and crossed over toward the front door three flights below.

The same sense of alarm that had startled me awake rekindled with a jolt—more insidious, more real, and more frightening. Tony Brandt did not make predawn house calls.

I got up, tucking my shirt in, and returned to my bedroom for some socks and shoes, moving quickly, stimulated now by the sure knowledge that bad news, of a personal nature, was making its way up the staircase.

I met Tony on the landing, already buttoning my jacket. "What?"

He stopped on the stairs, his hand heavy on the railing. His eyes were sorrowful and his face drawn. Before he spoke, the dread inside me spilled over and caught fire. "It's Gail. She's been raped."

I sat in his car, not focusing on the passing blur outside, my brain in a turmoil as we drove through the silent, empty town. "I was just with her a few hours ago."

I paused, unable to think clearly, and repeated the same question I'd asked him right off, feeling like I was acting in a play I'd been a spectator to a dozen times before. "How is she?" The nagging sense that this time I was the one under the lights, my performance being scrutinized, added to my anxiety.

Tony had told me she was okay. He went into a little more detail now. "She was knocked around some, but nothing's broken, at least on the outside."

"Did we get who did it?"

He shook his head. "She was at home. She never got a look at him. I haven't talked to her yet. Ron's on call this week—the hospital phoned Dispatch, Dispatch phoned him. He got hold of me when he found out who it was."

I rubbed my forehead and tried to appear calm, knowing he was debating how best to handle me. He was already looking at this as an investigation, and wondering if he should let me be a part of it. I had worked with rape victims and their friends and families before; I knew the toll it took on them. I could see his dilemma, and how imperative it was for me to win his confidence. I didn't want to be excluded from the one case where I would bring both my heart and mind most forcefully to bear.

"You were at her house?" he murmured, cutting into my thoughts and harking back to the comment I'd made earlier.

"She fixed dinner." And later we'd made love—quietly, tenderly—as two people who'd known each other intimately for many years. "She had a lot to do in the morning. I left so she'd get a good night's sleep." As I often had before.

He glanced over at me, but I left it at that. No predictably emotional self-recriminations for not having been at the right place at the right time. Not out loud; not under scrutiny.

We pulled into the hospital's parking lot and walked up the ramp leading to the emergency room. Countless times, I'd come here to gather preliminary statements from victims of domestic violence, or assault, or vehicular mayhem, or rape. But never before feeling like this. To me, rape is murder without a corpse—it kills a piece of the spirit, leaving the victim alive to haunt us all with the violence of the crime. But while always sympathetic in the past, I'd never before had such a vested interest in the survival of that spirit.

Ron Klesczewski met us outside the nurse's station. Rarely the most self-assured of men, he was among the most conscientious, and the expression on his face spoke clearly of his distress. "I'm real sorry, Joe."

I nodded. "Thanks. Where is she?"

He pointed vaguely down the hallway. "They're doing the rape kit on her now—room four. Shouldn't be too much longer."

I started down the corridor. The tension in Ron's voice climbed a notch. "You going in there?"

I hesitated. Had I been the one in need of a friendly face, Gail's would've been the first I'd have wanted to see.

But our roles weren't reversed, and I realized with the chill of experience that in all probability, and despite the duration and intensity of our friendship, she would yearn for comfort from those of her own sex.

Standing there, my hand almost on the doorknob, I felt swelling up inside me the same combination of anger, sorrow, and frustration that I'd suppressed in Tony's car. But again I was stuck, my colleagues discreetly watching me from a distance. For the second time since learning of the assault, I struggled to reverse my own emotional tide.

A gray-haired nurse opened the door to room four barely wide enough to slip out. I caught her eye as she was about to pass me with what looked like a urine sample in her hand.

"Will you be going back in there soon?"

She answered cautiously, a hint of suspicion in her voice. "Yes."

"I'm Joe Gunther. Gail Zigman is a friend of mine. Would you tell her I'm here, that if she wants me, I'm available?"

Her face cleared and she smiled at me. "Sure."

I returned to where Ron was filling Tony in on the details. Brandt held his hand up as I approached, interrupting him. "Better start from the top, so Joe can hear it all."

Ron nodded, but I could sense his uneasiness. Rape was something we usually discussed in self-consciously clinical terms, occasionally lapsing into morbid humor to hide our own discomfort. Now, none of that applied. My relationship with Gail was no secret, and she'd been accepted as one of the department's extended family.

Ron's voice was conspicuously flat. "It happened two hours ago, about two-thirteen, according to her clock radio. She caught sight of the time just before he put a pillowcase over her head."

I knew that radio well. At eleven-sixteen last night, I'd been prompted by its oversized green numbers to leave Gail's warm side, put my clothes back on, and leave. She'd laced her arms around my neck as I'd leaned down to kiss her goodnight, and I'd taken advantage of the gesture to give her breast a last caress.

"What was the very first thing she remembers about the attack?" I asked.

"That's almost it. He must've been real quiet, or she was sleeping like a log, 'cause the first thing she knew, he was on top of her, pulling the pillowcase off the pillow to bag her. Her arms were already tied down."

That surprised me. "How?"

"He fixed lengths of rope to the bed frame and then rigged slipknots around each of her wrists. Not tight enough to wake her up, I guess, but enough to lock her up when she tried to get free."

I frowned. Gail was a sound sleeper. There'd been times I'd gotten into bed next to her and the first she'd known about it was waking up in the morning. But she'd been unusually tired on those occasions, unlike last night.

Ron was still talking. "He tied her legs down the same way

after he threatened her with a knife and warned her not to put up a fight."

I rubbed my eyes with my fingertips, trying to visualize a generic victim instead of Gail. I noticed the nurse I'd spoken to earlier going back into the examination room.

Brandt interrupted for a moment. "Did he use the knife?"

Klesczewski glanced at me nervously. "He nicked her a couple of times to prove he had it. Pinpricks, really. They aren't bad, Joe."

I felt my heartbeat beginning to pick up speed, not wishing to ask where those pinpricks had been placed, and suspecting the worst.

"On the phone, you mentioned she had some bruises," Brandt said. "How'd she get them?"

The door down the hallway opened again and the nurse gestured to me. With a sense of relief, I walked away from Ron's descriptions. At some point, I'd get all the details and look at them critically, professionally, and categorize them as Brandt was doing. A rapist rarely attacks just once, and he rarely changes style from assault to assault. If we matched his MO to others already on file, we could probably identify him.

But right now I wasn't interested.

Pleasantly, even supportively, the nurse blocked my way to the door, placing her hand gently on my arm. "Joe, Gail asked me to thank you but said she wasn't up to a visit just now. It's been quite an experience."

I glanced beyond her, so wanting to just push her aside and barge in. In my gut, despite my earlier rational analysis, I couldn't help feeling a simple hug would be of some help—especially in this sterile setting. But I nodded instead, unhappily aware of who that hug was meant to soothe the most. "Okay."

She steered me gently farther down the hall, toward another examination room. "We were wondering if you could help us out a little. We need a blood sample from you for the kit."

I nodded again. My semen would still be in Gail, and would have to be differentiated from that of her attacker. All part of the protocol—the gathering of evidence. It made me think of what Gail was going through now, giving urine and blood samples, having her thighs swabbed with moistened Q-tips, her pubic hair

combed out with a fine-toothed comb, her wounds photographed—
everything documented and confined in dozens of small and large
aseptically clean white envelopes.

I looked down into the nurse's warm hazel eyes, nestled in a fine
webbing of sympathetic wrinkles. "Sure. Lead the way."

She sat me down in a small room and had me roll up my sleeve,
quickly and efficiently wrapping a tourniquet around my upper
arm. Her voice was clear and bright, much younger than her appearance. "I'm new in town. One of the other nurses was telling me
you're the chief of detectives in Brattleboro."

"That's right."

She shook my right hand. "Elizabeth Pace. Pleased to meet you.
I'm sorry about the circumstances."

I understood she was trying to lighten me up a bit, perhaps help
me over the rejection I'd received at Gail's door. Her effort made
me bite back my gloominess, although I refused to play along
completely. "How's she doing?"

Elizabeth Pace hesitated, pretending to be judging a vein the
size of a small child's finger—something she could have stuck with
her eyes closed. "You've probably dealt with rape victims before."

"Yes."

She swabbed the spot with alcohol, making the vein glisten. "I
came from Boston. We had a lot of them there. We ended up
cataloguing them, among ourselves, from the off-the-wall hysterics
to the dead-eyed catatonics. You probably do the same kind of
thing in your work."

She lanced the vein with a needle attached to a Vacutainer
hub and quickly slid a vacuum tube in. A small squirt of blood
quickly filled the tube. "Given that sliding scale—and the assumption that all those women are in some form of shock—I'd
say your friend is taking it pretty well. She came here right
away, told us to call the police and her friend Susan Raffner,
who then contacted Women for Women. She's been helpful and
cooperative from the start."

Raffner was the head of Women for Women, a high-profile crisis
and counseling center that often worked with us on rape cases, and
of which Gail was a founder and a board member. The two of them
had been friends and allies through many a political battle.

Pace withdrew both the tube and the needle, released the tourniquet, and placed a cotton ball against the puncture wound. "Bend
your arm to keep that in place a few minutes."

She sat back and appraised me for a couple of seconds. "You've
known her a long time?"

I appreciated her professional directness. This was obviously a
woman of considerable experience in dealing with people, and she
was paying me the courtesy of being honest.

"A lot of years," I admitted.

"In my book, that makes you both victims, except nobody's
going to spend much time on you. Part of that's as it should be—
her needs are greater. But if you two are going to get on with
things, you better not forget that you took a shot here, too. Get
some help—it'll benefit both of you, especially over the next few
months. It's not going to be easy—you're going to be asked to put
your feelings at the back of the bus."

She grinned at me suddenly. "But you knew all that, right?"

"I've had a taste of it already."

We stood up and she ushered me to the door, patting my back
like a supportive parent, although we were probably close to the
same age. "You ain't seen nothin' yet. Treat her gently, okay? She's
a strong woman, but right now she's got invisible *Fragile* signs
stamped all over her."

I shook her hand again. "Thanks. And welcome to town."

I went back down the hallway, still passing Gail's door with
regret but feeling a little less isolated.

The lobby outside the nurse's station had been abruptly transformed from a bland, overlit, near-empty patch of linoleum to a
tension-filled convention of mutually distrustful people, clumps of
whom were clustered in separate corners. In descending order of
numbers, there were a half-dozen patrol officers, reinforced by several sleepy-looking off-duty people; three sharp-eyed representatives
of Women for Women, including Susan Raffner; a growing number
of curious hospital personnel; and three people whose presence there
caused my heart to sink—Ted McDonald, from WBRT, the local
radio station, and a reporter/photographer team from the *Brattleboro
Reformer*.

I found Ron Klesczewski surrounded by blue uniforms, giving

out orders to seal off Gail's house and property and to start some fast preliminary street inquiries in the hope of glimpsing at least one ripple in the town's social swampland before alibis and plausible denials smoothed the surface back over.

Tony Brandt, wearing his political hat, was standing with Raffner in the center of the room, speaking earnestly and quietly and occasionally glancing over to make sure the three media people were staying—as requested—temporarily out of earshot.

I waited for Ron to finish with one of the patrolmen, and tilted my head in the direction of the reporters. "How'd they find out so fast?"

He shrugged. "Don't know, but considering the crowd, I'm not surprised."

"They know it was Gail?"

He didn't answer directly. "She's a pretty big name in town; a lot of people know where she lives. We've had to use the radio to get our people out to her place, and both the *Reformer* and BRT have scanners."

I nodded. He put his hand on my arm and added, "They're usually pretty good about keeping the lid on names."

I saw that Tony and Susan Raffner were parting company, so I joined him as the Women for Women contingent headed up the hall toward Gail's room. "Trouble?"

He smiled thinly. "No—just staking out turf. I basically told her we would pull out all the stops—like we always do—and she basically told me we better do a hell of a lot better than that. All very polite." He glanced over to where the reporters were looking increasingly impatient. "Maybe I'll have better luck with them."

He left me to watch Raffner and her colleagues knock on the door to Gail's room and walk in. I hesitated a moment, groping for a reasonable excuse for what I was about to do—Gail had said she wasn't up to seeing visitors, albeit a while ago; she obviously was receiving people now, and her door had been left open.

For the third time that night, fueled by flimsy logic and pent-up emotions, I walked down that corridor, unsure of my motivations—or of what I expected to see.

At first, loitering in the doorway, I didn't see anything except the backs of the three women I'd followed, lined up in a tight semicircle around a chair in the far corner of the room. Then one of them bent forward to receive the hug I'd been longing to give, and over her shoulder I saw Gail's face—pale, swollen, her eyes shut tight with longing, a dark bruise beginning to take hold of her left cheekbone. Her bare arms encircled the neck of her friend, and I clearly saw the red welts the rapist's bonds had left around both her wrists. The sight left me rooted in place, without a word to say.

Her eyes opened then, and she took me in for a long couple of seconds before murmuring, "Joe."

Gail's visitors turned to face me, their expressions stern, even vaguely hostile, their usual professional demeanor transformed by the emotional toll of having to tend to one of their own.

I stayed put, thoroughly daunted by the anger I felt radiating toward me. Gail motioned to me to come nearer, and as I did, two of the women flanking her draped protective hands on her shoulders. It was not how I'd envisioned our encounter, and it triggered a small but resentful response deep inside me—toward the man who had done this to my best friend, toward the women around her who obviously lumped me with him, and toward Gail herself, for not allowing us this moment alone.

Fully revealed by the others who'd moved aside, Gail sat in an oversized, green hospital gown, her arms and legs pale and skinny by contrast, looking as frail as a lame child. Her swollen face, crowned by a tangle of disheveled dark hair, made her head look enormous atop a thin, almost shrunken body. The effect was so startling I instinctively crouched before her and reached to hold her hands in my own, my throat tight with emotion.

That twin gesture caught her by surprise, and made her jump and grip the arms of her chair. I dropped my hands immediately, embarrassed that my own professional training had been so easily overridden.

"I'm sorry," I muttered, painfully aware of the others all around, looking down at me. "How are you doing?"

She smiled faintly. "I've been better."

"I wish I'd been there," I added without thinking.

There was a predictable but silent stirring at this traditional male cliché, but Gail embraced its intent. She nodded and said, "I do, too."

I found myself groping for something to add, something other than what was crowding the front of my brain and which would do her no good at all—about how we would catch the guy and take him to the cleaners; that I wouldn't sleep till we had; that I wished we could turn the clock back a few hours.

"Is there anything I can do?" I asked instead.

"Catch the guy," Susan Raffner answered immediately.

I didn't take my eyes off Gail's. "Would you like to stay at my place? I could bunk out on the couch, or at the office."

Gail shook her head. "No, that's okay."

Susan Raffner's voice was softer and she touched my shoulder. "I'll put her up at my house for a while—lots of room. Lots of people, too, when she wants the company."

I conceded the point, and felt slightly foolish about my suggestion. "Thanks, Susan."

I paused a moment, trying to find the right words, knowing I'd done poorly enough already. Gail was looking at her hands in her lap—an obvious sign I'd overstayed a welcome I'd never received in the first place. Fighting the desire to at least touch her hair, I rose and stepped back.

"Well, I'll get out of here. Let me know if I can do anything to help." I looked around. "Any of you—day or night."

Raffner nodded her thanks. Gail didn't move.

I took another step toward the door. "They'll have to come back and ask you more questions—probably later today."

Gail's head shot up. Her cheeks were wet with tears. "You're not going to be on this case?" Her voice was incredulous, rich with betrayal.

I opened my empty hands to her, burning with anger that I couldn't immediately grant her one request. "I can't say. They may not let me."

Her eyes blazed at me. "I want you on it, Joe."

I pursed my lips and nodded. "Okay. I'll make it work somehow."

She looked at me a moment longer, her expression softening, becoming distant again—mourning the loss of something precious and irreplaceable. She went back to studying her hands.

I moved to the door, at once eager and reluctant to leave. I paused there and glanced back at her, at her friends beginning to close around her once more.

"I love you, Gail."

There was no response.

Chapter Two

The lobby, as in some Alice-in-Wonderland dream, was totally empty again, aside from Elizabeth Pace, alone and behind her curvilinear counter, who was talking on the phone. She waved at me and smiled as I passed through the electronically triggered double doors that led to the ambulance loading dock outside.

The brittle air came as a relief, slightly stinging my cheeks and lungs as I drew in a deep breath. I walked to the edge of the loading dock and stood there a moment, overlooking the parking lot, whose features were softly emerging as the harsh, unnatural sodium lights faded against the far gentler but more pervasive gray glow of the looming dawn.

I was so overwhelmed by the feelings inside me, I was having a difficult time making sense of them. Moreover, I felt an urgent need to do so—and get on with the job at hand.

Because that was the primary issue here—to do the job. I didn't have the opportunity of escaping to the daylong demands of an accountant, or a backhoe operator, or a logger—of burying myself in something totally apart from what had happened to Gail, and, through her, to me. My job was to eat, breathe, and live what she'd just been put through, not only because I was paid to do it, but because Gail had specifically requested it of me. That meant, despite Elizabeth Pace's well-intentioned advice, that I was going to have to batten down some of the psychological hatches she'd urged me to throw open, and hope that the pressures behind them wouldn't blow out at the wrong time or place.

There was, however, one nugget of solace in my awkward position. Of all the gremlins that conspire to torture the mind of a rape victim, the conviction that her attacker is still out there, waiting to attack her again, is one of the most terrifying. And my job was to bring that guy in.

Assuming they let me try.

"How's she doing?" The voice was Tony Brandt's, coming from the dark far corner of the loading dock.

I turned to see him leaning against the hospital wall, his hands buried in his trouser pockets, smoking his omnipresent pipe. "You still here? I thought you'd be at the scene by now, or updating the board."

Gail had recently been made chair of the town's board of selectmen, currently a group of notoriously fickle people—and not to be left outside the informational loop for long.

He smiled and pushed himself away from the wall to join me. "Already have—by phone. We're meeting in a couple of hours so they can shovel on the outrage, and I can tell them I can't tell them anything yet." He paused a moment to launch a couple of pungent clouds into the atmosphere, and then rephrased his opening question. "So, how're *you* doing?"

I hesitated before answering. We had been friends a long time, and had been allied in some tough political wars. He was someone I greatly respected, and who'd consistently earned my trust. I knew his inquiry went beyond its simple wording.

"I was just asking myself the same question. I'm not sure yet— part of it'll probably depend on Gail."

"You get to talk to her?"

"A little. She's pretty closed down. I don't think I'm what she needs right now."

"Ah," he nodded. "The sisterhood."

"Yeah." I turned that over in my mind a couple of times, seeing both sides of it—understanding it in our terms. "Kind of like cops when they get in a jam."

He chuckled. "Okay."

"She wants me on the case, Tony."

He worked on his pipe a bit, finally taking it out of his mouth and staring into the bowl for inspiration. "That's not exactly kosher. The state's attorney might have problems with it."

"Do you?"

He parked the pipe back in his mouth. "Not in theory. You're the best investigator I've got, and given Gail's prominence, and the SA being in a tight reelection bid, I'm going to need the best."

"But . . ."

He nodded slowly in agreement. "Right: 'but . . .' People could scream conflict of interest, and the SA's opponent could make political hay out of it, especially if we don't nail our man right off. Plus, if the case gets to court, as the last person who saw her before the attack, you'd be a prime witness. All a little awkward."

He turned and looked straight at me. "And there's the personal side to it. How're you going to perform? I noticed you weren't too eager to hear the details from Ron a while back. You and Gail have been together for years—might as well be married. Psychologically, it would be like investigating your own wife's rape. How would you handle it, if our roles were reversed?"

I wasn't going to make it that easy for him. "The same way you're probably going to. You've been thinking about this since Ron first called you—I saw you checking me out in the car. So what've you decided?"

He shook his head and snorted gently, amused at my stubbornness. "I'm putting you in charge, but not alone. Everything you do, think, or even dream about has to be flown by me first. Nothing happens without my prior knowledge, and everything is shared with the SA and his investigator immediately."

An indefinable part of me found its footing with those words, anchoring all my other mixed emotions, if only tenuously. I made myself believe that Tony Brandt had not only just helped me out, but Gail and the case's outcome as well.

Still, I couldn't ignore that he'd chosen the bolder of his options—something the state's attorney was likely to remind him of, and perhaps use against him if things went wrong. "James Dunn is going to love this."

Brandt jumped off the loading dock and began walking toward his parked car. "I've already told him. He doesn't, but he'll survive."

We drove to Gail's house together. A converted apple barn, the house was the sole remnant of a farm that had once dominated a hill overlooking Meadowbrook Road in quasi-rural West Brattleboro. It

stood alone now, the other buildings having long since been disman-
tled or moved, reminiscent of a frontier outpost of two hundred
years ago—tall, weather-beaten, built of rough, dark wood. Gail
had purchased it for near nothing over a decade ago, and had turned
it into a bright, soaring, multilevel cathedral of a home, filled with
plants, ceiling fans, colorful art, and intimate lighting. It was a
hidden showcase of prime real estate, and went a long way in
demonstrating why she was the town's single most successful realtor.

At the moment, however, it looked more like the police-department parking lot. Tony had to park halfway up the long driveway,
behind a string of patrol cars. We went the rest of the way on foot.

As we'd turned off the road, I'd noticed both WBRT's and the
Brattleboro Reformer's cars perched by the edge of the ditch. "How'd
you fare with them?" I asked, as we trudged up the steep slope.

"We played footsie a bit. They asked me if it was Gail, or if
she'd been hurt, or if we'd caught the guy; I mostly said, 'No
comment.' I also made it crystal clear I'd be pretty pissed if they
divulged any names. They looked shocked I'd even suggested it."

"You talk to Katz about it?"

Stanley Katz, once the *Reformer*'s "cops and courts" reporter, had
recently been made editor-in-chief by his Midwest owners, right
after he'd surprised them with his resignation—a true example, we
thought, of the Peter Principle run wild. But Katz, despite his
ambition, his cynicism, and his total lack of manners, had always
showed integrity. I just hoped this sole virtue could withstand his
bosses' thirst for wider circulation.

Tony seemed to have been thinking along similar lines. "I didn't
see the point. He'll be coming to me soon enough—he's got too
much bloodhound in him to leave it to some reporter. I did tell
his boys—and BRT—that they are not allowed on Gail's property,
but they'll probably try what they can."

He suddenly stopped and put his hand on my shoulder, the fog
from his breath shrouding his face in the chill morning air. "I'd
prepare myself for the worst, though. This could turn into a three-
ring circus before it's done, and I'd be amazed if Gail's anonymity
survived. Which means she—and you—will be front-page news.
You might want to consider that before we finish this climb."

I nodded and started walking again. "My being involved depends on you and Dunn. I'm staying till one of you stops me."

The front door of the building led out onto a broad deck, which in turn had a flight of steps connecting it to the driveway. We had just set foot on the deck and greeted the patrolman guarding the entrance when Ron Klesczewski stepped out through the sliding glass door, a nervous smile on his face.

"They let you on the case."

I smiled back at his obvious relief, although he didn't need me as much as he thought he did. I wouldn't have made him my second-in-command if he didn't have the wherewithal to do the job himself. But his lack of self-confidence, perhaps due to my constant presence, never allowed my belief in him to be put to the test. "You may regret that they did."

Brandt interrupted the obvious denial already half formed on Ron's lips. "He's on it, but he's not running it, at least not by himself; we'll be co-leaders on this. Is Todd Lefevre here yet?"

Ron scrutinized our faces quickly, trying to gauge my view of this unorthodox command. Like most cops everywhere, he saw the chief as a bureaucrat only—not a street cop—despite the proof, given time and again over the years, that Tony functioned easily in either role. "He got here about five minutes ago—he's inside."

He stepped away from the door and ushered us across the threshold. Todd Lefevre—the state's attorney's criminal investigator—was standing in the center of the building's main room, admiring its huge, bright space, extending high overhead, interlaced by enormous, ancient cross beams which supported, here and there, a varying assortment of staircases and lofts.

He turned as we entered—a small, round man with a pleasant, bookish look about him—and came over to shake my hand. "Hi, Joe, I was real sorry to hear about this."

"Thanks, Todd."

"J.P.'s set up in the bedroom," Ron explained. "He asked we keep the traffic down to a minimum, and that everyone stay on the brown paper till he's had the whole place checked out."

Lefevre, as diplomatic as his boss James Dunn was not, bowed out. "You go ahead. I've already had a quick look around—I'll talk to you when you're done."

Ron, Tony, and I followed the brown-paper runner that J. P. Tyler—the forensics member of the squad—had laid down across the floor and up a long, narrow staircase to the uppermost loft, tucked under the sloped ceiling some thirty feet up. This was where Gail had established her bedroom, in the walled-off equivalent of a tall ship's crow's nest.

As Ron had said, the house was essentially empty, in order to preserve J.P.'s sacrosanct "field of evidence." Still, I felt the presence of strangers everywhere, something the butcher paper underfoot did little to dispel.

All three of us paused at the top of the stairs and surveyed the bedroom before us. Dominated by a king-sized bed awash in light from an enormous skylight, it looked like a war zone—the pictures askew on the walls, the dresser swept clean of its bric-a-brac, the closets and drawers disemboweled, their contents resting on the floor and furniture like freshly fallen snow. The only sign of any order in this mess was a perversely precise display of Gail's more revealing underwear, hung neatly along the upper edge of a lamp shade.

A sudden flash from Tyler's camera caught me unawares, startling me, and finalized the room's transformation from intimate retreat to crime scene.

I stared at the bed he was photographing, its covers pulled all the way to the foot, exposing an unnaturally vast expanse of bottom sheet, wrinkled in the middle, stained here and there by minute spots of crimson. I remembered Ron's comment about a knife— "Pinpricks, really, just to prove he had it." The bed took on the vague aspect of a laboratory table.

"Any semen stains?" Tony asked, his tone a little brusque, as if the question were as much to challenge my objectivity as to get an answer.

"A few," Tyler answered, still focusing. He then lowered the camera and turned to face us, seeing me for the first time. Normally, his scientific detachment at a scene rivaled his inanimate equipment's, but he looked suddenly uncomfortable now, a reaction for which I silently thanked him. To his face, however, I merely nodded and said, "It's okay."

He looked at me clinically for another second and then nodded, satisfied. "What did she say about ejaculate?"

Ron cleared his throat, clearly embarrassed. "I didn't ask. We didn't talk for long—she was pretty upset—so I just stuck to the immediate stuff, like did she see the guy, or know him."

I stepped away from the doorway, fighting my own growing discomfort. I nodded toward the stains on the sheet, "Some of those are probably mine. I was here last night. What else have you found?"

Tyler took my cue and moved on. "Nothing much so far, but I only got here a few minutes ago, just long enough to take a few overall shots." He pointed along the bottom edge of the box spring. The rope slipknots Ron had mentioned at the hospital hung limply from the metal frame, two on each side, like a demented child's preparations for a miniature mass hanging. "Looks like common clothesline—the more she pulled against them, the tighter they got."

Ron added, "She told me she finally freed herself by shifting to one side as far as possible, cutting off the circulation to one hand until the rope loosened enough for her to slip the other hand out."

"What else?" I asked, swallowing against the tightening in my throat.

J.P. looked contemplative. "It's a messy scene, from a pretty angry guy. The underwear on the lamp shade might've been to taunt her, or us later on. Or it might've been to turn him on. Hard to tell. It's all definitely a display of power and control, from the ropes to the knife to the destruction. Was her bedroom usually pretty neat?"

"Yes, she's very tidy," I said, nodding. "So what does it all tell you?"

Tyler, befitting his scientific bent, had taken several training courses in rape psychology, some on his own time, and therefore had a better knowledge of it than the rest of us, who tended to rely on our past experience alone. He shrugged slightly. "Fast attack, preplanned, with a specific goal in mind. I noticed before I came up here that the disturbance seems to be confined to this room only. She lock up at night?"

"Generally." I looked to Ron. "How much did Gail give you?"

"She didn't see him or recognize anything about him. He didn't say much, and then only in a whisper, so she couldn't identify his voice. He came out of nowhere, and left right after he'd finished. She said she didn't notice any damage to the house except for here."

"You said she saw the clock before he bagged her. Did she look at it later?"

He nodded. "She freed herself at 3:37. She wrote it down 'cause she knew we'd want to know."

Tyler whistled. "Did he beat her up?"

"Why do you ask?" I countered, cutting Ron off.

He pointed at our surroundings. "Big mess, took a long time, a little knife play, a lot of pent-up violence. They usually don't stop at beating on the furniture."

Ron spoke up then. "She's actually not too bad physically—he nicked her a few times with a knife, but not enough to require stitches, and only whacked her hard a couple of times, just before he split."

There was a slight pause in the room as we contemplated what had happened here just a few hours earlier. I was struck by the way the references to violence had been confined to fists and a knife. It seemed to me the biggest source of violence hadn't even been mentioned.

J.P. frowned. "No knife here. I'll check the kitchen, but if he brought it with him, that's another indicator this was preplanned."

"You think anything was stolen?" Ron asked of no one in particular.

J.P. looked at me. "I would doubt it—maybe a single article, kind of like a souvenir. What do you think?"

I shook my head. "Too hard to tell the way things are now. The TV and stereo are pretty fancy, and they haven't been touched. She keeps her jewelry in that box over there."

I pointed to a hinged cherry case with an inlaid maple design I'd bought her years ago. It was lying on the floor, unopened, half under one of the night tables. J.P. gingerly stepped over to it and opened it, his hands clad in ghost-white latex gloves. It was full of the things I'd grown used to seeing Gail wear.

Tyler replaced the box exactly. "Later, you might get her to do an inventory. If anything is missing, my bet's on something personal." He glanced at the lamp shade.

"Jesus," Ron muttered to himself.

Tony Brandt cleared his throat and spoke for the first time. "J.P., you set for what you need?"

Tyler nodded. "I'd like Ron to help me go through all this with tweezers, but that's about it. Dennis is running the show outside, from the boundary line in toward the house. You might ask him if he needs more people. Otherwise, I'm okay. The fewer inside the better, as far as I'm concerned."

Brandt had his hands in his jacket pocket, fidgeting with his pipe. I knew he was dying to fire it up, something he never did at one of Tyler's scenes, for fear of leaving a shred of tobacco behind. He was obviously getting restless as a result. "Okay, then. We'll get out of your hair."

He turned on his heel and was about to work his way down the long staircase, with me behind him, when Tyler stopped us with a question: "You going to talk to her again soon?"

I answered. "We'll try to—kind of depends on her. Why?"

"It's a gut reaction so far, but I'd say the guy knew her—well enough that she'd recognize him if she's given the chance."

I nodded and went after Brandt, reflecting wistfully that no one in that room, including myself, had referred to Gail by name.

We found Todd Lefevre outside on the deck, chatting with the patrolman on guard. Lefevre's was an unusual—and highly envied—job. A law-enforcement officer, he belonged to no department. His only boss was the state's attorney, and his jurisdiction extended as far as the SA's. Lefevre could run his own investigations, delegate them to other officers, or cooperate as he was doing here. He worked with sheriffs, municipal departments, the state police, or any relevant federal agency, and could, if the job required it and the money was available, travel anywhere outside Vermont's borders to do what he had to do. The only downside was that he existed on the SA's say-so, and on the state legislature's willingness to fund his position, both of which definitely blunted the appeal. Not only was James Dunn a weak excuse for a human being, but from a one-time high of eleven state investigators, there were now only three full-timers left.

Chances were good Windham County would be allowed to keep one of those, but for the first time in his career, all bets were off concerning Dunn's future—and therefore Todd's—at the polls. Dunn's opponent, Jack Derby, was as low key and appealing as the state's attorney was not, and he seemed to have all of Dunn's ability, judging from a very respectable twenty-year career as a trial lawyer. Dunn's acknowledgment of his own vulnerability was highlighted by a sudden newfound interest in popular opinion, complete with awkward appearances at Rotary lunches and Red Cross fund raisers.

Todd didn't seem concerned by any of it, however, remaining as affable and easygoing as always, and he greeted us with none of the election-time heartburn I knew a major case like this ignited in his boss. Perhaps the prospect of Todd's own potential unemployment was offset by a secret enjoyment in finally seeing "the gargoyle" sweat. In any case, I knew he was too discreet to tip his hand either way.

"Tyler working his magic?" he asked as we joined him.

Brandt nodded, crossing to the railing. "Yeah, with Ron. How's Dennis doing?"

Lefevre chuckled. "He's got 'em organized like a bunch of boy scouts on parade."

Almost cut off from view by the far corner of the building, we could see a long line of patrolmen, traffic officers, auxiliary members, and even a few borrowed state troopers marching slowly across the field under the supervision of Dennis DeFlorio, the detective squad's weakest link. A good-ol'-boy with a limited imagination, and ambition only for his pension, Dennis was never good enough to give me hope, or poor enough to give me cause to replace him. He did, however, have an unflagging good sense of humor, never pretended he was better than we knew him to be, and always did what was asked of him. I was confident that if something could be found out in that field, he would probably come up with it.

"Where're Sammie and Willy?" Lefevre asked conversationally.

I turned away from the distant search line and looked at him. We had worked together before, and with pleasure. For years, he'd been both the liaison to Dunn's office and the man who inherited our cases after arraignment, when the SA officially took over control. But things would be different this time. Without having discussed it with Brandt, I knew Todd would be nearby from the start—the price Dunn was exacting from Tony for allowing me on this case.

I smiled, and accounted for the two missing members of my squad. "On the street, squeezing their snitches."

He nodded. Brandt had hitched one leg up onto the railing and was stuffing his beloved pipe with tobacco, glancing at the two of us without a word.

"So what's next?" Todd asked.

I appreciated his courtesy, granting me the illusion of leadership, but I waved a hand toward Tony. "I would guess a door-to-door inquiry's being made right now."

Brandt nodded, his cheeks puffing eagerly behind a balloon of smoke.

"Then I guess it's time to talk to Gail," I quietly conceded.

Brattleboro is an unusually mixed bag of a town. An icon of the previous century's industrial might, it has an imposing downtown of stolid red-brick buildings, a few obligatory tree-lined neighborhoods of impressive Victorian showpieces, and a vast number of standard, modest, updated nineteenth-century homes—in good or poor shape depending on the locale. The whole thing rests on a broken-backed, topsy-turvy, creek- and river-creased patch of land, and looks like some oversized historical plaster diorama that's been dropped by mistake and abandoned. Its few modern touches—a Dunkin Donuts right at its heart, and a dreary commercial strip heading north out of town—barely make an impression. It remains a town that the architectural ravages of the optimistic, taste-free fifties and sixties essentially bypassed.

Sprinkled throughout, however, just off the well-traveled thoroughfares, Brattleboro has a contrasting scattering of neighborhoods unique unto themselves. They are poor or middle class or shyly redolent of old money, but they all share a separateness from the whole, as if, during the town's early evolution, hidden genetic strains of other far-distant communities were subversively introduced.

One of these enclaves clusters around the Chestnut Hill Reservoir—a football-field-sized, cement-lined pond with a potentially commanding view of the town in three directions. Curiously, the potential is all that's there, since the surrounding trees have been allowed to slowly shut out the urban scenery, leaving only glimpses of what might be available. In the same vein, the standard trappings of an exclusive, remote, dead-end block have all been dressed down. The houses are muted to dullness, the street and lawns nondescript, and the reservoir itself, historically the town's first private water supply, is almost ugly—concrete-wrapped and encircled by a rusty chain-link fence.

It was overlooking this dark, brooding, cold slab of water that Susan Raffner had her home, and it was there that Lefevre, Brandt, and I, in two separate cars, negotiated the narrow, potholed street— twisting up like an urban goat path—in order to speak with Gail.

The uncharacteristically chilly weather set the mood of the place—the low, gray sky leaching down into the tentacles of the trees all around. The foliage was still green and full, but in this light it all looked somber and cold, our breath collecting in vaporous clouds about our heads as we emerged from the warm cocoons of our cars.

Raffner's house fit the tone set by its neighbors—large, dark, shingle-sided and unimposing—and like them, it murmured comfortably of a hundred and fifty years of generations spinning away through endless successive life cycles. It was through the echoes of those embracing ghosts that we made our way across the frost-dappled lawn, up the porch steps, and to the front door. It was still early, not even eight o'clock.

Raffner answered the door bell, her face poised between suspicion and hope. "You catch him?"

"Not yet," I answered. "Could we come in?"

The hopefulness died, but she opened the door wider and invited us to enter. "So what are you doing?"

"Everything possible. You know Todd Lefevre, from the state's attorney's office?"

She shook her head, and I finished the introductions, which she just barely acknowledged. Except for a cursory glance at Todd, she kept her eyes locked to mine, her intention to get a fuller answer clear. We were still standing around the lobby, and Raffner made no move to extend her hospitality.

"Gail told the first officer she spoke to that she had no idea who this guy was. We have teams in the streets conducting interviews; we have a forensics unit going over Gail's place with tweezers; and we've got people covering her grounds and neighborhood.

Something like this doesn't happen in a vacuum—for one thing, we're already pretty sure he knew her—"

Raffner snorted. "I could have told you that—he raped her in her own bed, for Christ's sake."

I held up my hand. "I meant there's a good chance she knows him, too, even though she didn't recognize him. That's probably the reason for all the cloak and dagger. If we can combine her memories of the attack with what we get from our investigation, it might be enough to come up with a name."

She looked at all three of us doubtfully. This was hardly the first time she'd dealt with this kind of situation—part of Women for Women's role was to escort rape victims through the legal system— and my request was certainly mundane enough. But Susan Raffner was used to dealing with "clients"—not members of her own board of directors. For her, as for us, this attack had become personal, and the trauma of it had cut through all our professional defenses.

"So you want to talk to her now? All three of you?"

Tony Brandt answered for me. "No—just Todd and Joe. I have a selectmen's meeting to make."

Raffner was slightly mollified. "That might be a little less intimidating. Let me go upstairs and check if she's up for it, then maybe you can see her."

Todd and I stood in the entrance hall for some fifteen minutes, checking out the wall hangings, staring out the windows, and generally paying homage to whatever psychological mood Susan Raffner was establishing.

When she finally gestured to us from the top of the stairs, we discovered how thorough she had been.

Gail was located in a bedroom overlooking the reservoir, but she wasn't in bed, which stood, fully made, to one side. Instead, she was sitting in an imposing wingback chair by one of the broad windows with the light to her back, dressed in a heavy, full-length caftan. Her feet were resting on a small ottoman and she wore a shawl around her shoulders. Despite her pale and hollow face, the overall effect—while blatantly orchestrated—was one of security and peacefulness, almost of regality.

It may have bolstered Gail's own psyche—I certainly hoped so— but it did nothing for me. My eyes locked onto hers from the moment I entered the room, and in them I saw only the pain, the exhaustion, and the despair of a woman in mourning. Once again, I felt a trembling at the center of my chest. I found myself yearning to embrace her, and unwilling to speak—knowing I couldn't do the first, and would have to do the second.

Todd Lefevre covered my initial paralysis by introducing himself, explaining what he was doing here, and asking permission to run a small tape recorder he'd pulled from his pocket, all while Susan Raffner and I found our seats—she comfortably by Gail's side, and I next to Todd on one of two unstable-looking straight-backed chairs Raffner had placed in the middle of the room like penitants' stools.

By the time he'd turned his machine on, I had found my voice. Leaning forward in my seat, elbows on my knees, getting as close to Gail as the staging allowed, I asked her, "Do you feel you can talk a little?"

She nodded. "Yes."

It was said with determination, belying the circles under her eyes and the gauntness of her cheeks, but its brevity spoke also of a need to conserve energy. This interview had to be done, but it would cost her, and she knew it. It was then that I noticed, under the caftan's long, roomy sleeves, that her hands were gripping the arms of her chair like a child's on a wildly swinging Ferris wheel.

"Would you feel more or less comfortable with me asking the questions? Or even being in the room? I can wait downstairs if you want."

Her face hardened, tight with impatience. "Come on, Joe."

I stopped hanging back. "You told Ron you didn't see your attacker—didn't recognize anything about him. Now that a little time has passed, has anything come to mind? Some phrase maybe, some allusion he made that might place him in context?"

Her forehead furrowed in concentration. "He didn't say much, and he whispered."

"What kinds of things did he say?"

"Orders at first—telling me not to kick after he got off my legs to tie them down."

"He'd already tied down your hands before you woke up, right? How could he have done that?"

Her face flushed abruptly. "I don't know; I was asleep. Why don't you catch him and ask him?"

I straightened in my chair, stung by her fury. I'd anticipated an awkwardness between us—not that she'd react completely out of character. It emphasized that our intimacy could be a real liability here, leading me to expect the even-keeled rationality I'd grown used to. The first rule in interviewing rape victims was to absolve them of any notion that the attack was their fault. I'd inadvertantly cut a corner there, assuming Gail would understand where I was heading. Her failure to do so told me that the same love that had driven her to want me here could just as easily turn to resentment if I presumed too much.

"I'm sorry." I pressed on, "He ordered you to cooperate while he tied down your legs. Is that when he used the knife? To persuade you?"

She nodded silently, her eyes downcast, the color draining back out of her cheeks.

"How did he use the knife, Gail?"

"He pricked my breasts; he said he'd cut off my nipples if I fought him."

I paused a moment, steadying my voice. "What words did he use—exactly?"

"His voice was very calm—the whisper, I mean. He didn't seem excited at all. He said—" She stopped, apparently thinking back. "He said, 'I'm going to get off your legs now; if you move a muscle, I'll cut your tits off.' Then he pricked me with the knife, and said, 'With this.' "

"What happened then?"

"He tied me down. I didn't move." There was a tremor in her voice, and she looked—I thought almost apologetically—at her friend Susan.

Raffner squeezed her shoulder and kissed her forehead maternally. "You did the right thing. Your life was what mattered; you did it to save your life."

"Did he ever use the knife again?" Todd asked in the brief lull.

Gail shook her head.

"But he did beat you," I added.

"At the end, just before he finished. He seemed suddenly frustrated—angry for the first time. It was the only time his voice changed. He said, 'You snotty goddamn bitch.' And then he hit me."

"Where?" Todd asked.

"In the stomach once; on the breasts a few times; and once across the face—hard."

I focused again on the livid bruise that rested on her left cheek like an enormous birthmark, and tried not to play out the violence in my head. "Why do you think he became frustrated? Couldn't he get hard?"

Her face underwent a subtle change, as if some deep-seated pain had just reasserted itself. It wasn't a grimace, but more a drawing out—a sudden thinning of her features, as if her entire soul was recoiling. "He was hard—the whole time."

I decided to step away from the subject a bit, to give her time to get used to the idea that we would have to ask her for all the details—if not now, then eventually, and probably many times over. "Your room was a mess—drawers pulled out, closets emptied. When did he do that?"

"Sometime in the middle. He stopped and I could hear him, going around the room."

"After he'd completed the sex act?" Todd asked.

All three of us looked at him, caught off guard by his choice of words. He didn't seem fazed.

Gail finally shook her head. "If you mean ejaculate, he didn't. He just stopped."

Todd looked confused. "He didn't ejaculate at all?"

"No."

I was intrigued by that, wondering if it explained his flash of anger at the end. "Did he say anything before or while he was trashing the room?"

"No."

"Did he seem violent—throwing things, breaking them?"

"No. I mean, yes, he threw things, but I don't remember much breaking. Something broke—I think it was that plate I bought in Mexico I had hanging on the wall from a wire—and he said, 'Shit' when that happened, but that's the only thing I remember. A lamp fell over, but I don't know if it broke or not."

"Gail," Todd spoke up again, unburdened by my emotional caution, "I hate to have to do this, but I want to ask you some questions about the rape itself—what this guy did, how he did it, in what sequence, for how long—things like that. Not only to help nail him, but so we can build a legal case for my boss. Chances are good this man's done this before, maybe even developed a style. If we can find a record of that, it might end up being just like a fingerprint."

"He wore gloves," Gail blurted out impulsively, influenced by Todd's last image.

"Through it all?" I asked, struck once again by her attacker's peculiarities.

"Not when he touched me—mostly—but I could hear him putting them on before he tore the room apart . . ." She hesitated. "And just before he hit me."

I put my hand on Todd's arm to stop him from going on. "Gail, what did he do with his clothes? Did he have them on when you first woke up?"

She shook her head. "He was naked."

"But you heard him getting dressed after he was finished?"

"Yes," she murmured.

"Where was he when he was doing that?"

"By the door."

I nodded to Todd that I was finished, and he began his detailed questioning, prompting her to take all three of us through her ordeal step by step, virtually movement by movement. He paused occasionally to ask if she felt like taking a break, but every time she urged him to continue, although all of us could see the toll it was taking on her.

I was grateful he was there, to do the job I doubted I could have done alone. Watching Gail reliving the event, her body still sore and throbbing from its brutality, her voice quavering toward the end, was more than I would have allowed. And yet, the three of them knew better than I—knew that she had to partake in her own reconstruction, and perhaps play a hand in the capture of her tormentor—or forever remain his victim.

Finally, two hours and several tapes later, Todd punched the *off* button on his recorder, the sharp metallic click making Gail start with surprise, her nerves frayed and hypersensitive. "That's it. You did a super job. I'm sorry we had to put you through it. And I'm afraid, as I said earlier, that this won't be the last time, either. To be honest, especially if we get this guy to trial, there's going to be times you wished you'd never called the police. But you did the right thing."

He gathered his equipment together and turned to me. "Is there anything more you wanted to ask, Joe?"

I looked at his blandly pleasant face—an unsettling mix of everyone's favorite Uncle Charley and an IRS auditor—with something approaching wonder. He'd been so perfect through it all—concise, polite, accommodating, solicitous, and efficient, to Gail and me both—that it almost challenged his sincerity. That viewpoint was mostly fueled by my own ambivalence, of course, but knowing it didn't help any. I was feeling increasingly disenfranchised, unable to be either the grieving partner or a sisterly friend, or even, I was beginning to think, an objective cop.

I turned to Gail, shoving all this to one side. "It's a bit of a long shot, and I know you've got a lot on your mind—a lot to work through—but if you can take some time to think about who might have done this to you, it would help."

Gail's eyes took on a bewildered look, glistening with tears. "I've tried, Joe."

The pain in her voice was saturated with despair and bafflement. Still, I persevered. "You've been looking for a monster. Think about normal people—men who struck you as just a little odd— too attentive, maybe, or too quiet, or who showed up at odd times with odd excuses. We're looking for anything out of the ordinary."

She shook her head at the vagueness of the suggestion, muttering, "So many people."

I stood up, and Todd followed my example. I hesitated, then leaned forward and touched the back of her hand gently and briefly. It was cold and unresponsive, and after I straightened back up, she tucked both her hands into the opposing sleeves of her flowing robe as if she'd suddenly felt a chill.

I groped a moment for the proper platitude—"We'll get him," or "You'll be all right," or "At least you're alive." I'd already tried "I love you" at the hospital, and had walked away feeling drained. I finally gave it up, said, "Take care. I'll come back to see you soon," as if I were addressing some octogenarian in a rest home, and took my leave.

Susan Raffner followed us downstairs and ushered us through

the door. She grasped Todd's forearm as he passed by her. "Thank you. That was the best interview I've ever seen."

He nodded and smiled sadly. "Sorry I had to do it at all."

She stopped me too, as Todd made his way down the stairs and toward the car. "I've got a problem with you, though."

I stared at her, my face rigid, the dormant rage in me giving a tiny lurch, like a tremor across a field of thinly crusted lava.

But she leavened her words by laying her hand gently on my arm. "I know what you're going through, Joe, but you can't expect her to hold your hand. She doesn't need to worry about you."

"I don't expect her to."

That was at best suspect, and Raffner knew enough to ignore it. "She also doesn't need you to bottle it up inside. Find someone to talk to—someone professional. Don't try to tough it out—it'll only do you both dirt in the long run."

I heard the echo of Nurse Pace's counsel earlier—except that lurking within Raffner's soothing tone I heard the subtle implication that she would be keeping a critical eye on me.

I nodded, but didn't respond directly. "Thanks for being there for her, Susan. Let me know if she comes up with any names."

She frowned slightly, nodded without comment, and closed the door behind me. I turned away and walked to the edge of the porch. The smooth, black surface of the reservoir met my gaze—ugly, wrapped in concrete, awaiting winter's frozen glaze. That's what they all expected from me, I thought without blame, despite their conciliatory words: a quick, solid solution, delivered without screwups. And they were right.

Chapter Three

My apartment was down the hill and two blocks over from Susan Raffner's house. I had Todd drop me off so I could shave, shower, and get properly dressed. It had been just a few hours since I'd been catapulted from my sleep by some primordial instinct, but I felt totally drained, as if I'd been up for days.

But there was a familiar inner momentum slowly picking up speed, fueled as it always was by the first faint stirrings of an investigation coming to life. Even now, with so many of my own emotions in play, the steadying instincts of over thirty years of police work were beginning to settle in. The sad irony remained, however, that the very questions lending me stability were the same ones torturing Gail: Who did it? And why?

I watched myself in the mirror as I prepared to shave—placing the lathered brush just below my right sideburn, working the creamy soap down one cheek, across my chin, and back up the other side. Methodical, practical, a habit born of endless repetitions. Gail's attacker had neatly stored his clothes before waking her up, had put on gloves before trashing the room and again before running the risk of hurting his hands by striking her. He'd covered her face, protected himself by tying her down, spoken only in a whisper, had shown very little emotion, and had come prepared with rope and knife—a neat and tidy man, not easily seized by impulse. Gail had been a carefully chosen target, and raping her had been the reward for good planning.

I'd given Gail a difficult assignment, asking her to conjure up possible suspects. Any public figure, but especially an outspoken, successful, left-wing feminist, drew resentment and contempt from far beyond her knowledge. Any vote she'd cast as a selectman, any unorthodox stance she'd publicly taken, could have lit the twisted, vengeful fuse this one man so tenderly cultivated. Separating him from his surroundings, based on the very subtleties I'd told her to think about, would take some doing.

Unless, as Todd had mentioned, he'd done it before.

An hour later, I stepped out of my corner office on the first floor of the Municipal Center and handed a single sheet of paper to Harriet Fritter, the detective squad's secretary, or "clerk," according to the current politically correct nomenclature—although Gift from God was more the way I thought of her.

She looked at it wordlessly over the top of her half-glasses, her snow-white eyebrows colliding in silent fury. Over the years that Gail had visited me here, Harriet and she had formed their own friendship.

"That's the MO of this morning's rapist, or at least what we have so far. I'd like copies sent to the Vermont Department of Corrections, state police, SA's office, and the sheriffs' and local police departments in all surrounding counties, including Massachusetts and New Hampshire. And see if you can't set up an appointment for me with Lou Biddle at Probation and Parole—this afternoon if possible."

"How's Gail?" was all she asked.

"A little shaky—determined as hell. How many people know she was the victim?"

She looked slightly apologetic. "Probably everyone in the department. She's like family because of you; it hit people hard. Are you worried her name will get out?"

I began walking toward the door leading to the building's central hallway. "Tony says it's just a matter of time. It might help if we can nail this guy first."

I left her staring at the information I'd typed up, sadly shaking her head.

I crossed the hallway to the police department's other half, where Dispatch, the officer's room, and the chief's office were located. I was buzzed through the main entrance by Dispatcher Maxine Paroddy, and walked straight to Tony Brandt's door. A fog bank of pipe-tobacco smoke told me of his presence somewhere within.

Brandt squinted up at me from his computer console like a distracted mad scientist surrounded by toxic fumes. "You back?"

"Have been for a while—just wrote up the MO for distribution."

"How was Gail?"

The ever-present question. "She's hanging in there. She insisted on giving Todd a full statement; he said he'd have a transcript to you this afternoon."

"Learn anything?"

"The method was thought out, careful. Off the bat, I'd say he's smart, doesn't want to be caught, and she knows him. He took too many precautions to avoid being identified. That probably means he's local, too."

Brandt made a sour face. "Great. What did J.P. come up with?"

"Don't know yet. I was about to head back up there, but I thought I'd check in first."

He looked glumly at the computer screen for a second, and then checked his watch. "Todd at his office?"

"He was headed there when I saw him last."

"All right." He hit a couple of keys on the computer and stood up, reaching for his jacket. "I'll come along."

"There's no need; J.P.'s probably almost done anyway. I just want another look around."

Tony was putting the jacket on. "Sounds like a good idea."

"I'll be right back," I tried one last time.

He stopped, one arm in a sleeve, and looked at me levelly. "Get used to this, Joe. Trips to the can you get to take by yourself. Everything else, you have company." He waved a hand at my obvious irritation. "I told you that at the start. I want you baby-sat."

We walked to the rear parking lot in silence, and both got into my car. The temperature was merely cool by now, warm enough to unlock those smells of earth and trees that Brattleboro managed to retain despite its urban appearance.

"You having problems with this arrangement?" he asked.

"No; it was more for your sake."

He went along with the lie. "Don't worry about it—I could use the break."

But I'd seen his wary expression just before he'd insisted on coming, and I remembered the meeting he'd had with the board of selectmen while we were interviewing Gail. Before that meeting, he wouldn't have been so compulsive about following the guidelines he'd arranged with Dunn. "I take it the board's not too happy with my being on the case."

He hesitated slightly. "They have their political concerns."

"Which are high-pitched enough to put you in this car."

He was silent for a minute, as I got us out onto High Street, headed toward West Brattleboro. "Let's call it preventive mainte-nance," he finally said. "A down payment of good will. If the shit hits the fan, maybe they'll remember how we kowtowed. Besides, that was the deal with Dunn."

I sighed at the familiarity of it all—how every major investiga-tion came fully loaded with politicians, press people, and "concerned citizens" with ulterior motives. I was grateful Tony Brandt seemed content with his hybrid role of half cop, half politico, catching most of the flak so we could focus on our jobs.

But I sensed an additional factor in his reasoning—one that explained why he wasn't putting too much blame on the board. I was the potential loose cannon in all this, not our predictable, hand-wringing town leaders. I carried the gun, gathered the facts, and it was my lover and friend who'd been raped. Despite his apparent support, Tony Brandt was obviously less trusting of my state of mind than he was letting on, and happy to use politics as an excuse to keep me company.

"You having second thoughts about me?"

He gave me a surprised look. "No. Why?"

"Everyone else sounds pretty dubious. That's a lot of people to ignore."

"They don't know you."

I left it there, forcing him to listen to the echo of his own doubts. He finally shifted in his seat to better face me, and added, "I'd be an idiot if I wasn't concerned, Joe."

I smiled for his sake. "True—so ask."

"All right. Now that you talked to her, how're you handling it?"

"Not well, at first, but I think I've got it now. The one way I can help her and myself is to do the job."

"That simple? And what happens after we catch the guy?"

I shrugged. "None of it's simple—it's just all I've come up with. I guess I'll see what happens next—to both of us."

Gail's property loomed ahead on the left as we climbed the road, its entire two acres encircled by a single, pathetic-looking yellow ribbon, repeatedly stamped, "Police Line—Do Not Cross." At the entrance to the driveway, which now held only a handful of cars, we were stopped by one of our own patrolmen, and by a woman emerging rapidly from a parked Volvo, who ran to cut us off. Brandt groaned.

"Want me to keep going?"

"No," he muttered, rolling down the window.

Mary Wallis was one of the women who'd been attending Gail at the hospital, and one of Tony's prize antagonists. An outspoken advocate of women's rights, she was dedicated, hard-working, and utterly dependable when it came to the cause, but she could also be dogmatic, narrow-minded, and combative—the type of partisan that made feminists like Gail and Susan Raffner true connoisseurs of a gift horse's mixed value.

"Hi, Mary," Tony called out. "What are you doing here?"

She was obviously not in a sociable mood. "I've been looking for you. What've you found out?"

Brandt looked apologetic. "We've got everybody working on it, Mary—"

Her eyes narrowed, "Which means you're stuck. What about Jason Ryan?"

Tony turned briefly and looked at me. I merely raised my eyebrows. Jason Ryan was well known to us—and anyone else who regularly read the letters to the editor in the *Reformer*. A local restaurant owner, he was a major town crank, finding conspiracies under every rock and proclaiming his discoveries from any available pulpit. The police department was one of his supposed regular dens of iniquity, apparently a clever cover for a major drug ring, among other things.

"What about him?" Tony finally asked.

"Have you questioned him? He threatened Gail at the last selectmen's meeting—said he knew exactly what she needed to get her off her high horse."

Gail hadn't mentioned it to me, although that came as no surprise—it sounded like the kind of thing Ryan leveled at almost everyone he met. But this was no time to be dismissive. I leaned forward to better make eye contact. "What was the nature of the disagreement?"

"He was there to protest the wording of a sexual-harassment clause in the new town employment guidelines. He got ugly over it, raving about the dykes and fags and whatnot."

"Sounds pretty typical," Tony said softly.

It was the wrong response. Wallis stuck her face closer to his. "You should know, considering how long it took you to upgrade the wages of your own female employees."

Brandt's voice went flat. "That was years ago. I had to follow the town attorney's rules of procedure. You can't change everything overnight."

She opened her mouth to respond, but I interrupted. "Mary, this run-in with Ryan, did Gail get into it with him, or did he just foam at the mouth a little and take off?"

She let go of the door, shaking her head in disgust. "Jesus. One of your own men had to come in and escort Ryan from the room. He was threatening her, for God's sake, and you don't know a thing about it."

Tony muttered, "Let's go. We'll look into it, Mary—thanks for the tip."

She looked at him grimly.

I drove by the patrolman who'd been listening to all this with a half smile on his face—the small joys of hearing a boss reamed out in public—and continued slowly up the long, steep driveway.

Brandt rubbed the side of his nose with his finger. "That was a little embarrassing. Did you know anything about it?"

"Nope. Gail never mentioned it, and it wasn't in our daily reports."

"The board met last Thursday, didn't they? Let's find out which of our people was asked to throw him out. I think we ought to dig into this a bit."

I smiled as I parked and cut the engine, wondering who was talking—the cop or the politician. Both sounded worried.

All the earlier activity had ceased. There were no more lines of searchers crossing the field like grouse hunters looking for lost change, no reporters lurking at the boundary lines. The house, apart from four cars parked outside, looked empty and forlorn, standing out against the flat, gray sky, its windows blank. As we slammed our doors, a patrolman sheepishly stepped out onto the deck from inside.

We climbed the outside steps to join him. His name was Marshall Smith—a native Floridian who always took on a slightly bereaved look around this time each year, as summer's warmth began to wilt. He was wearing a coat, unlike us, and it was tightly buttoned up.

I opened the door for Tony and motioned to Smith to follow suit. "No point getting cold. Where's J.P?"

Smith pointed across the broad central space of the house. "Downstairs bathroom. You just missed Ron—left about ten minutes ago."

We found Tyler standing on the toilet seat, scrutinizing the sill of a single high window, and muttering into a small tape recorder.

"Find out how he got in?" I asked after I'd heard him snap the recorder off.

J.P. pocketed his machine and picked up the camera from the top of the toilet tank. "I think so; from the evidence, I'd say it was through one of the living-room windows." He focused on the window sill, took a shot, and then climbed down.

"What about that?" I pointed at the high window.

"It was locked and painted shut. I've documented all the windows, just in case it comes up later."

That fitted Tyler's character perfectly—a scientist in cop's clothing. His job description was as broad as the rest of ours, encompassing all the usual duties of a small-town detective; but where some of us relished working the streets and the snitches, J.P. was most at home in forensics. I often wished we had both the budget and the business flow to have him specialize only in that.

"You about finished?" I asked him.

"Yup. That was my last stop." He led us toward the living room. "As far as I can tell, the guy entered through here, using a knife or a shim to slide the lock back on the window."

He kneeled on the sofa in front of the row of sash windows and pointed to the middle one. "This is the intriguing part, and what makes me think whoever did this was invited inside the house at least once before: See this lock?"

He manipulated the ancient clasp that swiveled from the top of the lower window frame to grasp the bracket attached to the bottom of the upper frame. It swung to and fro so loosely that he barely had to touch it. "Just slipping a blade up between the frames from the outside is enough to pop this open. In itself, that's no big surprise—these are notoriously lousy locks—but this is the only one in the house that's this loose, and the only one of the older windows to open easily. In fact, all the others are either jammed or painted shut, or are newer windows with more pickproof locks."

Tony frowned and unconsciously pulled his pipe from his pocket and began filling it. Tyler's not protesting was a sure sign he'd finished his search.

"Any prints outside the window?" I asked.

J.P. shook his head. "Ground's dry and hard. Dennis and his crew didn't find anything outside. I did come up with something here, though." He pointed at the sofa he was still kneeling on. "A trace of vegetable matter. Assuming he did enter this way, he had to step on the sofa to get to the floor, so I'm hoping what I found came off his shoe."

I looked dubiously at the dozens of house plants that Gail had placed on almost every flat surface available.

Tyler answered my question before it was out. "I took samples of all the plants to rule them out. I'd also like to remove the lower half of this window and replace it with plywood. Some tool marks were left on the wood and the lock. If we find this guy, we might be able to match his pocket knife, or whatever he used, to the marks."

I nodded my approval and turned to face the building's interior. "So you think he entered here, went straight up to the bedroom, and then left by the front door?"

"Yeah." Tyler led us from the living room to the staircase leading up to the bedroom. "And by now, I'm almost positive he brought both the knife and the rope with him. I found Gail's knives in a rack in the kitchen, all arranged by size. There don't seem to be any missing, and they're all clean as a whistle."

He looked back over his shoulder as he began climbing the stairs. "Of course, the guy could've used one of them and washed up afterward, but I didn't see any evidence of that. As for the rope, there's none in the house that matches what he used. Joe, did

Gail have a sports knife or a pocket knife tucked away anywhere? Something he might have found easily and used?"

I thought about that for a moment. "She has a Swiss Army knife she carries in her purse, or on her belt when she goes camping. She didn't say it was missing."

"You might double-check, and ask her about the rope and the window lock, too, just to see if something comes to mind. Maybe some visitor made a comment she'd remember about the lock."

Tony, by now trailing an aromatic cloud of smoke, spoke up. "How long ago did she have the newer windows put in?"

I shook my head. "I don't know—maybe a year. I'll ask her for the name of whoever installed them."

We arrived at the top of the stairs, where J.P. stopped us at the threshold, looking directly at Tony. "I want to preserve this room at least another twenty-four hours—even put a guard on it so we can guarantee its legal integrity, if you'll let me."

Brandt nodded. "I think we can do that—sure." He removed his pipe and cradled it protectively in his palm.

Satisfied, Tyler turned to the room like a lecturer to his blackboard. "I'll have to compare my notes with Gail's statement to nail down the sequence of some of this—I can't tell if he trashed the place first and then raped her, or vice versa—but I have a pretty good idea of how he moved around the room."

He took a couple of steps forward, being careful not to disturb anything. "In a way, it's like an archeological dig—you know that, generally speaking, whatever's at the bottom was put there first. So all I had to do was link various articles on the floor—and how they were layered—to similar items still left in the drawers and the closet. That way, I could roughly trace his progress around the room, figuring out which drawers he'd emptied first and last."

"Which told you what?" Tony asked.

Tyler pulled a sheet of paper from his pocket. "Here's the crime-scene sketch I did of the room. I left out a lot of the clutter to clarify what was where, but you can see the guy's progression—very methodical. He toured the room in a clockwise direction, wiping out things as he went."

"Telling you he's repressed, compulsive, and angry as hell?"

Tyler looked at me and tilted the flat of his hand back and forth in an equivocal gesture. "Maybe; I don't have the psychology training to take this too far. The best I can do is establish a pattern—something we might find in somebody else's files."

Brandt coughed gently and cleared his throat. "Yeah—not ours. This doesn't ring any bells with you, does it, Joe?"

I shook my head. "I've already circulated the basics to surrounding departments. J.P., if you could translate what you just told us into something for them to check against—and send it out in a second bulletin—it might help. Then we can cross our fingers this bastard didn't come from California."

I looked at the rope nooses still hanging from the bed frame and felt the familiar twinge in the pit of my stomach. "What else was left behind?"

The contented gleam burned brighter in Tyler's eyes. "A few things, actually, some of which won't be his—like your fingerprints, hair, and—" He suddenly stopped, realizing his blunder.

I got him off the hook. "Semen."

His face, for the first time to my knowledge, flushed bright red. "Right. Anyway, barring those, I still think we have a couple of hair samples, the tool marks, the vegetable matter I found downstairs. And this . . ." He pulled a white envelope out of his jacket pocket and held it open to the light.

"What is it?" Tony asked.

"Looks like a fiber," I answered, squinting at a tiny comma of red material suspended in the middle of the envelope like a microscopic goldfish in a bowl. "Where'd you find it?"

"Right here." J.P. pointed to the door frame opening onto the bathroom, catty-corner to the door in which we were all standing. There was a thin sliver protruding from the rough, natural-wood frame, about half a foot up from the floor.

"I'll be damned," I muttered.

"What?"

"Gail said he was naked when he attacked her, but that she could hear him putting his clothes on afterwards by the door—right here."

"You or she have any red-wool shirts?" J.P. asked.

I scratched my head. "Sure. Christ, those are common as dirt around here—at least shirts with red in them. You probably have one, too."

Tyler carefully crossed the room to the closet and lifted the corner of a dress that had been tossed on the floor. Beneath it was the sleeve of a red-plaid shirt. "Like this?"

"Yeah."

He shook his head happily. "Not the same. When was the last time you wore your shirt in this room?"

"I don't know; a long time ago, if ever."

He shoved the envelope back into his pocket, a pleased expression on his face. "Then this may be where he screwed up. Find the shirt in his possession, and this little baby," he patted his pocket, "will place him at the scene."

"Maybe," Tony cautioned. "Even if we do find the shirt, he might have sixteen different explanations for how a piece of it wound up here."

Tyler's smile was undiminished. That was a legal problem, and not his department. And I had to admit, I shared his pleasure. Regardless of how far it led—and despite my own skepticism—it was a step, and that's what these cases were built on.

I gave Tyler a thumbs-up. "Here's to that being the first nail."

He nodded confidently. "There'll be more. By the way, when we get back to the office, I'm going to need some fingerprints and hair samples from you, to rule some of this out."

For the first time, I didn't mind being intimately involved.

Tony and I left Tyler to do a final sweep of the place and were almost back to the car when I saw Dennis DeFlorio's grimy sedan, dust-covered and blotched with rust, nose into the driveway and grind up the hill to join us.

I waited for him, one arm crooked on the open door, my foot perched on the rocker panel, while Tony took advantage of the pause to fire up his ever-ready companion once again.

Dennis pulled alongside and heaved himself out—a round man, unhealthy in appearance, who even in a coat and tie looked somehow untucked and disheveled, an effect heightened by his pants being stuffed into the tops of a pair of laceless, ancient hunting boots. I saw Tony examining the entire package like a slightly dismayed anthropologist.

After he'd led the search of the grounds, Dennis had coordinated the neighborhood canvass, but he hadn't actually come face-to-face with me since the start of all this, and was the least successful at hiding his discomfort at my personal connection to the victim. He scratched his ear, looked at the house, the ground, the cars, and everywhere else but at me, and, aside from an undirected half wave of the hand, accompanied by a muttered, "Hi, Joe," he finally ended up addressing Brandt exclusively.

"Hi, Chief. Dispatch said you were here, so I thought I'd give you what we got so far."

Brandt smiled and nodded, transparently amused with Dennis's anguished pantomime. "Shoot."

DeFlorio pulled a battered notebook from his pocket and flipped it open. "It's not a great neighborhood for this—not too many houses, and they're pretty far apart—but so far I got a jogger goin' by around ten, a dog barking maybe an hour later. The hottest lead is a car leaving this driveway a half hour after that—"

"That was me," I interrupted.

Dennis pursed his lips, obviously taken aback, but then carried on, his eyes glued to the page, still ignoring my existence. His voice, however, was just a shade flatter, "—another vehicle a few hours later, and then two male voices talking in the road about half an hour before dawn."

"Explain that last one," Brandt said.

"It's a little vague. I think it might've been two guys walking— for exercise, you know? The person who heard it said there was no sound of an engine—just two voices going by slowly, talking normally."

"You find out who they might've been?"

Dennis shook his head. "But not everybody's home. At work, you know? And if they were exercising, they could've come from a mile away or more. I just did the local area. I didn't mention it, but Ms. Zigman's car was also seen leaving her place at a little before four."

"Anything more on the second car you mentioned?" I asked.

He finally gave me a furtive glance, as if checking to see that I hadn't fallen to pieces. "Not too much—it might've been a truck, though, and technically, counting Ms. Zigman's, it was actually the third vehicle seen. The only one who heard it was an old guy who lives about three houses down. He was going to the bathroom when it went by; saw the lights through the window. Said he could tell by the way they jiggled and were high off the road that it was either a truck with a cap on the back, or something like a Bronco, with a squared-off look to it. It was a dark color anyway—like dark blue or green, maybe."

"He'd never seen one like it in the area before?"

Dennis was becoming more relaxed with my presence. "He might have. He said he'd have to think about it a little and get back to me. Maybe he's got something and maybe he just likes the attention. I guess we'll find out."

Brandt checked his watch impatiently. "So basically, except for someone seeing Joe's car leaving this driveway, we don't really have anything yet."

Dennis pursed his lips again, obviously put out. "It's a little early—and nobody told me Joe'd been here last night. I thought I had something."

Tony backed down. "No—you're right—we screwed up there. Should've told you."

"Dennis," I asked him, "what time was the truck or Bronco spotted?"

He checked his notes. "About four-fifteen."

That was disappointing. Gail had remembered three-thirty-seven as the time she'd finally freed herself. "What about anything before last night? Did anyone see anything unusual over the past week or so?"

DeFlorio shook his head. "No. I asked, but all I got was the usual: postman, UPS trucks, yard men, garbage truck, normal traffic . . . Stuff like that."

"The ten o'clock jogger?" Tony asked.

"Nope. There are a few regulars, but nobody running that late."

"You know that from the runners themselves, or from people watching them?"

"Mostly people watching. I talked to one woman who jogs, but she goes out in the morning, around eight. Everyone else I interviewed was pretty old—retired. I'll have to come back later to check on the ones who work. They're probably the health freaks." He made the last statement with understandable scorn, given his own physique.

I turned away and looked across the valley to the east, the distant gray mountains of New Hampshire forming an almost seamless bond with the dull sky overhead. Before this day was finished, we'd have dozens of reports like Dennis's, involving dozens of innocent people, that would have to be checked out, from the postman to the joggers to the old guy peeing in the middle of the night. Until something or someone fit the circumstances and the time slot of Gail's attack, we would have to cross and recross the terrain before us, looking at every detail like hyperactive bird dogs.

It wasn't the stuff of movies—but it was the way things worked. Somewhere out there, there was evidence to be found, people who knew things maybe they didn't even realize—all rungs on a ladder we had to build from scratch, hoping it would lead us where we wanted to go.

Chapter Four

I hadn't forgotten what Mary Wallis had told us about Jason Ryan. Upon returning to the Municipal Building, I went to find Billy Manierre in his well-tended cubbyhole built into a corner of the patrol officers' room.

Billy had been with the department longer than any of us. White-haired, avuncular, and no more capable of passing the department's physical fitness test than I would be of surviving a fall off a high cliff, he had evolved into more than the mere head of the patrol division. Over the decades, he'd achieved the rank of confessor and blue-collar guru. Always in uniform, and always even-natured—the calm in the midst of the proverbial storm—he generally held court from an office with the most-used—and most-comfortable—guest chair in the department, supposedly lifted from the new courthouse across the street.

He was sitting at a typewriter parked on the edge of his desk when I poked my head around the door. There was a form rolled onto the platen, but Billy wasn't filling it in; he was staring at the keyboard with the stolid indifference of a frog in a pond, seemingly willing it to do his work for him.

"Not inspired?" I asked.

He sat back and smiled at me wistfully. "It's hard doing things you don't see any point to. Have a seat. Tell me how you're holding up."

"I'm all right. Focusing on the job helps."

"And Gail?"

I sat down slowly, wondering when my answer to that would begin to hold more promise. "I don't know. Not a hell of lot's ever happened that we haven't been able to talk about . . . sooner or later . . ." I left it hanging. It hadn't been my intention to use him as a sounding board, but stimulating that kind of impulse in people was part of Billy's talent. When he'd been in his prime and on the street a lot more, it had made him a very good cop.

He smiled now and folded his hands across his ample belly. "Give it time. She knows you're there. Sooner or later she'll let it all out—not that you came here to listen to any words of wisdom from me."

"Who knows?" I answered truthfully, "I could've gone elsewhere to dig up what I'm after. Don't sell your talents short."

He looked pleased. "So what do you need?"

"I heard Jason Ryan got a little carried away at the last selectmen's meeting, and that they called on us to escort him out. Nothing's in the files—you know anything about it?"

He was still for a moment, mulling it over. I knew he knew—one of the other secrets to his success was that nothing happened in the department, or the building, for that matter, that he didn't know about. The question he had to be pondering, therefore, was how much trouble this little oversight could cost one of his people.

"Problems?" he finally asked.

"Probably not. I just want to talk to whoever did the escorting. Ryan's been presented as a suspect."

Billy's eyes grew round. "On the rape? Ryan? Jesus, I don't see that."

"Maybe not."

He nodded solemnly. "Talk to Al Santos."

I pushed myself out of the chair. "He out on patrol now?"

"Yeah—Maxine'll find him."

I moved to the doorway and looked back at him, giving in to an irresistible urge. "Why wasn't anything filed on Ryan?"

He gave me a sorrowful face. "Oh, Joe—all that paperwork for nothing. He was just doing what he always does."

I smiled and waved good-bye to him, crossing the officers' room to get to Dispatch and Maxine Paroddy next door, but in fact I wasn't all that amused. I wouldn't have traded Billy Manierre for the best that New York or Boston or L.A. might have to offer, but I also knew that sometimes innocuous events—like Jason Ryan's little outburst against a woman who was raped a few days later—should damned well be in a file somewhere, paperwork or not. It was always possible that a warning sign like that might be noticed before it was too late.

Maxine Paroddy—ax-handle thin and highly efficient—was perched on her rolling secretary's stool, gliding across the dispatch room's polished floor to answer the radio, a phone nestled in the crook of her neck. She acknowledged the short message on the microphone, gave me a wink and a be-with-you-in-a-second gesture. Then she rolled back across the room, pulled a file from a drawer, and read from its contents into the phone, all with the grace of a dancer.

"What's up?" she asked, after she'd hung up. You did not sit down to chat with Maxine. It was a waste of her time.

"Al Santos?"

She gave me a quick smile and pointed to the radio. "That was him checking in. He should be pulling into the parking lot right about now."

Santos was our New York City Police Department transplant, on the payroll for years by now, but still boasting a trenchant Bronx accent and a big-city union man's ingrained prejudice that rank, like class, should have strictly defined boundaries. I didn't give him the chance to get out of his cruiser once he'd cut the engine, but slid into the passenger seat next to him.

"Hey, Lieutenant. How's it goin'?" His grin looked disarmingly bright beneath his thick black mustache, but his eyes watched me carefully. "I was sorry to hear about your girlfriend."

I didn't bother responding, both because I was tiring of it and because I knew he didn't much care one way or the other. While we'd always been cordial to one another and had never crossed swords, his approach to me over the years had made it clear I was a "suit" first and foremost, and where he came from, suits were annoying, baffling, highly capricious creatures.

"I heard you threw Jason Ryan out of a selectmen's meeting the other day."

Santos chuckled easily, his eyes unchanged. "Yeah—and he was somethin' pissed about it, too. Kept bitching about his constitutional rights; called me a Nazi." His voice darkened suddenly, the suspicion briefly rising within view. "He suing us or somethin'?"

"Not that I know of. What was he so worked up about?"

He relaxed slightly, one potential bomb defused. "Dunno—they just called me once they got sick of him."

"Was he angry at anyone in particular?"

Santos thought back a moment, and then he looked at me with his eyes wide, abruptly comprehending. "Holy shit—he was laying it on your old lady pretty . . . I mean, he was real mad at Gail Zigman. You thinking he did it to her?"

"I don't know, Al. I'm just fishing around. What did you actually hear him say?"

He looked at me silently for a moment, and I was surprised by the renewed look of distaste on his face. It occurred to me that something in my tone had pushed one of his rank-conscious buttons—as if I was looking for answers without divulging my reasons—a typical "suit" stunt.

"You know the mouth he has on him," he finally replied evenly.

I was impressed how irritated I was by that answer, and his attitude in general. I expected better from a fellow officer, especially during a major investigation, and the passing references to "girlfriend" and "old lady" returned to me with less innocence.

"Did he say anything threatening, either in their presence or when you were alone with him?"

"Nothing he hasn't said before—called her a 'flatlander dyke,' and said the board was pussy-whipped." He hesitated, perhaps worried that he'd overplayed his nonchalance, and tried for a shortcut, "Well, you know."

I smiled good-naturedly, disguising my growing anger. "Yeah—nothing new there. And I suppose Gail handed it right back to him?"

He took my reaction at face value and smiled back. "Hey—you know how it gets sometimes."

It was a neutral enough response, but I had my suspicions. My interest in Ryan temporarily faded. "Give a woman a title and a gavel, right?"

He rose to my expectations of him. "Yeah, right."

"So Ryan was just blowing off steam?"

"Pretty much; I mean, he was disrupting the place. They did right to call me."

"But what he was saying didn't amount to much—in your book?"

"Not really." Santos stole a glance at his watch.

"Just out of curiosity, did he suggest taking her down a few pegs while you were escorting him outside?"

Santos shifted slightly in his seat, perhaps sensing something unusual in my persistence. "Don't take this personally, Lieutenant, but he did say something about a good fuck setting her right."

I could feel the pressure building on my temples, but I kept my voice level. "You didn't fill out a report on it, did you?"

"Didn't see the point," he admitted.

I turned to face him, feeling free at last to vent some of my rage. "How about now that she got her good fuck? Were you thinking about filing a report now?"

He looked both surprised and angry that he'd been set up, predictably missing the point. "It was the local nut case shooting his mouth off, Lieutenant—it didn't mean anything."

I threw the door open and swung out, welcoming the fresh air on my face. I leaned back inside the car where Santos was sitting stiffly, his eyes straight ahead like an adolescent wishing all adults would vanish. "You know that for a fact, do you?"

"Yes, I do." His voice was barely audible.

"You better hope you're right, Al, or we'll talk again with more company. Don't ever pull this kind of shit again."

My fury grew exponentially as I walked back to the office—not just at Santos, whose error had been no worse than Billy's laxity, but as much at myself. Instead of immediately seizing Al's information as the possible lead it was, I'd used his procedural sloppiness, and his predictable sexism, as a target for my own frustration. Knowing what Santos and his buddies would later make of this episode made me feel exposed, and did nothing for the professional demeanor I was struggling to maintain.

I headed back to the squad room reluctantly, wishing I could invent some excuse that would keep me on the street, at least for the rest of the day. What had happened to Gail was just a few hours old—a fresh crime with fresh leads. Statistically, that gave it "quick to solve" potential. People's memories would be sharp;

any covering up would be either ongoing or slipshod; and the combination of Gail's status and the SA's political needs would allow for a no-expenses-spared, all-out investigation. That was the good news.

The downside was all inside me, and had been building steam since Tony had pulled up to my place this morning. That part of me didn't want to work around the clock, finding the man who'd turned Gail's life upside down. It just wanted to spend time with her, helping her to rebuild her equilibrium. I could rationalize that one role fulfilled the other—I was on the case, after all, at Gail's insistence. And I knew that giving her psychological "space" was not only sound, it was out of my hands. But none of that addressed my own emotional needs.

Nevertheless, as I reentered the Municipal Building, I began feeling slightly better—or at least more in control.

Harriet Fritter, not surprisingly, seemed to sense some of what was chewing at me. The even-tempered matriarch of an enormous gaggle of children, grandchildren, and at least one great-grand-child, she was a veteran observer of us all, and her sympathetic smile as I walked in was enough to move me up a few more notches.

"I got hold of Lou Biddle at Probation—he's calling a special intelligence meeting at Rescue, Inc., in forty-five minutes. He thought it might be more efficient for you to brief the whole group, instead of relying on phone calls or faxes."

The intelligence meeting was normally a monthly arrange-ment—a gathering of law-enforcement representatives from all the surrounding jurisdictions. It had operated discreetly for years, meet-ing on neutral ground, and served as an informational conduit that both cut the red tape and made for less formal relations among the participating agencies. That Lou had called them together—and in no time flat—was testimony to the support we could expect on this case. Brandt had been right about how Gail was being viewed, at least by those who wore a badge—she might as well have been my wife.

I thanked Harriet and asked her if either Sammie Martens or Willy Kunkle had reported back in from their respective sweeps of the town's nether reaches.

Sammie's head popped up from behind one of the soundproof

panels that separated the four desks set up in the middle of the room. "I'm here."

I went around the corner to find her climbing off her chair. Slim, dark, and almost overly intense, she was also as small as a teenage girl, with a similarly impulsive style. Over the years, I'd had to pour oil on occasionally troubled waters between her and her colleagues. Whether it was being the first and only woman to have been made detective in our department, or just a natural competitiveness that bordered on the cutthroat, her drive could make her difficult to deal with. Only Willy Kunkle, infamous in his own right, seemed totally unaffected by her.

Her expression was not encouraging. "I chased down almost every connection I have, Joe. There's nothing stirring out there. And there's a lot of interest—everyone knows who the victim was, and they're all dying to be on the inside. If any of them knew, I'm pretty sure I would've heard about it. I'm real sorry."

I shrugged it off. My conversations with J. P. Tyler had already braced me for bad news. The meticulousness of Gail's attacker— the preplanning, the caution he'd taken to conceal himself—had persuaded me we wouldn't find him hanging out in a bar, bragging about his latest score.

"I don't think this was a spontaneous assault anyway. Did you compare notes with Willy?"

She nodded. "He didn't find anything either. He's getting coffee in the officers' room, if you want to talk to him."

The door to the hallway opened and Ron Klesczewski walked in, purposeful and obviously full of news. I turned back to Sammie. "I'd like to talk to both of you, actually. Round him up and bring him back over here, will you?"

Sammie left, and I shepherded Ron into my office cubicle, parking myself on the corner of my desk. "What've you got?"

"I'm setting up a command post in the extra room—bulletin boards, a dedicated phone line. Billy's given me one guy out of each of his shifts to man it. We've already started classifying those neighborhood witnesses by what they saw and at what time, and Dennis is chasing down the ones he missed at their work places instead of waiting for tonight. We figured the sooner, the better. With any luck, we'll construct a chronology of the whole night and then see what sticks out."

I raised my eyebrows. "Does Tony know about this?"

Ron smiled. "He authorized it. I don't know if it's James Dunn or the board—or maybe both—but the chief's catching some serious heat on this."

I remembered Tony's pessimism about keeping Gail's name under wraps, and what would probably happen once it got out. "I think he's just preparing for the worst. You doing all right coordinating it all?"

Klesczewski nodded emphatically. "Oh, yeah. I like it—tips are already starting to come in. It's interesting, separating the bullshit from the solid stuff."

"Good. Keep at it. Run things from the command post, keep me and Brandt updated, and use the patrol division to chase down leads as you see fit. Get Dennis to help you out. If you see the need for a squad meeting before Brandt or I do, call it yourself. Before too long, you're going to be in a better position than any of us to know the overall picture, so throw your weight around a little."

I was pleased to see the satisfaction in his eyes. His youthful insecurities were hardening with time, and while he'd always have problems with someone like Willy Kunkle, I no longer harbored Tony Brandt's ebbing skepticism that I'd backed the wrong horse as my second-in-command.

Sammie Martens and the infamous Kunkle were loitering outside my door—she almost at attention, a note pad clutched in her hand, and he typically leaning against the wall, sipping his coffee, and gazing out the window, looking bored. I waved them in as Ron happily departed for his newly established nerve center.

There is a media-hyped misconception among many people that the only discernible difference between most cops and the people they bust is the badge in their pockets. In my personal experience, that's mostly bunk—except with Willy. He was a cynical, hard-bitten, nasty-minded street cop with a withered, crippled left arm he kept from flopping around by anchoring its hand in his pants pocket. He had no friends that I knew of, no pleasures outside his job, and no discernibly pleasant characteristics. He'd had a wife once, whom he'd taken to beating and who'd left him years ago, and he'd once fallen so far into the dumps that I'd thought we'd have to fire him. Instead, a sniper's bullet in the arm had retired him on permanent disability.

That should have marked the end of his career, except that I'd encouraged him to challenge the town under the Americans with Disabilities Act to get his job back. He'd never thanked me for that apparent folly, but he'd never given me cause to regret it, either. For as bitter and disagreeable as he could be, he understood the workings of Brattleboro's least-desirable social circles like no man I'd ever met. And while he talked like them, acted like them, and at times even appeared indistinguishable from them, Willy Kunkle was positively driven to putting the "bad guys" in jail. He was, like a highly motivated but disturbingly hostile attack dog, unbeatable at his job. I just never had him tour the schools upholding the department's image.

"Sammie tells me you didn't have any better luck than she did."

"Nope."

"Did either one of you hear Jason Ryan's name come up while you were poking around, in any context at all?"

Kunkle's cup froze halfway to his lips. "Ryan? Don't you think it's a little early to get that desperate?"

Sammie merely shook her head.

"He threatened Gail just a few days ago—got so unruly at a board meeting, Santos was called in to throw him out."

Kunkle shrugged instead of responding.

"I'd like you two to check him out—discreetly—especially what he was up to all last night. Find out if he's been mouthing off about Gail, and see if you can nail down exactly what was said at that meeting."

Kunkle made a face, drained his Styrofoam cup, and tossed it into my trashcan. He easily—even gracefully—shoved himself out of my guest chair with his powerful right arm.

Sammie, more polite, was looking at me dubiously. "You want us both on this?"

"As far as it makes sense—I want it fast and thorough. There is one other item, though. J.P. thinks Gail's attacker entered through one of the living-room windows, and that he knew which one to choose beforehand. She had several windows replaced about a year ago, by whom I don't remember—some local outfit. We're thinking one of the workmen might have scoped her place out back then."

They both nodded at that one, knowing full well that similar patterns had proven out in the past, in both rape cases and robberies.

Kunkle headed out the door, but Sammie lingered a moment, looking a little uncomfortable. "I'm sorry about what happened to Gail. Must be tough when it's someone you know."

I didn't argue the point.

The next several hours were spent at Lou Biddle's emergency intelligence meeting—discreetly held in the back room of the local ambulance squad—where a dozen of us culled through reams of files from Vermont's Department of Corrections and those of law-enforcement agencies from most of the towns and counties around Brattleboro, including several from Massachusetts and New Hampshire.

The mood was not encouraging, however. Stimulated already by Tyler's faxed circulars, these people had already given their files a preliminary survey, all without a "hit." Now, each of them discussed their second and third choices, mentioning the presence of a knife, the blindfolding of a victim, the use of physical restraints, the timing of an attack, or the fact that it had taken place in the victim's home. And while I gratefully accepted even the most remote possibilities, I did so without much hope.

I was thanking all those around me for their help when the pager on my belt erupted with its familiar chirping. As the rest of the people in the room began gathering their things and filing out the door, I used a nearby wall phone to call my office.

Brandt answered immediately. "You finished there?"

"Just now."

"You better get over to the *Reformer*. We just heard through the grapevine that Gail's name is hitting the headlines tomorrow morning."

I didn't answer at first. Tony had predicted this would happen, and I'd even made a certain feeble mental effort to prepare for it. But now that it was becoming reality, I felt caught totally off guard.

"That information's from the paper itself," he added. "One of our friendlier contacts. Sorry."

I smiled bitterly at that. "Does she know yet?"

"I have no idea."

I weighed my options—to see Katz at the paper, to try to see Gail, or to do nothing—and tried not to let my feelings get the better of me.

I thanked Brandt for letting me know, gathered up the files and gave them to Todd Lefevre, and told him I'd meet him at the office—that I wanted to quickly swing by the newspaper first. Whether it was a lack of concern, or a perceived look in my eye, he asked me no questions and didn't insist on joining me.

I drove over to the *Reformer* offices in a simmering rage. The *Brattleboro Reformer*, once a reputable small-town blend of global and community news, had been going through rough times. Purchased a year ago by a Midwest news conglomerate, it had been reduced to a *USA Today*–style tabloid, its front-page banner changed from traditional black to sensationalist red, all its articles reduced to one-page news bites, and its old editor and much of his staff either encouraged to leave or downright fired.

One of the few holdovers, just barely, had been Stanley Katz, who'd actually already begun working for the *Rutland Herald*, in the western part of the state, before he was lured back. In the old days, as a writer, Stanley had delighted in making the police department miserable, motivated by a conviction that his efforts kept us honest. Now, rehired as editor-in-chief, he had loftier—and we thought more realistic—goals in mind, such as saving his paper from bankruptcy. Its brief and trendy foray into nouveau journalism—an unappealing package in a politically hard-nosed town—had been costing its owners a bundle, and everyone knew that Katz had his hands full.

Knowing all this convinced me that, in an effort to stem the tide, he'd reverted to the take-no-prisoners journalism of yore.

But there, it turned out, I was wrong. The first person I met at the *Reformer* building, exiting the front door, was Susan Raffner.

Of course, the sexual assault of a prominent citizen had taken place—name or no name—and Women for Women was a logical place for a paper to seek background and quotes. But there was something in Susan's eyes as we approached one another, an odd look of challenge that made me stop in my tracks and rethink my notions about Katz.

My reaction startled her slightly, and saved me from repeating the gaffe I'd just committed with Al Santos. "She knows what she's doing, Joe."

There was only one *her* between us, and only one thing *she* could have done that would have brought Susan and me together at the *Reformer*.

"You're just the messenger."

She flared at that. "She's done an amazingly courageous thing, entirely on her own. She's a strong woman—you know damned well the only reason I'm here is because she's in too much pain to do this in person. I'm proud to have carried her message here. If every abused woman had her guts, and everybody else stopped tiptoeing around this issue, we might start putting an end to it. Day after day, I listen to women who've been beaten or raped or mentally tortured, and I try to give them support and counsel, and all the time I wish I could say, 'Stand up for yourself—plaster the walls with this bastard's name. Tell his boss and his co-workers and his drinking buddies and everybody else what he does in his spare time.' But I can only murmur that kind of advice, and then be understanding when it's ignored. Who gains the most through an abused woman's silence? It sure isn't other women."

I was stunned at my own thickheadedness. I should have known Gail would honor her own philosophy with action, especially at this worst of times. It was testament to my own lack of balance that I'd totally overlooked the obvious.

But my speechlessness stood me in good stead. Susan Raffner, her face still pink from her impassioned outburst, gave me a sympathetic smile. "Sorry—I'm taking all this a little personally. You're probably the only cop who doesn't need that lecture."

I smiled back weakly. "I wouldn't bet on it. Do you know how Katz is going to handle it?"

"Front page, with a head shot of Gail. They're going to run a statement from her, an interview with me, and an updated story—I guess about what your people are doing." She suddenly looked embarrassed and passed her hand across her forehead. "Is that why you're here? When I saw you, I just assumed you were going in to try to stop it."

I shrugged, not wanting to justify her stereotype, and happy to leave her slightly off balance. "Don't worry about it. Give my love to Gail."

She called after me as I moved toward the building's front door, "Do you have anything new to tell Katz?"

I stopped and faced her. "It sounds like a cliché, but we're doing everything we can. I'll tell him we're following a variety of leads—some quite promising—just to make whoever is out there sweat a little. But I'll tell you privately we don't have squat yet. We will, though. We'll find the guy."

She merely nodded, accepting it at face value.

I half turned away again, and then paused. "Could you do me a favor?"

"What?"

"Tell Gail I'm proud of what she did."

Chapter Five

I didn't hunt down Stan Katz immediately. I borrowed a phone at the receptionist's desk to call Brandt. I'd let Raffner assume why I was at the *Reformer*, but I knew better than to stick my neck out much farther. This was the last place Brandt wanted me visiting, especially alone.

I confirmed to him that Gail's name was being released and gave him what details Raffner had told me about Katz's plans.

"So how do you want to play it?" he asked once I was through, acting much cooler than I would have in his shoes.

"If we let them quote us now, it sounds more like we're part of the overall plan—backing Gail up. It might help pacify the Mary Wallises of the world."

"Does Katz know you're there yet?"

"No. Want me to wait for you?"

There was a long pause—Tony weighing the options before him—before he surprised me with his answer. "No. Do it alone."

I waited for him to explain his reasoning, but that was all he said. I finally filled in the void by muttering, "Okay—I'll let you know how it goes."

The *Reformer*'s home was a new, informally laid-out building, with a large central room filled with clusters of computer-equipped desks. People came and went largely unchallenged, pausing at the receptionist's counter only if they needed directions. I therefore made my way to Katz's small, windowless office without being announced, and was settling myself into his guest chair before he even noticed my arrival.

He looked up abruptly from the paperwork he'd been studying. "Joe—Jesus Christ. Small world."

I smiled and nodded at the typed sheet still in his hand, hoping to impress on him that my visit and Raffner's were coordinated. "That Gail's statement?"

He looked at the paper as if it had appeared from thin air. "You know about this?"

"Sure—we applaud her courage."

He paused over my use of "we." "The PD help her make up her mind?"

I gave him a suitably disappointed look. "Come on, Stan, does that sound likely? I would've thought Susan set you straight on that. You're not going to butcher another story, are you?"

He sighed slightly. "Spare me."

"It's department policy that the release of the victim's name be her decision alone, but we're always grateful when and if she does. Makes our job a lot easier."

"And I guess you could stand all the help you can get." He smiled.

I kept playing the bland diplomat and planted another optimistic kernel. "We always appreciate any help, although the investigation's coming along pretty well."

"Meaning what? Suspects?"

"Meaning just what I said."

Katz pursed his lips and glanced back at Gail's statement, obviously hoping for a way to get under my "official statement" tent flaps. "How will her identity being known help you guys? Won't it just mean more pressure?"

"Only on whoever assaulted her. Now everyone who knows Gail will be trying to think back to any suspicious event they may have witnessed between her and another guy. We certainly encourage that."

"So you don't have any suspects."

"I didn't say that." My spokesman-ese was getting more fluent by the second. "No investigation is built in a vacuum. The more supporting evidence, the stronger the case—that's a quote."

Katz smirked in response. "Swell—original, too. If that's all you got, why're you here?"

"Didn't want you thinking we were anything other than support-ive of Gail's decision."

He tried challenging my implication that Women for Women and we were closely allied. "Raffner didn't mention the police at all."

"That's why I'm here. Susan's main concern is Gail, as it should be. Mine is that the *Reformer* not get it in its head that Gail and we aren't in full communication. She's been an asset to this investigation from the start, and her letting you publish her name is just another example of that."

Katz sat back in his chair and crossed his hands across his narrow stomach, realizing he was getting nowhere fast. He chewed on his lower lip for a moment, apparently pondering how to get to me. "What's it like being the victim's companion?" he finally asked.

I stood up to go. This was exactly where my being the police-department mouthpiece could seriously backfire. "I hope you never get to find out."

"Why not share it? You're human, too. People would benefit hearing about this from a cop."

"Maybe, but not now." I moved toward the door.

"You don't want to give ammunition to the people who think you shouldn't be within a mile of this case, right?"

"Talk to Brandt and Dunn about that. I do what I'm told to do."

I expected some sarcastic crack following that, but he surprised me by letting out an exasperated laugh. "My God, Joe, doesn't what happened to Gail piss you off just a little?"

I looked at him without answering.

He suddenly left his chair, crossed over to the door, and closed it. "Off the record—just you and me: How're you holding up? Has Brandt set anything up to protect you if the shit hits the fan? 'Cause I'm already getting phone calls from people wondering how the hell you're going to stay impartial."

I dearly wanted to be gone from here. "Like I said, talk to him."

He shook his head. "I got the official line, Joe—I'll run it like you want me to: 'The police and Raffner and Gail are cozy as all hell.' This is just for me."

I looked at his face more carefully then, startled by his apparent candor, and noticing for the first time how exhausted he seemed. I began to understand what was eating at him—it had less to do with my position and more to do with his. "I guess things were a little more clear-cut back when you were a hired gun."

He went back to his chair and sat down heavily. "I went after the story, pure and simple. I fought you guys to get it, and I fought the editors here to run it the way I wrote it." He paused a moment before adding, "I've had to widen my views a little."

I sighed inwardly, feeling less on the spot. At the beginning of this conversation, his blatant intention had been to lead me into an indiscretion, even, I suspected, after he'd shut the door and played "off the record." But I sensed now he'd slipped off that track, distracted by the pressures of his new job. He was sounding like a man who had no one to talk with.

"The owners breathing down your neck?"

"They don't know this business—not at this level. They saw USA Today go through the ceiling and thought, 'Hey—why not us?' All their money comes from shopping malls and condo villages. They have no idea a tabloid tattler just raises the hackles of a town like Brattleboro."

I thought of the damn-the-torpedoes ambition that had marked most of Katz's career as a reporter. "And you hope Gail might be the story to turn them around?"

He caught the tone of my voice. "Look, we're not exactly best friends, but we have worked together in the past, right? And besides the all-reporters-eat-shit paranoia you guys call normal, have I ever really stuck it to you—at least when you didn't deserve it?"

"That's too many qualifiers, Stan. If you were a used car, I don't think I'd buy you."

He became abruptly more animated. "Cut it out. I'm trying to do something you ought to be supporting here. The shopping-mall kings want short, dirty details and peek-a-boo photos. I want this paper to be a public forum, where this town can share its views—"

"Like it used to be."

"Fine—only better, but if I don't get the PD to help me, it's not going to work and the paper'll go down the tubes."

"And you'll be out of a job."

His face fell into a scowl. "That's not the point. I can get another job."

"But your résumé wouldn't look as good."

He began to respond angrily, but I gestured to him to wait. "All right, all right. I'll pass this along to Tony. But if you want us to open up more to you, you'll probably have to make some show of good faith."

"Like what?" His eyes narrowed instinctively.

"Tony's the one to work that out with, but—just as an example—I don't think it would hurt if you let us see some of the articles you're about to print concerning us, just so we can correct the mistakes."

His jaw tightened. "No way."

I reopened the door, relieved at least that my involvement in the case had been forgotten for the moment. "Well, like I said, it's not my department. Talk to Tony. In the meantime, giving us a fair shake in the paper might help win him over."

He nodded distractedly, his enthusiasm blunted by my unsympathetic self-interest, and he didn't even look up as I left. I did understand his position, even though I'd made little effort to show it. He'd never had the responsibilities he was facing now, nor had he ever had to build bridges of mutual trust, at least not of this magnitude. And time was running out for him. The paper's circulation was dropping.

As I walked through the darkness to my car, I wondered what a thawing out between the paper and the department might entail, and how far Katz was willing to go. After all, how much credibility do you give a man under pressure?

The irony of the question—and that I was the one asking it—was not lost on me.

Driving slowly down Putney Road, back toward town, the disappointment I'd felt following the intelligence meeting returned in force. Despite what I'd told Stanley, not finding an MO that clearly fit the case was a serious setback. It meant we had nothing to help us differentiate among the growing number of suspects already coming our way. Tyler had gloated over his single strand of red wool and said, "This little baby will place him at the scene." But it was a precarious boast at best, and would be a downright hollow one if we never found a *him* in the first place.

I was about half a mile from the end of the Putney Road commercial strip, close to where it dips down to the bridge which connects it to one of Brattleboro's older and more affluent residential neighborhoods, when my portable police radio put out a call to a nearby restaurant for a reported brawl.

I paid little attention to this—it being a natural for a patrol unit—until Dispatch followed the call with an inquiry of my whereabouts.

I keyed the mike and answered, "M-80 from 0-3; I'm on the Putney Road near the bridge."

"This one might be of interest to you."

I took my eyes off the road and glanced quickly at the radio, as if some further explanation might appear in spectral writing. With half the town monitoring our radio conversations—a practice so peculiarly widespread, we referred to our unseen audience as *scannerland*—some of our messages became cryptic to a fault. I therefore knew better than to ask for details, and merely responded, "10-4. 0-3 is responding."

The restaurant in question was located right at the edge of the Retreat Meadows. Once a flood plain of fields belonging to a local drug-and-alcohol rehabilitation facility named the Retreat, it was now, thanks to a dam farther down the Connecticut River, a scenic, lake-like pocket that marked the confluence of the Connecticut and the West rivers. The restaurant's broad verandah had become an idyllic platform for watching canoeists, fishermen, and outboard-motor enthusiasts in summertime, and ice fishermen and skaters during the winter months.

No one was watching now, however. Not only was it jet black by now, but the action was most distinctly in the dirt parking lot to the restaurant's rear. As I left the Putney Road and cut back down a narrow switchback leading to the shore, my headlights picked up a large throng of people clustered around two stationary vehicles.

I stopped at the crowd's edge, let Dispatch know I'd arrived, and was told a patrol unit was about five minutes away. Relieved by that bit of news—these kinds of disputes were famous for drawing indiscriminate blood—I removed my badge from my pocket and, using it as a combination calling card/battering ram, began slowly to edge my way into the center of the crowd.

I heard the fight before I saw it, and so recognized at least one of the participants. Mary Wallis's authoritative voice cut through the night air like the railing of an outraged nun. I immediately began to rue Dispatch's apparently warped sense of humor.

My dread, it turned out, was justified. When I reached the front row of spectators, I found that Wallis had fixed her wrath on none other than Jason Ryan—our unlikely primary suspect. He was sitting in his car with the windows up and the doors locked, nursing a split lip with a bloody handkerchief. She was standing next to the car, yelling invectives and finally pounding on his driver's-side window with her shoe.

My appearance, signaled by the parting of the crowd, caught both her attention and her rage. "Why isn't this man in jail?"

I approached her and gently reached for the shoe. "As far as we know, he's done nothing to deserve it."

She waved the shoe menacingly in the air, distracting me from making good eye contact with its owner.

"Nothing? What about Gail? You of all people should know what he's done."

My hand closed on the shoe. Her arm didn't relax, which made us look locked in a dance step, but at least I felt a little safer. I looked at her carefully. "Mary—what are you doing here?"

The window of the car rolled down a few inches, enough for Ryan's scratchy, whining voice to be added to the chorus. "Arrest that bitch. She hit me—fucking bitch hit me with her goddamn shoe. That's assault and battery."

I heard the door mechanism click as he began to open up. I kicked the door shut again with my foot and glanced at him briefly. "Stay in the car or I'll let her loose. I'll get to you later."

Looking like an ad for Arthur Murray lessons, I moved Mary a short distance away from the car, still in front of an enthralled and speechless crowd. I could hear a comforting siren approaching from afar.

I shook her arm a little, as a reminder. "Would you put your shoe back on, please? You'll catch cold."

She looked up at our entwined hands and flushed with embarrassment, suddenly conscious of the absurdity of her situation. The arm finally descended. "I came here for dinner. Not to confront him."

"You met by chance?"

She nodded.

Around us, the dark crowd of faces and the trees beyond them began pulsating with the reflected blue lights from the arriving patrol car. Two officers waded through the parted spectators, barely restrained smiles on their faces. "Got this one locked up, Lieutenant?"

I pointed at the people now fading away, the fun over and the risk of personal involvement just beginning. "Grab a few of them and get statements. And don't let the guy with the bloody lip out of his car. I want to talk to him."

I turned back to Mary Wallis, who was obviously starting to reflect on the trouble she might be in. "Where did you see him?"

"At the bar."

"And he approached you?" I was making it easy for her to build a face-saving story, knowing very well her honesty was almost as rigid as her dogmatism.

She didn't disappoint me. "I went up to him and asked him if he raped Gail."

My eyes widened a bit. "Just like that."

She scowled at me. "Yes, just like that—what did you expect? I thought you people would have him in jail by now."

I held up my hand to keep her calm. "I take it you weren't being conversational at the time?"

"I didn't scream at him—I merely asked him for the truth."

"And what was his response?"

"He began abusing me—swearing at me, using foul language."

"Did he touch you at all?" I was hoping we could counter his assault charge with one by her—and maybe get him into jail where we could sweat him a bit.

She shook her head. "He didn't have to. His words were enough—they were sexually violent, and I considered them grounds for self-defense."

"Meaning you hit him."

Again, her face darkened with anger. "This is incredible. Not twenty-four hours has gone by since a prominent woman in this town—your own partner—was raped by that man, and you're giving me the third degree because I hit him."

"If he presses charges, it'll be worse than that. You might end up spending the night in jail."

She stared at me, openmouthed.

I shook my head, muttered, "Stay here—I'll see what I can do," and went to talk to the two patrolmen, who were standing side by side behind Ryan's car, finishing their notes.

"He yelled at her, she whacked him, he ran for cover," the older one said, with a veteran's economy of form.

I thought for a moment. The patrolman seemed to have read my mind when he added, "And he never so much as brushed up against her."

"But the language was good?" I asked.

He chuckled. "You know the man, Joe—worst mouth in town."

I nodded and borrowed the note pad he'd used to gather statements. "Okay, good. Why don't you two keep Ms. Wallis company for a few minutes while I try something."

I went around to the passenger side of Ryan's car, motioned to him to open up, and looked in. "How're you doing, Jason?"

"Not too fucking good. You goin' to bust that bitch?"

I noticed his lip, though swollen, had already stopped bleeding, and that the cut was apparently on the inside of his mouth, where it wouldn't show. "Well—" I squatted down to get a better view of him in the dome light. "That might prove to be a two-edged sword."

"What the fuck you talkin' about? Look at my goddamn face. She hit me, for Christ's sake."

"After you provoked her with some pretty strong language. We have a roomful of very impressed witnesses."

He fairly exploded. "Language? What the hell's going on here? She accused me of raping your fucking girlfriend, and you're talking about two-edged swords? Did all your fucking witnesses turn into dummies when that happened?"

"No, no. They got it right. They also saw you hightail it for your car and lock the doors against a small woman with a shoe. That got a few laughs. How much do you weigh?"

Several expressions chased across his face as he began seeing where

I was headed. "What was I supposed to do?" he finally asked a little lamely, "punch her out? You would've nailed me for sure."

I glanced over the patrolman's notes once more. "You could've tried to defend yourself. You 'ducked and ran,' according to these people. One said you screamed."

"Horse shit I screamed. What the fuck's goin' on here, Gunther? You jerk me around anymore and I'll sue your ass to hell."

I put the note pad into my coat pocket. "Straight? Okay, you press charges against her, and I'll make sure the eyewitness accounts get circulated all over town. You don't press charges, and I'll also make sure she stays out of your way—with a restraining order, if necessary."

He didn't react immediately. Ironically, for a man whose prose made sewage look clean, his self-image was important to him. What he saw in the mirror was a bastion of conservative rectitude, attending town meetings and writing letters to the editor as a saint might stand by the front door of a brothel, warning all of the sins within. My offer, though painful, had its impact.

He glanced out the window at Wallis and the two patrolmen. "What's to stop them from blabbing?"

"Me. Some word might get out from the crowd that was here, but that'll just be gossip you can deny."

There was a long pause as he stared out the windshield, considering his options. What he finally said both surprised me and helped explain his decision, which had less to do with vanity than I'd thought. "I didn't rape your girlfriend."

"You said all she needed was a good fuck."

"I say that to a lot of people."

"Saying it that time made you a suspect."

I expected outrage, but he looked at me, genuinely startled. "But I didn't do it. I wouldn't do that."

I let it stand at that. I didn't want to pursue this without seeing what Kunkle and Martens might have dug up about Ryan's whereabouts last night. I gestured toward Mary Wallis. "So what about her?"

He frowned and touched his lip. "Tell her to stay the fuck away from me, and that if I hear one more crack out of her, I'm suing for libel. And that goes for you assholes, too. Shut the fucking door."

I drew back and complied. He fired up the car and spun its rear tires leaving the parking lot. Across the now-empty space, I looked at Mary Wallis. "You're off the hook, with a few provisions."

My first opportunity to see Ron Klesczewski's handiwork came at around eight o'clock that night, not long after I'd filed a report about my meeting with Stan Katz, and a private memo to Brandt concerning the parking-lot spat I'd just arbitrated.

Ron's command post reflected his penchant for order and tidiness. The room directly down the hall from the detective bureau—normally a wasted space in search of a proper function—had been transformed into a data-management center of classic design. Bulletin boards, desks, phones, *in* and *out* trays, rows of open cardboard filing boxes were all arranged clearly and logically, without clutter or duplication—an efficient bureaucratic information funnel, designed to guide every scrap of incoming intelligence, no matter how trivial, to an easily locatable parking spot.

I hadn't expected to see much activity at this time of night. I knew Ron would be there—his personality dictated he'd probably move a cot in before long—and I knew at least one officer from each patrol shift was assigned to be there. What I found was four times that number of people, all of them immersed in work, shrouded by the sounds of typewriters, telephones, muttered conversations, and the vague odor of overcooked coffee.

Sammie Martens was the first one to see me standing in the doorway. Listening on the phone, she waved me over to where she'd staked out a claim at one end of a long folding conference table.

She jotted down a few notes, thanked whoever it was at the other end, and hung up, explaining, "Still canvassing Gail's neighborhood."

She rose and led me to one of the bulletin boards, which had been covered horizontally by a six-hour timetable, divided into columns fifteen minutes apart. The legend, *Time of Assault*, occupied the centermost column. Reading from her freshly obtained notes, Sammie filled out an index card with "car sound—southbound—unwitnessed," and stuck it with a pin under the 4:00–4:15 label.

She stood back and explained the team's progress so far. "We're filling it up little by little. Some of them, like Dennis's old guy going to the john, are pretty specific; others, like the one I just got, aren't worth too much."

I pointed to the only entry in the 3:30–3:45 column, a card stating, "Burgess returns home." After freeing herself and pulling the pillowcase off her head, Gail had locked the time at 3:37. "What about that one?"

"Timothy Burgess—lives over a mile down the street. One of the patrolmen working with Dennis found him. Rock-solid alibi, seen leaving one place and arriving home. We checked him for priors just to be sure. Nothing."

I scanned the entire board, noticing that even I made an appearance. "Anything interesting at all, even if it doesn't fit the timetable?"

Sammie shrugged. "Maybe."

She marched back to her table and pawed through a pile of notes, extracting a single sheet. "Harry Murchison, works for Krystal Kleer Windows and Doors. He was half the crew that installed two of Gail's windows last year."

She handed me the sheet—a printout from the Vermont Department of Corrections. "One count of sexual assault and battery, for which he served time, and an arrest for sexual molestation, which never made it to court. We haven't contacted him yet, nor have we run him by Gail to see if he rings a bell."

She hesitated a moment, and then added, "Are you planning to see her soon?"

I handed the sheet back. "I don't know. Probably. You been able to check out what Murchison was doing last night?"

"I asked around his neighborhood a bit—low profile. He has a girlfriend with a noisy kid, they like loud music, and they put down a fair amount of beer on the weekend, so they're not too inconspicuous. But the closest I could get to pinning down his whereabouts was whether his truck spent the night at home." She paused, apparently for effect. "It didn't, at least not the whole night. When the woman I spoke to went to bed at midnight, the truck was still gone. When she got up early this morning, it was there, and she says she thought she heard it coming back 'sometime in the middle of the night,' to quote her."

My mind was running through the various ways we could get

closer to Mr. Murchison without tipping our hand. "He on parole or probation?"

Sammie shook her head. "I thought of the same thing. No, he's not, so we can't use a parole officer to help us out. Except for maybe getting chummy with his girlfriend, I don't see how we can get close."

"Maybe one of our snitches will. Where's Willy?"

She rolled her eyes and smiled. "Out there somewhere, poking around in other people's laundry. This is his kind of case. I'll try to find him and tell him to work on that."

I glanced back at the bulletin board with the timetable. "You said Murchison has a truck?"

"Yeah—a dark-blue pickup with a cap. Could've been the one the old guy saw."

"God bless old bladders," I muttered.

Sammie hadn't heard me. "Willy checked out Ryan, by the way. As far as we can tell, he had dinner with friends, wrapped things up a little before eleven, and went home to bed, the last part being speculative. He lives alone, the neighbors don't have a clear view of his house or driveway, and they hate his guts anyway, so they aren't too interested. Besides that, Willy found out he has a couple of bicycles and that he likes to ride at night, probably to look through people's windows. He could've snuck out on one of them after pretending to hit the sack. Nobody would've heard him, and he doesn't live that far from Gail's place."

I nodded, half to myself, my eyes on Ron Klesczewski, who'd left his computer terminal to refill a cup of coffee at the urn near the door. I didn't tell Sammie about my recent chat with Jason Ryan, or the fact that for some reason I'd believed him when he'd told me of his innocence.

"I suppose you heard Gail's name is being published in tomorrow's paper?" I asked.

"Yeah." Sammie's response was bitter.

"It was her choice—you might want to spread that around before everyone starts dumping on the *Reformer* prematurely. Besides, it might be helpful—we won't have to tiptoe around quite as much, and maybe we can start pulling people in and pressuring them a bit. Thanks for all your work, Sammie. You ought to think about getting some shut-eye."

"You too," she said quietly as I walked over to see Ron.

"We've been working on the intelligence files Todd dropped off," Ron said as I approached, "and we may have a couple of hits."

He pulled a folder from one of his neatly arranged file boxes and read me two of the names I'd heard earlier at the intelligence meeting. "Barry Gilchrist and Lonny Sorvin. Both of them are in town, both have MOs that at least partially fit the bill, and, as far as we can tell, both have daily schedules that would've allowed them to do the assault. I contacted their parole officers and we're arranging for interviews tomorrow morning."

I glanced at the files, familiar with their contents. Neither one of them had struck me as prime during the meeting, but I wasn't going to fault Ron's enthusiasm. My instincts weren't infallible, and the textbook approach had put a lot of guilty people behind bars.

He reached into another box and handed me a sheet of paper. "That came from Gail—somebody dropped it by early this afternoon. It's a list of men she thinks could have done it. Ryan's on it."

I felt a slight tingle at the nape of my neck as I took the sheet. "How far have you gotten on this?"

He picked up on the urgency in my voice, which triggered his dormant insecurity. "I gave it top priority—over the intelligence files even. I figured if she gave us those, she must've had good reason. Problem is, there're some twenty names, and we want to do them right—not move too fast. So far, we've dug into about half of them."

I pointed at the list. "I take it the ones that're crossed off were misses?"

He looked over my shoulder. "Yeah—Dan Seaverns is out of town. I talked to him in Salt Lake City, just to make sure. Johnston Hill's mother died two days ago and he's been dealing with that—with witnesses. Philip Duncan was at a late dinner party, lasted till two-thirty. Mark Sumner was there, too—I think it was some realtor blast—they work in the same office. Anyhow, that checks out, too. Richard Clark was home in bed, according to his daughter—"

"His daughter?"

"Yeah. Dennis did that one. Little unorthodox, I guess, but he intercepted the daughter at school this afternoon, got into a big conversation, and found it out."

"How would she know where her father was at two in the morning?"

"They sleep in the same bed—the whole family does."

I shook my head and pointed at the last entry, not crossed out. "What's 'Peter Moore's people' mean?"

"That's the hottest one we have so far. Didn't Sammie tell you about him? Peter Moore runs Krystal Kleer—the people who put in Gail's windows last year. I guess Gail didn't know their names, but Harry Murchison's the one we're interested in."

The phone had rung during this conversation, and a patrolman now held it up in the air and pointed at me with an inquiring look on his face. I leaned over Ron's table, picked up his phone, and punched the one blinking button.

"Gunther."

"Hi. It's me." Gail's voice—soft, sounding a hundred miles away—warmed me like a fire on a cold winter night, giving me all the comfort I was yearning to give her. "Could you come over?"

"I'm on my way," was all I said.

Chapter Six

The circle of houses on Chestnut Hill was somber and quiet, the only signs of life a glimmer here and there from a crack in some curtain. They looked chilly and withdrawn, buttoned up against a second night of record-cold air. The reservoir around which they clustered was as much a bottomless hole of cold air as a slab of opaque water.

I parked opposite Susan Raffner's home and got out, pausing a little, the vapor from my breathing dissipating the glow from the porch light. Raffner's parting words last time still echoing in my head, I had mixed feelings being here, knowing I would have to watch myself with utmost care. The Gail I'd come to visit was not someone I felt I knew—she was frail, fractured, and struggling to recover, and I had no time-tested, familiar ground to fall back on if things got emotionally complicated.

Susan opened the front door before I could ring the bell, smiling and ushering me in as a friend—a comforting change due, I thought, to her misunderstanding about why I'd been at the newspaper office so close on her heels. "She's upstairs, Joe, waiting."

I nodded and headed for the stairs.

"Joe?"

I looked back at her, surprised by the gentle tone of her voice. "Thanks for helping Mary out this evening. I know she could've gotten into a lot of trouble."

I smiled at her. "Thank Ryan's vanity."

Gail was in a different chair this time, close to the now-rumpled bed, and lit by a single soft shaded light that gave her face a gentle glow. Still, she looked exhausted, her eyes weary and drooping, her cheeks gaunt. She sat as if she'd been dropped from a great height and was utterly incapable of movement.

But she did move. She saw me against the gloom of the hallway, smiled tiredly, and extended her hand to me.

I crossed the room and took it in my own, noticing its coolness and frailty, and I sat on the bed next to her, resting both our hands on my knee. "How're you getting along?"

"I don't know," she said simply.

"I wish I knew what to do."

She squeezed my hand then, and smiled again. "You're doing fine. I'm sorry for what I'm putting you through."

"You're sorry?" I burst out. "You had nothing to do with all this. My only problem's been not knowing how to act. Last time I was here, Susan told me to put a cork in it and concentrate on helping you."

She actually laughed briefly. "The head lioness." She paused, and then looked me straight in the eyes. "Susan gave me your message. Releasing my name to the paper wasn't easy. Your support meant a lot."

Feeling guilty by now, I kept quiet.

Gail didn't notice. "I feel like half of me's looking in, and the other half's looking out. I've spent so much time with rape victims, working with Women for Women, guiding them through all the emotional stages . . . It's strange being on the other side. I have all these feelings, and halfway into them I start thinking, 'Oh, right—that's the guilt kicking in—typical.' Or, 'Why aren't I mad yet? Oh, yeah—that comes later.' It gets pretty confusing."

I knew some of those stages myself. "I saw the list you sent—that's a good sign, isn't it? Fighting back, regaining control?"

A look of pain crossed her face and I worried I'd overstepped somehow. "God, I'm a long way from there . . . And putting a list together of all the people you think could have . . . There were so many of them."

Tears began to trickle down her cheeks. "I can't stop asking, 'Why?' I'm not a bad person. I've had disagreements with people, but I've never wished them harm. What did I do?"

I let go of her hand and rubbed her back gently in a slow, circular motion. "You didn't do anything, Gail. You were a target."

Her anguish intensified. "But he planned it, right? He spent a long time thinking about it. He didn't just wander by."

I wondered if telling her more would help—not that I had much to tell. "He planned it, but he wasn't as careful as he thought. He made a few mistakes, and those'll lead us to him. The point to remember is that he attacked what you are, not who you are."

She passed her hand across her forehead. "I wish I could remember more about him—something that would help."

"You have . . ."

A dog barked outside, once and not loudly, but Gail started as if stuck with a pin.

"You okay?" I asked in alarm, remembering a similar response when Todd Lefevre had snapped off his tape recorder early that morning.

She sat back in her chair and rested her head against its high pillow, her gaze on the opposite wall. The light hit her face directly that way and made it look like a marble mask. "I can't relax—little sounds set me off. I'm so hyper they actually hurt."

I glanced at the rumpled bed. "Have you tried to sleep?"

She rubbed her forehead and smiled, embarrassed. "I remember how peaceful I felt when you left me last night . . . I'm scared to fall asleep, Joe. I try to rationalize it, but I'm scared of everything—noises, sleep, going back home. I'm scared going down the hall to the bathroom, for God's sake."

I heard the hollowness of my own words: "It's going to take time."

A crease appeared between her eyes, and her voice darkened. "Yes, Susan comes by every once in a while and drops off one-liners like that."

I began to rethink my approach, remembering what she'd just said before the dog barked. "You want to talk about the case? I hadn't been planning on it, but there are questions you could answer. Maybe it would help."

After a slight hesitation, she nodded.

I tried to organize all the details running around my head into some kind of order. "Let's start with something minor. J.P. was wondering if you still had your Swiss Army knife."

A mix of expressions crossed her face—bafflement first, as she wondered why J.P. would care, followed by a frown as she figured it out for herself. "Yes, I do," she answered in a near whisper.

"Okay. Another easy one: Do you have a wool shirt or piece of clothing that has red in it, other than the red-and-black check in your closet?"

She thought about that one for quite a while, the reason for it totally eluding her. "No. That's it, as far as I can remember. I have other red things, but not wool."

"Do you remember me wearing red wool in your bedroom in the last year?"

Her eyes widened slightly. "He left a strand of red wool behind?"

I nodded. "We think so, unless you can place anyone else in that room wearing something like that."

She shook her head emphatically, obviously heartened. "No, I can't."

"Good. Harder question now. Can you remember anything else about the attack that you might not have mentioned this morning? I'm thinking specifically about those few seconds just before he put the pillowcase over your head—you called it a blur."

She sighed and closed her eyes briefly. "I need to do this—get it out."

It was a statement to herself, not a question, but it still stimulated an answer from me: "Not if you don't want to."

Her eyes reopened, more purposeful, reminiscent of the Gail of just yesterday. "No, no. It's okay." She paused. "It was my breathing that woke me up—or the difficulty I was having. I felt something heavy on me. For a split second, I thought it was you—that I was dreaming, or that you'd come back. I opened my mouth and his hand pushed my head to the side—that's when I saw the clock, and when I realized what was happening. It was almost clinical, as if something inside of me snapped to the outside and said, 'You're being raped—remember everything you can. Joe will want to know,' as if it was happening to someone else."

I waited for a couple of seconds, and then asked, "Did you ever catch a glimpse of him?"

She shook her head. "It was too dark. He fumbled around with the pillowcase for a couple of seconds—that's when I first realized my hands were tied, because I tried to push him off—and then he pulled it over my head. After that, I couldn't see a thing."

"Was he trying to get the case off the pillow, or just having a hard time getting it on you?"

"It was already off the pillow. My head was flat on the mattress. He'd done all that before waking me up."

"Okay—a little off the subject: On the list you had delivered to the police department this afternoon, you marked down, 'Peter Moore's people.' I know you meant Krystal Kleer, but did that refer to when they installed those windows last year?"

Again, she looked both embarrassed and angry. "It's so crazy, wondering who, of all the men you've set eyes on, was the one that finally raped you. It could have been anyone, Joe. It could have been a counter clerk at a shop, or a gas-station attendant, or even someone reading the newspaper and seeing my picture—someone I'd never even seen before."

I reached out and took her hand again. "Maybe, but something made you write the window people down. What was it?"

She took a deep breath, doubt clouding her earlier determination. "Probably nothing—certainly nothing that anyone can do anything about. It was the equivalent of a wolf whistle in the street, or someone leering at you . . ."

"One of them did something like that?"

She squirmed in her seat, still trying to avoid the inevitability of what she'd set in motion, the impact her words might have on others. "It wasn't that obvious, or that direct. It was more a feeling I got from one of them—the way he looked at me."

"Did you get a first name or a nickname?"

"No. That's why I wrote it down the way I did. He was tall— over six feet—with black hair tied back in a ponytail and bright blue eyes. That's what kept bothering me when they were here. It was so obvious every time he looked at me, because of those eyes."

"But he didn't do anything physical—touch you or anything?"

"No . . . It wasn't a touch. It was creepier than that. I offered them both coffee, and I served it on a tray in the living room. I was wearing a work shirt with buttons down the front, unbuttoned at the top, and as I leaned forward to put the tray on the low table, the one with the blue eyes stood up slightly, so he could see down my shirt. It was so blatant . . . I jerked my head up when he did it, at first wondering if he was going somewhere, because of how quickly he'd gotten to his feet, but he just stayed there, watching me. No apologies—he didn't try to pretend he was looking at something else, like most men do. He just kept looking until I put the tray down—I damn near dumped the coffee—and then he smiled at me. Nothing was said, but I felt like it had been. I left right after that—told them to close the door behind them. I had to get away—I felt I'd been trespassed upon."

I almost asked why she hadn't told me anything about it before I realized what a predictably masculine response that was.

She apparently sensed the question anyway. "Later, I felt kind of foolish. It's hardly the first time something like that's happened. Every woman knows most men'll try to catch a glimpse either up her skirt or down her blouse. It's an obnoxious fact of life."

I felt distinctly uncomfortable, recalling how often I had done just that. "Did you ever see him again?"

"No. It was a quick job—only two windows. They were done the same day they began. But I never wanted to use Krystal Kleer again . . ." She stared off into the distance briefly. "And now I feel I may have gotten this man into a lot of trouble."

"Not unless he did it. Let me go back a bit. When you served them in the living room, it was in front of that row of older windows behind the couch, right?"

She nodded.

"Did you see either of them showing an interest in those windows—examining them in any way?"

"No. They were just sitting there. Their backs were to them." She leaned forward and rubbed her eyes with the palms of her hands.

I stroked the back of her head. "You okay?"

"It's just this headache—I've had it all day."

"You had any aspirin?"

"A couple, a long time ago."

I was rubbing her back again, acutely aware of how thin and frail it felt. "When was the last time you ate anything?"

I felt her sigh—it was eloquent enough.

I got off the bed and circled around in front of her, squatting down to look into her face. "Look, I know lying in bed hasn't been a big success, but why don't you try it one more time while I get hold of some more aspirin and maybe a sandwich or some soup at least. You need something inside you or you'll get sick, on top of everything else."

She didn't resist as I pulled her gently out of her seat and guided her to the edge of the bed. I propped up the pillows and set her down against them, covering her legs with a blanket I found draped over the footboard.

She held onto my forearms as I finished tucking her in, her eyes brimming with tears again. "Joe—what if he had AIDS?"

I felt my heart skip a beat. "One thing at a time. We'll run blood tests and rule it out, but you can't worry about it right now. Just work on what you can get your hands on." I kissed her cheek and straightened up. "Let me get you something to eat."

I found Susan downstairs and we quickly put together a small plate, along with some orange juice and two aspirin, but when I returned to the upstairs bedroom, Gail had finally fallen asleep.

I watched her for a few minutes, seeing how shallow her breathing was; every once in a while, her fingers would twitch, or her brow suddenly furrow. I could only imagine what nightmares were clashing inside her, and hoped with all my heart that they would soon be put to rest.

Chapter Seven

I couldn't go home that night. For entirely different reasons, my place was no more appealing to me than Gail's was now to her.

I returned to the department around midnight. I'd now been up for some twenty hours. The command post was ghostly in its emptiness, like a battlefield stripped of warriors—all except for a single policewoman from the graveyard shift, who presumably had been instructed on how to continue the sifting process that Ron had been overseeing all day. She was young and relatively new on the force, not an uncommon occurrence in a town the size of Brattleboro, whose police department was often used as a stepping stone to other, more lucrative jobs in law enforcement elsewhere. Particularly in the patrol section, we had quite a few people who were inexperienced, underpaid, overworked, and yet were expected to have at least a passing knowledge of every aspect of a police officer's duties.

But spreading our resources thin was the only way we could afford to maintain a "full-service" operation, and it usually, if sometimes just barely, fit the bill—as long as no major cases came along to throw us all into turmoil.

Which is what was worrying me now. Unless something broke soon, the personnel allotted to finding Gail's attacker would begin dwindling in direct proportion to the growing pile of other cases.

I grabbed a chair and pulled it over to the bulletin board with the timetable that Sammie had shown me a few hours ago. Additions had been made since then. Actual names written under older labels, like "voices heard walking by" and "jogger headed south," indicated that real people had been linked to events, and—because Ron had written them in black ink and not red—that they'd also been eliminated from the suspects list. The pickup with the cap, going by at four-fifteen, was still unidentified, however, and its status had been upgraded by an accompanying red question mark. Harry Murchison, window installer, was going to merit an interview soon.

I wearily got back to my feet and crossed over to Ron's long file-covered table. The young patrolwoman looked up as I approached. "Hi, Lieutenant—how're you doin'?"

"Hi, Patty—hanging in there. Found anything interesting?"

She made a small face. "I'm just cross-indexing witnesses with things they saw, to see if anything shows up hinky. I'm working on UPS trucks and garbage pickups and what-have-you. I guess they're lookin' for someone casing the place out, but so far I don't see it."

I went around the table and sat next to her, my interest pricked. "I didn't know we'd rounded up that kind of information yet."

She paused in riffling through a folder, happy to be interrupted. "Oh, yeah. Billy turned half the afternoon shift over to this—we've had people all over town. Everyone's really psyched, you know, because . . . well, you know," she finished lamely, knowing of my ties to Gail and suddenly embarrassed by her own enthusiasm.

"I appreciate it," I said for her benefit and patted a pile of folders she'd put to one side. "These the ones you're finished with?"

"Yeah."

I pulled them over in front of me and opened the top file. Patty glanced at me, obviously disappointed at being left with no other option besides getting back to work.

Folder by folder, down through the pile, I began to reconstruct activities I'd known nothing about—all credits to Ron's efficiency. Fanning out from the immediate canvass of Gail's neighbors, the investigation had reached far afield to reconstruct a whole month's prior activity on her street. There were interviews of rural-route postal carriers, utility-company employees sent out to remove a broken branch from the wires, a Federal Express driver from Keene, New Hampshire, who'd delivered a package two weeks ago. Residents had been queried about any parties they'd held recently, guests or visitors they might have had, or any unusual occurrences that might have caught their attention—from strangers lurking to dogs barking at odd hours. Wherever possible, names had been taken down to be checked against the computer networks available to us.

While I'd never panned for gold, it struck me as being a similar process—patiently washing through thin covering layers, watching for the tiniest glint.

I struck such a glint at 2:35 in the morning, long after Patty had abandoned me to find some company by the coffee machine across the hall.

I'd been going over files covering events over two weeks old, and I was by now pretty thoroughly immersed in the neighborhood's residents and their habits. Like an overeager new arrival on the block, I'd made the effort to remember everyone's name, whose pets and children belonged to whom, what their hobbies and interests were, and even which ones I tended to like or dislike, for whatever reason. Their voices, as reflected in the canvass transcripts and notes, took on individuality, and over the hours I grew familiar with the neighborhood's daily cadence.

It stuck out, therefore, when cranky old Mrs. Wheeler hired a one-time yard man to give her lawn a final mowing before the frost settled in.

He hadn't done anything to bring attention to himself, hadn't gone up and down the street drumming up additional business, hadn't sat in his car at lunch and watched people's comings and goings. He'd merely appeared one day in a beaten-up, ancient station wagon, unloaded some hand tools and an old mower from the back, done the job, and left, never to be seen again.

And that's what caught my eye. In a neighborhood with a regular, predictable rhythm, his appearance—as mundane and uneventful as it had been—was nevertheless unusual.

The interview with Mrs. Wheeler, neatly indexed in another of Ron's folder boxes, revealed two other things: that Mrs. Wheeler's regular yard man had suffered a garage fire a few weeks back, destroying much of his equipment and forcing all his customers to fend for themselves until the insurance came through; and that the temporary, one-time replacement had been named Bob Vogel. The tantalizing possibility that the fire, Vogel's appearance, and Gail's rape were interrelated was inescapable, if as yet totally unfounded. Unfortunately, the name of the regular yard man, seemingly incidental at the time of the interview, had not been recorded.

I crossed the room to where Ron had set up a computer terminal and unleashed the machine onto Bob Vogel's scent. I began with a quick name search of our own criminal files, although I was pretty sure that if Vogel had been a client of ours, I would have remembered him. I was therefore not too surprised to come up empty-handed. I switched to Meadowbrook Road—Gail's street—and launched a query for complaints originating from there that might have featured either Bob Vogel or his vehicle within the last month. Again, I found nothing, and, again, I wasn't too surprised. I moved next to the Vermont Criminal Information Center's databank for an overview of all the state's criminal offenders. This time, the absence of Vogel's name was a little more troublesome—it meant either I was barking up the wrong tree, pursuing an alias, or that Bob Vogel had appeared from out of state.

I paused to rub my eyes. Despite the adrenaline that had accompanied my little discovery, I was beginning to fade, and knew I'd have to call it quits soon. I straightened my back, stretched, and called up the FBI's National Criminal Information Center to gain access to the Interstate Identification Index—the Triple I—a listing, by state and/or municipality, of most people with felony records.

Realizing this was my last swing at getting any quick results—and that lots of legwork lay ahead if it failed—it was with a small sigh of relief that I finally saw, "Vogel, Robert" appear on the screen. I called up his file and sat back, admiring how close we'd come to missing him, even while doing all the right things.

Robert Vogel was on probation in Vermont on a Massachusetts burglary charge, which explained why Lou Biddle hadn't thought to bring his file to our intelligence meeting, and why I hadn't found him in my search of Vermont law breakers—a non-Vermonter, nonrapist, his name had never come up.

My real satisfaction, however, lay in what the computer showed Vogel to be. It turned out that although he was still paying society for burglary, he'd already paid his legal dues for rape by serving a full four-year term in a Massachusetts penitentiary; he'd also been previously charged with two additional rapes, neither resulting in conviction.

I stared at the screen for several minutes, its fluorescent green letters hypnotic in their intensity, before I suddenly realized that despite my excitement I was on the brink of falling asleep. *Soon*, I thought, *soon*, as I switched off the computer and slowly walked over to the fax machine. I typed up a brief note for Lou Biddle to call me as soon as he got to his office, punched up his number, and sent it off over the wires.

At that I straightened, stretched, and gave in to exhaustion, satisfied that the day had at least ended with a shred more hope than it had begun.

Four hours later, I rued the enthusiasm that had prompted the sending of that fax. Lou Biddle's voice on the other end of my phone not only gave me no joy, it was even, for the first few moments after I picked up, a complete mystery to my sleep-clotted brain.

"Joe, what the hell's the matter? You sound sick."

I cleared my throat and struggled to open my eyes against the light from my bedroom window. "Sorry—long night. Do you have a Robert Vogel in your files, on probation here for a Massachusetts burglary?"

"Not in my files, but maybe one of the others has him. Helen, probably. I'm sex offenders only."

"Could you find out? Now?"

There was a moment's surprised hesitation. "Sure. Hang on."

I spent the five minutes he left me hanging getting tiredly out of bed. Just before he returned, I wondered how Gail had fared through the night—and what use I was going to be to her if I kept up this pace. I realized now that, despite the promising end results, last night's marathon had been more than a little self-indulgent, triggered by some subtly pervasive urge to vaguely mimic Gail's ordeal with one of my own making. It had been exactly the type of display I'd been struggling to avoid.

Nevertheless, Lou sounded duly impressed when he got back on the line. "I got him. How the hell did you dig this guy up?"

"He mowed the lawn of one of Gail's neighbors a couple of weeks ago. You free for the next hour?"

"Next half hour, yeah."

"I'm on my way."

The local probation and parole branch of Vermont's Department of Corrections was located a mere stone's throw from where Mary Wallis had hammered Jason Ryan with her shoe—down among a cluster of buildings bunched together on the flats between the water's edge and the high bank on which the Putney Road was perched. Fifteen minutes after hanging up on Lou Biddle, I pulled into his parking lot.

I found him in his office, comfortably settled in an ancient tilt-back office chair, a cup of coffee cradled in his hands and his feet propped up on his desk.

He pointed to a coffee machine by the door. "Help yourself. You look like you need it."

I gratefully followed his suggestion. "Did you get a chance to read that file?"

He leaned forward and pulled it off his desk. "Yup. You may have a hot one here. Three rape charges, the last one with a sentence. He served the rape in full and is doing the burglary on probation."

"I take it they were connected?" I asked, clearing his guest chair of a stack of books and sitting down.

"Yeah. The burglary kicked in because he was witnessed entering the apartment window of the woman he assaulted."

"She lived alone?"

"Yeah. He attacked her in her bedroom in the middle of the night—tied her down using slipknots, threatened her with a knife, blindfolded her . . . The whole ball of wax. I'm sorry I didn't hand him over to you yesterday."

I reached for the file, my exhaustion turning to adrenaline. "Not to worry—who'd you say his probation officer was?"

"Helen Boisvert."

"What's her reading on him?"

"Dunno—I just ran in and grabbed the file. She's in, though, which is just as well, 'cause I've got to hit the road."

I took the hint and stood up, thanking him again for the coffee.

Helen Boisvert had worked for the department of corrections for over twenty years. Originally from the state's so-called Northeast Kingdom region—remote, sparsely populated, and proudly inde-pendent—she'd been brought up on society's fringes, one of six kids of a dirt-poor logger and his wife. Her highly regarded abilities as a probation officer were due in part to the fact that only her own moral strength and determination had stopped her from becoming one of her own clients. Half her siblings had spent time in jail, and two of her brothers had met violent deaths. But as she'd told me once, extracting herself from that environment and ending up in corrections, after earning an M.A. in psychology, was as natural to her as an Eskimo training to be a cold-weather scientist.

She was nestled in an office just like Lou's, which looked more pleasant but smelled a lot worse, due to its occupant's lifelong addiction to cigarettes. She was lighting one up as I walked in.

"I hear you're interested in one of my boys," she said through the smoke.

I returned her file to her. "Bob Vogel—but not for burglary."

She raised her eyebrows, immediately following my lead, and tossed me that morning's *Brattleboro Reformer*. "You think he did that?"

Knowing that it was coming, even with Gail's blessing, didn't make the front-page story any easier to take. "Selectwoman Raped at Home" ran from one edge of the page to the other, across several related articles and a photograph of Gail at a recent meeting. I returned the paper without reading it further. "It's a possibility."

"Interesting."

"Why do you say that?" I asked, struck by her tone of voice.

"Because this took place night before last, and he missed his meeting with me yesterday morning."

"Have you talked to him since?" I was suddenly worried he'd already taken off.

"Oh, yeah—he came in later. Said he overslept, that his alarm didn't go off. Interesting coincidence."

"How did he seem?"

"A little nervous I might nail him for messing up, but otherwise he was the same as always."

"Which is?"

She took a deep drag, finishing the cigarette, and ground it out in an already half-full ashtray. I imagined her forceful personality allowed her to flaunt the state's no-smoking rules. "Bob Vogel is an unrepentant shit," she finally said. "He toes the line with me because I can pull his chain, but we both know it's a waste of time.

As soon as he's free and clear, he'll be back in trouble—unless he's already jumped the gun."

I removed the jacket I'd been wearing against the fading morning chill and placed it on the floor next to my chair. "Lou said Vogel's last assault fit the MO of the guy who raped Gail—what about the two rapes he didn't get prosecuted for? Were they the same?"

Helen pulled another cigarette from the pack lying on her desk and lit up. "I couldn't say for sure. I only know about the last one, and even there I don't have all the details. He moved up here ten months ago, and we only got this preliminary file about four months back, which is par for the course—they're either drowning in cases down there or they don't give a damn, depending on the office.

"Anyhow, the outline you got from Lou about sums up what I've been told—the big difference being that he used a nightgown to blind his victim instead of a pillowcase. Which helped nail him, as it turned out—not only was he seen going in through the window by a neighbor, but the nightgown slipped off enough so the victim got a look at him. She pulled him out of a lineup."

"Lou mentioned a knife."

Boisvert made a face. "Yeah—he cut her nipples a little, I guess to get her attention. A real bastard."

"What else did he do?"

"Everything shy of killing her, as far as I can tell. The rape lasted several hours, with intermissions for the knife play and beatings. The woman ended up having her jaw wired."

"Did he trash the bedroom also?"

She looked uncertain. "I suppose—there was mention of a lot of destruction."

I changed subjects slightly, realizing I was nearing the limit of her knowledge. "Did all three rape victims live in the same area?"

"Two in Greenfield, one in North Adams. None of them knew one another, and none of them knew Bob. He's a stalker."

That made me think of Vogel's one-day employment at Mrs. Wheeler's. "Was part of his technique getting handyman jobs near where the victims lived?"

She shrugged and shook her head. "I don't know. Like I said, we actually don't have all that much on Bob yet. What I do know mostly comes from my conversations with him. The file only highlights the bare bones on the last assault—the one that landed him in the pokey."

"How did he get off on the first two?"

"Screwups; technicalities. You'd have to check it all out with the Massachusetts people, but from what he told me, the system served him well. For that matter, four years for what he did to his last victim was a slap on the wrist."

There was a pause, during which I digested some of what she'd told me. There was no longer any doubt in my mind that we had a "hit"—someone who, from a distance at least, fit our profile to a gnat's eyelash.

"It sounds like he talks about the rape a lot."

Helen made a dismissive gesture with her hand before grinding out the second cigarette. "Lou should be handling this guy—he's a sexual offender. It's only the burglary technicality that makes him mine. But let's face it, *burglary* means he entered by force—not that he was out to steal anything—so we don't spend much time talking about how to jimmy windows or fence TVs. Besides, Bob Vogel reminds me a lot of some of the guys I grew up with, including a couple of my brothers. I don't like him, and I don't see him living to a ripe old age—at least not on the outside. But I do know what makes him tick." She grinned suddenly—so immersed in this world she no longer saw the incongruity. "I guess you could say we get along."

"Lucky you," I muttered, to which she only laughed, and reached for another smoke.

I had copies made of all the information I needed concerning Bob Vogel, including his home address and place of employment, and went straight to my office, despite the fact that I still hadn't shaved or showered.

Ron Klesczewski's expression told me I should have tended to those small details first. "Are you okay?" he blurted as he looked up to find me looming over him at his temporary, paper-strewn desk.

I gave him the file I'd secured from Helen Boisvert. "Get the records on this guy—his Massachusetts rap sheet is inside. And see if you can locate a police officer who knows about him, either from North Adams or Greenfield. I'd like to talk to him."

He flipped open the file and stared at the name at the top of the first page. "Robert Vogel?"

"He did a one-day handyman stint for one of Gail's neighbors. I found him in your files." I saw J. P. Tyler waving to me from the hallway door. "Okay?" I asked Ron.

He still looked a little startled, but nodded firmly, regaining his composure.

"What's up?" I asked Tyler in the hall, as he led me down to the detective bureau, where he'd converted a cramped janitor's closet into a makeshift laboratory.

"Two things: One, I tried to match the pubic hair I found in Gail's bed to either you or her and came up empty, which means it came from the attacker."

It was nice of him to be so diplomatic. In fact, I knew damn well such an argument wouldn't hold up in court. A third person's pubic hair found in a de facto conjugal bed did not necessarily involve a rapist. For our purposes, however, it was good enough.

"All I can get from it, though," he continued, "is that the guy was Caucasian and dark-haired."

We entered the detective squad office and went not to the tiny lab, but to Tyler's desk. "The second thing I have higher hopes for."

He held up a small baggie with a tiny fragment of organic material in it. "Remember this? The vegetable matter I found on the couch near the window? It's Russian olive—a cross between a screen bush and a small tree. It can grow to twenty-five feet, has small silvery leaves and berries."

I knew better than to ask him the relevance of this. J.P. had his own style, and it often involved some minor theatrics.

"It's not a rare plant—you see it planted by the side of the interstate sometimes. Developers like it because it's cheap, hardy, and easy to handle, and it makes them look like nature lovers when they surround their junky architecture with it."

He looked at me with a pleased expression. "The point is, there ain't a single Russian olive on Gail's property."

"How 'bout Mrs. Wheeler's, two houses down?"

I should have known better. "She doesn't have any either—no

one on the block does—which means the assailant left it behind inadvertantly, just like the fiber sample from his red wool shirt."

"Gail told me last night she still has her Swiss Army knife," I volunteered, my memory jostled by what he'd just said.

Tyler nodded. "Well, we expected that. That's good, though, 'cause when we find this guy, we can check all his knives for traces of blood. Even if he wiped the blade off on his pants, we might still find something. And the window lock I removed might come in there, too. I know for sure a knife was used to jimmy it open. I might be able to match the marks to the blade."

I reflected on that for a moment, impressed at how impersonal it could all be made to sound. "That it?"

"For the moment. The DNA analysis won't be here for weeks, and we're not expecting anything there anyhow. I've pretty much done all I can do with fingerprints. You're going to get dozens of other people's prints in most houses anyhow—guests, workers, people like that—and Gail's was no different. I haven't had a hit with any of them, except yours and hers, of course."

"What about Harry Murchison, the window installer?"

Tyler smiled apologetically at the vagaries of his beloved science. "No. We know he was there, but it was over a year ago—it's hard to expect a print to survive that long."

I finally asked a question that had been chewing at me since Gail had first brought it up. "Do you know what they heard back on Gail's blood tests?"

He looked at me quizzically. "I don't think they found anything. What were you after?"

"No sign of HIV or AIDS?"

His mouth fell open slightly. "Jesus, I'm sorry. I should've thought of that." He looked suddenly embarrassed, and his words came out slowly and carefully. "No—the test was clean . . . for the moment. That's good, of course—a good sign—but you shouldn't take it as gospel, not yet. She ought to have another test in a month or so—and periodically for every six months after that—just to be sure."

I thanked him and went into my small corner office. I sat down at my desk and dialed Women for Women.

Susan Raffner was on the line in a few minutes. "Hi. What's up?"

"Nothing specific. We may have a lead, but we need to check it out thoroughly. I was just wondering how Gail fared last night. I didn't want to call her at your place in case she was sleeping."

Susan's voice saddened. "She's not doing much of that. She woke up right after you left. I ended up putting her in bed with me—it seemed to calm her down a little."

"What about something to help her sleep?"

"I'm not crazy about that stuff—her system's messed up enough as it is—but I did ask her. I think she's planning to sleep days and stay awake nights, if she can."

"Is that a good idea?" I asked.

"No, but it's her own decision, and that *is* good. The more she takes charge of things, the better. She just feels too vulnerable to sleep at night. It'll pass with time." There was a pause on the line before Susan added, "Did you see the paper this morning?"

"Saw it—I didn't read it."

"Katz played it pretty straight—the editorial's a little heavy-handed, but sympathetic. He did say a few things you probably won't be too happy with, like how the paper's going to make it a mission not to let this just slip by. The quote was something like 'keeping a spotlight on the wheels of justice.' "

"Great," I muttered.

"I know how you feel, Joe, but we agree with him, and we're planning to help him out. We're going to keep this in the news."

"I realize that," I said without enthusiasm.

"And Gail's going to be a part of it."

Despite my unhappiness, I appreciated the sensitivity in her voice. Even believing as she did that I was wholly supportive of Gail's identifying herself as the victim, Susan still understood the pressures such a decision placed upon a couple. After years of locking horns with her on purely technical grounds, finally I found it oddly comforting that she was there as head of Women for Women, even as she prepared to make my professional life miserable. It was the sign of someone, as irony might have it, that I could trust.

"I know that, too," I answered. "And I know that's what she thinks she needs. I just don't want everyone else's enthusiasm running her over."

"I'll keep an eye on it, Joe. And, by the way, your coming over last night made a big difference. I think you should drop by any time you feel the urge, as long as you keep the same tone. I'll tell the others you might do that."

I thanked her and hung up, ignoring the fact that "keeping the same tone" might be easier said than done, depending on my own emotional mood swings.

I pulled open my bottom desk drawer and removed an old electric razor, with which I did an approximate job on my face, using my fingertips in place of a mirror. The shower would have to wait. I knew that with this morning's headlines, the political natives were going to be at least restless, and perhaps arming for battle.

I crossed the hallway to Brandt's side of the building, only to find him putting on his jacket and preparing to leave.

"I was just about to round you up. Dunn wants to see us—I think he's getting sweaty palms."

I accompanied Tony back out to the hallway and upstairs to where the state's attorney had his offices on the top floor. Dunn's request—and Brandt's reaction—were in perfect keeping with my own concerns. The SA had been a fixture in the county for the past fifteen years, a feather in the community's cap when he'd first been elected as a highly respected prosecutor with big-city credentials. He'd been slumming then, a fifty-five-year-old flatlander, newly retired from handling big criminal cases in New York, and his run for office had reflected that lack of desperate hunger so common among office seekers. Dunn had felt free to say whatever was on his mind, regardless of the consequences, because he'd literally had nothing to lose. It had even seemed to some of us in those days that, were he elected, he might not choose to serve, having found something else of more interest. This curious nonchalance had worked well in his favor, being misinterpreted by both press and public as courage rather than arrogant indifference.

Time had worked its devious alchemy, of course, eroding the man's lack of ambition—and the public's gullibility—with the result that he was now as driven to hang onto his position as a growing number of people were to see him replaced.

Having the chairwoman of the board of selectmen raped, therefore, with no suspect in jail and both these facts in banner headlines, was not good news.

He greeted us silently from behind a large, gleaming, imposing cherry-wood conference table, looking like a bad caricature of some egomaniacal dictator. Before him, in pointed isolation, lay a single copy of the morning's newspaper, face up. We were not invited to sit.

He extended one long, manicured finger and tapped the newspaper gently with it, looking me straight in the eye. "Why wasn't I told about this?"

I hesitated a moment, weighing any number of possible responses, and finally settled for, "I didn't think of it. Sorry."

"You guys made me look like an idiot. Alice Sims called me up at the crack of dawn and asked for an on-the-record comment, and I had to ask her what the hell she was talking about. She said you and Raffner's crowd cooked this up together."

Alice was Stan Katz's "courts-'n-cops" reporter, covering his old beat. She was young and aggressive and dying to make an impression, just as Stanley had been before her. I was sure Dunn was right that she'd make the most of this communications glitch, and felt badly that I'd dropped the ball. I didn't like Dunn, but it did none of us any good to make it appear the police and the SA weren't talking.

Dunn continued coldly, "She also told me that Jack Derby had weighed in with his own homespun country-cracker bullshit about the plight of women in this violent society, and how bravery like Ms. Zigman's was an example of how to stem the tide—or some other highly original piece of crap."

He pushed aside the paper and laid his thin, pale hands flat on the table's shiny surface. "Are you two gentlemen counting the days until Mr. Derby moves into these offices? Perhaps you think he needs a little help?"

I had seen James Dunn pull the imperious magistrate before— it was one of his better acts. But it had always been directed outward, at a suspect or a reluctant witness. Turning his vitriol on us, especially on purely political grounds, was a mistake I knew Tony was not going to take in stride.

Brandt walked around the end of the long table to join Dunn on the other side. The latter looked taken aback by this gesture and, as Tony approached, even faintly alarmed. He shifted in his chair and raised his hands vaguely over his chest, as if prepared to physically defend himself.

Tony, however, smiling thinly but affably enough, merely pulled out the chair right next to Dunn's, sat in it, leaned back, and placed his crossed feet on the immaculate tabletop, all the while reaching into his jacket pocket to remove his pipe and pouch. Dunn's theatrically staged and imposing set dissolved. As an afterthought, I sat down on the edge of the table, instead of standing like an abashed schoolboy.

Tony's voice, despite his mild appearance, was ice cold. "Want to run that by us again?"

Dunn looked ready to explode. "How did Derby know about this before I did?"

Tony focused on stuffing his pipe. "The paper knew about it before we did, and the paper's endorsed your opponent. How do you explain it?"

The SA's eyes narrowed slightly as he stared at me. "What do you mean, the paper knew about it before you did? She's your goddamn girlfriend, for Christ's sake."

I decided to play Brandt's bland game. "She called them, an informant there called us, and I went over to their office to make it look like we were all coordinating. Katz bought it. You just slipped my mind. I am sorry about that. I'm afraid I was scrambling for cover myself."

Dunn's lethal gaze shifted back and forth between us. Tony lit up and his pipe erupted into a cloud of smoke. "Was there anything else you wanted to talk to us about, James?"

It was a graceful offer from someone who would have been entirely justified in simply walking out of the room. Dunn grudgingly recognized it as such.

"Yes. How is the investigation going?" he asked, switching gears.

Brandt spoke as if the conversation had just begun. "Fine. We've got two possibles from among the files Joe collected at the intelligence meeting yesterday, and a third one Gail gave us of a guy who replaced a couple of windows at her house a year ago—"

"And Jason Ryan," I added, "who said she deserved what she got, a few days before the rape. We also have a guy from Massachusetts on parole here on a burglary rap who has a long history of sexual assault."

Tony gave me a quick glance, since I hadn't had a chance yet to update him on Bob Vogel. He also was not one who enjoyed being left out of the informational loop, especially with Dunn on the warpath.

Dunn looked at his watch, eager to get this over now that it had blown up in his face. "I take it Todd's being kept abreast of all this."

"I haven't seen him this morning," I said, "but I'll fill him in."

Dunn stood up and walked to the door that led to his private office. "All right. Let me know when something develops."

He closed the door behind him, and Tony and I looked at one another. "Can't imagine why the race is so close," Brandt muttered.

Lunch was a combination of brown-bag sandwiches and chips, ordered-in slabs of glistening pizza, and a mismatched assortment of carrots, pickles, cookies, yoghurt, soda, and one Twinkie, belonging to Dennis. Sitting around the least-cluttered conference table in the command post were the entire detective squad, Brandt, Billy Manierre representing Patrol, and Todd Lefevre from the SA's office.

Ron Klesczewski was running the meeting. "Of the two possibles gleaned from the intelligence meeting—Lonny Sorvin and Barry Gilchrist—Sorvin looked the most likely. They had both blind-folded their victims in the past, but only Sorvin used ropes and spoke in a whisper. Neither one of them broke into their victims' homes, neither one had used a knife, and neither one had stripped naked prior to sexual contact. Still, they were the only ones that even came close to fitting the MO of the guy we're after. Also, given their jobs and generally known habits, they both had the opportunity to commit the rape in question.

"On the strength of that, we had them interviewed by their parole officers. They were asked to account for their movements in detail, and then we had their stories checked out. As far as we can tell, they're clean."

"Who did the checking? Us or Corrections?" Brandt asked, slightly confused by Ron's syntax.

"I did," Dennis DeFlorio answered. "I talked to family members in Gilchrist's case—Sorvin lives alone—and friends and neighbors of both of them. Harriet's transcribing my report. Maybe I'm wrong, but I kind of think we'd be wasting our time with them. Just my opinion, of course."

No one challenged him, much to his apparent relief, so Ron plowed on. "We finished going through the list of people Gail submitted, and except for Harry Murchison, we came up empty. But since those were the people she suggested herself, we gave them a second going-over. The only iffy pair were Philip Duncan and Mark Sumner, who were at a party together until two-thirty—after the rape began. Since each had spoken for the other concerning that time, and their friends could've been covering for them, we looked for other witnesses for corroboration. Unfortunately—or fortunately, I suppose—we found them. Both a waitress and a bartender confirmed the time."

"This place was still open at two-thirty?" Billy Manierre asked.

"It was a special party at the Redtop Inn—the dining room was reserved for the whole night. Ethan Allen Realty's just been bought out by some businessman from Boston, and I guess he wanted to show his new employees what a great guy he is."

"So what about Murchison?" Brandt interrupted, impatient with Ron's methodical approach.

"I've been checking him out," Sammie answered. "And he's still a good candidate. I went to Krystal Kleer pretending I wanted a mirror cut to size, and I got into a conversation with the woman at the desk. According to her, Murchison is a grade-A sexual harasser, making comments, copping feels, and generally being a pain in the ass. She said even some of the customers complained and the boss had to stop sending him out on the road.

"I looked into the two sexual priors against him—an aggravated-assault conviction and a dropped simple-assault charge. The first involved a woman he was seeing and who'd broken off the relationship; he waited for her one night when she got back from work, forced her inside, threatened her with a hammer, and then raped her, apparently hoping the ecstasy of the experience would make her see the error of her ways."

Everyone but Kunkle remained studiously silent at the bitterness in Sammie's voice. Kunkle laughed.

"Murchison did three years for that and got out almost three years ago. The simple-assault charge was eight years ago and didn't stick because the girl he had sex with was too flaky—she only came forward because her parents forced her to, and she kept changing her story. The state wasn't all that sure who to believe."

"What was the background on that case?" Todd Lefevre asked.

"Backseat groping at a lover's lane. The girl was a well-experienced minor. He claimed he didn't know how old she was. There was no violence, but her first story—the one she came in with accompanied by her parents—was that he'd forced the situation. There don't seem to be any parallels with our case, unlike the rape he was convicted for. Willy did the legwork on his whereabouts the night before last."

We all looked expectantly at Kunkle, who took his time finishing off a Coke. I filled the gap by asking Sammie, "Did you run a picture of Murchison by Gail, just to make sure we're talking about the same window installer?"

She hesitated. "I wasn't sure I should—not this soon after."

"You better get me a mug shot or something. She said the guy had almost electric blue eyes."

Sammie was already nodding, "That's him—the receptionist even said it was too bad they belonged to such a creep."

Willy put his can down and wiped his mouth against his sleeve. "Okay: Harry Murchison is a definite maybe—the truck fits the old man's description, and we know from his neighbor he spent at least part of the night away from home. Turns out he had a fight with his girlfriend—something about her drinking too much beer at a party they were both at—and she had to catch a ride home with a friend. Murchison lit out for parts unknown.

"I put together a list of his drinking buddies—most of it from his ex–parole officer—and tried to see if I could trace his movements that night. Up to about the time of the rape, I got him drinking at a guy's house near West Dummerston, but then he disappears. They ran out of booze and Murchison took off, either in search of another watering hole or someplace to pass out besides home. With more time, I might be able to pin down which one. One interesting thing, though—the quickest way to get back into town from the place in West Dummerston is Meadowbrook Road."

"So the truck the old guy saw was Murchison's," Dennis said.

But I saw the problem with that. "Maybe—Willy said Murchison left his buddy's around the time the rape began—that's two-thirteen—and the witness didn't see the truck till . . ." I glanced over my shoulder at the board, "four-fifteen—over half an hour after Gail got loose, and twenty minutes after her own car was seen leaving for the hospital."

"He could've waited, to watch her leave," Ron suggested.

I didn't argue the point. "I'm not ruling him out—it's just a discrepancy we need to remember. Keep digging, okay, Willy?"

He nodded once without looking up, his eyes on a distant pickle.

Ron hesitated, and then resumed running the meeting. "Robert Vogel is next. I assume you've all read the updates, so you know basically who he is. I made some phone calls after Joe gave me Vogel's file, and talked to an assistant DA in Massachusetts who knew a little about his case. From what he told me, it does look like we should put Vogel on top of our list."

Ron shuffled a few pages in front of him and extracted a single sheet of notes he'd presumably written to himself during his phone conversation. "Bob Vogel is twenty-eight years old—and a dark-haired Caucasian, which fits the samples J.P. recovered from Gail Zigman's bed. As far as law enforcement in Massachusetts knows, he's committed three rapes, the last of which landed him in jail for a fully served four-year sentence. As your updates make clear, he's now out on a burglary probation, being monitored by our own department of corrections.

"The interesting thing about this man is that his record shows a learning curve, as if each rape taught him how to improve on the next. In the first attack in North Adams, he held his victim down by the neck and got scratched for his efforts. The next time, he used tape on her wrists and ankles; and on the third outing, he used the slipknots. Same thing with the blindfold: first time, nothing; second time, he ordered her to keep her eyes shut; third time, he used her nightgown."

"And now he's into pillowcases," Sammie muttered.

Ron continued speaking. "In all three instances, the women were single, lived alone, and didn't know Vogel personally, although they may have seen him around town. Also, all the attacks were made in the middle of the night, all of them involved a knife— although he actually used it the third time only—and all of them lasted several hours."

"Were the second and third rapes committed in North Adams?" Lefevre asked, taking notes of his own.

"No. After the first one landed him in court, and ended with a hung jury and a dismissal from the judge, Vogel moved to Greenfield. That was about eight years ago, when he was twenty. The second one occurred a couple of years after that, but it never got to court. The prosecutor couldn't run with it because the investigation was botched—illegal searches, a broken chain of evidence, a few other things. The officer in charge turned out to have a drinking problem and was let go right after, but the case was a wash. The ADA I talked to was pretty bitter—even though they nailed him good and proper the third time, the court had to sentence him as a first-time offender. That's why he got off so light."

The similarities between Vogel's record and the MO used on Gail prompted an outburst of questions as Ron paused to sip from his coffee mug.

"Why don't we just pick him up?" Dennis suggested.

"Does he have an alibi for the night before last?" Lefevre asked.

"How did he set up the three rapes?"

Ron swallowed quickly and held up his free hand. "Hold it, hold it. All this is based on a single phone call. I got the name of the Greenfield cop who worked on the last two attacks, but I haven't talked to him yet; nor have I seen any paperwork. There're a lot of holes to fill."

"And we don't want to pick him up until we have them filled," I answered Dennis indirectly. "If we grab this guy before we know most of the answers, we could open ourselves up to a nasty surprise. The press and a lot of other people would have a field day with that. We need to put Robert Vogel under a microscope before we pick him up, not only for an alibi, but for more details on his MO: Did he ever wear gloves? Did he strip before assaulting these women? Did he whisper? Did he trash their rooms or houses? There's a lot to do yet."

I turned back to Ron in the answering silence. "What else?"

"A couple more things on Vogel—I'm having the arresting officers' affidavits faxed to us, since they're part of the public record, but court transcripts and other closed documents'll take a little longer."

Todd Lefevre got the hint. "I'll get on it—just give me the particulars after we're through here."

Ron nodded his agreement. "Okay, next suspect on the hit

parade: Jason Ryan. While Willy was prowling the streets checking out Murchison, he also dug a little deeper into Ryan's supposed activities, which at last report amounted to going home to bed. Were you able to find out if he snuck out later?"

Kunkle gave a disgruntled shrug of his shoulders, typical for when he came up empty-handed. Both his personality and his crippled arm dictated that he should outperform anyone around him. So not doing so tended to make him sullen. "I've got one witness who says he might've seen him on a bike, but if I'd pushed him harder, he also would've said it was pink and had wings. Ryan's going to stay a question mark until we get lucky."

Ron was obviously disappointed. "That's it for me. Since the paper came out this morning, we've been getting a steady stream of calls, some of them interesting, some of them loony, and the rest in between. Ryan's a popular suggestion, mostly among women callers, and there've been about ten men who called in suggesting Gail faked the whole thing for publicity. One guy claimed Dunn did it for votes—he didn't explain how that worked. I was thinking that if we fed the *Reformer* a few more details, especially about the timing of the attack, we might get another lead."

I gave Ron credit for an impartial presentation, purposefully downplaying the buzz that the evidence against Bob Vogel had stimulated, but there was no denying which name had suddenly hit the top of the charts.

Still, I wanted to play it by the numbers, this time more than ever. Not only did I have Gail's interests in mind, but I knew damned well that if we pushed too hard and somehow screwed up, there'd be more hell to pay than any of us could imagine. The upcoming election, Gail's willingness to have her plight politicized, and the fact that Bob Vogel had escaped prosecution once already through a policeman's incompetence, all combined to make me especially wary. The moment we let Vogel's name become publicly linked to this case, we would begin to lose control of it—Dunn, Women for Women, and Stanley Katz, among others, would see to that.

I therefore supported Ron's suggestion. "Okay. We should stress that we're currently building a case, but that we'd appreciate all the corroborative help we can get—anything heard or seen that might be linked to the specific time and location of the assault."

I was looking at both Tony Brandt and Todd Lefevre when I said this. They both silently nodded their agreement. "All right. Ron, why don't you put together a press release, then."

I got to my feet and began pacing back and forth across the front of the room. "It would be dumb denying Bob Vogel is now number one. But I don't want that overshadowing that we have at least two other strong likelies—Murchison in particular—plus Christ knows who else that might pop up. What we need to do, therefore, is to divide into teams and hit all three suspects with equal strength."

"I'd like you on the Vogel team," Brandt said quickly and clearly.

"All right, since I'm partnered with Todd and/or the chief anyway, we can make that one team. Willy, you've done most of the digging on Murchison. How 'bout you and J.P. keep on him?"

Willy gave a barely perceptible nod, but I knew I'd done him a favor. Besides Sammie, whom he liked because of her devotion to the job—and because she was one of the few people who regularly told him to drop dead—J.P. was Willy's favorite partner. Polar opposites personally, they'd forged a mutual respect, knowing that each had special abilities the other didn't.

Unfortunately, all this also predicated who would form the last remaining team. I looked at Sammie, my expression as supportive as I could make it. "And you and Dennis tackle Ryan."

Her face remained studiously impassive, which for a naturally expressive person told me a lot. I wondered if she'd be in to see me shortly after this meeting.

I returned my attention to the whole group. "Each team should be seen as a core grouping only. I want to leave Ron running the command post, and it's to him that all of us should report. That way, if any team develops a need for more manpower or resources, Ron's the man to talk to. Ron, in turn, will either pull people from the other teams, depending on what they're up to, or he'll go to Billy for help. Ron will also be responsible for forwarding any information he might get to the appropriate team, as well as giving all of us general updates on all three investigations."

I turned to the one member of the department whose importance was constantly underrated, except by me. "Harriet, that means you'll be running the day-to-day details for all of us, plus keeping track of Ron's paper flow. If you ever feel you're beginning to drown, I'm sure Tony can find it in the budget to pay for a temp."

Harriet gave me a look that suggested the possibility of that was remote at best.

I stopped pacing and stood before them in silence for a couple of seconds, slightly tongue-tied by what I felt I had to add. "I'd like you all to know, by the way, that I appreciate all the hours you've been putting in—personally, as a friend. It means a lot. Thank you."

There was a predictably awkward silence following this, diplomatically broken by Tony Brandt pushing back his chair and announcing that it was time to get back to work. In the slightly overplayed hubbub that followed, J. P. Tyler came up to me just as I was about to leave the room.

"Since you're handling Vogel, I thought you might be interested in this." He held out a small, slightly silvery leaf.

I held it quizzically between my fingers.

"It's from a Russian olive—like the one I found on Gail's couch. After we talked this morning, I drove out to West Bratt to where Bob Vogel lives. There's a Russian olive right in front of his trailer."

Chapter Eight

Todd caught up to me in the hall as Harriet informed me, "Billy wants to see you."

I smiled at that, watching Billy's large form slowly lumbering toward his office. Something was bothering him, and typically he wanted to air it on his own chosen ground—using Harriet as an emissary so his plans wouldn't be upended. I thanked her and followed Todd around the corner, out of the flow of traffic emerging from the command post.

"How do you want to divvy things up?" he asked.

"I'd like to close in on Vogel—just a hair. Scope out his neighborhood, learn his daily routine, maybe follow him around a bit. I don't want to flush him out yet, but maybe we can find out what he was up to the night before last. Ron's going to try to set up a meeting with the Greenfield cop who worked Vogel's last two rapes, so I thought a little hands-on research might be appropriate beforehand."

He glanced back at Harriet.

I followed his meaning.

"Yeah, I'll see what's up with Billy first. You've got to make a few phone calls for Ron anyway, right? Could you make a couple for me?"

"Shoot."

"Call Mrs. Wheeler. She hired Vogel because her regular man's equipment was destroyed in a fire. I'd like to know how she heard about Vogel. Also, we need to get the regular yard man's name from her and chase him down. That fire sounds pretty convenient."

Todd began heading toward the stairs. "Why don't you have your chat with Billy and then come up to my office? See if I got lucky."

I nodded my agreement and started down the hallway, pausing as I heard Tony's voice behind me. "Susan Raffner informed me just before the meeting that they're planning an 'awareness march' down the middle of Main Street tonight, complete with handheld candles. They want to wind up surrounding the court house—'an unbroken circle of light,' quote-unquote."

We fell into step side by side. "Is Gail going to be part of it?"

He smiled grimly. "Right at the front." It looked like he wanted to say more but thought better of it.

"I take it you're not impressed."

He paused in front of the unmarked door to the officers' room, suddenly giving vent to his frustration. "I'm impressed that a woman fresh from being beaten and raped and having her name plastered all over the paper would think it a good idea to march down Main Street advertising the fact. I know she's committed to her principles, Joe, and I hope you don't take this wrong, but if I were her, I'd choose a different way to straighten out my life."

I merely looked at him and raised my eyebrows. He respected Gail, and liked her. He also knew there wasn't anything he or I could do to change her mind once it was set.

He finally shook his head, muttered, "What a pisser this is," and continued down the hall.

I found Billy ensconced in his cluttered office, like mine separated from a larger, outer room by an aquarium-like window. He'd surrounded himself with the memorabilia of a lifetime in police work—pictures, citations, antiquated equipment, and mementos from favorite cases—in a way that reminded me of a bear trapped in a small museum.

He nodded genially at me when I entered and offered me a mug filled from his own private coffee urn.

I sat in his fancy guest chair. "I don't think so, thanks. I'm about fifty-percent coffee as it is. What's up?"

He pursed his lips and pulled on his chin, settling his bulk more comfortably in his own chair. He was a man who enjoyed the social niceties, often lamenting the rush of the modern world. But he was also obviously feeling ill at ease.

"Scuttlebutt has it you really reamed Al Santos. Thought you weren't going to do that."

I sighed. Not my finest hour. "Yeah—probably overdid it. He pissed me off."

"It was as much my fault as his—should've reamed me, too, when I first told you it was him."

"All right, consider yourself reamed." I knew, however, that he was after more than that. So I added, "I nailed him as much out of frustration as for what he did—I could've apologized, but then I figured I better leave it alone. The more they think I'm on the warpath because of Gail, the more careful they'll be to cross every *t* and dot every *i*. If we find this man, I don't want him to walk because of anything we did or didn't do."

Billy was quiet for a while, looking out the window at a few of his officers working at their desks or milling about the other room. "That's one way to look at it, I suppose."

"As against what?"

"They start talking about how this one's maybe screwing up your objectivity. They know damn well if it had been their wife or girlfriend, there's no way in hell they would've been allowed on the case. Maybe that's a good rule."

I'd been expecting the objection, but not from within my own ranks. That was unsettling. "Are you saying I should have another chat with Santos?"

Billy shook his large head slowly. "I wouldn't do that." He hesitated, honesty with a friend being something more easily praised than practiced. "Just don't give 'em any more to feed on."

A half hour later, I climbed the three flights to the rabbit warren of short hallways and minute offices that made up the SA's domain. As with most old buildings that had been designed for one use and converted to another—in this case a school built in 1884—the torture showed in the details. Some offices were merely wide spots along a hall, others looked like big broom closets with little air and no windows. Lefevre's eight-by-eight office did have a window, but it was placed a good five feet off the floor, probably to dissuade any student's wandering eye. The window was open in an effort to dissipate the sauna-like heat that routinely rose—summer and winter—from the floors below.

"Any luck?" I asked Todd, poking my head through his doorway.

He got quickly to his feet. "Yeah—couldn't believe it—three calls, and I got everything I was after. You ready to go? I need some fresh air."

Brattleboro has a fair number of mobile-home parks, planted like sentries around its outer perimeter. Some have been there for decades and share the same rooted look of any middle-class suburb, complete with above-ground pools, detached garages, and paved driveways. Others look considerably more ravaged by time and economics—clusters of rusting, swaybacked boxes, their mobile days long gone, arranged haphazardly along grids of rutted, trash-strewn dirt lanes. These latter groupings are small and few in number, and are usually relegated to the no-man's-land between the town's outermost civilized fringes and the true boonies—away from the paved thoroughfares, out of sight of most of the populace, and out of mind for most public-health and code inspectors. Bob Vogel's address was in one such backwater, at the very edge of West Brattleboro's town line.

I waited until we were on Route 9 before asking Todd what he'd dug up.

"Talked to Mrs. Wheeler. Story hasn't changed—her regular guy told her he couldn't service her until his insurance settled, and Vogel dropped in out of the blue. He did the job well and disappeared. The regular guy's name is Ned Barrows.

"I called him next and talked to his wife. The fire that trashed their equipment was in the garage—wiped out his two lawnmowers. Interesting, since he also has two snowblowers, neither of which was touched."

"Do they think it was arson?"

"No. She said they had no reason to. They just assumed an oily rag started it, or maybe the sun coming through a window and superheating a small gas spill. Barrows apparently isn't too neat and tidy."

"A little farfetched, isn't it?" I asked.

"Maybe. You won't find their insurance company arguing with you. That's why they haven't settled. Barrows is an on-call fire-man—dealt with the blaze himself out of embarrassment. I called his adjuster and was told they think the whole thing is pretty murky, including the spontaneous-combustion part. The only catch is, Barrows had undervalued his equipment to save on the premiums, so he's actually going to lose money on it, even if they do settle."

"So it's possible Vogel torched the mowers just to get the job at Mrs. Wheeler's," I muttered half to myself.

Todd continued, "I also called Helen Boisvert, and she told me that Vogel currently had a night job with New England Wood Products, a lumber manufacturer up around Jamaica—the four-to-midnight shift."

I was struck by the location—the town of Jamaica was a good forty minutes away, and one of the ways of getting there involved Meadowbrook Road. "How long's he been there?"

"Four months. He must've been moonlighting when he worked for Mrs. Wheeler."

I slowed the car by a peeling, barely readable wooden sign announcing Treetops Mobile Park, and turned off Route 9 onto a dirt lane in such poor shape it looked more like a track.

"Did Boisvert know about that?"

Bracing himself against the car's lurchings over the potholed, mangled road, he answered, "Indirectly. She said he does do odd jobs for extra cash sometimes. He tells her about them when she asks, so she's never thought much about it. They're always outside, and she's never heard a complaint. She double-checked on him at first, calling after he'd done a job and asking the employer how he behaved. She gave it up when it never led to anything."

I stopped the car and checked my watch. "Well, if he's still working nights, he must be gone by now—it's almost three-twenty-five."

We looked over at what had once been a beige-and-silver trailer, shoved up against the base of a large evergreen. It was decorated in mottled earth colors now, weather and neglect having conspired to concoct an enviably effective camouflage. Over the top of it, someone had built a pitched tarpaper roof, supported by rotting, warped beams at each corner, presumably to supplement the trailer's own leaky roof. Skirting the home's edge, sheets of ancient, shredded plastic had been duct-taped to cut down on the annual winter cold. The windows were small, stained, and blank, showing no curtains, lights, or signs of life. Between the battered metal front door and the road was a weed-choked jumble of rusting, broken debris, some of it almost fully returned to the earth, along with one garbage can holding a bulging plastic bag, and an exhausted example of J. P. Tyler's famous Russian olive. Chained to the evergreen were a rusty, prehistoric, but apparently valued bicycle, and an equally ancient lawnmower.

"Home sweet home?" Todd asked in low voice.

"According to what Ron gave me." I killed the engine, swung out of the car, and approached the trailer.

As I did so, I heard a noise to my left and saw a man emerging from a half-wrecked home similar to Vogel's. He had long, stringy hair and a struggling, wispy beard and looked like a turn-of-the-century ad for the terrors of consumption.

"He ain't in." The voice was jagged and harsh—a smoker's half croak.

I made a show of seeming disappointed. "Damn. When's he get back?"

"Late—night shift."

Now I looked surprised. "This is Bob Vogel's place, isn't it? The handyman?"

That brought a half smile to the neighbor's haggard face. "I don't know how handy he is."

"He does yard work, right? A friend of mine recommended him."

He rolled his eyes. "Some friend."

"Not a good idea?"

He equivocated slightly. "I don't know—I'm not in a hiring position. Maybe he's a frigging green thumb. I wouldn't try getting sociable, though. He's a dick-head."

"I'll keep that in mind. Is there somewhere he hangs out where I might find him tomorrow?"

"Try the Barrelhead." And without further ceremony, the human scarecrow moved off, climbed into a car I'd thought was abandoned, and drove away under cover of an explosive, rank-smelling smoke screen of burned oil.

Todd had slid over to the driver's side of my car and rolled down the window to eavesdrop on this conversation. I looked up and down the street for other signs of life, found none, and turned back to Todd. "Pull around in a U-turn."

He did as requested, stopping right next to Vogel's garbage can. As quickly and unobtrusively as possible, I pulled the fat plastic bag from the can, tossed it into the car trunk, and got into the passenger seat.

Lefevre shook his head slightly and smiled as he slowly negotiated our way back out of the trailer park. "You're not going to ask me to help dig through that, are you?"

"Might be interesting."

"So might the disease you catch from it."

The radio on the seat between us muttered my call number. I picked it up and answered.

"Ron says the Greenfield investigator you wanted to talk to is on his way up here. You available?"

I hesitated briefly. What I'd been hoping to do was drop the garbage bag off with Tyler and go see Gail. All day, I'd been pulled by the twin desires of running the investigation and keeping her company—knowing full well the former not only held the higher priority, but was also what she'd prefer I'd do. Nevertheless, having spent most of the day at it, I now dearly wanted to take a break and see how she was faring, especially in light of tonight's planned march down Main Street. It was reluctantly, therefore, that I told Dispatch I was on my way in.

Todd noticed my lack of enthusiasm. "Problems?"

"No, no. I asked Ron to locate the guy. I'm hoping he can fill us in on Vogel's past." That much was perfectly true, of course, but I sensed from his silence that Lefevre was waiting for a fuller response to his question.

"It's just tough pretending all this doesn't mean something personal to me," I continued.

"Maybe you shouldn't try so hard."

I looked at him directly. "I'm not so sure. Billy—among others—seems to think I'm losing my grip. At the *Reformer*, Stan Katz questioned the wisdom of having me involved. Even Tony had to shove me down your boss's throat, and only succeeded by guaranteeing I'd have a twenty-four-hour baby-sitter. I'm what's due the devil because we're shy on manpower and the case is too hot. Which doesn't mean a lot of people won't find it convenient to pin the tail on me if something goes haywire. Part of me wants to focus on Gail and on getting her—and us—back on track. Part of me wants to do my job and nail the son-of-a-bitch who raped her. And I know that by trying to do both I'm basically tripling my chances for screwing things up royally."

Todd was honest enough not to argue the point, which was just as well. My own description fell short of my true feelings. Gail's rape had triggered inside me the exact same emotions of sorrow and loss, albeit to a lesser degree, that probably would have attended her death. The bizarre twist, of course, was that she hadn't died. She was alive, vibrant with her own pain and suffering, and her living thwarted the conventional closure that would have followed her funeral.

It was a paradox that gave credibility to a phrase I'd always held in contempt—that rape was a "fate worse than death." While I still didn't completely agree with that, I was beginning to understand it.

Chapter Nine

Detective Jim Catone was in his mid-thirties, built like a wrestler, and had been with the Greenfield Police for over ten years. What I wasn't prepared for was the intensity of the man. As he entered the command post, escorted by Harriet Fritter, I had the distinct impression of a man under temporary—perhaps only marginal—control. It went a long way in explaining why he'd impulsively driven north to see us, rather than waiting for us to do the courtesy.

When I commented on this last point, after introductions had been made, he fixed me with a piercing look. "Lieutenant, I'd travel a whole lot farther to nail this guy. It's a pleasure."

I nodded silently. We were seated around Ron's central-most conference table—Brandt, Lefevre, Ron, and myself, with Harriet taking notes—all of us looking positively disinterested in contrast to our visitor's almost carnivorous eagerness. I finally felt obliged to mention, "Bob Vogel is at the top of our list, but he's still only a suspect. We don't actually have anything on him yet."

Catone mashed his hands together as if he were compacting a snowball. The muscles running up under his shirt cuffs fluttered and bunched. "You will—I guarantee it."

"When did you first come across him?"

"Six years ago, after he raped Wendy Polan. We screwed up the investigation, but he was as dirty then as he was when he got off for doing the same thing to Ginny Davis two years before that in North Adams.

"I'd been on the force just four years. I was still in uniform but being groomed for plain clothes. I worked with the detectives a lot, so I was involved in the Polan case from the start." His voice darkened slightly. "In fact, I was the one who discovered her. Her neighbors heard her screaming and called us. We found her strapped to the bed, beaten and bloody, half out of her mind, his come dried on her face—like a piece of meat. It broke her. She was completely changed after that. 'Course, our fucking the case up didn't help— we told her that helping us would put this scumbag behind bars. So she did. She spilled her guts to us, she picked him out of a lineup, let herself be humiliated by the DA and the defense attorney. She put herself through hell and none of it even got to court."

We all glanced at one another in uneasy silence. His intensity told me Catone wasn't a man I'd ever want working for me, but listening to him convinced me that he was just the historian we were after. I finally asked, "You knew Polan from before?"

He looked up, his expression softening a bit. "She went to the same high school I did—a few grades behind me. She was a pretty girl—popular, fun to be with. I never got to know her that well, but she sort of stood out in a crowd. You couldn't help noticing her."

"Our records are pretty slim still—we're having Massachusetts send up their files. She was single, right? Living alone?"

He nodded. "Yeah—bottom apartment in a three-story building—an old converted family home."

"How did Vogel gain entry?"

"He broke a back window—just enough to reach the door lock."

"She didn't hear anything?"

"He used a glass cutter. Besides, she was asleep and the bedroom was on the other side of the house."

"Had he cased the apartment beforehand?"

Catone shrugged. "I don't know. We never really got to talk to him, at least not without his lawyer there. We thought he must've. I mean, he had to have staked the place out to know she lived alone, and to pick a time when the upstairs neighbors were gone on vacation."

"We were told Vogel and Polan didn't know each other."

"Right—she'd never set eyes on him before that night."

"During the rape, he told her to keep her eyes shut?"

He smiled for the first time. "Yeah—of course she peeked. A rocket scientist he ain't. Even with Katherine Rawlins, the third woman he raped, he messed that part up, wrapping her head in her nightgown and not noticing when it slipped."

"Can you outline his approach?" I asked. "What were the common denominators between the two rapes you investigated?"

"I can do you one better—I researched the one he did in North Adams, too. All three were single women—"

"Prominent?" Brandt suddenly asked. "You mentioned that Wendy really stood out in a crowd. Were all three distinguishable that way, either through their looks or what they did for a living?"

Catone looked stumped for a bit. "Wendy was the prettiest. I only saw a photograph of Ginny Davis—the North Adams girl—she was the youngest, and sort of plain. She worked as a store clerk. I don't remember anything about her that stood out."

"How 'bout age?" I asked.

"Each one was a little older than the next. How 'bout yours?"

For a split second, I considered how we were referring to these women. Catone had begun by talking about Wendy Polan in almost reverential tones—now all four of Vogel's victims were beginning to sound like car wrecks. "Mid-forties," I answered.

He pursed his lips. "That's a bit of a jump, but it fits. Ginny was eighteen, Wendy, twenty-three, Katherine Rawlins, twenty-nine. Rawlins was a lawyer, and had been quoted in the paper off and on. I suppose that makes her small-time famous, if you stretch it a bit."

"Let's get back to his general approach," I prompted.

Catone nodded. "All three happened in the middle of the night, all were illegal entry—once by unlocked door, twice by window, although Rawlins's was half open because of the weather. All were done on the victims' beds, and all of them lasted from two to four hours. The last two involved bondage, the first was forcible restraint. All three involved a knife—"

"Only used the last time?" Brandt interrupted again.

"Right. We already talked about the blindfold angle. Let's see . . ."

"Did he trash the bedrooms?"

Catone's eyes widened. "Yeah—totally. It depended on how close the neighbors were, but if he could get away with it, he busted televisions, lights, pictures, you name it."

"Any ritualistic displays of the victims' underwear?" Lefevre spoke up for the first time.

"The last time—he draped Rawlins's all over the lamp shade."

"And she was also the only one he used his knife on, is that correct?" Todd pursued.

"Right. Cut her nipples."

"And broke her jaw." Todd consulted some notes he'd written to himself. "What was the sequence of all that?"

Catone's expression had changed subtly during Todd's questioning, recognizing as we all did the growing similarities between his cases and ours. His eyes seemed to take on an extra glow, and an enthusiastic flush colored his cheeks. It made me think of a basketball fan in the last quarter.

"He tied 'em down first—all except the first one—and then he threatened them with the knife to get 'em to cooperate."

"Did he speak in a whisper?"

"Yeah, he did—the last time. Rawlins described it as 'stage sexy,' like Vogel was trying to win her over. We thought that's why he got so violent with her, because she didn't buy the act and told him to fuck himself." He glanced at Harriet suddenly, who'd taken no notice. "Sorry—her words—not mine. That's when he broke her jaw."

Todd held up his hand. "Hold it. Let me back up a bit. The whisper wasn't to disguise his voice?"

Catone looked blank for a moment. "She didn't know him—why bother? He was just doing a Latin-lover routine."

Lefevre paused to write something on his note pad. The rest of us were interested enough in his line of questioning that we waited patiently for him to resume. "How about gloves? Was he wearing any?"

Again, Catone smiled. "He probably wished he had. When he broke her jaw, he also dislocated his little finger. That's one of the things that helped nail him. Rawlins heard him scream with the pain, and when we picked him up, he was wearing a splint."

"So, presumably, breaking her jaw came at the end of the attack."

"Yeah. He split right after."

Todd made another notation. I spoke up during the pause. "You mentioned he was violent with the others, too. Aside from the rape itself, what did he do?"

"After he'd finished with them and trashed their stuff, he beat 'em up."

"He hit them all in the face, or just Katherine?" Todd asked quickly.

"Just Rawlins. He punched the others in the stomach and breasts—Rawlins got it there, too—the face was an extra, probably because of what she said to him."

"Was he naked during the attacks?" I asked.

He hesitated, thinking back. "I'm not sure exactly—it wasn't something we focused on. He had his shirt off with Rawlins—she commented on his chest hair—but he kept his pants on. I don't know about Ginny Davis. Wendy mentioned a T-shirt, but I don't know about the pants."

"The files we're expecting might have that," Todd muttered.

I reached back to early in the conversation. "You mentioned Wendy had seminal fluid on her, indicating Vogel ejaculated during the rape. Did he ejaculate with all three women?"

"He couldn't get hard with Ginny, but he came with both Wendy and Rawlins."

"Several times? You mentioned he spent several hours with each of them."

He nodded. "Twice each with Rawlins and Wendy. Vaginally and orally with Wendy—vaginally only with Rawlins, I guess because of the nightgown around her head."

I had other questions—mostly technical ones—which I thought would be better answered by the dry, emotionless paperwork already headed our way. As helpful as Jim Catone had been, I didn't want to rely too much on him—or be influenced by his blatant prejudice.

Ron did have a question, however. "You said Vogel trashed the bedrooms of these women. What about the rest of the house?"

"He left them alone, except where he'd broken a window or lock to get in."

"That reminds me," Brandt said, "in trying to figure out if he cased the victims' homes, did you ever find out if he got jobs in the area, or pretended to sell door-to-door?"

Catone shrugged. "We checked on that but came up empty. We

never figured out why he chose the women he did. They were of different ages, backgrounds, appearance. Something about each of them caught his eye. We all had our theories, but nothing really made sense."

"You're absolutely sure he did them all?" I asked quietly.

I'd been saving this question for last, figuring it might stimulate more than a simple yes or no. We'd all had cases go sour, or stolen from us in court, but I'd rarely met anyone so emotionally hooked on a case. You learned to live with your losses in this business, and you trained yourself to stay as coolheaded as possible.

His reaction didn't disappoint me. He leaned forward, fixing me with his dark, impassioned eyes. "You're damned right I am. That son-of-a-bitch is dirty as hell, even if he did beat the system two out of three times." He held up his hand and began counting off on his fingers. "First time—the victim ID's him right off the bat. Says she scratched him, and he's got the marks to prove it. He's got no alibi and his prints are all over her place. That one got to court, but the jury deadlocked, the judge threw it out, and the DA didn't have the balls to try it again."

"Why the deadlock?" I asked.

He sat back suddenly, disgusted. "Defense argued it was a consensual deal gone bad—that the girl changed her mind and screamed rape."

"They bought that?" Ron blurted.

"Only because Vogel's lawyer twisted it around. She showered after the assault, took a long time reporting it, messed up her story—she did everything you're not supposed to do. In a nutshell, the jury didn't like her, and maybe didn't trust her, and the lawyer played on that. But there was no doubt about Vogel's involvement. But the judge bought it, said that considering some of the sexual positions she described, she had to have been a willing participant, since a simple twitch of the hips would've ended it. I mean, Jesus, they didn't even focus on the knife, or the fact she was scared shitless. The DA fucked up, if you ask me."

Brandt interrupted gently. "And with Wendy Polan?"

Catone held up a second finger. "I know you're not supposed to blame a fellow officer, but that fiasco rests entirely with Walter Huss. The bastard was hitting the bottle—got the wrong address on the search warrant of Vogel's apartment, lost the chain-of-custody

paperwork, and then made up a phoney story to cover his ass . . ."
He slammed the tabletop with his hand. "But Vogel was dirty
then, too. We just couldn't do anything about it. If you people
nail this creep, you'll make a lot of people real happy. I came up
here so you'd understand that—and so you'd know that if you need
any help south of the border, don't hesitate to call."

Brandt and I exchanged glances. It was obvious things would
have to get pretty desperate before either one of us took him up
on that. Nevertheless, he had brought the similarities between our
case and Vogel's MO into sharp focus. I no longer had much doubt
that we were on the right track.

I got to my feet and extended my hand, making it clear the
interview was over. "Jim, we appreciate your making the trip up
here. It's helped a lot. And I promise we'll keep you posted."

As further niceties followed from the others around the table,
Harriet closed her pad and gracefully escorted our guest back outside.

There was a long pause following his departure. Tony finally
looked over at Todd Lefevre and asked, "Well?"

Todd smiled and confirmed my own thoughts. "Well, I don't
think we'd ever want to use him in court, but I do think he's
confirmed we've got a hot one."

"With a few discrepancies," I added.

Brandt nodded. "Like the gloves and the lack of ejaculate?"

"Yeah, and the fact that he kept some of his clothes on in the
past. Also, he never got a job in the victim's neighborhood before,
to scope the place out."

Todd waved his hand in disagreement. "But his MO's evolved
from crime to crime. From tape to slipknots, from nightgown to
pillowcase, from showing a knife to using it. He's refined his style.
So now he takes all his clothes off, puts on gloves to protect his
hands, makes a display of the woman's underwear, even gets a job
to stake the target out. If you look at them all as a progression,
including Gail, I don't see much that doesn't fit. I'd bet Dunn
would have a field day painting exactly that picture to a jury—
and making it stick."

Since I happened to agree with him, I didn't argue the point. I
stood up and stretched instead, suddenly feeling the previous night's
lack of sleep. "Well, let's not forget how Greenfield dropped the

ball on victim number two. I'd just as soon go slow, take the heat, and get it right."

"Amen," Brandt said quietly. "Where're you off to now?"

I paused halfway out the door. I kept forgetting my agreement not to move around independently. "I thought I'd see a man about some garbage."

He wrinkled his nose. "Oh—right. Let me know what you find."

I walked down the hallway to a set of stairs that was awkwardly located in the middle of the floor, opposite the detective squad's front door. Earlier, returning from Vogel's trailer, I'd asked Harriet to locate J.P. and have him dissect the garbage bag I'd swiped. Having seen him do similar operations before, I knew where I'd find him.

The Municipal Building's basement is a wonderous throwback to a previous century—and to childhood nightmares. It is high-ceilinged and gloomy, strung along a twisting central corridor lined with mysterious blank doors and wired-off alcoves, complete with the distant rumbling of unexplained machinery and the sense—at all times—that one is never alone.

The police department had reserved several of those mysterious rooms for its own use, including a small gym and shower area, and it was to one of the least used of these that Tyler had retreated.

As I opened the door and crossed the threshold, I both blessed his consideration and cursed having set him to work. "Jesus Christ."

He looked up from his hunched-over position in the midst of a putrid, rotting semicircle of refuse, spread out over a large plastic sheet. He had Vicks Vaporub smeared under his nostrils and was wearing latex gloves. "You get used to it eventually." He dug the Vicks from out of his apron pocket and tossed it over to me. A box of gloves lay just shy of the plastic sheet.

"What've you found?" I asked, decorating my upper lip.

"So far? That this guy has one of the worst eating habits I've ever seen. His two major food groups seem to be Spam and peanut butter—I guess potato chips are considered roughage. As far as I can tell, he doesn't eat anything that doesn't come in a package, ready to eat. None of it even needs heating up, much less cooking. And he seems to have a fondness for cake icing, straight out of the can."

I pulled on a pair of gloves and got down next to him. The

sickly sweet odor that rose in waves from this glistening, mold-crusted mess made me slightly dizzy. "Anything else?"

He pointed to a segregated corner of neatly piled but slimy documents. "Third-class mail, mostly—same as we all get. The envelopes are all unopened." He suddenly extricated a small piece of paper from inside a half-finished can of marshmallow fluff. "Grocery-store receipt." He carefully placed it with a soggy pile of other like it. "It's amazing to me how little paperwork people like this collect. Besides a single electricity bill, I haven't found anything that links this guy to the outside world—no phone bills, letters, magazines, newspapers—nothing except lousy food, lots of cigarettes, and empty beer bottles."

"And junk mail," I added. I moved over and began gently peeling apart the various catalogues, flyers, and ad sheets, looking for something more personal that might have become mixed in with them. It was the usual haphazard collection, from local grocery-store inserts to mail-order brochures, along with three tantalizing offers from Ed McMahon to make "Robin Vogle" a millionaire.

Fifteen minutes and about half the stack later, I sat back on my heels, a barely perceptible buzzing pressing against the inside of my temples. "Bingo."

Tyler looked at me, his eyes narrowing. "What?"

I showed him a damp and incongruous Victoria's Secret catalogue, my finger pointing to the mailing label.

"Damn," he muttered, surprise mingling with embarrassment. Smeared but still legible were Gail's name and address.

Chapter Ten

My timing couldn't have been worse. Delayed by the meeting with Jim Catone and pawing through Vogel's garbage with J.P., I didn't arrive at Susan Raffner's until shortly before 7:00 P.M., long after any anticipated quiet moment with Gail had been overrun by the stress and commotion leading up to the march. When I was brought upstairs by a distracted Raffner, still clutching a cordless phone in her hand, Gail was in the company of several intense women, including Mary Wallis, who cast me a startled and embarrassed look.

Gail was speaking in a hard-edged staccato to a harassed-looking woman with a note pad. "Damn it all. I thought we'd made that clear from the start. It doesn't matter if we march around the courthouse from the left fork *or* the right—either way we look like a herd of goddamn cattle. The point is to divide there so that we meet at the common. We want to envelop the courthouse." She made a vase-like gesture with her arms, "Not walk around it like it was some puddle in the road. Where the hell's Susan?"

She turned to the doorway and saw me there. Susan was back in the hallway, talking quietly on the phone. Gail's face crystallized briefly—hard and angry, both too pale and too flushed in parts; and her eyes were red-rimmed and haggard—gleaming almost feverishly. She seemed totally thrown by my appearance. Her mouth opened slightly and her hand vaguely touched the side of her head, but for a moment nothing was said. I realized with dread that showing my face—especially this close to an emotionally charged public event—served only to remind her of why she was here, and undermined the protective, hard-driving persona she'd adopted for herself. Like a strong breeze on a house of cards, my appearance— for a brief but telling instant—was threatening and unwelcome.

She finally managed to mutter, "Joe."

"I know you're busy. I just wanted to wish you luck and tell you I'll be out there. I'll get out of your hair now." I waved awkwardly, turned, and bumped into Susan Raffner, who'd seen enough to understand what had happened.

She grabbed my arm and gestured to Gail, who was only slowly recovering her composure. "Why don't you both take five in my office? I'll sort things out here. I think we're in pretty good shape— not to worry."

She ushered us both out of the room and down a short hallway, steering us into a large, comfortable corner room filled with book-shelves, overstuffed furniture, and an enormous, cluttered antique desk. She closed the door behind her, leaving us alone.

Instinctively, I reached for Gail's elbow, startling her and making her pull away. "I'm sorry. I should've called or given you some warning. I just wanted to see you, to wish you good luck tonight— let you know I was here . . ."

She held up her hand, shaking her head. "It's okay. You just caught me by surprise. I hoped you'd come by—I guess I thought it would be earlier, and then I forgot all about it."

She looked at my face and half smiled, moving closer and taking my hand in hers. "I didn't mean to flip out on you. I feel a little like a juggler on center stage . . . I just lost my concentration for a second."

Her voice was still taut, but at least the cause of her tension was no longer me. She was one of the strongest women I'd ever met, but I knew—and I half suspected she did, too—that in the long run she was going to have to let down her defenses, allow the pain and the anger and the loss to flush through her, and then rebuild herself from the inside out.

But that time wasn't now. Now, she needed all the stamina she could muster.

Still, I felt bound to ask if she was thinking ahead. This was someone, after all, who was fully aware of how deep rape cuts the soul, even before she'd experienced it personally. "You sure you want to do this? So soon after?"

She gave a lopsided half smile and shook her head. "I'd really like to escape to a deserted island for a few months."

"That could be arranged," I said quickly.

She turned and settled into the huge, soft armchair near the window, looking exhausted. Again, she shook her head, but with no smile this time. "I can't, Joe. I need to stick this out."

We'd debated her beliefs too often for me not to understand what she meant. In her view, leaving town, even though wounded, would be to concede to her attacker, abandoning the very principles in which she and her colleagues put their faith. Besides, the die was already cast.

All of which left me with few options. "Would you like to know how the investigation's going?"

She didn't react at first, and then answered slowly, almost shyly. "Do you have a suspect?"

"We're looking at someone. He doesn't know it yet."

"Someone I know?"

"I'm not sure. I don't think so."

Her eyes widened. "It could be a stranger?"

"Possibly. If this is the guy, that's how he worked before." I probably should have tried Vogel's name out on her, but something told me she didn't want to know—not yet.

She nodded, studying the floor. After a few moments, she pushed herself slowly and awkwardly out of the chair, like a woman twice her age, and came to me. "Thank you—that did help."

"One question?" I asked.

"Sure."

"Are you on the Victoria's Secret mailing list?"

She actually laughed then, and looked slightly embarrassed. "I didn't ask for it. It was sort of an inside joke—feminist black humor. You found a copy at the house?"

I nodded and lied. "Yeah—it seemed a little out of character."

She touched my cheek then, and I was careful not to react beyond smiling.

"Thanks for being there, Joe."

I nodded. "Good luck tonight."

"Where're you going to be?"

"In the background."

She nodded wistfully, and as she turned toward the door, her face became more composed, a little harder—a face for the outside world. She smiled at me one last time as she left the room. "I like the eau-de-Vicks, by the way—very subtle."

Two hours later, I was standing in front of the darkened Municipal Building, high on the slope overlooking where Main Street split in two at the tip of the courthouse lawn like the water before a ship's bow. Heightening the image, a long, wide, undulating stream of flickering candlelight slowly flowed down Main from the south, breaking before and surrounding the building like phosphorescence, a credit to Gail's dramatic flair.

I crossed the steep lawn diagonally, seeing that Gail, Susan, and the other leaders of the march had opted for the route closer to where I was. I joined the crowd at the curb.

Illuminated as they were by the gentle flickering of their handheld candles, the women seemed both serene and somehow otherworldly, like harbingers of some truth only they fully comprehended. Certainly some of the people watching them were at a loss. As Gail drew near to us, her face upheld and her long hair loose and flowing down her back, I found myself next to two young men dressed in jeans, work boots, and denim jackets. They'd been chatting quietly together before I arrived, their hands buried in their pockets against the evening chill. The three of us—I standing slightly back of the other two—watched those women, united in a common cause, making a statement all the more powerful for its silent and symbolic eloquence.

One of the young men leaned toward the other slightly. "Is that the one that was raped?" he asked quietly.

His companion muttered, as if muted in awe. "Yeah. Third from the left."

"Pretty," whispered the first, "I'd fuck her in a minute."

Bob Vogel's station wagon was a twisted, rusting, spring-shot heap, the standard ornament on a run-of-the-mill backwoods Vermont lawn, and reminiscent of his next-door neighbor's. Except it was parked in the Jamaica lot of New England Wood Products, where Vogel worked the four-to-midnight shift.

Willy Kunkle and I were in my car far to the rear of the lot, beyond the reach of the anemic floodlights attached to the distant warehouse's corrugated walls. We were completely wrapped in a couple of thick wool blankets I kept stashed in my trunk for just such occasions. It was 11:45, and I was having serious problems keeping awake, even with the cold. Willy was snoring peacefully, wedged in the corner, looking utterly content.

For me, unlike for Gail and her colleagues, the parade had been a melancholy affair. They had been pleased by the attendance, the coverage—by several outside papers and radio stations, and even WNNE–TV from White River–and by the overall tone of the evening. Among other luminaries, Jack Derby—Dunn's opponent in the SA's race—made a speech, suitably brief and stirring, which hit home all the more by highlighting Dunn's absence. Afterwards, there'd been a song or two sung by the crowd, and then, on cue, all the candles but Gail's had been extinguished—over three hundred all at once—and Gail had quietly placed hers on the steps of the courthouse. It had been both theatrical and magical and had left many of the spectators wiping their eyes.

And yet I had left feeling depressed, the voices of those two young men still echoing in my ears, enhanced by several other comments I'd heard in the crowd. Gail and her supporters had their cause to rally around and their enthusiasm to maintain their faith. I just had a thorough working street knowledge of the odds stacked against them.

Naturally enough, Gail had been unapproachable following the rally. Flushed by their perceived success, her supporters had surrounded her like an enveloping cocoon and had virtually carried her away to Susan's house to celebrate. Stimulated as they were—or, perhaps, depressed as I was—I felt they were ignoring the look in her eyes, which I saw only from afar as she was whisked by. She appeared wrung out and haunted. I hoped Susan would find time to focus on her friend, and not get swept up in the fervor of making a well-timed political point.

It was in this bitter mood that I decided to personally step up the investigation of Bob Vogel—starting that night.

Willy Kunkle stirred next to me, peered at the watch on his

right wrist, and let out an exaggerated sigh. "You know what's going to happen, don't you? This schlunk is going to get in his car, drive home, and hit the sack, leaving us with butkus."

I checked my own watch; just a couple of minutes shy of midnight. "Maybe. You're getting overtime."

He grumpily buried himself slightly deeper into his blanket. "That's no shit."

A flow of people began spreading out from a small door in the building's side over the surface of the parking lot, to be absorbed here and there by dozens of cars. Vogel's heap remained ignored for some ten minutes before a narrow shape, otherwise indistinguishable from this distance, finally hesitated by its side, worked the lock, and then settled inside. A black, oily cloud erupted from the station wagon's tail pipe and drifted over the rest of the car on a gentle breeze, making the subsequent appearance of head- and taillights look like the distant glimmerings of a lighthouse on a foggy night.

"Jesus," Willy muttered, "couldn't we bust him on that alone?"

I waited for the car to make its way to the lot's entrance before I started my own engine and followed discreetly. There was enough traffic around that I wasn't overly concerned about being spotted, but we were a long way from West Brattleboro, and I didn't want Vogel to get a fix on my headlights too early.

Jamaica is located near the Stratton Mountain ski resort, a couple of state parks, and a scenic reservoir, all of which make it a magnet for "seasonal visitors," in chamber-of-commerce parlance—"flatlanders" to the locals so dependent on their money. As a result, the road passing through it, Route 30, is wide and well maintained—a quick and pleasant way to meander through several quaint villages on a forty-five-minute trip to Brattleboro. It was anticipating this trip that we eventually pulled out onto Route 30 and headed southeast, a good half mile and several cars behind Bob Vogel's belching, poisonous, but fast-moving vehicle, easily identifiable even at this distance because of its mismatched taillights, one of which had been made vaguely legal by covering a bare white bulb with pink-tinted cellophane.

We hadn't gone more than a mile, however, to the center of Jamaica village itself, before our travel plans were abruptly revised.

"Where the hell's he going?" Willy asked as Vogel turned right off of Route 30 and then almost immediately left at a fork in the road.

I slowed down at the corner and waited until the taillights ahead were over the crest of the hill he'd taken. "Beats me—that goes to Wardsboro."

Willy's voice became peevish as he realized that his hopes of a quick trip back to Vogel's place were about to be thwarted. "I know that, but if he took Route 100 farther down, it would take him half the time."

"Maybe he plans to stop along the way." My interest, unlike Kunkle's, had suddenly sharpened, dissipating my earlier fatigue. "Who do we know around here?"

Willy hesitated a moment, grasping the gist of my question. "How 'bout Freddie Gibbons?"

I shook my head. "I think he moved to New Hampshire. Besides, he was a car thief."

"Well, if anyone needs a car, this guy does."

We continued in silence for a while, keeping far enough back to catch only occasional glimpses of our quarry. After a quarter of an hour, the first houses of Wardsboro village slid by on either side of us, quickly joined by the church, the town hall, and a typical New England clustering of white-sided, green-shuttered homes. Willy muttered, "Better close up—Route 100 is just ahead."

I sped up slightly, saw Vogel slow down at the stop sign, and then watched him turn left. "He's going the wrong direction, back north toward Route 30."

Now Willy's curiosity matched my own. "Did we miss something? A drop-off, maybe?"

I shrugged. "It's possible."

A few hundred feet farther on, Vogel veered right off of Route 100, crossed a bridge, and headed for Newfane, five or six miles farther along. At that point, nervous that even infrequent glimpses of us in his rearview mirror might tip him off—especially along this much more isolated dirt road—I killed my headlights and drove by moonlight alone.

This proved easier in theory than in fact. The moon was not full, the sky smeared with occasional clouds, and the air thick with the dust kicked up by the car ahead of us. Both Willy and I ended sitting bolt upright in our seats, craning forward in a futile effort to better see into the gloom, all while traveling at the breakneck speed set by our unsuspecting target. Several times, I had to swerve at the last moment to avoid the ditch, and once, despite Willy's last-second warning, I ran over something large and furry which made me break into a thirty-foot skid that almost put us into a tree.

We both knew this road ended up turning back into pavement above Newfane village, where thicker traffic would allow us to turn on the headlights and stop driving like two suicidal blind men, so our disappointment was keen—and in Willy's case vocal—when Vogel turned right onto Grout Pond Road, thwarting our hoped-for relief.

"What's that stupid son-of-a-bitch doing? We're going to get killed because this dumb bastard doesn't know where the hell he is."

But I was beginning to see a pattern. "He's avoiding the village—and Route 30 again."

Kunkle grabbed the dashboard as I half slid off the road on a curve, my rear wheels spattering gravel as they groped for some traction. "Why? He doesn't have any warrants."

"The car must be uninspected. If he gets caught while he's on probation, he could get his ticket punched—at least I think that's what he's afraid of. And at the speed he's going, I'd guess he takes this route every night—looks like he knows every curve by heart." We both hit our heads against the roof as I lurched over a half-buried boulder.

Whatever his reasons, Bob Vogel was wending his way home, by as straight a route as such linked dirt roads as Hobby Hill, Baker Brook, and Sunset Lake would allow. By the time we finally reached Route 9 in West Brattleboro and unobtrusively merged our headlights with those of the steady trickle of late-night traffic, the effects of a smooth road and clear vision were almost anticlimactic. We were so tired from trying to keep the car on level ground through sheer will power alone that we barely noticed such effort was no longer necessary.

I went beyond the turnoff for Vogel's trailer park as he pulled in, and parked in the lot of an abandoned garden center, across from an exhausted-looking motel with a stuttering, half-lit Welcome sign.

Kunkle sat back cautiously, as if unsure the seat was still behind him. "So what the fuck did that do for us?"

I flexed my stiff fingers. "We have to check his habits—same as you did with Harry Murchison. And this may have given us something to squeeze him with, if we need it."

He turned away and stared out the side window. I didn't blame him for being irritated. Above and beyond the danger of the wild goose chase we'd just survived was the fact that Willy was here purely to baby-sit me, as both Brandt and Todd Lefevre were unavailable. That might've been all right if Vogel had done something other than take the scenic route home, but now Willy obviously felt it well within his rights to make me pay for his disappointment.

Until I spotted a lone figure on an ancient bicycle wobbling away from the trailer-park entrance. "I'll be damned."

Willy followed my gaze. "That him?"

"It's the same bike he had chained up next to his trailer."

We watched him laboriously grind away at the pedals, his body bent over the handlebars, heading east toward the anemic glittering of West Brattleboro's outermost inexpensive restaurants, motels, and bars.

"What the hell's he doing on that thing?" Kunkle wondered out loud.

"If we're right about the car, he's keeping a low profile." I pointed to a long, nondescript building set back from the road slightly. "We are, after all, cutting right across the front door of a state-police barracks."

I followed him in several stages, moving only once I was about to lose sight of him. Within a mile, he wheeled up to the front of one of the town's more decrepit bars and leaned his bike against the wall.

Kunkle chuckled beside me. "The Barrelhead. At least I'll be able to find out what he's up to in there."

That the Barrelhead was one of Willy's listening posts came as no surprise. It was the Rainbow Room for Brattleboro's down-and-out. In constant jeopardy of losing its license, it was also where we found Willy himself in the old days when he'd still had both arms, a marriage in shambles, and been in a headlong rush toward alcoholism.

I killed the lights again and found a parking space far from the bar's front door. We got out of the car and stretched in the refreshingly cold night air. There were about six other cars in the lot, enveloped in the red-and-blue glow from the Barrelhead's neon sign. Jukebox music leaked from the building like secondary smoke.

We moved to the shadows by the side, where a small window decorated with a flickering beer sign allowed us a dim view along the length of the bar inside. Bob Vogel had just seated himself on a stool and was struggling out of his windbreaker, talking to the bartender. There were two other men at the bar itself, neither one of them close to Vogel, and several more among the booths along the opposite wall. A fat waitress in what looked like a black-satin nurse's uniform, complete with cap, lounged at the far end of the bar in an endangered long-legged director's chair, either uninterested or unable to tend to her flock.

"You still come here?" I asked Willy.

"Fuck you." He suddenly pointed at Vogel. "Well, look at that."

Having finally removed his jacket, Vogel revealed a filthy but solid-red wool shirt underneath.

"Did J.P. come up with a final analysis on that fiber sample yet?" I asked, knowing that Kunkle, despite his seeming disregard for everyone but himself, actually made a clandestine effort to keep up on every detail in a case.

"Yeah—said it showed engine oil and dirt stains, just like that," he said, pointing at Vogel, who by now was working on his first shot and beer.

We stood by the window for several minutes more to determine that Vogel was there for his own entertainment, and not to meet anyone. Then, after Willy relieved himself against the wall, we retired to my car to wait him out—again.

Willy settled into the folds of his blanket, awkwardly tugging it up around his neck, and fixed his eyes on the sporadic traffic passing by on Route 9 before us. "So—assuming we're only farting around with Jason Ryan because of Gail's dikey friends—we've got two real suspects, right? Harry Murchison and old Bobby in there?" He jerked a thumb at the bar.

"I remember six others from Gail's list of possibles, and two from the intelligence meeting."

He didn't hide his contempt. "Very diplomatic. You could throw yourself in there, too—you were the last one with her. And from what I hear, the DNA analysis won't come up with anybody else."

I didn't bother responding. His style aside, he was essentially correct.

"So how close are we to doing more than sniff through their garbage?" he persisted.

Willy was not a chatty man, nor was he given to seeking the counsel of others. It occurred to me therefore that he was curious about my reasoning. He wanted to know whether Vogel—whom we'd almost broken our necks tailing for no apparent reason—was becoming an obsession with me, to the detriment, perhaps, of Kunkle's assigned target, Harry Murchison.

I turned the tables on him. "You're the Murchison expert. What've you got?"

"He had motive, opportunity, and means—"

"What motive?" I interrupted.

"He's a grab-ass generally, and he made eyes at Gail enough for her to put him on her list."

I conceded the point with a nod.

"He also had the opportunity to preplan the attack when he was in her house fixing the windows. He might've even rigged one of them then. I interviewed the guy he worked with that day. He said they were out of each other's sight off and on the whole time. On both those points alone, he's stronger than Vogel. We don't know if Vogel and Gail ever set eyes on each other."

"Why did he wait a year between rigging the window and breaking in?"

Willy shrugged. "Why does any guy jump a broad? Something snaps. Maybe he rigs windows all over town. And it looks like it could've been Murchison's truck on Gail's street that night. Plus he has no alibi."

"We haven't talked to him yet. Faced with a rape charge, he'll probably come up with some explanation, even if it shows he was cheating on his girlfriend."

Kunkle scowled at the window for a moment. "So you're not buying Murchison?"

"Not like I buy Vogel. Like with the red shirt tonight—every time we take a look at him, he gives us something new. Did J.P. tell you we found a catalogue in his garbage with Gail's address on it?"

Kunkle's inbred restlessness shot to the surface. "So when do we get a warrant to search and bust the guy?"

He was echoing the same thoughts I'd been mulling over after the rally. My conclusion then held all the more true now. "As soon as we've answered every question we can on our own. When I sit down with Bob Vogel, I want to know more about him than he does—like why he drives home the way he does. And what he talks about in there." I gestured to the bar. "And what he was doing to make him miss his appointment with Boisvert the morning after the attack."

Kunkle merely nodded, apparently satisfied.

"It shouldn't be too much longer," I added. "Maybe a couple more days, especially if Dunn puts on the pressure."

The bars close at two during weekdays, and it had been after one when Bob Vogel had wheeled his bicycle into the Barrelhead's lot. Nevertheless, he looked much the worse for wear when he staggered outside exactly at closing time—the last to leave— and fumbled with his handlebars. It was with an element of relief that I saw he was too drunk even to get on the saddle, and contented himself with pushing his transportation homeward. I didn't need him flattened under some passing truck—not just yet.

Simultaneously, Willy and I swung out of the car and walked over to the bar's entrance. I faded back slightly to let Willy cover obviously familiar ground.

He pounded on the thick glass window covering the top half of the door.

The predictable answer was instantaneous and reflected the manner of the establishment: "We're closed—fuck off."

Kunkle pulled out his badge and tapped it against the window, calling out, "Hello, Ray."

A muted curse barely reached our ears, followed by footsteps and the sound of the lock being shot back. The actual opening of the door, however, was left to us, as we heard the footsteps retreating without further ceremony.

Raymond Saint-Jacques—short, squat, balding, and in dire need of a shave—was heading back behind the bar as we entered, like a mole seeking the sanctuary of his hole. The gargantuan waitress was still perched on her endangered chair, as oblivious to us as an overdressed fire hydrant.

Willy and I parked ourselves on two stools opposite Ray, who was now safely barricaded among his bottles and shot glasses.

"What do you want?" He kept a wary eye on Kunkle, which made me wonder about the full extent of their shared past.

Kunkle smiled. "We were working late. I told Joe what a wonderful place this was, and what a great conversationalist you were, and he said he wanted to meet you."

Ray stared at us sullenly for a few moments, fully understanding Willy's gist. He turned to the waitress, who'd done no more than breathe since I'd first seen her an hour ago. "Nora—go away. Do something outside."

Nora slid off the creaking chair with the delicacy of a dolphin in heels, and drifted off through a door leading to the back.

"What'll it be?" Ray then asked Willy.

"A beer. Joe?"

"Tonic water."

Willy laid two twenty-dollar bills on the bar; Ray served us our orders and stuffed the money into his pocket. He didn't make change. "What do you want?" he repeated, with no less hostility.

Willy took a sip from his beer, allowing me to ask, "You know the guy who just left? The one on the bicycle?"

Ray shook his head. "Nope—Bob somethin'."

"How long's he been coming in here?"

"A few months."

"Good customer? Pays his tab?"

"He's okay—a little behind sometimes."

Willy wiped his mouth and spoke, "Not a good guy, though, Ray—could cause you problems."

Ray merely stood still and looked from one of us to the other, a resigned look on his face.

"Does Bob talk about himself much when he's here?" I asked.

"He's usually working the bottle too hard."

"He have his ups and downs, like most of us?"

"I suppose."

"Night before last," Willy asked, "what was he like?"

"Wasn't like anything. He wasn't here."

"That unusual?"

The bar was as still as a confessional, the three of us utterly motionless. I could see in Ray's face that he was becoming interested, tipped off by Willy's comment about Bob's character and our having pinpointed the time we were interested in. Gail's rape had played big enough in the media by now—including the now silent television that hung above the bar—that Ray would have to have been brain dead not to know of it.

He finally said, "Yeah. It's the first night he's missed since I've known him. He came in later, though."

Willy jumped on that. "How much later?"

" 'Bout nine in the morning. He was in a real bad mood."

I poked at the ice in my untouched drink. "How so?"

We were all playing by different rules now. By telling us Vogel had messed up his routine on the night of the attack, and had appeared at the bar later in a depressed state, Ray had moved from informant to witness, whose statement would in all likelihood make it into court. All three of us knew that, and Willy and I knew further that we'd better tread carefully, making sure we couldn't later be accused of putting notions into Ray's head.

But the bartender was no stranger to the process. He and Willy went back a long way. He even seemed to bask in the moment a little, understanding the importance of what he was about to tell us, and knowing we could do nothing but wait for him to do so.

"You want me to freshen those up a little?" he asked with a smile.

Kunkle was not in the mood. "Cut the crap."

Ray Saint-Jacques looked pleased with himself. "All right. Look, I read the papers, like everybody, so I know about the rape, you know? It was sort of a hot subject that morning—even on the radio. Bob didn't start right in on it. He maybe knocked off a few at first, but later, after everybody else had pretty much left, he started in, saying shit like, 'Sure as hell I'm fucked now—they'll be all over me—don't even have an alibi—fucking broads.' Stuff like that."

I chose my words carefully. "Did he explain what he meant? Go into any detail?"

Ray laughed now, his entire mood changed by the conversation. "Well, shit, he didn't confess, if that's what you're after, but it was kind of creepy. It was like he was resigned to it. Most of my customers are a little paranoid, you know—got a record and all, or maybe just think the world's out to get 'em. But he didn't seem all worked up—just in the dumps."

"Did he explain why he didn't have an alibi?"

"Nope."

"He didn't say anything else?"

Ray grinned again and made a tossing-back gesture with his fist and thumb. "Too busy, you know?"

"He drink a lot?" Kunkle asked.

"No more'n the rest of 'em."

"That's not telling me a hell of a lot, Ray." Willy's voice had gained a touch of menace.

The bartender held up both hands in mock surrender. "Hey— it's the truth. He drinks, but he always gets out the door. That's more'n I can say for some of 'em—remember, Willy?"

Kunkle glared at him.

"Has he been drinking more in the last forty-eight hours?" I asked.

He tilted his head to one side, looking thoughtful—or at least pretending to. "Could be, you know?"

That didn't satisfy Kunkle. "Has he or hasn't he?"

Ray's voice suddenly went surly, as if he understood that with me there, there was little Willy could do physically to back up his aggressive tone. "What the fuck am I—his nanny? He has, all right?" He stepped away from the bar, grabbing both our glasses and dropping them into a sink of greasy water at his waist. "I got work to do before I can turn in. Are we done here?"

I slid off my stool. "For the moment."

"Good. That'll be six-fifty."

Willy stood and leaned across the bar, his powerful right hand sprayed out on its surface as if he might vault right over it. "Don't, Ray. I could come back alone."

The fat man glowered, but kept quiet.

Outside, breathing in the cold, medicinal air, I asked Willy, "How reliable is he?"

Kunkle smiled confidently. "In legal terms? He's as good as gold. I've used him on four affidavits in the past, and every one of them stuck."

"Let's hope we're on a roll, then," I muttered, and headed for the car.

Chapter Eleven

Pending Dunn's approval, we had all that we needed for a search warrant of Bob Vogel's trailer—enough circumstantial evidence linking him to Gail's rape to convince a judge we had probable cause. I didn't write up the affidavit as soon as I got back to the office, however. I still wanted to determine that our guess about why he traveled the back roads to commute from work was correct, and for that I needed to contact both the department of motor vehicles and Helen Boisvert, Vogel's probation officer, neither of whom would be available until morning.

I also wanted to get some sleep before tackling this next crucial step. Cops march to ever-more precise legal drummers as they follow an investigation toward its hoped-for finale in court, and the further they proceed, the more paranoid they become, increasingly convinced that something they do or don't do will result in some lawyer destroying their case. I didn't want to embark on that road with the little sleep I'd gathered over the last two days. The trade-off of a little time lost for a clear head in the morning seemed more than a bargain.

I therefore left my office at 3:30 A.M.—after dictating my daily report for Harriet to transcribe later—as exhausted as I could ever remember feeling, and virtually sleepwalked the few blocks to my apartment, not trusting myself to drive.

But things didn't turn out the way I'd hoped. Throughout the few hours I'd planned to spend sleeping, I kept working and re-working the case in my mind, reviewing the steps we'd taken, the facts we'd amassed, knowing of the general scrutiny that awaited our results. For as soon as that affidavit was filed, it would become part of the public record, available to Katz and his colleagues, to Susan Raffner and hers, to Dunn's opponent, Jack Derby, and to the selectmen and any other politician or advocate with a point to make. Headlines would follow, speeches by Dunn, Derby et al., debates in the press, more marches and demonstrations—and through it all, I hoped, Gail might begin to find solace knowing that the man who had permanently affected her life was about to be similarly treated.

Assuming we'd done our jobs right.

As a result of all this mental thrashing, I returned to the office in as bad shape as I'd left it—my eyes burning, my temples tender to the touch, and my head resonating with a buzz as pervasive as an overworked boiler in the basement.

As I crossed the threshold, Harriet's expression told me I looked as bad as I felt. "I know, I know. Bad night. Could you do me a favor? Contact DMV and run a license check on Robert Vogel—find out if he's legal, and if he has a car registered to his name."

She nodded wordlessly, and allowed me to escape to my glassed-in cubicle without any maternal admonitions.

I sat heavily in my chair, wishing to hell I could somehow shake off my exhaustion, or at least make it less visible, and looked up Helen Boisvert's number in my address book. I called her emergency private line and was met by a voice both preoccupied and irritated.

"Helen, it's Joe Gunther. I'm sorry to butt in but I need a quick piece of information about Bob Vogel."

"Fine—come by in forty-five minutes."

I pushed harder, still reluctant to reveal more than I thought she needed to know. "It's real quick, and I'm scrambling for time."

There was a pause, followed by a half-strangled, "Shit—hold on."

I heard her talking to someone in the background, explaining that she needed privacy for just a few minutes.

"What do you want?" she asked when she got back on the line.

"How does Vogel commute to work?"

There was dead silence. I imagined her struggling with the urge to rip the phone out of the wall, but her response when it came was strangely placid. "Hold on a sec—let me grab his file."

During the pause, Harriet poked her head in through my door and half whispered, "Bob Vogel has no driver's license, and no vehicle registered in his name."

I gave her a nod as Helen got back on the line. "He car pools with a guy named Bernard Reeves. Did Bob do something to screw that deal up?"

I should have been more tuned in to her peevish state of mind and kept my mouth shut. But I was operating at low voltage, and feeling a little guilty about keeping her out of the loop. "He's driving around the back roads like a rumrunner."

I heard the click of Helen's lighter being ignited in the background. "That little peckerhead. You got any other questions?"

I quickly requested Bernard Reeves's address and phone number and let her get back to work.

Bernie Reeves's phone was answered by a cheery-voiced woman. Without identifying myself, I asked for Mr. Reeves.

Her voice immediately chilled. "Are you selling something?"

I looked at the phone in surprise. "No. I'm just looking for some information, and I heard Mr. Reeves was the man to call."

"About New England Wood?" She had regained about half of her previous good humor, obviously disappointed I was not calling for her.

"Indirectly, yeah."

"Why don't you call back in about two hours? He's still asleep— he works the night shift."

I thanked her and hung up, not even remotely interested in waiting two hours. Bob Vogel's personal file still hadn't arrived from the Massachusetts Department of Corrections, which meant we were on the brink of getting a search warrant for someone we still knew too little about. The opportunity to at least nail down Vogel's peculiar commuting, therefore, despite its presumably mundane explanation, played larger in my mind than it might have otherwise. I grabbed my coat from the hook behind the door and told Harriet where I'd be, too tired to bother lining up someone to ride shotgun.

Reeves lived along the no-man's-land stretch of Western Avenue between Brattleboro and West Brattleboro—a narrow umbilicus, half residential, half commercial, that had linked the two communities for over a hundred years. Despite West Bratt's long-lost political and municipal independence from its overwhelming neighbor, this stretch had still resisted becoming more than a minimal concession to the alliance. West Brattleboro prided itself on its separate identity, even though it had little left to show for it.

The address Helen Boisvert had given me fitted a modest, tidy, one-story frame house set back from the street on a steeply sloped, well-tended, quarter-acre lot—as unique to this town as swing sets, the Lions Club, and fast-food franchises.

I parked in the driveway and rang the front-door buzzer protruding from under a small wooden sign proclaiming this "Bernie and Edith's."

A small, middle-aged woman with short, suspiciously gray-free hair greeted me with a quizzical but pleasant, "May I help you?"

I showed her my badge, a gesture I generally bypassed unless I was either treading on legal thin ice or trying to make an impression. "I'd like to speak with Bernie Reeves."

She recognized my voice. "You just called here. I told you he was asleep."

"I understand that, but I'm afraid I need to talk with him now."

Her eyes widened and her shoulders slumped in fear. "What's wrong? What's happened?"

I smiled encouragingly. "This doesn't involve you directly, Mrs. Reeves. I just need some information—but I need it now."

Defeated, she backed out of my way and invited me in. "I'll go get him."

I stood for a few minutes in a small, overstuffed living room, its windows lined with glass and porcelain trinkets, its curtains and furniture decorated with clean but faded flowers. Two recliner armchairs separated by a small table faced a large television set whose blank, shiny screen seemed poised to mesmerize at the touch of a button. It made me think of some predatory magician taking a brief nap.

Mrs. Reeves returned with her husband in tow, bleary-eyed and disheveled, still tucking his shirt in over a well-founded beer gut. He looked at me warily but without fear as his wife moved to one side.

"What's up?" he asked. His voice was neutral but pleasant— that of a man with nothing much to hide.

I showed him the badge I was still holding in my hand. "I was wondering if we could chat a little—in private."

Mrs. Reeves furrowed her brow angrily and left without a word. He smiled as she went and lifted his eyebrows at me as she slammed a distant door behind her. "That didn't win you any points. She's going to give me the third degree anyway."

"Sorry, but I'd like to keep this confidential for at least a day or two."

He pointed to the sofa and sat in one of the armchairs. "I can hold out that long—depending what it's about."

I settled on the edge of the sofa and watched his face carefully. "Bob Vogel."

His eyes narrowed and his mouth turned down, half in disgust, and half, I thought, in apprehension. His hands found one another and his fingers knotted together nervously. I was glad I'd decided to do this in person, instead of on the phone.

"What about him?"

"According to his probation officer, you're supposed to be his car pool to and from work. I gather that's no longer true."

He opened his mouth to speak, thought better of it, and paused. His face had become pale. "Why do you care?" he finally murmured.

"When did you two stop riding together, Bernie?" My position on the edge of the sofa gave me a little leverage over him, trapped as he was in the embrace of the soft chair. I let my voice take advantage of the implied authority.

"A month—maybe a little longer."

"You knew you were supposed to contact Helen Boisvert, didn't you? What happened?"

Reeves glanced out the window behind me, apparently hoping some gorilla's arm would suddenly appear and whisk me away. "I meant to. I guess I forgot. Didn't seem like that big a thing."

The tension in his voice told me otherwise. "Why didn't you call her?"

"He said I shouldn't tell," he almost whispered.

"Did he threaten you?"

Bernie Reeves nodded toward the back of the house, where his wife could be dimly heard moving about in the kitchen. "Her. He said he'd take it out on her if I told anyone."

"You guys get in a fight?"

Now that his secret was out, Bernie regained some of his composure, his voice strengthening slightly. "It was all right at first. The supervisor asked me to help him out since we were on the same shift and didn't live too far apart. I figured Vogel had done his time, and if the company was willing to take him on, that was okay with me. He gave me the creeps, though—talking the way he did. I guess he picked up on my not liking him much. Said he didn't need me acting superior and that he'd get him his own car. That's when he told me not to tell anyone or he'd come after Edith."

"Why didn't you call us, or Boisvert? You knew he was on probation. Either one of us could have yanked his chain."

He gave me a look of utter contempt. "That son-of-a-bitch is crazy. He said that no matter what happened to him, he'd come back sooner or later—that he never forgot anyone who fucked him over."

Reeves shifted angrily in his seat and tried to paint a slightly more stalwart portrait of himself. "I might not have cared much for myself, but Edith's alone here most nights. What the hell could I do?"

I shook my head, utterly unswayed. I had spent a professional lifetime listening to people convince themselves that their self-preservation was the same as high moral ground. As far as I could see, Bernie Reeves's spinelessness had eventually led to Gail's rape.

I struggled to keep my voice neutral. "You said Vogel gave you the creeps. What did you mean by that?"

"When we started the car pool, I tried to make small talk, you know? Break the ice a little. I didn't know the guy—we work in different sections of the plant. I thought I'd be friendly. But whenever we talked about women—you know how you do with another guy—he got really weird. When we talked about girls in the plant, say—he'd say things like, 'She'd look better with my dick in her mouth,' or real violent stuff, especially about women who stood their own ground or were a little snotty to him. We've got some tough ones at the plant."

That single word cut through the weariness clouding my mind. Gail's attacker had called her a "snotty goddamn bitch."

"Is that how he described those women? As snotty?"

"You mean, is that the word he used? I guess so. I couldn't swear to it."

I paused, disappointed by his faulty memory. "Did he ever talk about what he'd done with women?"

His lips tightened and looked uncomfortable again. "A little."

"He told you what he'd done time for."

It wasn't a question, but he answered anyway by the way his eyes suddenly dropped to his hands.

"What did he do, Bernie? Start bragging?"

He nodded, back to whispering again. "I told him I thought he was twisted. He pulled a knife and made me swear to keep quiet. And he said the car pool was over—that he'd take care of himself, and that I better keep quiet about that, too, or he'd do to Edith what he'd done to those others."

"And you believed him."

He leaned forward then, no longer tentative or doubtful of his motivations. "Damn right I did. He scared the shit out of me. I didn't know if he was going to cut my throat or not. What did I care if he drove himself to work? It sure as hell meant more to him than it did to me, and I wasn't about to risk my life over it. I just wanted to be rid of him."

"Did you see him after that?"

Reeves shook his head emphatically. "I'd see him from a distance, maybe, but I'd steer clear. He didn't mess with me, and I sure as hell didn't mess with him."

"So you don't know what he was wearing at work two nights ago?"

"Nope. Didn't even see him."

I stood up and walked over to the front door. "Did he have any friends at the plant, that you know of?"

Having made his confession, Bernie Reeves regained his home-owner's authority. He made a gesture as if to usher me out. "I told you what I know, and that was probably too much. The way you people work, I'm probably knee-deep in shit by now, right?"

"Everything's relative, Bernie. Thanks for your time."

Despite my ambivalence about his character, I felt Bernie Reeves had done me a double service. As I drove back toward the center of town, I now knew we'd gathered more than enough for a warrant—and I was personally convinced that we had the right man.

My optimism was apparently catching. The Municipal Center's

parking lot, normally pretty dormant, was teeming with activity. Cars and trucks bristling with antennas and sporting flashy logos of newspapers and radio and TV stations from as far away as Burlington were parked at odd angles all over the lot, their owners either fiddling with equipment or clustered in small groups sipping coffee from Styrofoam cups. A news conference, a big one, was in the offing.

But my own confidence deflated suddenly at the sight, and settled unhealthily with the exhaustion pounding softly at my temples. I continued driving, parked around the corner, and entered the building from the far side, dreading the start of a circus that could only do us harm.

I went straight to Tony Brandt's office, finding him, as I thought I might, in close company with James Dunn. They had their backs to the door as I entered, both of them standing over Tony's desk, studying the contents of an open folder.

"Isn't it a little early for a press conference? We don't even have a search warrant yet," I blurted out, my sense of self-preservation dulled by lack of sleep and irritation.

They both turned and looked at me.

"I don't think so," Dunn answered at his chilly best.

"Where the hell have you been?" asked Tony, "I've been looking all over for you." His own anger ran deeper than it needed to, which told me the press conference was not his idea.

"Interviewing Bernie Reeves, Vogel's ex–car pool partner to and from work."

"Alone?" Dunn asked. I saw Tony go still, obviously ruing that he'd brought the subject up.

"Yes. It was only a background talk. He'd make a good witness. Vogel bragged about his past rapes and fantasized about committing sexual violence on women at work. He even pulled a knife on Reeves to keep him quiet about dropping the car pool."

Dunn jerked a thumb toward the window and the reporters milling about outside. "Do any of them know you've been working alone?"

I felt my cheeks flush and struggled to keep my voice level. "I haven't been. I wanted to check this one thing out before drawing up an affidavit. I wanted every detail covered before committing ourselves in public."

Dunn gave me a withering look. "We had more than enough for a search warrant early this morning. That's what those reporters are doing out there. The warrant's in the bag—unless you screw it up. I've already handled enough questions about you as it is, so don't add to my problems."

In the strained silence that followed, Brandt explained, "Santos got chatty with Alice Sims."

Mention of the *Reformer's* courts-'n-cops reporter gave Dunn a second wind. "And now Katz is thinking that a little human-interest piece on the trials and tribulations of a certain cop with a big personal stake in this case—whose boss thinks he's Sherlock Goddamn Holmes and lets him work on his own girlfriend's rape— might make interesting reading. So if you don't like the timing of this press conference, keep in mind that it might just keep your ass out of hot water."

Brandt let out a small sigh and began guiding me out the door. "Vogel's jacket came in this morning from Massachusetts. Why don't you compare notes with Ron while we dance with the media? It won't be long. Work up a rough draft of the affidavit in the meantime."

I paused at the door. "Katz did ask me about a feature piece. I turned him down."

Brandt's murmur was beyond Dunn's earshot. "Don't worry about it. He talked to me, too, very reasonably. This Santos thing's just got the SA worked up. And we do have more than enough for a search warrant."

I, too, kept my voice down. "What if we come up empty? We'll all look like idiots. Why not wait the few hours it'll take us to check the trailer out? Then he can talk till he puts 'em all asleep."

Brandt sighed and glanced over his shoulder. Dunn had gone back to studying the press release. "There was a bad poll this morning." He paused, knowing how hollow that sounded. "And Jack Derby's holding his own press conference in an hour."

He raised his eyebrows and smiled tiredly. "I can't tell a state's attorney what to do. I can only recommend that he's full of shit, and *that* only diplomatically. His entire staff is against this, too."

Given the threat to the case, that came as no comfort, but I nevertheless did as Tony suggested—I checked in with Ron Klesc-zewski at the command center, and used him and his by-now voluminous files to draw up the most careful and thoroughly re-searched warrant application of my career. If this thing was going to blow up in our faces, the police department was not going to be the one needing surgery. In the back of my mind, however, an unacknowledged bell kept sounding that, despite all my care, I was too tired to be doing such detail work.

I knew some of the hoopla was inevitable. Gail's own candlelight march had kicked it off, and even it had been the mere overture to a media/politics/public-relations carnival that was going to play on the front page for weeks. What was unsettling me was James Dunn's reaction. Although never a mellow man, he was powerfully self-restrained, and had never before left the boundaries of his office to meddle with police procedure on such a personal level, and at such a hysterical pitch.

He had also never made any bones about his dislike of sex-crime prosecutions, of how they hinged more on appearances and prejudice than on the solid evidence he cherished. As far as I could see, the combination of just such a case and an increasingly desperate reelection bid was apparently pushing him to some sort of edge.

Driving my fogged brain through the wordy intricacies of the affidavit, I kept wondering how the pressures on Dunn might affect his performance. Given his almost irrational behavior now, how safe was Gail's case in his hands?

Such meanderings were interrupted by a patrolman sticking his head into the room, informing me that Dennis DeFlorio was on the radio. I crossed over to Dispatch. Dennis had taken over the discreet surveillance on Bob Vogel, stationing himself well out of sight in the trees ringing the trailer park. He was calling in on a special frequency, not commonly found on the recreational scanners around town. Nevertheless, he made all his references as oblique as possible.

"Joe, our boy just got a visit from Probation, accompanied by a sheriff's deputy."

I checked my watch. It was late morning. I'd spoken to Helen Boisvert just a few hours earlier. She hadn't mentioned she was scheduled to visit Bob Vogel. This was not good news.

"Why was the deputy there?"

"Pure baby-sitting—just Helen following the rules. He never left the car."

"Anything happen between her and her client?"

"They weren't happy with each other. She yelled something at him when she left and he gave her the finger after she turned her back."

"He still there?"

"Far as I know."

I turned to Maxine Paroddy, the day-shift dispatcher, suddenly alive to how thin the ice had become under Dunn's—and our—feet. "Who do we have out in West Bratt, or nearby?"

She answered without hesitation. "Santos and Smith, in separate vehicles. I've got two other units close enough to the interstate to be there in under five minutes."

"Get all four of them rolling and tell them to convene at the state-police barracks down the road. Lights but no sirens till they get near, then go with the flow of traffic. I don't want to spook this guy unless it's already too late."

I turned to Ron, who'd followed me across the hall. "Where're Dunn and the chief holding their press conference?"

"Upstairs—the boardroom."

"Get Brandt and bring him here—now—but don't tip off the reporters that something's up."

I turned back to the radio. "Dennis, you within sight of the trailer?"

"Negative. I couldn't raise you on my portable, so I had to go to higher ground. Too many trees or something."

More likely antiquated equipment, I thought. "Get back to your observation post. I'm sending you backup—four cars. They should be there in exactly eight minutes for the bust. You're in command."

There was a surprised silence. Dennis had obviously thought he was calling in with an informational tidbit, not a summons for reinforcements. "What's the charge?"

"Driving without a license and operating an unregistered vehicle. But he may be armed. So be careful and do it by the numbers."

DeFlorio gave a strictly neutral "10–4," and returned to his post.

Maxine, operating the other radio, looked over her shoulder at me. "First two units are standing by at the barracks."

I nodded but didn't answer. After a minute's silence, I yielded to impulse. "Call Parole and Probation and see if you can locate Boisvert. Maybe she's back by now."

Brandt walked in a moment later, looking grim. "What's up?"

"I'm worried Boisvert might've tipped Vogel off. I'm sending a team in to arrest him for his vehicular violations. I figured that would hold him till the search warrant is issued."

Brandt nodded. "Okay."

Maxine added. "The second two units are in place, and Boisvert is still out."

I checked my watch. "Tell them to hit the trailer in four minutes."

She turned back to the transmitter and passed the word. We could hear the cryptic replies, the tension in the officers' voices filling the air like static. The room was deadly silent, each of us listening, balancing what we knew should happen, based on our training and past experience, against what might go wrong. Both Smith and Santos were members of the department's special reaction team—what used to be called SWAT before Hollywood made the term politically unpalatable—and Dennis, for all his slovenly habits and slow-witted reputation at other times, was at his best in these types of operations, his nature abdicating to adrenaline and years of practice. All of us in the dispatch room would have preferred a more thought-out, coordinated approach, but we were trained to respond to the unexpected, and no one questioned my judgment.

The four minutes came and went; a few more were added to them. I could visualize the trailer surrounded, the area secured, positions and equipment checked, an attempt made to rouse someone from inside, and finally the forced entry, made low and fast, shotguns ready, men fanning out, their hearts hammering under bullet-resistant vests.

The radio finally came alive; Dennis again: "He's gone, Joe. Nobody's home."

Chapter Twelve

James Dunn sat at his empty, highly polished desk, staring at his neat, interlaced fingers, as if impressed by their utter stillness. I was, too, actually. I figured the news of Vogel's disappearance would send him through the roof.

But the SA was no longer the politician scrambling for headlines in the wake of a bad poll; he was in operational mode, in which he was at his best.

He finally looked up from his hands at the three of us—Brandt, Todd Lefevre, and me. "You talk to Boisvert yet?"

I nodded. "She said she confronted him on the illegal driving and that he accused her and the state of a double standard—telling him to earn a living and contribute to society, and then trying to send him back to the slammer for driving without a license when he'd done nothing to deserve it."

"Is that what she threatened him with?"

"At first. She told me she calmed down a bit after hearing his explanation and gave him till the end of the week to come up with a solution."

"But she heard about his driving to work from you, right?"

Here it comes, I thought. "Yes. I'd discovered he wasn't registered with DMV. I had to fly it by her to make sure she didn't have an explanation, but I didn't tell her why we were asking. I guess I also hit her at a bad time. Anyhow, she grabbed a convenient deputy instead of one of our guys as an escort—another reason we didn't know what was going on—and she acted on her own. I should have guessed she might, from her tone of voice. My screwup."

"True," was all he said in retribution. After another pause, he mused, "Doesn't seem like enough to make him run. What else did they discuss?"

"She did say he was pretty paranoid about the rape. He kept connecting her visit to our investigation—which she knew little about and he only suspected we were conducting—accusing her of trying to lock him up on a technicality to buy us time till we could nail him with the big one."

"Which is exactly what we almost did," Dunn muttered. "Nice try, by the way."

His mildness was almost unnerving. It was possible the same cold, logical thinking that made him good in a courtroom had just saved me from being crucified—but it was hard to believe.

"So," he said in a livelier tone, "where do we stand, having told the world we all but have the cat in the bag?"

Brandt gave him a detailed rundown of the manhunt we'd set into motion—alerting all area enforcement agencies, poring over Vogel's records for personal references that might tell us where he'd run to, and contacting DMV to put a flag on all inquiries concerning unlicensed drivers who might fit Vogel's description.

"And," Lefevre added, "the affidavit for a search warrant's been finalized by this office and delivered to Judge Harrowsmith for signing."

Dunn nodded. His voice was almost conciliatory when he spoke. "All right, that's good for the moment, since we're still the only ones who know Vogel has gone missing. In twenty-four hours, however, that will probably change, and if we still haven't located him, I'll be asking the state police to take over the investigation." He looked up at Tony Brandt.

Brandt didn't so much freeze as crystallize. For a moment, I saw them lock eyes like opposing force fields, each apparently hoping pure energy alone would atomize the other.

Tony finally took a discreet deep breath and countered, "I understand the pressure you're under, but that might not be in your best interest. We know more about Bob Vogel right now than the state police will learn in a week of going through his files—and that's a week in which Vogel could disappear forever."

"They have better resources than you do."

"Perhaps, and if we think Vogel has left the area, we'll call on those resources."

Dunn's voice became the icy knife I knew all too well. "He's already left the area, Tony. Your staff saw to that."

Brandt ignored that bullet for the sake of the battle. "People in his position don't run for distance, James, they run for cover, and they run for places they know personally. We're not just faxing other departments to keep their eyes open—we're telling them where to look and who to talk to, according to Vogel's own files. The state police could do no better."

Dunn didn't answer at first. Then, finally, the hands came alive, slipping free of one another as he pointed to the exit. "Good. You'll have twenty-four hours to prove your point."

Bob Vogel's trailer was dark and cluttered, and looked like a cyclone had blown through it. And it stank—of dirty clothes, stale sweat, rotting food, and mildew. The small refrigerator oozed the gaseous sweet odor of a biological time bomb waiting to be unleashed.

To Tyler and Kunkle—Tyler's unlikely but preferred companion for detailed searches—it was all as rich as an untapped gold mine. The two of them, gloved and masked, surveyed the dim premises with interest. I, in contrast, stood in the narrow doorway, imagining only the owner of this rat hole emerging to violate Gail in her clean, airy, sweet-smelling home. That someone with so little to offer could wreck such damage turned my stomach.

"Let me know if you find anything," I told them, before returning outside to the relative pureness of the surrounding decrepit neighborhood, where the other members of the squad were foraging around and under the trailer and picking through the abandoned station wagon.

I stood in the middle of the rutted dirt lane, breathing the cool, fresh air so much at odds with the setting. The weather-beaten, broken-backed trailers were strung out along the road haphazardly, as if thrown away, and shared a disturbingly imperiled appearance—as if the earth were swallowing them up in imperceptibly slow bites.

Whether it was the disappointment following Vogel's disappearance, Dunn's display of overwhelming self-interest, the unslacking melancholy that had dogged me since the attack on Gail, or just plain exhaustion from too many days without sleep, I suddenly felt overwhelmed by lassitude. The damage to Gail had been done, her attacker identified—to my satisfaction at least—and the subsequent process attending both those facts—her healing and his eventual capture and prosecution—put in motion. My role was soon to be diminished to that of the loyal supporter. I was to be attentive, encouraging, helpful if possible, but essentially useless until forces beyond my control had run their course. Once caught, probably by some other agency than ours, Bob Vogel would be in James Dunn's manipulative hands, while Gail's recovery depended mostly on her own abilities to rally and rebuild her life. It all left me feeling strangely empty-handed.

Brandt, who had broken with protocol to join us in the field, came up beside me in the middle of the road.

I guessed he was going to ask how I was doing, or maybe how Gail was faring—both questions I was in no mood to answer at the moment—so I sidetracked him with what I intended to be small talk.

"I was surprised Dunn let me off so lightly, even if he does plan to hang us all in public in twenty-four hours."

Brandt chuckled and loaded up his pipe. "There won't be any hanging. He'll just write us off as well-meaning boobs. And he sure as hell isn't about to land on you, especially now."

I glanced over at him, puzzled. "What's that mean?"

He took his time lighting up, sending out large smoke signals into the air. When he was finally satisfied, he removed the pipe from his mouth and peered into its bowl, as if curious to see how that had happened.

"It means," he said at last, "that our state's attorney can become a little cynical when the pressure's on." He pointed his pipe stem at me. "You are in the public eye, a nice guy, a good cop, and Gail's lover. In that same light, Helen Boisvert is an antagonistic, introverted crank with no political allies and a low profile—meaning the public doesn't know who she is and doesn't care that she also happens to do a good job."

"He's going after Helen?"

"Not necessarily. Dunn held that premature press conference

this morning solely to steal Derby's thunder, telling the media we were closing in on a prime suspect. He gave no names, detailed no strategy, and still managed to sound upbeat and in control. It was a gamble that worked in the short term, because an hour later, Jack Derby gave a sincere and heartfelt dog-and-pony show, but he lacked the goods Dunn pretended to have. Point one to Dunn, something he felt he needed, since Derby had stolen the limelight at the candlelight march."

Tony nodded toward the trailer. "If this search results in enough evidence to trigger an arrest warrant, that'll be point two, showing Dunn to be the experienced old hand he claims to be, and maybe giving him enough of an aura that Vogel's skipping out will seem like a minor detail, easily remedied, especially if he throws us out and brings in the state police."

"But if the aura's not enough," I concluded bitterly, "then Helen gets crucified with a great show of reluctance."

Tony raised his eyebrows. "You got it." He was quiet for a moment, seemingly lost in reflection, his eyes on the distant tree-line, which was tinged with the first colorful signs of the coming foliage season.

He turned and looked at me carefully. "If this thing works out, and we flush Vogel out, Dunn's going to own him. We'll do the paperwork and the background research and all the rest as usual, but Bob Vogel is going to sit on the SA's velvet pillow—his golden key to reelection. And nothing better happen to threaten that. For whatever reasons, James Dunn is playing for keeps this time, and I don't think anyone should forget it."

He checked his watch suddenly and murmured, "Well, I better get back," as if our seemingly impromptu little chat had been the sole reason for his visit.

I was still mulling over Tony's ominous prophecy when I heard Tyler calling me from the trailer's front door an hour later, the white dust mask he'd been wearing dangling like a miniature feed bag from around his neck. I slid off the car hood I'd been using as a bench and crossed over to him.

"I think we got him" was all he said, gesturing for me to follow him inside.

They'd opened the windows, so the smell was less intense. In a bizarre reversal of the norm, their search had actually tidied things up a bit. Kunkle was standing in what passed for the kitchen with a triumphant look on his face, but he left the exposition to Tyler.

"Everything's been sketched, photographed, and documented, so you don't have to tiptoe too much, but you might still want to watch what you touch."

I gave him a quizzical look, which Kunkle responded to more bluntly. "The guy beat off a lot, all over the place, including on the mirror."

I repressed an involuntary shudder, much to Willy's satisfaction. "What've you got?"

Tyler stepped over to the counter next to the cluttered, greasy sink, and pulled open a drawer. Inside, among other utensils, was a newly bagged and labeled carving knife—short, broad, and ugly. "First: a knife, stained with what a preliminary field test tells me is blood. Obviously, Waterbury'll have to check it out, but I wouldn't be surprised if it matched Gail's type."

He stepped through to the narrow hallway in the waist of the trailer and pulled open a closet door. Hanging from a nail on the inside was a loop of cotton rope similar to the small nooses we'd found dangling from Gail's bed frame. Tyler merely pointed at it, adding, "Item two. Again, I'll have to match the cut end to what we've already got, but it looks likely."

I nodded and continued following him down the hallway and into the bedroom, passing the bathroom door with its smeared full-length mirror along the way. "Watch yourself," Kunkle chuckled, as if warning me against a chained rat.

Tyler stood at the far side of the disheveled, foul-smelling double bed. What sheets were still on it were stained dark and covered with scab-like blotches. Despite having visited countless places as bad or worse, I felt my throat tighten.

"This is the gold mine," Tyler resumed, in a singularly odd metaphor. "You can tell he favors the right side of the bed."

"No shit," Kunkle murmured.

"I reasoned that if he were to hide anything under the mattress, it would be on the side he wasn't occupying." He lifted the mattress so that the light from the window played on the box spring and asked, somewhat indelicately, "Item number three—look familiar?"

Spread out like a crushed butterfly was a scanty pair of women's underwear, gaudy and colorful, with a small red heart sewn on its crotch. Gail had bought it as a joke several years earlier.

I merely nodded. Willy had the rare good taste to keep quiet.

J.P. gestured to a pile of clothes in the corner, on which the red shirt Willy and I had seen Vogel wearing earlier was perched at the top. "The shirt speaks for itself, but this . . ." he moved to another closet and pulled down a small box from the back of a high shelf, "is the real bonanza, if you ask me. The kind of thing prosecutors love. It was actually tucked even further out of the way, between the roof and the false ceiling, behind one of the acoustic panels."

The box contained several four-by-five glossy photographs, which Tyler spread out carefully on the bed with his latex-clad fingertips. "These still need to be dusted using fancier equipment than I've got. If they're as hot as I think, it'll be worth the effort."

I leaned forward and studied them. They were of various views of Brattleboro—of its sidewalks, crosswalks, and storefronts—but all of them featured Gail, alone or chatting with other people, dressed for summer weather in a tank top and shorts, and looking, to my saddened imagination, remarkably youthful, happy, and carefree. The pictures had obviously been taken on the same sunny day, close to one another in time, as if the photographer had found his quarry outside and downtown, and had shot off a half roll in quick succession.

I straightened back up. "That's eight photos. You find any others?"

Tyler shook his head. "No, but they were in a Green Mountains Lab envelope with the negatives." He patted his pocket. "And the negs match the prints. I'm guessing he shot these and left the rest of the roll unexposed. Probably either he or the lab threw the blank film away."

"How 'bout a camera?"

There was a pause. Willy and J.P. glanced at each other. Tyler finally said, "Guess not."

I rubbed my aching eyes with my thumb and forefinger. "We'll have to check into that. Anything else?"

"There're about thirty porno magazines under the bed," Kunkle said.

"Kiddy or adult?"

"Straight adult—no boys, no kids. Some of the girls look like teenagers, but that's pretty standard."

There was a long pause, and I realized that I'd trampled their euphoria with my lack of enthusiasm. I took a deep breath, trying to override the humming in my head, and gave them both as genuine a smile as I could muster. "Looks like a home run, guys. You might as well collect all this and log it in. It's about as strong a basis for an arrest warrant as Dunn could ask for. Thanks."

Tyler smiled back sympathetically, but Willy just shook his head. "Go to bed, boss. You're falling apart."

Bed, however, was out of the question. As I walked into Ron Klesczewski's operations room, intent on escorting the arrest-warrant affidavit all the way to the judge's pen, I was stopped by the gleam in Ron's eye. He cupped the phone in his hand and murmured, "I think we got something."

I waited while he continued listening to whoever was on the other end of the line.

He finally said, "Hang on a sec," and looked at me again. "This is Wilma Belleview—she's the sheriff's dispatcher in Newfane. She just got a call from a power-company guy at Harriman Station asking if there've been any MVAs in the Jacksonville–Harriman Dam area. One of their field men was supposed to be working at the Glory Hole out there but he's not answering his radio."

MVA stood for Motor Vehicle Accident. "He have a history of wild driving?"

Ron shrugged. "I don't know, but Wilma told them she'd call around. VSP and Wilmington PD drew blanks, so she thought she'd try us on a long shot." He moved over to one of the neat paper piles on his table and retrieved a single, slim folder, his enthusiasm gaining momentum. "The point is, one of Vogel's big enthusiasms a few years ago, when he was still living in North Adams, was fishing and hunting around the Harriman Reservoir. He and his buddies did that a lot, and they once got busted for trespassing onto the dam, trying to piss into the Glory Hole."

Dulled as I was by fatigue, I was becoming infected by Ron's energy. "How long ago did the field man head out there?"

"Early this morning."

"Was his radio working when he left?"

"Yup. What do you think?"

I held up my hand instinctively, as if to slow down oncoming traffic. "I don't know yet. How's the sheriff handling it? They have anyone in the area?"

"Not really, and there haven't been any MVAs. They weren't planning on doing anything."

No reason for them to, I thought, and pointed at the phone still clenched in Ron's hand. "Better let your friend off the hook."

Ron looked at the receiver in surprise, muttered his thanks to Wilma, and hung up. "Should we send someone out there?"

I sat down in one of the metal folding chairs clustered around the table. "How often did he visit the area?"

"Every hunting season, fished there every summer, all through his teenage years and into his twenties, at least according to family and friends." He waved a hand across the stacks of files and folders before him. "I didn't find anything recent, but it was obviously an old stomping ground."

"We had any other nibbles?"

Ron shook his head.

I rubbed my forehead. I was so tired by now, I could barely function, much less jump at the notion of traveling forty-five minutes to the far end of the county because some power-company field man was playing hooky. "When did Harriman Station first try to contact their guy?"

"Three hours ago."

"Long-time employee?"

Ron had asked all the right questions before me. "Seventeen years—rock solid."

Despite his eagerness, or perhaps because of it, I merely felt more drained as I said, "Okay. I was going to wait for J.P. and the others to bring back what they need for an arrest warrant and then see the process through, but I might as well keep out of their hair and do something more constructive. I'll pick one of them up on the way out of town and check out your Glory Hole."

I got to my feet slowly, ignoring Ron's look of disappointment at being left with his paperwork. "Then I'm going home for some sleep."

* * *

I didn't go into great detail with Sammie Martens when I picked her up outside Bob Vogel's trailer park, and—after giving me a quick glance—she didn't ask for any. She merely listened to my directions, accepted that we were being stimulated in large part by a hunch of Ron's, and took over the wheel as I slouched down into the opposite corner and closed my throbbing eyes.

I didn't need to admire the passing countryside. Like many people living in southern Vermont, I was intimately familiar with the Harriman Reservoir and its surroundings. Hanging like a seven-mile-long twisted streamer from Route 9's rigid curtain rod, the reservoir nestles in a bunched-up cluster of steep, stocky, tree-choked hills vaguely reminiscent of the Appalachians—a setting unlike any other in the state. Coming south off of 9 onto Route 100, roughly paralleling Harriman's jagged shore, it is easy to think that Vermont's been mysteriously left behind, perhaps because the driver is not actually crossing the Green Mountains, but moving among them as they mingle to become the Hoosac Range leading down into Massachusetts. It is, for locals at least, a recreational area of choice, and a place I and many of my friends visited often.

Even the so-called Glory Hole was familiar ground. A hundred-and-sixty-foot-wide concrete, curved funnel that looked like a gigantic suction hole in some child's nightmare, it sat, as if floating, some thirty feet from the dam that had formed the reservoir back in the 1920s and which, back then, had been one of the largest earthen dams in the world—two hundred feet tall, eight hundred feet long, and thirteen hundred feet wide at the base. During extremely wet years, when the Glory Hole's role as spillway was called upon to protect the dam from any eroding overflow, people from miles around would gather at a convenient cliff high above the hole and look straight down, transfixed, as millions of gallons of water slid over the lip of the funnel and vanished as into the bowels of some gargantuan toilet. It was a frightening, mesmerizing, deafening sight that no first visitor ever forgot, and which pulled people back time and again, whenever the waters swelled beyond their prescribed boundaries.

Now, however, was not such a time, for weather or tourists. The summer had been relatively dry, the weather was becoming cooler with each passing day, and it was too early for either leaf-peepers or deer hunters. The place, I noticed, opening my eyes as Sammie pulled off Route 100 onto the long, paved dead-end access road leading to the dam, was deserted.

"You see any power-company trucks?"

She shook her head. "Haven't seen much of anybody. You really think this is where Vogel headed?"

"I don't know . . ." I hesitated. "To be honest, I think the main reason I'm out here is just to take a break. No reason he couldn't have, though." The gap in the rocks and trees to our right indicated the approach of the scenic cliff top, high above the spillway. "Pull over when you get near the fence."

She stopped by the side of the road and pointed to the dam, which angled off below us to the far shore. A road capped its crest, and a small yellow pickup truck, looking like an abandoned toy from this distance, was parked with its driver's door open. "There's one of your mysteries solved."

We got out of the car and approached the chain-link fence blocking the top of the cliff. Far below, the bone-dry Glory Hole, no less hypnotic for the absence of rushing water, came into view. It was fringed by a circular wooden pier, below which taintor gates hung to further control the water level if necessary, and from which two narrow wooden catwalks extended like clock hands—one toward the quiet, still, massive dam, and the other to the top of a concrete tower, crowned by a small shed, which stood alongside the Glory Hole, slightly farther out in the water, and which presumably functioned as a vertical service tunnel.

Our attention, however, was drawn to none of this, for near the center of the spillway's funnel, just shy of where the downward curve began its dizzying plunge toward the black hole in the middle, the small, motionless shape of a man lay spread-eagled. One of his hands extended high above his head and was wrapped around an iron ring, set into the concrete for service crews to hook their ropes. And below him, trailing like a kite tail and vanishing into the void at his feet, was a thin bright ribbon of blood.

Chapter Thirteen

J esus Christ," Sammie muttered, ducking down, her eyes already scanning the area around us. "You think he's still alive?"

Squatting next to her, I craned my neck to look at him again. "He's got a firm grip on that ring, not that that necessarily means anything."

I cupped my hands around my mouth and shouted. "You down there. Can you hear me?"

For a moment, nothing happened. Then, almost imperceptibly, one leg moved about eight inches.

"Jesus," Sammie repeated. "If he lets go, he's had it."

I scuttled back to the squad car, not knowing what we had— if the man had fallen by accident, if he'd been pushed or shot, and, if so, whether his attacker was still nearby, perhaps sighting on the two of us right now.

I unhooked the mike from the car's radio. "M-80 from 0-3."

Dispatch answered immediately, "Go ahead, 0-3."

"I'm at our intended destination with one civilian down, possible hostage situation, unknown and unlocated perpetrator. Get me all the help you can, including an ambulance and a high-angle rescue team, but stop them at the entrance to the access road until I give further word."

The reply was crisp and unemotional. "10-4. M-80 out."

Sammie joined me crouching by the open door. "So now what? That guy doesn't look like he has too much left in him."

I pulled two armored vests from the back seat, handed one to her, and slipped into the other without attaching the Velcro tabs. The exhaustion that had been dragging me down for untold hours, clogging my brain and affecting my concentration, had vanished completely, replaced by an almost frightening hypervigilance. "This road hits a hairpin curve about two hundred feet farther downhill and then doubles back to a parking lot on the dry side of the dam. We should have pretty good cover and a safe approach to the Glory Hole from there—assuming no one's waiting for us."

"Right," was all she said, before slipping on the vest, circling the car, and getting back behind the wheel.

The sylvan peacefulness of moments ago had been abruptly wrenched into something almost perversely opposite. Without a single hostile sign or sound, our surroundings now were threatening and dangerous—the trees potential sniper nests, the rocks and bushes obstructions to a clear, safe view all around. We rolled the car slowly down the hill and around the corner, our eyes straining against the dark green of the bordering trees for anything suspicious, dimly aware of the massive bulk of the dam growing to our right as we circled around below its potentially protective shoulder.

As soon as we got to the small parking lot at the end of the road, some thirty feet below the dam's crest, we raided the car trunk, and, lugging a shotgun, a radio, a coil of rope, a pair of binoculars, and some extra ammunition, we made our way though the bordering trees up the steep slope to the top. To our left, extending eight hundred feet to the hills across from us, and several thousand feet down to a seemingly tiny streambed far below, was the vast, open, grassy sweep of the dam's restraining slope. Normally a sight of inspiring beauty and industrial ingenuity, it was now just a potential killing field of gigantic proportions—a place to avoid at all costs until the threat, if any, could be located.

Just shy of the narrow utility road where the abandoned pickup stood, we ran out of tree cover.

Sammie—small, athletic, almost wiry—was barely breathing hard after the strenuous climb. She crouched by the last tree trunk and looked around at the quiet countryside. "How d'you want to play it?"

I wiped the sweat from my forehead with my sleeve. "The road's got a low cement wall on the water side. If we tuck up close to that, it ought to protect us pretty well from everywhere except the cliff we came from."

She looked over her shoulder. "What about from the trees?"

"The angle from the top of the dam ought to cover them—just keep low once you get there."

She pursed her lips, took a deep breath, muttered, "Right," and took off across the last twenty feet at a dead run, her feet digging into the slope like a sprinter's. I watched all around as best I could, knowing there was little I could do with a shotgun in any case, and was infinitely relieved when I saw her reach the top and roll out of sight across the road.

I waited a few seconds, hearing only birds and the gentle breeze among the leaves overhead. Then I too set out, feeling slow and clumsy, slipping in spots where Sammie had run like a teenager. When I got to the roadway and rolled across it as she had done, clutching the shotgun parallel to my chest, my relief came more from just being able to rest than from any newfound sense of protection. I lay flat on my back, staring at the cloud-dappled sky, gasping for air. Sammie crouched beside me, peering over the top of the low cement wall.

"What d'you see?" I asked, trying to speak as normally as possible.

"Nothing."

I struggled to a sitting position, first checking the few spots nearby from where someone could draw a bead on us, and poked my head over the wall. The contrast with the scene now to my back—a miles-long view down a narrow, stream-cut valley, seen from the very top of what amounted to a manmade mountain—contrasted violently with what I saw before me. Just five yards below me, the water of the reservoir stretched out so near to where we were hiding that it was almost like standing up in a boat.

I shifted my gaze to the Glory Hole, where, between the circular dock and the concrete edge, I could just see the top of the man still hanging on for his life. The catwalk leading from the shore to the dock above the spillway was about twenty feet away, but there was a locked gate cutting off access. My eyes went to a small object lying at the intersection, where the second catwalk connected the Glory Hole to the maintenance access tower with the shed on it.

"Hand me the binoculars," I asked.

Sammie took the shotgun from me as I focused the field glasses on the object.

"It's a tool box," I muttered, "lying between the wounded man and the shed on the access tower."

"So if he was shot and fell backwards over the railing, the bullet must've come from the shed."

"Right." I handed the binoculars back to Sammie and cupped my hands around my mouth again. "You in the Glory Hole. This is the police. If you can hear me, try to raise your free hand."

Sammie had the glasses trained on him. "He moved his fingers."

"Okay," I shouted, "we saw that. I need to ask you some questions. Move your fingers for yes; stay still for no. You got that?"

"Yes," Sammie interpreted.

"Have you been shot?"

"Yes."

"Is the shooter still around?"

Sammie paused, about to say no. "Hold it, he moved his hand. Better take that as an 'I guess so.' "

"You think he is, but you're not sure?" I shouted.

"Yes," Sammie said softly, "no doubt about it."

"Was he in the shed?"

"Yes."

"Was he alone?"

"He's hesitating again . . . There it is."

"You only think he was alone?"

"Right."

"Have you been there a long time?"

"Yes."

"Can you hang on much longer? Are you secure there?"

"Not a twitch, Joe."

"Can you move at all?"

"Still nothing."

"Shit," I muttered, "by the time everyone gets here, he'll be down the toilet—literally." I cupped my hands again. "Can you hang on for another ten minutes?"

"Yes, but he didn't put much into it."

"All right. We're on our way, but we've got to be careful, okay?"

"He gave us a thumbs-up." Sammie looked at me. "The manual says no life is worth your own."

"We don't even know the guy's still in the shed," I countered.

Sammie eyes grew wide. "Where the hell else would he be?"

"He might've had a boat, and that shed leads to something down below. That's what the tower's for."

"You know that for a fact?"

I didn't answer her. The radio between us squawked instead, "0-3 from M-80."

I picked it up. "Go ahead."

"You have two Wilmington units at the entrance of your access road, two sheriff's deputies five minutes out, a Dover unit and a VSP unit, both about ten minutes out. What's your status?"

"Still the same. We're about to reconnoiter. You better get the state police tactical support unit rolling just in case. And tell the Wilmington units to approach cautiously and to stage at the parking lot below the dam. We're on the crest road."

"10-4. M-80 out."

Sammie gave me a smile. "I get the feeling the manual is about to be thrown out."

I went back to looking over the wall at the spillway. "Just edited a little, but we are going to wait for the Wilmington people."

"Then what?"

"Then I run out onto the catwalk, shoot off the lock, drop down onto the edge of the Glory Hole with the rope and pull that poor bastard to safety, all while you and the others riddle that shed with covering fire—if need be."

"The need being that he put a bullet in your head?"

I gave her a shrug. "All right, riddle it anyway—there'll be three of you—and we'll send our apologies to the power company later."

"And if there's another shooter somewhere?" she persisted.

"Come on, Sammie, this ain't the movies. We both know that's probably Bob Vogel in there, and even if he did have a friend backing him up, he'd be long gone by now. People like that don't risk their lives for each other."

But I could tell from the look in her eye that I was preaching to the converted. Sammie Martens—more than most of my other officers—rarely shirked a fight. The only girl and the youngest child in a large, dysfunctional family of boys, Sammie had run away from home, joined the army where she'd received combat training, and was constantly taking refresher courses in hand-to-hand fighting, rappeling, special weapons, and whatnot. She was single and childless and almost grimly determined to climb the ranks. I thanked God regularly that mixed in with this lopsided package was also a good sense of humor and an ability to laugh at herself—sometimes.

Right now, however, she was struggling to be diplomatic. "Since we're waiting for people from about four different police agencies, don't you think you ought to stay here to coordinate them, and let me go out there? You are in command, after all."

Again, according to the manual, she was right. But it was my idea to take the risk, and I couldn't shake the notion that behind her concern for protocol lay a deeper worry that I might not be up for the job. I hadn't been the only one to notice the toll that run up the hill had taken—or to know that I hadn't had any sleep since Christ knew when. Nevertheless, whether fired by ego or a sense of responsibility, I wasn't interested in a debate.

"No," I answered curtly.

She looked at me a moment longer, making her private peace with the idea, and then nodded her acceptance.

High up on the cliff, we saw the Wilmington police car roll by, and a few minutes later, two tense young men with shotguns joined us on the service road.

While I busied myself with the coil of rope and replaced the soft-nosed bullets in my pistol clip with metal-jacketed ones—better suited for blowing the padlock apart—Sammie explained the plan and positioned them to give me maximum coverage.

I shuffled over to the narrow cut in the wall that led to the pathway and the fenced-off catwalk beyond, stuffing the portable radio into my pocket. Now that the other two officers were here, there were enough communications to go around.

Sammie joined me, her eyes bright. "You sure about this?"

"Just so long as you pulverize that shed."

She patted my back. "Okay—good luck."

I waited for the first explosive shotgun blast to pepper the near wall of the shed before bolting from cover and sprinting down the path toward the gate, my eyes scanning back and forth for any sudden movement. At the gate, I positioned myself as far from potential ricochets as I could, turned my face away, and fired one bullet into the center of the padlock, feeling tiny shards of metal slice into my firing hand.

The lock was mangled but still fast.

I positioned myself again and heard a shout from the wall. I glanced up at the shed in time to see a quick shadow and a flash of light amid the shattering of wood and glass from the shotgun pellets, and felt a section of the chain-link right next to my ear shatter under the impact of a bullet. I fired two quick shots at the lock, without much care this time, and saw the fractured remnants of it spin off into the water below.

I threw my shoulder against the gate, and ran as fast and as low as I could toward the circular dock above the spillway, by now totally deafened by the explosive crescendo behind me. Glancing repeatedly up at the disintegrating shed, I tied one end of the rope to the inside metal railing and threw the rest of the coil in the direction of the wounded man, who'd turned his head to watch me, his face grimacing with pain.

Just as I hooked one leg up to go over the railing myself, I heard a series of rapid, muffled shots from the shed, and saw a large chunk of the wooden wall, almost level with the tower's decking—and below where most of the shotgun blasts were hitting—come flying away, carried off by the bullets that had created it. The shooter inside, presumably lying on his stomach, had created a firing hole by simply blasting one out.

Not bothering with the niceties of rappeling, I pulled out my own pistol again, emptied half the clip in the direction of the hole. I felt one bullet bite into my Kevlar vest near my heart, and jumped.

It was a longer drop than I'd thought, and the impact of the bullet, while doing my body no harm, had nevertheless given me a rotational punch, which meant I was twisting in the air as I fell.

I landed on my feet, barely, but given the downward slope of the concrete surface, plus my own lack of balance, I tumbled headlong into a forward roll toward the gaping center of the Glory Hole, feeling as I went the pull of the ever-increasing pitch.

It was the wounded man who saved me, throwing the coil of rope at me with his free arm, using up what little strength he had left. As I hurtled past him, out of control and scrappling at the rough cement with my fingernails, my arm became entangled in the rope. There was a ferocious jarring as the line drew taut, damn near dislocating my shoulder but arresting my fall. I hung there, my feet dangling over the small, circular void of the Glory Hole's center drain, hearing my pistol reverberating off its sides as it hurtled down some two hundred feet to the bottom.

I stayed motionless for several seconds, trying to regain my bearings, wondering if I had the strength to pull myself up. There was silence all around, as if the fall had damaged my hearing. In fact, only the shooting had stopped, and I slowly became aware of a small rush of water below me from a small inlet port drilled into the drain's side. Gradually, as if emerging from a fog, I heard the muffled squawking from the radio still in my pocket, and, from yet another quarter, a repeated but feeble, "Hey, Bud . . . Hey, Bud," that came from the wounded man, now stretched out way above me.

I could just see the soles of his work boots over the curvature of the spillway—the ribbon of his blood extending past and below me like some parody of a lifeline—and realized with a start that he had no idea whether I'd made it or not. "I'm okay. Thanks for the save."

There was no answer.

"How're you holding out?"

I could barely hear him. "Not good."

I straightened myself out against the concrete, putting the rope between me and the rough surface, wincing at the friction burns that now covered both my hands. Slowly, I wriggled my way up, improving as the slope lessened, until I could gather my feet beneath me and half walk, half pull myself level to the wounded man.

Once there, I wrapped the line several times around my middle, anchoring myself, and then looped the end of it around the man's chest, under his armpits.

"What's your name?"

"Frank." His voice was a whisper.

I snugged the loop up and tied it off. "Do you know where you're hit?"

"The chest, I think."

I gestured to the wooden taintor gates that controlled the amount of water pouring into the spillway during flood season. "I'm going to go up there, secure this line, and pull you up after me. Okay?"

Frank barely murmured his assent.

Using the rope hand over hand, I step-walked the rest of the way to the edge of the Glory Hole, almost to flat footing, and carried out the anticlimactic conclusion to my almost fatally flawed plan, wondering whether Sammie would have done a better job or ended up dead at the bottom of the drain.

I pulled Frank up to me like a deer carcass, and then carefully rolled him onto his back. The front of his khaki uniform was drenched in blood. "How're you doin'?"

He blinked up at me several times, as if trying to decipher my words. "I feel kind of numb."

"Can you wiggle your hands and feet?"

"I guess." He moved his extremities very slightly.

"How's your breathing? Any pain?"

"Not much," he murmured.

"When did you get hit?"

"I don't now—maybe twenty minutes ago."

That caught me off guard. "Why didn't you answer your radio? They've been trying to raise you for hours."

"It stopped working after I headed out this morning." He gave me a weak smile. "That's why I was going to the shed—to report in."

I shook my head at the providence of pure luck, and finally pulled the radio from my pocket. "Sammie—you there?"

"Jesus Christ, Joe. Where the hell you been?"

"Busy. This guy's secure now, but he needs help fast."

"The ambulance is here, but we still don't know if the scene's safe."

"Hang on." Ignoring the pain in my hands, I reached up and grasped the edge of the circular dock above and chinned myself up until I could look along the length of the second catwalk to the remnants of the shed on the access tower. The damage was extensive, a good part of both shore-facing walls tattered and torn enough to threaten the whole structure. I could see into it, however, thanks to all the extra impromptu windows, and could even see through it to the daylight on the far side. It looked completely empty.

I dropped back down and retrieved the radio. "Sam, I think you can go ahead. He must've ducked below surface. Send a recon team in to secure, though. He may be setting us up."

"Can you give us cover?"

"Negative. I lost my gun. Bring me a backup, will you?"

"10-4."

Frank was weakly tugging at my pant leg. I squatted down to hear him. "He can get away."

"How?"

"Through the spillway tube—the outlet's a half mile from here. The tower has its own tunnel, leading to a bypass chamber. That used to be it—a dead end. But we cut a connector passage from the chamber to the spillway tube just last week. It hasn't been sealed yet. He's a got clear shot." He stopped and breathed heavily, catching his breath, wincing with the effort.

A shiver of adrenaline tickled the nape of my neck at again losing the man who had both raped Gail and now tried to kill me. "Okay, don't say any more. We'll get him."

I could hear the recon team approaching cautiously along the first catwalk, so I chinned myself up again and swung one leg onto the dock to save my strength.

Sammie saw me and hurried forward, her eyes glued to the shed. She squatted down next to me and helped me up with her free hand. "How's the guy doin'?"

"Hanging on by a thread." I took the gun she handed me. "We're going to have to go after the shooter."

She looked at me, surprised. "Why?"

"Because he's got an out. There's an underground connector to the spillway outlet about a half mile away."

"Shit," she muttered, and moved as quickly as a panther across to the second catwalk and up to the shed, her shotgun held at the ready, I and two other men in her wake.

The shed was empty, and in the center of its debris-strewn floor was a trap door leading to a steep metal ladder. Damp, cold air drifted up out of the opening like the mist from a fresh grave.

I turned to one of the officers that had accompanied Sammie—a state police sergeant from the Brattleboro barracks. "You know where the spillway outlet is?"

He shook his head. "But there's a power-company rep on the dam."

"Good. Get him to show you and seal it off. Better yet, if you have the manpower, seal it and send a team in to meet us partway. Sammie and I'll be heading down from here. If this guy feels he's being pinched in the middle, he may chuck it in—assuming he's not already gone."

The sergeant left, stepping around the medical personnel on the curved dock, who were already beginning to lift their backboarded patient up over the railing.

I turned to the remaining officer, from the Dover Police Department. "You have a flashlight I can borrow?"

He pulled a heavy brain-basher from his belt and held it out to me. "What'd you want me to do?"

I glanced over at Sammie, who was standing grim but ready at the edge of the black rectangular opening—a mirror to my own eagerness to get this done, once and for all. "Stay here and keep in touch by radio. And do what you have to do if he gets by us and doubles back."

A young man with probably no more than a year on the force, he looked at me with wide eyes. "Could he do that?"

"He could if he kills us both," Sammie muttered.

Chapter Fourteen

I stood next to Sammie, eyeing the narrow opening to the vertical shaft of the maintenance tower, a few remaining notes of caution struggling to be heard in a tired, overworked mind. "Wish I knew what we were getting into."

She kept watching the entrance as if it might suddenly come to life. "According to the power-company guy I was talking to on the dam, we're now standing on top of something like a hundred-and-seventy-foot-tall underwater missile silo—a twenty-foot-wide cement tube sticking straight out of the mud with a zigzag ladder running down one of the inside walls."

"What's at the bottom?"

She shrugged. "Beats me—that was about the whole conversation right there."

"Well," I gave in, "guess we better get to it." I stretched out on my stomach, poked the powerful flashlight beam over the edge of the hole, and, after a slight pause during which no bullet came flying up to blow my hand off, I cautiously stuck my head over. Sammie joined me.

Below us—indeed, beneath where we lay—was a seemingly bottomless, smooth-walled, misty pit, the dampness of which formed a slight fog, thick enough to defeat the flashlight's ability to reach the bedrock. The ladder was fastened to one glistening side, zigzagging back and forth at sharp vertical angles from one narrow platform to the next, like some misplaced urban fire escape.

It appeared almost puny in comparison to the void all around it.
The whole thing gave me vertigo, a feeling enhanced by the realization that the thin metal flooring I was stretched out on was all that
was saving me from a free-fall into the void.

"How the hell're we going to make a safe approach into that?"
Sammie asked softly. "Put down some covering fire and follow it
in?"

I'd never been a big one for fireworks, especially if I had no idea
where they were landing. "No. In the dark," I countered, switching
off the light and swinging one leg over the edge, "and in silence."

Silence, however, was not my first priority. I wanted to enter
the silo fast, before anyone could draw a bead on my silhouette
against the highlighted entrance. I therefore descended the first
stretch of ladder in a barely controlled free-fall, trusting my memory
to judge the distance to the first platform. It was a graceless, noisy
effort, compounded by Sammie following right behind me and
virtually landing on my head, but it was worth it—no sooner had
we collapsed in a heap than a muzzle flash spat at us from far below,
and the walls around us exploded with the reverberations of a pistol
shot.

Lying on my back, my feet still entangled in the rungs, and
with Sammie lying on top of me, a second shot rang out, the bullet
ringing harmlessly off of metal somewhere above us. I felt Sammie's
small muscular body tense against mine.

"Don't move," I whispered in her ear, "give him a couple of
minutes."

We lay there, barely breathing, listening. Below us, mixing
with the subtle sounds of dripping water, of vague and distant
mechanical noises, we were both aware of someone moving, possibly
seeking a better angle for another, more accurate shot. I was distinctly aware of how little of my body my Kevlar vest actually
covered.

"Okay," I murmured to Sammie after two very long minutes.

She got off me like a shadow, and I rose just as quietly, leading
the way to the next ladder heading down.

Our environment now was radically different from what it had
been moments earlier, when we'd been lying on the floor looking
down. There, we'd been in the light, in the open, surrounded by
the cool, dry air of a normal fall day. Here, all was dark, damp,

and tomblike. The metal rungs of the ladder were slippery and wet, the cement to which it was attached smooth with the same calcium skin that coated cave walls. And despite our silence, I felt surrounded by sound—the rustling of clothes, our virtually suppressed breathing, the mere brushing of a hand across a hard surface. I felt I was locked in a huge, wet, very cold echo chamber, the only available warmth threatening to come from the end of an invisible gun barrel somewhere far below us.

Things did not improve as we progressed. The moisture increased along with the cold, tickling the hairs in my nose and reaching down my collar like a draft. What little light there'd been from the trapdoor became absorbed by the mist, reducing the entrance above to a hazy, pale rectangle with no radiance or effect. Reality became solely what I could feel beneath my hands. All sense of smell was suffused by the dampness and the cold, and hearing became clogged by a minute cacophony of drips, sighs, and subtle shiftings—the living sounds, I came to think, of the millions of tons of water all around us, held at bay by a few feet of seventy-year-old cement.

Several more flights and I stopped, letting Sammie come up next to me until her ear was inches from my mouth, a fact I could by now only determine by touch. "I'm going to go to the far end of the landing and turn my flashlight on to see what's below. You stay here, ready to shoot anything that moves."

Her hand touched my cheek, turning it, and her lips brushed my own ear. "Why take the risk?"

I ignored the doubtfulness I heard in her voice. "I want to speed this up if I can. He's not worried about getting his ass shot off like we are, so he's probably making good headway by now, especially if he knows about the way out."

"You hope," she whispered back. "You turn that light on, and that's what he's going to shoot at."

I put my hand on her back. "Just do it, Sam," and I gave her a small push.

I counted to five to give her time to position herself, during which I heard her gun being slipped from its holster. Then I held out my flashlight, pointed it down, as far from my body as possible, and leaned far over the low railing.

I pushed the *on* button.

There was a blinding, dazzling snowstorm of light—the halogen glare of the torch bouncing off a billion tiny particles of moisture, all suspended in the still air. In that paradoxically clear instant, as if frozen by a camera's electronic strobe, I found myself hanging in midair, far beyond the comfort of the thin iron railing, between an invisible roof and a murkily distant, shiny-wet floor, still far, far below. In that moment, before I could orient myself, I felt I was being sucked into the void, drawn away from my precarious perch by the sheer immensity of the swirling emptiness, momentarily numbed by a surge of the penned-up exhaustion I'd been holding off for too long.

"Joe," Sammie shouted, still standing in a classic shooter's stance, aiming down, but with her eyes wide and staring at me in alarm.

I watched dumbfounded as the light slipped from my hand and spiraled down, and I grappled with the railing to regain my balance. Everything went dark as the big flashlight smashed to pieces below us.

"You okay?" she asked in alarm.

I fought a sudden impulse to sit down where I was and give up—let others finish the job. "Fine, fine—just lost my footing."

Her own light came on and searched the bottom of the silo, revealing a catwalk crossing to the opposite wall, several huge pipes with calcium-encrusted valves, and the rough-hewn, solid-rock surface beneath it all. At the foot of the catwalk was another ladder, which slipped through a narrow opening between the bottom of the silo wall and the uneven floor, almost like an irregular drain.

There was no one in sight.

"Go," I told Sammie, shrugging off my momentary inertia. "Fast as you can."

She moved to the top of the next ladder, but paused there a moment to reach out and touch my arm. "You sure you're feeling up to this."

I nodded. "Go. I'm right behind you."

Finally unleashed, she fairly flew down the remaining flights, at times taking controlled leaps from level to level, using the slippery handrails like guide wires to stabilize and slow herself. I followed as best I could, but she'd already thoroughly checked out the bottom of the silo and was crouching at the top of the ladder leading through the slit in the rock by the time I caught up to her. From our vantage point, all we could see was that a larger chamber opened up below us on the other side of the narrow opening. We could also see that in order to squeeze through the slit and get beyond it conventionally, we'd have to descend feetfirst, hugging the ladder, and offer our backs to whoever might be waiting.

"What'd you think?" I asked her.

"Be a good place for an ambush. How 'bout a headfirst recon?"

I nodded and stood at the top of the ladder. Sammie slithered onto her back between my legs, a flashlight in one hand, her pistol in the other, and began to slide down the ladder headfirst, her shoulder blades to the rungs. As her hips went by and the weight of her body threatened to pull her straight down the rest of the way, I caught her and lowered her slowly as I might a rope, grabbing her thighs, then her knees, and finally her ankles. Using proper harnesses and climbing gear, it was the same way we trained to attack upper-story windows from the roof—showing the smallest target, and having our hands and weapons available for use. It looked funny, but it worked.

"Clear," she finally said. She stored her light and gun, took hold of the rung just below her, and did a controlled flip to land right side up as soon as I released her ankles. I climbed down conventionally and joined her in a short, six-foot-diameter tunnel, hewn entirely out of the bedrock. Here, the cave effect was complete—the calcium leaching that had covered part of the cement walls in the silo, giving their rough, manmade surface the smoothness of polished stone, had taken over entirely down here. The rock ledge, long ago scarred by dynamite and pick, had been filled in and softened by decades of gentle, mineral-rich water drippings, until it now resembled the butter-colored grottos of tourist attractions like the Mammoth and Carlsbad caves. There were even stubby stalactites and stalagmites reaching out for each other on both sides of the tunnel's beaten path.

The most startling evolution, however—and a most uncomfortable one—was the moisture in the air. From dampness to mist, we had reached a subterranean level of perpetual drizzle. Water trickled down the walls and dripped from the low, vaulted ceiling in a steady, light rain, increasing the effects of the cold, getting into our eyes, and—worst of all—cumulatively creating enough noise to mask whatever slight sounds the man ahead of us might make.

Sammie, not surprisingly, paid no attention to these effects, nor did she give any indication of having noticed the change in weather. By now filthy, drenched, and with her shoulder-length hair plastered flat to her head, she moved quickly to the sharp turn at the far end of the chamber and crouched with her back to the wall. She took a quick look around and retreated, fast enough to draw fire but stay out of harm's way, repeated the gesture a little more slowly, growing in confidence that there was no immediate threat, and then finally stuck her head out boldly and turned on her flashlight.

"Damn."

Since the tunnel we were in was aimed in the direction of the spillway discharge tube, I'd been hoping that the bypass chamber—and its newly cut link to the tube—would be readily available. But switching positions with Sam, I discovered the source of her disappointment. Around the corner was another tunnel, four feet in diameter, angled down well over forty-five degrees, and equipped with a metal ladder lining its bottom like the rails on the downside of a roller coaster. Making matters worse, the artificial rain was so intense here that visibility—even with Sam's powerful light—didn't exceed twenty feet. And the ladder seemed to stretch well beyond that.

"We'll be fish in a barrel," Sammie said. "One shot in our general direction and we'll be hit, either straight on or by ricochet."

I unclipped the radio from her belt and tried to raise the Dover policeman we'd left on the top of the silo.

"Go ahead," he answered.

"What's the word from the spillway outlet? Anyone there yet?"

"Negative. There was some sort of communications breakdown."

Sammie had killed her flashlight, but I could feel her exasperated eyes on me. "Have they started out?" I asked.

"Oh, sure. A few minutes ago."

I couldn't tell if it was a statement or a question. I handed the radio back without comment, the remnants of my exhausted mind now totally and vengefully set. My voice, as I heard it, was a calm and reasoned contrast to how I was feeling. "He could've killed you when you were hanging from your toes. The fact that he didn't shows he's headed out of here, fast. And now I guess we're the only ones likely to stop him."

I could feel Sammie's practical hesitation. "It's a shooting gallery, Joe," she reminded me softly.

"Could be," I answered brusquely, pulling the extinguished flashlight from her hand and heading down the ladder awkwardly, facing out so I could quickly answer any gunfire that might come up at me. After a moment's pause, I heard Sammie coming after me.

It was dark beyond imagination. I remembered as a kid, closing my eyes, pretending I was blind, staggering into furniture until I hurt myself. Back then, despite my best attempts, there'd still been a hint of light that had filtered through my eyelids. But not now. The darkness here was surgically absolute. With my eyes wide open, stinging with the water that fell into them from the rocky ceiling just above, I could see no more than if I'd been dead.

The descent was longer than twenty feet; longer than fifty, before I gave up trying to guess. My shoulders aching from the unnatural position I'd chosen, my body soaked and freezing from the drizzle, and my head now pounding with the tension of not knowing what might be three feet in front of me, I was about to come to my senses and let Bob Vogel's fate be dictated by somebody else when my foot slipped off the last rung of the ladder and I collapsed onto a wet, uneven, stone-strewn floor, dropping the second flashlight. Sammie, coming on strong right behind me, kicked the back of my head by accident.

"Jesus—you okay?" she whispered urgently, searching for and retrieving the light.

For the second time, like a pair of Keystone Kops, we disentangled ourselves and tried to take our bearings, murmuring like bomb-carrying conspirators even though I'd made enough noise to reach through three walls.

Judging from the little we knew, this was the famous bypass chamber—a room carved out of the rock like some prehistoric beast's fossilized burrow, and equipped, as far as our outstretched fingers could tell us, with several very-large-diameter pipes, all with massive in-line gate valves.

"So where's the famous door?" Sammie hissed after several minutes of groping around in the dark.

"I think I've got it." What I'd found was a rectangular piece of plywood, standing on its narrow end and leaning against one of the rough walls. "Turn on the light."

The effect of the light was again spectacular. Even with my eyes almost completely shut in anticipation, the power of the beam was like an electrical shock, leaving both of us momentarily rooted in place like stunned rabbits. Nevertheless, it revealed what I'd feared it would—a totally empty room through which I was now convinced our man had passed on his way to a clean getaway.

I'd also been right about the doorway. The plywood sheet half covered the jagged entrance to another small, short tunnel, the making of which had produced some of the rubble we'd been picking our way through carefully until now. The short tunnel was also empty.

"Turn the light off again," I asked.

We both stood still, regaining our night vision, realizing that finally it might actually do us some good. As I'd sensed with the light on, there was a glimmer emanating from beyond the small tunnel ahead of us—that and the steady, gentle rush of flowing water.

It reminded me of the small inlet port at the mouth of the Glory Hole, where I'd been hanging from the rope by one hand. The water peacefully splashing through it and vanishing into the void had been equally at odds with the circumstances, which instinctively told me now they were one and the same. "The discharge tunnel's up ahead."

I squeezed by the plywood and was about to follow the dim light to its source, when we both heard our names being called out from far up the slanting shaft behind us.

I handed the flashlight to Sammie through the gap. "Find out what they want."

She retreated to the foot of the ladder and shouted back, "Who is that?"

The sound of the rushing water muffled the response, but Sammie, turning on her light as a beacon and shouting back about the ladder's length and condition, indicated friendly troops were on the way and confirmed my pessimism about our chances of catching Vogel. I turned away and continued on to the discharge tunnel.

The connecting passageway was low enough to require stooping to get through it, so its contrast to the twenty-by-twenty discharge tube at the other end brought me up short. I hadn't expected a tunnel as high and as wide as a two-story building, several hundred feet underground.

The water ran down its middle, the dim light from the outlet some eight hundred feet downstream reflecting dully off the ripples. There was a slight mist in the air, which gave the small distant silhouettes of several approaching men a ghostly, almost dreamlike quality.

I was just beginning to ponder the chances that Vogel might still be hiding somewhere in the gloom between us when I heard Sammie step up behind me.

I turned to face her, a little surprised. "I didn't hear you coming."

"That's the point, asshole."

I smelled his breath in my face just as his right fist came up hard against my side. It wasn't a punch, really—in fact, its lack of strength surprised me at first. I wondered why he'd bothered sneaking up behind me if all he was going to do was give me a weak shove.

I opened my mouth to call out to Sammie, and made to step into him, to throw my weight against him and throw him off balance while I brought my gun into play.

But nothing happened. No sound came out of me, no part of me moved. The gun stayed where it was, hanging from my right hand. All my instincts transformed into something more primeval, some basic force that told the rest of me that neither fight nor flight were appropriate any longer—that all was secondary to the primary task of keeping my heart from stopping.

I realized suddenly, as if overtaken by a riptide of unbearable sadness, that, for reasons I had yet to discern, I was dying.

That's when I felt the knife blade slip slightly, somewhere deep inside me, like a chip of ice swallowed on a hot day—only harder, colder, and much more frightening. I remembered seeing myself as if in a movie, quickly slipping on the Kevlar vest and forgetting to fasten the two Velcro straps on the side.

Bob Vogel stepped away from me, and his breath was replaced by the pungency of the underground water whose sound now swelled up in a crescendo. He slipped from my vision like a bad dream. I heard shouts to my left—from the narrow passageway—but muted and far off. There might even have been a gunshot. I paid no attention to any of it.

I felt my knees hit the ground hard, jarring my entire body, but without sensation. Things tilted slightly as I toppled onto my side like a slowly falling tree, and then the loud water was running by my cheek, even filling an ear. I blinked several times, trying to keep the splash of water out of my eye. From this angle, almost swimming on its surface, the water looked enormous—like a huge, moonlit river, rushing to the sea in a tumult.

I thought of how Gail would enjoy a scene like this.

When the pain kicked in at last, from my very core, it felt like lava. The river turned to fire, and I thought maybe it would carry me to Gail. After all, hadn't the same man killed us both, each in our own way?

I took comfort in that—the only comfort I could find—just before I stopped thinking altogether.

Chapter Fifteen

What I remember comes to me in private mental snap-shots—some slightly fuzzy or badly framed, some of people, others of ceilings, ambulance roofs, or views of the sky. All of them are in random order. The one constant theme, like music accompanying a slide show, is the pain. It is the pain, I've come to think, that stimulated my taking the snapshots in the first place. Whenever it hit badly enough, I came into focus, more or less, just as a dozing concertgoer might be jarred awake by an occasional off-key note, before nodding off once more.

There are many clear, full-face, but troubled portraits of friends—Tony, Ron, Sammie, Gail, Billy . . . even my younger brother Leo, a butcher from Thetford and the gentle custodian of the remnants of my family. All there, I knew, to lend me comfort, to see how I'm doing, but all looking as if they've lost their best friend. There is one of Willy, of course, that's a little different. He's farther away, standing straight and viewing from a distance. When I wasn't taking photos but just leafing through them until the next spasm woke me up—I came to think he was looking at me as he might a dead dog in the street. But then he's a special case; and he did show up.

Toward the end, more lucid, although still keeping to myself in dark unconsciousness, I knew that's what was going on—that they were visiting me—fitting themselves awkwardly in between the IV poles, the electronic monitors, the EKG machine, and a bunch of other equipment that kept a steady watch on me. But having no memory of their visits apart from these disjointed images—and judging solely from their expressions—I knew I wasn't doing too well.

I eventually found that out for myself when the familiar painful stimulus led to a moving picture instead of a still. I watched in grimacing fascination as a young nurse, her face still, her eyes watchful, manipulated something below my line of sight. It was dark all around us, the only light coming from a freestanding gooseneck lamp she had beside her, and the familiar green, red, and amber glow from the various instruments plugged in all around me.

"Ow."

She stopped, and turned to look at me, her face darkening in the shadow, which in turn highlighted the whiteness of her teeth as she smiled. "Good morning."

I moved my head slightly to take in the surrounding gloom. "Morning?"

"Figure of speech. It's 2:00 A.M. How are you feeling?" Her voice was soft and clear.

"Not too good. What are you doing down there?" To me, my voice sounded like it was coming from inside an echo chamber and my throat hurt like hell. I didn't know if I was whispering or shouting.

"Changing your dressing. Sorry if it hurts a bit."

I caught my breath at an extra jolt, remembering how painlessly the knife had slipped in. "He did a hell of a job, I guess."

She smiled again, her eyes back on what she was doing. "That he did. He said lots of other people would've died from less. You're a tough guy, Mr. Gunther."

She hadn't known whom I'd meant, and I was too tired to explain it to her. Also, there was something uplifting in the way she spoke, after all those grim-faced snapshots, and I didn't want to ruin the mood. I passed out instead, launched on a new career of collecting movie loops—small segments of action, usually of nurses like her, sometimes of doctors—always brought on by the pain. Some of these loops had dialog, occasionally as coherent and reasonable as that first one, but they tended to be a little repetitive. The time of day and concern for how I was feeling were two popular subjects. And there were other times when the movie and the soundtrack were completely out of whack, when lips moved without sound and words floated by out of context. I got more of those grim looks at those times, and eventually, like a precocious toddler, I learned to keep my mouth shut when the audience frowned.

A breakthrough came when I woke not from pain, but from a gentle pressure on my forehead—something warm and smooth—a caress—and I opened my eyes to see Gail looking down at me.

"Smile," I asked her.

She smiled—genuinely—the pleasure reaching the small crinkles near her eyes. "Hi. You're looking better."

I waited for the pain, for the lights to fade and the movie to end as usual—some of them had been that short—but nothing happened. I took advantage of it to study her more closely, in the flesh, instead of in the recesses of my mind. *She* didn't look better. Her eyes were bloodshot, her hair tangled and unwashed, and her cheeks gaunt and shadowed with exhaustion.

"You look terrible."

The smile spread to a chuckle. "Thanks a lot—you're to blame for most of it."

I felt a familiar tug on my ability to focus—my brain longing to return to its black hole of peaceful contemplation. My sight darkened and blurred. But I didn't want to go this time. I shifted my weight slightly, and the hot poker did the rest—my eyes cleared and my mind resurfaced.

That obviously wasn't all it did, however. Gail suddenly leaned forward, her expression intent. "Are you okay?"

I unclenched my teeth. "Yeah—sorry." I raised an arm to touch her, to set her at ease, and saw a thin, almost bony hand come into view—pale, slightly wrinkled, and scarred by several old IV sites along the forearm. Instead of squeezing her shoulder, I flexed my hand several times, as if at a loss to explain its function.

She interpreted the gesture. "You've been here a long time, Joe. Weeks. You came close to dying a few times."

Her tightly controlled voice suddenly meshed with her ravaged appearance and I felt terrible about my earlier flip comment. I put the stranger's hand to use and gripped her arm. "Gail, I thought about you—about being with you—just after he stabbed me."

She smiled again. "Swell."

I held onto her harder. "No. It was strange. It was peaceful, and didn't hurt. I was just lying there in the water, thinking of how nice it would be to be with you. You were the one thing I could think of that helped."

The words sounded awkward to me, unfamiliar and slightly juvenile. I was angered at my own lack of eloquence, knowing without being told of the hours she must have spent by my bed, putting aside her own pain so she could accompany me through mine.

"I guess it worked" was what she said, but the smile lingered in her eyes.

I wanted to ask her how she was doing, if her own suffering at the hand of our mutual nemesis had eased any since we'd last visited. I wanted to find out what had happened to Bob Vogel, and what her reaction was to that. But it was all beyond me. My vision closed in again, I saw my hand fall away from her arm, and this time I couldn't bring myself to move. Just as I shut down, I saw Gail lean forward to kiss me.

The next visitor I knew about was Leo, my brother, who woke me up as any truly professional butcher might—by getting a firm grip on the meat of my upper arm.

He smiled as I opened my eyes. "Jesus, Joey, you're scrawnier'n hell."

I focused on his tired face—broader and darker than Gail's. "You don't look so hot yourself," I croaked, clearing my throat.

He slipped his arm behind my neck and tilted my head up to receive some cool water from a cup with a bent straw hanging out of it—his years of tending our invalid mother showing in his gentle dexterity. "I knew you'd want some of this—all that crap they had stuffed down your throat. I couldn't believe it."

I finished sipping and he laid me back, suddenly peeling back my upper lip and looking at my teeth. "Boy, we ought to do something about that, too. I brought a toothbrush, okay?"

I stared in wordless amazement at the brush he whipped out of his shirt pocket, his tired eyes gleaming with the bright glow of success. "That's another thing I knew they wouldn't think of. Has Gail tried to kiss you yet?"

"I don't . . . I think so. I've been kind of groggy."

He burst out laughing and produced a crumpled tube from another pocket, from which he slathered a thick dollop onto the brush. "God, no wonder she hasn't said much—must still be catching her breath."

I blinked a couple of times, trying to banish the tendrils of a deep sleep from my brain. "Leo, what's been going on? Where am I?"

He raised his eyebrows and dipped the brush into the cup. "You don't know? Open your mouth."

I raised a hand to hold him off. "Don't. I can do it."

He handed it over cheerfully. "I doubt it."

I took the brush and tried to use it, my fingers trembling with the effort. After only a couple of strokes, my entire arm felt heavy, and I missed my teeth completely, delivering a swatch of foam across my chin.

Leo shook his head, satisfied by his foresight. "Give me that. You're making a mess." He took it away and set to work, neatly and gently. "You're in Lebanon, New Hampshire—the Hitchcock Hospital—and you've been under for three weeks, Joey—gram-negative septicemia—that's what they said you had. Fancy for blood poisoning. What the knife started, your own guts spilling into the rest of you almost finished. You had the docs scrambling a couple of times. Bad fevers, seizures, times you were delirious—you gave 'em a run for their money. They tell me you lost forty pounds just lying here. By the way, who's paying for all this?"

I gurgled something, and he shrugged, "Oh, right. Sorry. Here—" He brandished the all-purpose cup. "Spit."

I spat.

"The reason I ask, you got first class all the way—police escort for the ambulance from the dam; helicopter ride up from Brattleboro; the best surgical team they had to offer here . . . You know how long they worked on you?"

I knew better than to try to answer. When Leo was on a roll, there was no point trying to stop him.

"Eight hours. Gail and I were sitting outside the whole time. They tried getting us to go home, but forget that. Anyway, it was the same bunch working on you the whole night. I thought docs were a little overpaid, you know? But when I saw the head guy—

when he came out to tell us you'd pulled through the operation—
he looked like he'd earned his keep. That son-of-a-gun looked beat.
You know what I mean?"

He punched me gently on the shoulder and then immediately
leaned over me, his eyes inches from mine. "Damn, you okay? Got
a little carried away. That didn't hurt, did it?"

"It's okay, Leo."

He was already massaging the shoulder with his big paw, doing
far more damage than he had with the punch. He suddenly stopped
again and took my face in his hands, as he might a small child's.
His face was serious and troubled, in abrupt contrast to the beaming
expression he'd been showering on me so far. "You're doing okay
now, aren't you? Feeling better?"

I tried to nod between his hands, and muttered through puckered
lips, "Fine—a little tired."

"I know you've been banged up before—even out like a light
for a couple of days—but this time . . . I don't know . . . You
really had me scared. You actually died a couple of times, you
know that?"

I tried shaking my head politely, with less success.

He glanced up at the machines clustered around me. "Hadn't
been for all this stuff—and all the people here—you would've been
history." He paused, his eyes gleaming brightly. "You scared the
shit out of me."

He gave me a quick kiss on the cheek, said, "Don't do it again,"
and disappeared as magically as he'd appeared.

My days became more normal after that. I woke up when most
people normally do, I had conversations with beginnings, middles,
and ends, and I began to feel more a part of, if not the regular
world, then at least a highly regimented corner of it. Then I was
moved from Intensive Care to a regular room, and introduced to
the far less pleasant realities of physical therapy—a harsh enough
contrast to make me yearn for the good old days of suspended
animation.

I was in the rehab gym, bathed in sweat from both exertion and
pain, when I got my first news of what had been happening outside
the hospital walls. Tony Brandt appeared on the threshold one day,

and came over to where I was sitting slumped on the bench of a Universal weight machine, trying to catch my breath.

He perched trimly on a barbell rack and smiled at me. "Lifting your own weight already?"

I answered with a short, exasperated laugh. "More like the weight of three gerbils—if that."

He tilted his head and looked at me appraisingly. "You look pretty good. Some guys would kill to lose forty pounds in their sleep."

I just looked at him sourly.

His voice softened subtly. "How are you?"

Ever since I'd woken up, that had been the topic—for me, for the doctors, nurses, therapists, for my friends. I spent so much time either responding to that question or pondering it myself—my fingers gingerly running along the long tender scar that extended from where Vogel had stuck me in the side, right across my belly to where the surgeons had gone in to patch me up—that I was beginning to wonder whether obsessions could be picked up like germs. I didn't want to leave this hospital feeling like every bowel movement should be up for appraisal.

"I'm getting better," I answered blandly and changed the subject. "I heard we got Vogel, but nobody around here knows the details."

Brandt gave me a rueful glance. "Has Sammie been by?"

I reached back into my catalogue of mental snapshots. "Yeah, but before I was conversational. Why?"

"There's some controversy about whether Vogel gave up before she nailed him with her flashlight, or the other way around. According to him, he thought just the two of you were behind him—that the rest were coming from the other end—and that he might be able to get around you. But he said after he knifed you, supposedly in a panic, by the way—hear the insanity plea coming?—that he realized you two had reinforcements, so he gave up, raised his hands, and then got nailed by Sammie. She put him in the hospital, too, but just overnight."

I wiped my face with a small hand towel and straightened up, feeling a little stronger after my rest. "Tell her thanks when you see her. You realize the rest of his story is total bullshit. He knew we weren't alone. Sammie shouted up the ladder to the others just before he stuck me. He heard them as clearly as I did. Is that how he's trying to weasel out of this? That he gave up and we creamed him?"

Brandt pulled a face and shook his head. "That's just his first line of defense. He also says he was innocent—another con framed by the pigs—and that he ran off because he was convinced we were going to persecute him. He said he's never set eyes on Gail Zigman and that on the night in question his car broke down on his way back from work, and that he spent a couple of hours underneath it jury-rigging a repair."

"What kind of breakdown?"

"Punctured oil pan. We checked the car out and found the repair, all right—he put a screw in the hole—but we also went to the place he said it happened, and the road's clean as a whistle. According to his own testimony, there was oil all over when he was through."

"Did he go for help anywhere?"

"Nope. Supposedly, he didn't want to draw attention to himself or the illegal car, so he did it all on his own. He said it was a long time before he found out what was wrong, put the screw in, replaced the oil, and went on his way."

"He had extra oil?"

"Yeah—says he uses almost as much oil as gas."

I nodded in agreement. "Car smokes like it was on fire. And of course he happened to have the perfect screw for the job."

"Naturally. And when we hit him with the discrepancies, he went stone cold on us. Told us we were a bunch of fuckers out to get him, and that he'd see us in court."

"What?" I asked, surprised. The popular technique was to stall the process until damn-near all the principals were dead of old age. "Who's his lawyer?"

"Tom Kelly—he got the nod from the state when the public-defender's office claimed conflict of interest."

"Is Kelly playing the see-you-in-court angle, too?"

Brandt scratched his head. "I don't know. It's a little early—they haven't even had the status conference yet. After the oil-in-the-road story blew up, Kelly approached Dunn with a plea, but he withdrew it in mid-negotiation. Now, no one knows what he's up to. He asked for a change of venue, of course, but there was a wrinkle there, too. He said he'd accommodate Dunn by requesting an out-of-county jury instead of actually moving the trial. According to Kelly, that's because he's being sensitive to Dunn's schedule, since Dunn's out politicking every minute he can find. But according to the scuttlebutt, Kelly made the offer so he can humiliate Dunn on his home turf. Of course, that only works if Kelly's got a secret weapon, and as far as any of us can see, all he's got is the last deck chair on the *Titanic*."

"What was the plea they were working on?"

"Well, given the rape and the attack on you—not to mention shooting the power-company guy—he's looking at a life sentence, easy. I think Dunn was offering fifteen to thirty on the rape alone before Kelly lost interest."

"What's Dunn's attitude?"

Tony rolled his eyes. "He's licking his chops. He knows damn well the case won't come to court for a year or more, especially with Kelly acting so cagey, so he's going around to every rubber-chicken banquet in town bragging about putting Vogel in jail in record time. He's making hay off you, too, since your getting stabbed makes Vogel look guilty as hell. And it's working. The press is buying it, Women for Women has said it was a job well done, although they've started a 'justice watch,' as they call it, to make sure Dunn doesn't let Vogel off with a slap on the wrist. Jack Derby is trying his best to inject a little reality—pointing out that Dunn didn't have anything to do with Vogel's arrest—but that just looks like sour grapes. Dunn's making out like a bandit in the polls. Kelly backing out of the plea process just made it sweeter."

"You smell a rat?"

Brandt shook his head. "Oh, no. Tom Kelly's a good guy, but this is a tough one for him. You built a strong case, and he's got an asshole for a client. He's going to have to come up with something awfully flashy to beat it. Far as I can see, it looks like Dunn's been handed a prize bull at no cost. I think Kelly's being secretive for his own sake, not because he has anything."

From across the room, my physical therapist looked up from another of her patients and gave me a stern look. I sighed and shrugged apologetically to Tony. "I better get back to it, before she has me doing laps. One last thing, though—how did the power-company guy turn out?"

"Better than you. They pulled a bullet out less than an inch from his heart. He's already back at work part-time, doing paperwork."

I shook my head at the workings of fate. "I wonder why Vogel hung around after he shot him?"

Brandt made a face. "That much we did get out of him. Vogel thought the poor bastard had gone all the way down the Glory Hole—that he was dead and out of sight. It was going to be dark in a couple of hours. He doubted anyone would come hunting for the truck before it was due back in, so he was planning on waiting till nightfall and then hitting the road. Lucky for us." He paused awkwardly, and then smiled. "Well . . . lucky for some of us."

He rose and patted me on the shoulder, I thought a little gingerly. "Speaking of which, I know what you're going to say, but you've got a Medal of Honor coming your way."

"Oh, please."

"It's not just for you. It makes the department look good, too. We can make it very low-key—a private ceremony."

I made a face. "I'm really not interested, Tony."

He looked down at me as if I was becoming more trouble than I was worth. "All right, here's another argument for accepting it. James Dunn is organizing an award of his own for you—some sort of 'outstanding achievement' plaque from the State's Attorneys' Association."

"Jesus Christ . . ."

"If you'd agree to the Medal of Honor, it would steal some of his thunder, and you could insist that both awards be given at the same time, in private. Otherwise, he might just bushwack you with a bunch of press people and slap you with it like a subpoena, whether you like it or not."

I let out a deep sigh. "Let me think about it, okay?"

He shrugged good-naturedly. "Sure—when do your doctors think you can come back to us, by the way?"

"A few more days here, then three weeks at home with my mother and Leo. They're only twenty minutes away, and these folks want me back in every three days for a while to check me out."

"Gail'll be there, too?"

Gail had been a constant presence since I'd come out of my coma, keeping me company, bringing me newspapers and books, watching TV with me when I became too tired to do anything else, including sleep. She was commuting from Thetford, where she'd been staying with my mother and Leo, like some career-path traveling nurse, displaying much of her old take-charge stamina and making few references to her own troubles. Tony's question made me realize how much I'd become used to her being continually nearby.

But distracted by that thought, and pondering the unaccustomed ripple it caused across my emotions, all I said to him was, "Yes, she will."

Tony had taken my self-assessed physical prowess as a joke. In fact, a bench press of three gerbils wasn't far off the mark. Several days later, when I left the hospital under Gail's supervision, I did so in a wheelchair—and not because of the hospital's insurance requirements. I could only manage a few dozen feet before dizziness and exhaustion set me down. The septicemia had sucked my energy down to near empty. Tony may have been right about my having found the perfect diet, but I knew replacing the lost weight with muscle would be hard work, even if I was already brushing my own teeth.

My dread was compounded by the expression I'd seen on Leo's face as the physical therapist outlined my training regimen earlier. He'd rarely been so receptive. I knew that, bighearted to a fault, he was going to fix me up as good as new in record time—or kill me in the process.

Which made him a co-conspirator with Gail, since she'd already told me that she'd cornered the hospital nutritionist and designed a diet for me. Notions of raw tofu and cold bean gruel filled what was left of my panicky imagination.

Initially, I'd planned to return to Brattleboro, transfer my records, my case, and my outpatient status to Brattleboro Memorial Hospital, and recuperate at home on Spam and fruit cocktail. But that, it had been made clear early on, was out of the question. Not only did Leo use the excuse of a prolonged and long-overdue visit with our mother as a pretense to torture me—but Gail also had seemed eager to stay away from Brattleboro. I didn't begrudge her the tactic; I also didn't miss the irony that I felt more useful to her as an invalid than as a friend during her time of need.

As partners, however, Leo and Gail made a distinctly odd pair. As exuberant as Gail was thoughtful, as boisterous as she was quiet, and as physical as she was cerebral, my brother—on the surface— seemed made of the very stuff Gail was not. In addition, his passion for cars from the fifties and women with short attention spans were precisely those qualities which Gail tended to view with suspicion. And yet the two of them had hit it off from the first time they'd met, some fifteen years before.

Gail was not alone in her generous view of Leo. I think most people saw him in the same light that my mother's generation had revered Will Rogers, he who'd never met a man he didn't like. Leo was one of the world's optimists. A butcher who ran his own shop far off the beaten track, just down the hill from where he'd always lived with our mother, he'd created such a reputation for honesty and goodwill that people drove dozens of miles to do business with him. To enter his shop was not only to be guaranteed good meat at fair prices, it was to have your anxieties momentarily washed away by his nonstop cheer and compassion. He greeted everyone equally, with enthusiasm and an eye for their troubles. He had an encyclopedic memory for names and, more important, remembered from visit to visit the course of people's lives, which imbued in his customers the same trust they might have reserved for a respected psychologist. For a small-town, high school–educated meat man, his was an impressive aura, all the more so since he was totally unaware of its effect.

So I was tucked under the wing of these two oddly compatible friends, and driven across the Connecticut River to the Thetford farm where I'd grown up.

It wasn't a farm any longer, actually. The fields had been sold off to a neighbor after my father's death. But my mother and Leo still owned the house and barn, and we all three still referred to it as "the farm." It was located off the connector road between Thetford Hill and Thetford Center, where Leo had his shop, and despite its proximity to the new interstate, it retained for me all the isolated sweetness of my early memories. Before and during the Second World War, when I and certainly Leo were too young to enlist, we'd been the closest knit as a family—my youthful, vigorous, well-read mother, who'd injected in her sons a love of reading and a respect for all people; my much-older father, soon slated to pass away—taciturn, hardworking, undemonstrative, and gentle; and the two of us.

That, however, was then. Now, my mother was in a wheelchair, restricted to the ground floor and reduced to watching TV, her cherished reading victimized by failing eyesight, and Leo, for all his charm and parochial success, was running the risk of becoming an overage roué, tooling around in rough-looking vintage cars and dating women who shared his disinterest in commitment.

That, in any case, was my dour state of mind as we drove up to the place. It was a mood that Leo, Gail, and my mother—when at last I was wheeled into the living room to greet her, wheelchair to wheelchair—worked instinctively to overcome, filling the evening with good food and chatter, almost to excess.

When it was finally over, and Leo was putting our mother to bed, I looked over at Gail sitting on the same sofa I'd bounced on as a child, her long legs stretched out, her head tilted back against the pillows, her hands slack beside her. She looked like a loosely assembled collection of tired body parts.

"Well, I guess that's done."

She gave me a sad smile. "Was it that bad?"

"No," I admitted. "Maybe a little unreal."

"It's a lot to deal with, Joe. You and I aren't the only walking wounded around here."

I realized my sadness earlier had a secret sharer—one who'd been living here for several weeks now.

"So what's the bad news?" I asked fatalistically.

She smiled to lighten my concern. "It's nothing dramatic. Your mom's starting to slow down a lot, and pretty suddenly. She has to go to the doctor more often, she gets tired more easily, her innards aren't functioning as well as they used to . . . 'I'm just winding down' is how she put it to me—but I also think what happened to you sort of brought it into focus for both of them."

I sighed and shut my eyes momentarily. So much happening in so short a time, leaving everyone at loose ends.

"That's not to say she won't live another twenty years," Gail added hopefully, if without much conviction.

I opened my eyes and looked at her again. "And Leo?"

She paused, searching for the right words. "I think he's worried he might lose the center of his universe."

I thought about the butcher shop, his adulating clientele, his unending string of girlfriends, the car collection in the barn—Caddies, Mustangs, Corvairs, what-have-yous, all under tarps, all used for special occasions, like a selection of suits hung in a closet. So much window dressing for what had always been Mom and Leo. I saw for the first time the fragile thread by which Leo's life was held together. Not that my mother's dying would destroy him—I gave his inner strength more credit than that. But Gail was right—it would break his heart, and perhaps leave him ruing some of the choices he'd made along the way.

In that, I realized watching Gail, he wasn't alone.

Gail had moved a double bed into what my mother had proudly titled the library, knowing that few other farmhouses in the state had an entire room that could be so called. My father had catered to this one presumption, and had lined the walls of an erstwhile parlor with floor-to-ceiling shelves, which my mother had eventually filled with an eclectic, much-read collection—a passion for the two of us of an evening, my father being content to watch the fire and smoke a pipe, while Leo built models and read car magazines.

It was the heart of the house, as far as I was concerned, and I was grateful Gail had thought of it.

I did notice, however, as I slowly and laboriously undressed, that I was not to sleep here alone. A night table by the left side of the bed had a small collection of Gail's things, and some of her clothes were neatly piled on a nearby chair. I could tell by the wrinkled pillow next to mine that she'd been using this room for some time.

I was pleased by that, but it made me wonder how to behave. Amid all the trauma that had befallen her, and the emotional, legal, and public uproar that had attended it—not to mention what my mishap had contributed—we'd never had a chance to get privately reacquainted. The prospect of sleeping with her, along with the sexual implications that carried, made me wary.

I climbed under the covers, naked, as was my custom, the bed's embrace a mixed blessing. Gail moved about the dimly lit room, busying herself with her few belongings, avoiding looking at me, and finally broke the palpable tension in the air by grabbing her pajamas and leaving for the bathroom down the hall.

I lay on my back, my eyes on the ceiling, listening. The couch in the living room was long and wide enough to accommodate either one of us, should the need arise. There was even my old bedroom upstairs, which is where I'd thought she'd been bunking all along.

I glanced at the small lamp by her side of the bed, wondering if it would be helpful or too suggestive to turn it off, and thought again of the upstairs bedroom. Why hadn't she used it? Why had she instead moved in here, knowing it was the room I would occupy? Was it to get used to the idea? I imagined her lying here, as alone as I was now, considering the prospect of my eventual arrival just as I was anticipating hers. You always think these things will get easier with age.

I didn't hear her coming in her bare feet. The door just swung open and she was standing before me, in thin cotton pajamas, her toilet bag in her hand. She gave me an awkward smile as she crossed over to the chair she'd commandeered for her things, and put the bag down.

"You feeling okay? Dinner go down all right?"

I watched her standing in the middle of the room, her hands by her sides. "Yes. It was great. Where'd you get the bed?"

"Leo put it together. I think he got the frame out of the barn. I don't know where he got the mattress. Is it comfortable enough?"

I didn't answer, but kept looking at her. "Gail, I'd be happy to use the sofa—"

She stopped me with her hand, suddenly held up. "No. I did this on purpose. I need to find out if I can spend the night with a man and not feel afraid." Her voice was tight but strong, her convictions overriding her own nervousness.

She moved to her side of the bed and turned off the light. Gradually, my eyes adjusted to the milky moonlight that angled in through the uncurtained window. I saw her—in vague pale shadow only—quickly remove her pajamas. She slid into the bed next to me, and tentatively touched my chest with her hand. Instinctively, I put my arm around her shoulders and pulled her close to me, reveling in the familiar way she nestled her head against my chest, the smell of her hair rich in my nose. She draped her leg over mine and I felt the softness of her naked breasts and stomach against me. At that, a sigh—almost a shudder—escaped her.

"How's it feel?" I finally whispered.

She moved her face so her lips just touched mine. Her voice, wreathed in the sweetness of her toothpaste, was serious and thoughtful. "So far, so good."

I kissed her gently, and gave in to the best sleep I'd had in well over a month.

Chapter Sixteen

In some respects, I found myself spending the next week groping for an elusive past. I was in search of my former well-being, the easy communication I'd once enjoyed with Gail, and the comfort I'd always assumed would be there for me in my childhood home, but whose stability now seemed threatened.

The physical therapy set the rhythm. Leo eagerly supervised the hospital-dictated routine, but I felt driven to go beyond it, and did so in private, away from those I knew would caution me not to push too hard. There were no demands on me to rehabilitate rapidly. The calls I made to the office reassured me that all was well and progressing at its own legal snail's pace. But despite the pleasant setting, a string of inordinately balmy days, and the color-ful riot of the long-awaited fall foliage, I felt somehow under pres-sure, as if any regained strength might soon become a crucial advantage.

Apparently, I wasn't much good at keeping my anxiety under wraps. Pulling up a seat beside my mother one afternoon, no longer using a wheelchair but wobbly-kneed from a private workout, I was about to embark on what had become a daily ritual for the two of us—the viewing of her favorite soap operas. This time, however, she killed the sound with her remote and gave me a mother's careful scrutiny. "Why are you pushing yourself so hard?" she asked gently.

I wasn't surprised she'd noticed, but I still hadn't come up with a satisfactory answer. "I don't know."

"Is it Gail?" she persisted.

I looked at her in surprise. "What makes you think that?"

"She's still in a lot of pain. Maybe you think you need to be, too."

I was startled by the sophistication of the idea—and wondered if she might be right. Nevertheless, I made light of it, squeezing her hand. "My mother the shrink."

She wasn't amused. "Have you asked her what she's feeling? It might be easier on both of you."

I thought back over the week, at our initial night together, and at how, although tentatively, things seemed to be improving. "She's doing well. She doesn't brood on the attack as much—she seems more focused on getting on with things. She's a strong person. I think she's coming along."

"Is she sleeping at night?" my mother asked pointedly.

"Sure—I guess so. She wasn't at first."

"Then why does she nap so much?"

A small, wiggling irritation began welling up inside me, as if I'd missed something obvious because I'd been distracted by my own concerns. "She's been through a lot. Plus she takes care of me, helps Leo out at the store sometimes, and she's still trying to run things in Brattleboro. It takes a toll."

My mother patted my forearm. "She's still not sleeping at night, Joey. She comes in here after you fall asleep. She plays the TV, sometimes she reads, other times I imagine she just sits on the sofa and wishes she were someone else."

"How do you know that? Do you hear her?"

She laughed gently. "No. I'm sleeping fine. I notice things in the morning—a magazine's been put back on another pile, a bookmark's been moved up a hundred pages, the blanket on the back of the sofa's folded differently than it was when we went to bed."

I stared at her in astonishment. "The bookmark? You know what page she's on?"

She shook her head, obviously delighted with her prowess. Her eyes, however, remained serious. She didn't want me to miss her point. "This room is almost my entire world. The first things I noticed were obvious—the bookmark came after I started paying close attention."

She reached out and touched my cheek, her fingertips warm and smooth. "She needs you just like you need her. Helping you to get better has let her focus on someone besides herself—it's given her breathing room—but it's also helped her to hide from her own demons."

My eyes strayed to the screen. A beautiful man in beautiful clothes mouthed something to a beautiful woman and then stalked out the door. The woman stared at the camera with tear-stained eyes, her trembling mouth parted, before everything went blank for a station break.

"One last piece of motherly advice," the soothing voice said next to me.

I looked into those old, familiar gray eyes. "Don't stop now."

"Just be supportive. Don't confront her on her sleeping habits— or anything else. Time will help you out."

I didn't confront Gail on her nocturnal habits that night. I joined her instead, albeit without her knowledge. A half hour after we'd turned off the light—and about five minutes after she'd slipped out of bed for her nightly vigil in the living room—I propped myself up against the pillows in the darkness and began wrestling with my own doubts. Gail's mental health was certainly part of them—and I now knew for myself that my mother's concerns had been well founded. But there was something else, something that had first stirred inside me the day I'd talked with Tony Brandt in the hospital gym, and which the conversation I'd had with Gail tonight—before we'd both pretended to go to sleep—had put into sharp focus.

I had taken my mother's advice. Upon getting into bed earlier, I'd asked Gail if caring for me wasn't merely a way for her to avoid her own problems.

She frowned at the question, but didn't get angry. "Maybe, but that's probably not all bad. Before you were hurt, the rape was all I thought about—it took over my life."

"And now that I'm on the mend?"

She hesitated, and then sighed heavily, as if forcing herself to be polite. "I've been in touch with Susan. Women for Women have started a vigil to help keep Dunn honest, and they've held Katz's feet to the fire so the paper doesn't drop the issue now that Vogel is in jail. Next week, WBRT is holding a half-day call-in show I'm going to be on with other women, so the whole subject of rape can be discussed in the open—"

I reached out and took her hand. Her voice had dropped to a virtual monotone—a recitation of events in somebody else's life. "I don't care about that, Gail. I want to know how *you're* doing."

She pulled her hand away, the anger finally surfacing. "That's the point, Joe. You *should* care. Focusing on me doesn't address the issue. It just reduces the rape to the level of a mugging, or a car accident—something to be swept under the rug after all the right words have been said."

I thought ruefully of my mother's advice not to set up any confrontations. "You don't need to convert me—I'm a believer. But I also think the messenger should be as well taken care of as the message."

Gail didn't comment for a while. "Maybe you're right," she finally murmured. "I'm not doing all that well. I can't sleep at night, and sudden noises set me off like an alarm clock. I lock the door and jam a chair under the handle every time I take a shower. And I think I'm driving Susan and the others crazy with phone calls, trying to see if there's anything I can do."

She let out a shuddering sigh and stared at her hands. "I thought I could beat this, Joe. I know the routine; I've seen others go through it. But it's just not working."

"Are you seeing someone who can help?"

"I was, until you got hurt. I've called her a couple of times since I've been up here, when things got really bad, but I guess I thought I could cheat there, too."

"How bad do things get?" I asked, feeling guilty for not knowing.

"They pile up, bit by bit. When I go out, I think every man in sight is looking at me, and when I'm here alone, I'm afraid someone will come crashing through the door. I've felt so sorry for myself at times, I've started resenting you—thinking you got stabbed on purpose to grab attention away from me."

I shook my head, overwhelmed by what she'd been dealing with. "What did your therapist say?"

"She wanted me to come back to Brattleboro, or at least find somebody up here. She said I had to talk it out so I could deal with it up front—relive the rape in detail, admit my life has been permanently changed and then move on. I had to 'commit to heal,' in her words."

She lightly punched her own leg, her face tight. "It pisses me off. I know my life's been changed, but I can't shake what that bastard did to me—That's another thing," she added vehemently, as if I was arguing with her, "I have these fits of pure rage. I get so mad I start crying, and I can't stop." She caught her breath. "I just can't believe I can't beat this."

"Would you like to use me to talk it out?" I asked softly, referring back to her therapist's advice.

Her reaction was tentative. "It's supposed to help—make it something that doesn't eat me up from inside."

"Let's try it, then."

"I don't know, Joe . . ."

"It helped to talk about it the day after, didn't it?"

She thought about it for a few moments. "You're not too tired?"

"Nope. And it would make me feel better, after all you've done for me."

She finally agreed. Sitting back with her head against the pillows, my hand in hers, she went over in detail what Bob Vogel had done to her.

I listened carefully—asking a question now and then—slipping on my professional demeanor to keep my emotions in check. By the end, she seemed a bit more peaceful, her cheeks reddened by tears. She blew her nose, gave me a hug, and pretended to go to sleep, although she left again for the living room as soon as she thought I'd nodded off.

Sleep for me, however, was out of the question.

For now I understood what had been troubling me. It wasn't my physical wound, or her emotional one. It stemmed instead from a phenomenon I should have recognized much sooner.

As she'd recounted her purgative tale, my mind had begun catching on stray details of the account, like fine fabric snagging on rough skin. Questions had started to form, discrepancies to loom, and I'd been forced to face the strong probability that something—I didn't know what—had been missed earlier.

What I realized in my gut was that the case in Dunn's hands was perhaps fatally flawed.

Chapter Seventeen

Tony Brandt's voice on the phone was both hesitant and slightly defiant. "I hope you've gotten used to the idea of getting a medal."

It was midway through the second week of my convalescence, and all four of us had been playing cards in the living room following dinner. The group behind me laughed suddenly at something Leo said, and I stretched the telephone cord until I was just inside the front hallway. "Why?" was all I asked.

" 'Cause the ceremony's tomorrow morning, up where you are. Dunn's invited the press and a few flunkies—yours truly included—we'll do it in your front yard if the weather's good."

"Whether I like it or not."

"Whether you like it or not. 'Course, you could make us look like jerks and skip town for a while."

I waited for more, and then asked, "Is that a recommendation?"

He chuckled briefly. "I guess not. Wishful thinking. For a second, I could picture Dunn trying to explain where you were . . ."

"Is he going to graciously give me a call in an hour and ask my permission, or is that what you're doing now?"

The answering silence had no mirth in it. "Yeah," he finally admitted, "James is tied up till late tonight—asked me to do the honors. Apologies and all that."

"Right. What time?"

"Ten in the morning."

I digested the news, slowly accepting that there was little I could do about it without involving the department in publicity it didn't deserve. Brandt saying he was going to be there confirmed that, regardless of whatever furor might have preceded this decision, he'd lost, and now it was time for a proper stiff upper lip. "Tell him I'll be here."

Tony was more resigned than pleased. "Okay."

"Do me a favor, though, will you? Could you bring a synopsis of Vogel's case up with you tomorrow?"

There was a long pause. He knew I hadn't merely run out of reading material. "You working on something?"

"I just want to refresh my mind on a few points."

"All right," he said slowly. "Nothing up your sleeve?"

He didn't want to know—not really. I wasn't sure I did myself. "Nope. See you tomorrow."

Unfortunately, the next day was beautiful. The sky was a startling shade of electric blue, making a picture-perfect backdrop for the miles of gaudily dressed trees that swept down the valley from the farmhouse's front door. Even the giant maple in the yard was at its best—a wild craze of red and orange impressionist daubings, looming high overhead in a dazzling canopy. I shook my head with disgust at the whole display and slammed the door on it, returning to the kitchen.

It was not the happy gathering one might have expected on such an occasion, despite Leo's best efforts to make it cheerful. Reinforcing my gloom, Gail had barely said a word since I'd mentioned the ceremony the night before, and my mother kept looking nervously from one of us to the other, as if anxious to find out whose fuse was going to prove shorter.

I was troubled by Gail myself. There was no great love between her and Dunn, and the blatant opportunism of his little maneuver hadn't been lost on any of us. But there was something beyond that, and I was fearful it stemmed from my having asked her to recount the rape. I wondered if reliving the trauma had been exactly the wrong thing for her to have done. But despite several gentle attempts to get her to talk, she kept to herself. Perhaps Dunn's contrived ceremony was the last straw for her. She had, after all, come up not only to help me out, but also to get away from the turmoil and pressure that Brattleboro had come to represent.

So we ate breakfast largely in silence, and ended up retreating to our separate corners of the house to await the circus's arrival.

Our worst fears were well founded. The string of cars that eventually crested the driveway reminded me of the funeral cortege of some latter-day martyr. Not only were all the Brattleboro luminaries there in force, but the town's familiar media corps had been reinforced by a dozen more from around the region, including two TV trucks.

As I stood in the doorway, pointing out the cast of characters to Leo as they milled around like a bunch of actors on break, he shook his head and asked, "Who the hell did they leave behind?"

Brandt was the first to come over to shake hands, complimenting Leo as he gave me an appraising eye. "Nice work—he almost looks better than before he was run through."

"Jesus, Tony," I muttered, my eyes fixed on the throng.

He gave me a hopeless shrug. "It was out of my hands, Joe. I told Dunn we were tabling the Medal of Honor at your request, and he just said, 'Then I'll do it my way.'"

"What crap," I muttered.

"You know, what all of us admit except you is that you deserve this citation. Besides, we don't do this job for the money, Joe, and people like you give other cops something to be proud of."

I was too frustrated to answer, feeling I was being celebrated simply for surviving.

"Well," Tony filled the silence impatiently. "Let's get it over with."

From that point on, it was difficult identifying who was in control, as we were unsuccessfully posed in front of one photogenic location after another. I, my mother—included because she was deemed picturesque—Brandt, Dunn, and a sullen Gail, were shuffled from the front steps, to the base of the maple, to the bottom of the yard. Finally, at the outer limits of his patience, Dunn ended it abruptly by giving a short, clenched-teeth speech about what a wonderful fellow I was, and thrust his precious plaque at me as if he couldn't get rid of it fast enough—all before a semicircle of clicking cameras, tape recorders, and bulky TV camcorders.

When it was over, after Dunn had left and we'd returned to the house, fending off the crowd of reporters with a barrage of "no comments," Tony Brandt handed over a cardboard box filled with documents.

"This isn't everything, of course. I left out all the chain-of-evidence data, most of the legal mumbo-jumbo, and a lot of stuff I didn't think you'd be interested in—including the physical evidence, which stays under lock and key. That basically leaves the narrative documents—who did what when—the relevant technical paperwork, and a lot of photographs. That what you were after?"

I nodded at the box. "I really appreciate it, Tony."

We were still standing in the front hallway, Brandt having declined an invitation by my mother to stay for lunch. He looked at me long enough to force me to finally meet his eyes. "You going to tell me why you want all this?"

"I would if I could."

"Something must have got you thinking."

I shook my head. "It's not like I've got a problem. Gail and I were just talking the other night, and I started asking myself questions—niggly little ones. The answers are all probably in there." I pointed my chin at the box.

"And if they aren't?"

I raised both palms toward the ceiling. "I'll call you."

Tony Brandt mulled that over for a while, absentmindedly chewing his lower lip. "You realize this thing could go to court anytime. Dunn's only hoping it won't before the election."

"You think it might?" I asked, surprised. Dunn wasn't the only one expecting a drawn-out process. Virtually none of us had ever seen a felony case go in front of a judge in anything under twelve months—and that was considered fast.

"No," he admitted. "But you never know. Tom Kelly's still playing coy—no depositions, no continuances, no delaying tactics whatsoever. I just want to be sure that, regardless of when they go in, we've made damned sure Dunn's got everything he needs. If you've got problems, I want to hear them now. If Dunn ends up screwing up on his own, that's his problem, but I don't want him dropping the ball because of something we did or didn't do."

"I understand," I said neutrally, sensitive to the hackles I'd raised in his mind. "But I've got to do my job regardless of the timing."

He seemed to stop breathing for a moment, and then let out a long breath. "Just do it soon, okay?"

He moved toward the front door. I followed him out. "Things a little wild back home?" I asked, stimulated by his pessimistic tone.

"You been watching the news? Between the vigils, the public meetings, the media, and Dunn and Derby chewing on each other every day, this case is about the only topic in town. That crazy bastard Jason Ryan has annointed himself the Joan of Arc of the feminist movement, if you can believe that, and he's started passing out pepper Mace to damn near every woman he meets. So now the usual domestic disputes and parking-lot squabbles are starting to involve chemical warfare, with a few of our guys getting zapped in the process. The town's a zoo, and if you want my opinion, all it would take is for some loony to do something really crazy, to put us on the map big time."

Over the many years I'd worked with him, I'd rarely seen Tony Brandt so worked up. I patted his shoulder as we reached his car. "Look, I've probably just had too much time on my hands, and nothing else to think about. I'll read through what you brought me, refamiliarize myself with the case, and then drop it, okay? I don't think there's anything to worry about."

He turned and looked at me then, and echoed what was going on in my own brain. "I know you too well, Joe, and that scares the shit out of me."

I moved the box upstairs and spread its contents in orderly piles around my old bedroom, feeling an odd twinge of pleasure as I did so. I realized how much I'd been missing the job. Beyond any questions I might have harbored concerning this particular investigation, I found myself happy merely manipulating the tools of my craft. The eye-witness accounts, case reports, forensic sheets, and crime-scene photos passed before my eyes with a comforting familiarity, and were as welcome and rewarding as the exercises I'd been doing to retrain my muscles. I even kidded myself that perhaps my reason for asking for these documents had been sub-consciously therapeutic, with no bearing on the actual integrity of the case.

I was lost in this reacquaintance ritual when a knock at the door made me look up. Gail was standing quietly on the threshold, her expression guarded. "What are you doing, Joe?"

I felt suddenly and inexplicably guilty, as if caught in an act of lapsed faith. "Oh. Tony brought up a synopsis of your case—basically what he's handing over to Dunn. I thought I'd look it over again—it's been a long time."

She watched me in silence, her face impassive, her eyes taking in the carefully stacked piles. "Leo's looking for you."

I checked my watch in surprise. I'd lost track of time and had completely forgotten our afternoon training. Gail was already walking back down the dark hallway toward the stairs. I quickly got to my feet and went after her. "Gail . . ."

She turned in the gloomy light and faced me silently, her arms by her sides, her body tired and defeated. I reached out and held her shoulders, to no response. "Something's wrong. Was it our talk last night? Or Dunn and his stupid plaque?"

She smiled wanly and shrugged. "I'm just feeling a little blue. It's just part of the process. Our talk was good. I know it's what I'm supposed to do."

"Is there anything I can do to make things easier?"

She raised her hand then and laid it on my forearm. "Not unless you could give me amnesia." She shook her head, the smile fading entirely. "I think I'll take a nap. You go work out with your brother." She paused a moment, and then asked, "You're doing a lot better, aren't you?"

"I'm getting there. I still don't have much stamina, but the strength is coming back. Why?"

"I was just thinking that I wasn't doing much good up here anymore. Maybe I ought to go back to Bratt—help Susan out."

"Would that make you feel better?"

She slipped her shoulders from under my hands and turned away again. "I don't know. I'll take a nap first."

I almost skipped the soaps that day. After my workout with Leo, I returned to my paper piles and began to discover that nostalgia had played no part in my need to review what we'd done. Things no longer felt as solid to me as they had before Vogel stuck me with his knife. I still had no palpable evidence leading me anywhere, but I did have a growing list of questions that needed definite answers.

None of which eclipsed my concerns about Gail. Her abrupt emotional nose dive shouldn't have been unexpected. But it reminded me too much of the days immediately following the rape, when she'd been absorbed by her friends, and I'd ended up on the outside.

My mother turned down the sound before I even reached my chair.

"So what's going on?" she asked me bluntly.

I quoted Gail. "It's a process that has its ups and downs."

She shook her head impatiently. "I know that. Did you talk to her about that idiocy this morning?"

"I've tried. . . ." I stopped, and thought about the question more carefully, countering with a question of my own. "What about this morning? She's a politician herself. She may have thought it was a lousy thing to do, but she knows the game."

Again, my mother looked disgusted. "I thought you'd missed the point. I could see it by the way you handled things."

I rubbed my forehead in exasperation. "What are you driving at?"

She looked at me closely. "Where's Gail's award?" She then squeezed my hand supportively, sat back in her chair, and hit the remote, her message delivered. The earnest murmurings of insincere people filled the room.

I sat there beside her, stunned by my own shortsightedness. I was no longer in the mood to watch TV; nor did I want to further aggravate Gail by waking her up just to be contrite and make myself feel better. So I did what I'd done for most of my life, when the complexities of human nature outpaced me—I went back to work.

My weeks in a coma had given me distance from the case, allowing my mind to float free of the momentum and prejudice that had grown as we'd gotten closer to Bob Vogel. Now, that passion had been supplanted by an analytical coolness, granting me the chance to play devil's advocate with many of the clues we'd collected with indiscriminate enthusiasm.

For example: the rape itself. We had built strong, credible

bridges linking Gail's account, the evidence found at the scene, and Bob Vogel's MO. My perusal of Tony's selected documents told me that these bridges had been strengthened by corroboration and tailored for clarity.

So where was the problem?

While attempting to fit a person to a crime, police officers are supposed to probe for the loopholes, no matter how flimsy. Much of this falls into the "vagaries of human nature" department, such as, in our situation, the assumption that Bob Vogel had continued to learn from each of his previous assaults, altering the way he blocked his victims' vision, restrained their movements, and protected his hands by using gloves when he beat them.

My concern was that we hadn't questioned hard enough, instead caving in to the weight of attractive evidence and increasingly turning our backs on a significant number of apparently minor questions.

Such as: Why, after stealthily entering the house and removing his clothes—presumably to help shield his identity—did Vogel climb onto Gail before bagging her head? By so doing, he'd woken her up prematurely, and had run the risk of being identified.

Why did he whisper, when the two of them had never met, and there was no way she'd recognize his voice?

During the rape, he'd taken the time to go on a rampage, breaking lamps and tearing apart Gail's drawers and closet. But why had he been so methodical, working his way around the room in a clockwise direction? Why had he spared the fancy TV set— the largest target in the room—and why had he said, "Shit," when the expensive Mexican plate she'd had hanging on the wall fell and broke? Surely such destruction was the whole point of the exercise. Hadn't he called her a "snotty goddamn bitch," implying a wounded sense of social and financial inferiority—a factor which had played no apparent part in Vogel's previous rapes? It was an odd choice of words from someone whose vocabulary tended to wallow among the truly obscene—a phrase that sounded even vaguely effeminate.

And what about the means of entry? It had been easy to effect— the simple sliding of a knife blade across a window's loose lock— but that had been the only such vulnerable window in the house. An unlikely coincidence unless Vogel had been inside before, scoping things out—a supposition for which we had no evidence. Murchison, the glass man, had been a good suspect there, but—according to a forensics report from Waterbury—the blood-stained knife found in Vogel's trailer was a perfect match for the scratch marks on the lock.

And what about Vogel's presence in the area shortly before the attack? The neighbor who'd hired him to work on her lawn had positively identified him, but, to our knowledge, Vogel had never staked out his intended victims before in that fashion. Furthermore, assuming that he'd set fire to the regular yard man's equipment so he could legitimately get close to Gail's house, why hadn't he gone door to door afterward, pretending to offer his services to others? That simple ploy could have put him right at Gail's doorstep, and—if he'd properly conned her—might have gotten him inside.

I hadn't lost sight of all the evidence we had against Bob Vogel, or of the fact that his own actions, once he'd been accused, had hardly been those of an innocent victim. But I was troubled by what I was finding.

With the sun having surrendered to the room's overhead light, and the sounds of dinner being prepared in the kitchen below, I sat back from my research and stared at the floor in contemplation, Tony Brandt's words of caution echoing in my ears. If you're going to kick over the apple cart, he'd implied, do it now and don't be wrong.

What I needed was a sounding board, and of the two best ones I'd used in the past, one—Tony Brandt himself—was in Brattleboro, while the other was downstairs, slowly drifting away from me on a raft of her own misery.

Chapter Eighteen

I went downstairs, lost in thought, rationalizing how my problem and Gail's might be mutually redressed. I wanted someone to help me untangle—or at least confirm—the questions I'd been struggling with all afternoon. And Gail, as I saw it, needed some mental handhold she could use to help pull herself out of her depression.

Perhaps mercifully, I never got to put my theory to the test. By the time I walked into the living room, all three of them had been pulled out of the kitchen by the evening news and were clustered around the television in silence. I joined them quietly, standing to the rear, looking over the top of my mother's head.

After a brief, noncommittal smile at the camera, the anchorwoman behind the curving desk fixed us all with a serious look. "Earlier today, in Thetford, Vermont, Brattleboro Police Lieutenant Joseph Gunther was presented the State's Attorneys' Association's annual Outstanding Achievement Award. Last month, Gunther was stabbed with a knife while apprehending the alleged rapist of Brattleboro Selectwoman Gail Zigman. Gunther spent three weeks in a coma at the Hitchcock Medical Center and is currently recuperating at his mother's home in Thetford. *News at Six*'s Tony Coven covered the ceremony."

The anchorwoman was replaced by a young man in a ski parka standing in bright sunshine in front of our house, a microphone gripped in his hand like a relay-race baton. "The Outstanding

Achievement Award was presented by State's Attorney James Dunn to Lieutenant Gunther on the heels of one of the most publicized sexual-assault cases this state has seen in years—a case still awaiting trial, and which is of particular concern to James Dunn, who is currently in a neck-and-neck reelection bid against Brattleboro attorney Jack Derby."

The camera cut to footage of me standing next to a tense James Dunn. My mother was seated between us, and to my other side, cut off by the camera's tight framing, we could all see one of Gail's arms. Dunn all but speared me with the edge of the plaque and muttered a few words of congratulations before giving my hand a limp shake.

Coven's voice continued in the background. "Ms. Zigman made headlines last month because of her insistence not to remain an anonymous victim of rape. Instead, immediately following the alleged assault, she organized and led a candlelight march on the courthouse to publicize her message that rape is only encouraged by the silence of its victims."

The screen came alive with a phalanx of police officers escorting a manacled Bob Vogel from a heavily guarded van into an unidentified building, surrounded by a crowd waving placards and chanting.

"The missing figure in all this turmoil is the accused man himself. Robert Vogel, who was apprehended at the Harriman Reservoir immediately following the stabbing of Lieutenant Gunther—a bloody knife still in his hand—remains in high-security isolation at the Woodstock Correctional Facility, silent and defiant. Neither he nor his attorney, Thomas Kelly, have issued any statements to the press, nor have they responded to any inquiries made of them by *News at Six*."

Tony Coven reappeared before us. "Off camera, State's Attorney Dunn stressed that today's ceremony honoring Joseph Gunther was a simple act of recognition for a public servant who came so close to paying the ultimate sacrifice. Dunn denied that his own tight political race, and the significant role this case might play in his reelection, had anything to do with the timing of the award. *News at Six* learned, however, that Gunther himself didn't wish to be so honored, and has asked that the presentation of his own department's Medal of Honor be postponed until sometime after his return to work. For *News at Six*, I'm Tony Coven."

Leo burst out laughing at my sudden celebrity status. "See that, Joey? You're a hero."

But my eyes were on Gail as she pushed herself violently out of her chair and marched out of the room, her back and shoulders stiff with anger.

I patted Leo gently on the back as I moved around him. "Be back in a sec." I followed Gail into our bedroom. She'd already pulled her canvas bag out from under the bed and was filling it helter-skelter.

She didn't look up as I entered. "I'm going back to Brattleboro."

"Could we talk?" I asked, keeping my voice soft.

"What about? You're doing fine, and I need to get back to work."

"Neither one of us is fine, Gail. We need to sort this out."

She stopped packing and stared at me. "What are you doing with those files upstairs? And don't give me that 'I wanted to look it over again' crap. I know you better than that."

I could feel my face flush. "It was my case. There were some details I wanted to review."

"What details? Are you having problems with what happened? Is it becoming an 'alleged' assault to you, too?"

Her anger was white hot and all-encompassing, but instead of easing it as I should have, I bristled in turn, finally reacting to a stored-up critical mass of pain and self-denial. I ignored groping for an appropriately soothing response. "We both know you were raped, Gail. But it's my job to make sure Vogel did it. I've got to make sure we go into that courtroom with a rock-solid case. You're not the alleged victim—*he's* the alleged rapist."

"He stabbed you, for Christ's sake, and he raped three other women," she shouted, her fists clenched by her sides. "Isn't that enough? Why do you have to pick at everything? That bastard is guilty, Joe—let the son-of-a-bitch hang."

"I'll let him hang when I believe he did it."

She stared at me for a moment, and then returned to her packing. "Go away, leave me alone. Wrap yourself in your mother and Leo and your hero's halo, and let me get on with my life."

I caught my breath, stung by her reckless, damaging fury. Despite my sympathy for her plight, I was astonished at what it had suddenly unleashed—in both of us.

I left the room without comment.

*   *   *

Twelve hours later, I was back in the hospital, back under the knife.

Reacting to both Gail's blistering departure and my own growing reservations about the case, I'd pushed my training too hard. Consciously, the point had been to get better faster and return to the job; subconsciously, I wasn't so sure, although the looks Leo gave me as I sat writhing in agony on the way to the hospital told me he wasn't in any doubt.

My injury was not severe—a small internal tear, easily remedied. But it insured a few more days in a hospital bed and took a few notches off the hard-won gains I'd made so far. More important, it put me out of action just when I most wanted to get moving. Tony Brandt's call, a day later, made me regret my setback all the more.

"Dunn and Kelly had the status conference yesterday. Kelly asked for a speedy trial—standard enough—but it looks like he's going to get it. They have a judge and an out-of-county jury all lined up. The trial's set to begin in three days."

It took me a moment to digest what he'd said. A criminal trial, especially a major one, never came up this soon after arraignment. It could in theory—assuming both the prosecution and the defense agreed—but it never actually happened in practice. Not only were delaying tactics so common they'd become routine, but judges and courtrooms were at a premium, booked for many months in advance.

Normally, as a beleaguered cop who constantly complained about a snail-paced system, I would have been elated for all concerned. Given my newfound qualms, however, this was lousy news. "How come?"

"There was another change-of-venue case scheduled for the end of the week, complete with judge and courtroom, but they settled out of court about an hour before the status conference on the Vogel case. When Kelly demanded a speedy trial, the clerk offered it as a possibility—almost as a joke. He took it."

"So it's definite?"

"Dunn couldn't argue the point. He'd already said he was ready, and if he backed down now, he'd have a hell of a time explaining why. From what I heard, though, he went ballistic when he reached his office. He's convinced Kelly's got something up his sleeve."

"What do you think?" I asked cautiously.

"I'm not sure anymore. I've never seen anything like this. One thing I do know is that the judge'll be Waterston, from the old if-she-was-dressed-like-that-she-was-looking-for-it school. Maybe Kelly's pinning his hopes on that."

I didn't buy it. The judge would probably be a factor in the defense theory, but I respected Tom Kelly's abilities enough to know there must be more to it. "What about their witness list? Who do they have?"

Brandt's voice rose a note. "That was another surprise. Vogel's the only one on it, which means Dunn can't depose him, since he's also the defendant. But Dunn may not even get to cross-examine him, since Kelly isn't obligated to put him on the stand, so the prosecution's got no way of knowing what strategy they'll be fighting. Kelly could claim his client's innocent, or that he was insane at the time . . . He could even claim it was consensual sex that got too rough. Whatever he chooses, he's got Dunn in a pickle, since he won't be calling his witnesses till after the prosecution's shown its hand."

"Has Kelly deposed anyone?"

"Gail's the only one he's listed. You might warn her that he'll be calling her soon."

"She's gone back to Bratt."

I could hear him evaluating the tone of my voice. "I'll let her know" was all he said finally. "How long are you going to be on your back?"

"A few days, maybe—it depends," I answered vaguely. I was distracted by the sudden thought that Tom Kelly had more up his sleeve than just a mysterious strategy. It was possible that he had certain knowledge of his client's innocence, and needed only Vogel on the stand to prove it.

"Have you been able to get a reading on Vogel? Any rumors from cell mates or prison guards or anyone else?"

"Nope. Ever since he blew it with the oil-slick story, he's been stone silent." Tony's voice became guarded. "What're you after, Joe? Did you find something in those files I gave you?"

I sidestepped. "I'm just trying to figure Kelly's strategy."

Almost reluctantly, I thought, Tony admitted, "From what I've heard, Vogel is feeling no pain. I guess *defiant* is the word."

"Like he expects to stick it to us in court?"

"If I knew that, I wouldn't be biting my nails."

"Right," I muttered.

Brandt tried once more. "I get this feeling you're holding out on me."

I gave in just a hair. "I don't know, Tony—I've got a lot invested in all this. I'm worried I may have been sloppy."

His voice was solicitous, but he sounded vaguely relieved. "You didn't land this guy all by yourself, you know. We all did, and we got him on the evidence—better than a lot of other times. You just need to get back to work."

"I guess so," I agreed, but I knew we had different meanings in mind.

I returned to Brattleboro four days later, in the middle of the night, just as soon as I'd been able to get out of bed, use the bathroom, and put on my clothes, all without assistance. I knew there was going to be hell to pay from the hospital, whom I hadn't informed of my departure, but getting back to work had by now become a visceral need. I had to confront theory with reality—doubts with concrete answers—and thus stand with everyone else in their conviction that we'd put the right man behind bars.

One major obstacle to all this, however—aside from the fact that the trial had begun the day before, and that nobody now wanted to hear from a last-minute Cassandra—was that legally I couldn't return to work. Until the hospital officially released me, my doctors issued a clean bill of health, and the town's insurer gave me the nod, I couldn't be seen inside the Municipal Building in a professional capacity.

I was pondering how to get around this red tape, having slowly and painfully climbed the stairs to my third-floor apartment, when I fished my keys from my pocket and inadvertently inserted the wrong one into the lock.

I stood there for a moment, staring at the lock. I'd lived here for decades, always using the same key every day, and yet, after only a five-week absence, I'd goofed. It wasn't me I was thinking about, however. In a totally different context, it was Bob Vogel.

I returned the keys to my pocket and slowly returned downstairs, the question of where to start my private quest suddenly answered.

*   *   *

It had been well over a month since Willy Kunkle and I had tailed Vogel along the back roads between Jamaica and West Brattleboro, but while the route we'd taken had been new to me then, it seemed intensely familiar as soon as I pulled off of Route 30 forty minutes later and began retracing our trip.

This time, I wasn't following a distant pair of taillights with my own lights out, hoping to avoid notice and the ditch both; instead, I put myself in Vogel's position—a recent arrival to the region, traveling on roads familiar only for where they led, watching not for any memorable landmarks, but rather for the roving sheriff's car that would mean the end of my license and the probable revocation of my probation.

It had come to me, when I'd inserted the wrong key in my lock, that perhaps Vogel had done much the same thing with his proffered alibi—identifying not the place where he'd broken down and lost a noticeable amount of oil, but where he'd *assumed* the breakdown had occurred.

According to the statement he'd given Willy Kunkle after I'd gone into a coma, his car had quit "maybe four miles out" between Wardsboro and Newfane, just beyond where a narrow road or driveway took off into the trees on the right. We'd already determined that his car's odometer was on the blink, but Willy, who'd done the on-site investigation, had also discovered that there was only one place along that approximate stretch of road that fit the description.

I drove almost as fast as we had the other night, assuming that was the pace Vogel usually set for himself, and I made a pointed effort not to study the right side of the road with undue scrutiny. Nevertheless, the gap, when it came, was pretty evident, all by itself along an uninterrupted stretch of forest.

I stopped, delicately extricated myself from behind the driver's wheel, grimacing at the pain in my still-sensitive gut, and walked along the side of the road. Even allowing for the passage of time, there was no sign of an oil slick, despite extensive sweeps with my flashlight. I'd told Brandt that five weeks of inaction had probably led to an overblown imagination, but I hadn't actually believed that myself. I'd been dreading that, at first scratch, some overlooked truth would rear up and bite us all. Now that it hadn't, I was paradoxically disappointed. I got back in the car and resumed my way home.

It was then that my suspicions were given a second wind. A half mile farther on, I came across a second road to the right. Puzzled that Willy had reported no such thing, I pulled over and stopped again.

The answer became obvious as soon as I played my flashlight across the opening in the trees. There was no road, but merely a sizeable equipment yard for logging skidders and trucks, thinly screened from passing vehicles by a spindly row of saplings.

The catch was, as soon as I killed my flashlight, all that remained in the peripheral glow from my headlamps was the narrow dark gap and the presumption that it marked the opening of a side road. Willy, investigating during daylight hours, would have made no such mistake; for him, the yard had been as obvious as a parking lot.

In contrast to how I'd felt in the face of good news a few moments ago, I now felt a rush of excitement at this disturbing discovery. I quickly returned to where my car was parked and began scrutinizing the ground in front of it, concentrating—as per Vogel's testimony—just beyond the "road" to the right. Sure enough, even some five admittedly dry weeks later, the soil was dark and greasy with motor oil.

I continued searching, trying not to fall into the same trap that had apparently enmeshed Willy. Unlike him, I didn't want to stop at finding what I was after, but instead wanted to eliminate any possibility I might be wrong. Unfortunately, I was soon brought up short. Not surprisingly for an area opposite an equipment yard, I found several more oily patches, and with them the realization that all I'd done was to make the whole issue more muddled. Vogel might well have broken down just as he'd said, albeit confusing one site for another; but given the contaminated ground around me, there was no way I could prove it.

I stood in the cold night, reflecting on my growing ambivalence and the potentially dangerous game I was playing. If word got out that I was privately rattling the state's ironclad case—which I'd largely built myself—the restless army of Dunn observers would ignite like gasoline.

I snapped out of my trance suddenly and peered into the surrounding frozen gloom, my senses alarmed by something out of place. It had been a metallic sound, and perhaps a glimmer of light, both so subtle they could have been imagined. A car door perhaps? I shot a beam of light up and down the silent dirt road, but found nothing.

Fueled now more by instinct than by common sense, I got back into my car, turned it around, and headed back to Jamaica—to Vogel's former place of employment.

I parked in the dimly lit lot of New England Wood Products, pulled the file so labeled from the box Brandt had delivered to me, which I had stashed in my locked trunk, and headed for the supervisor's office.

Directed by a couple of employees along the way, I discovered the supervisor near the loading docks, talking to a group of workers. I waited for them to break up and then quietly introduced myself.

I showed him the list that we'd compiled of Vogel's co-workers, all of whom we'd interviewed previously, and explained that I was merely doing some last minute double-checking. "Did we miss anyone that Vogel might have worked with?"

He looked it over carefully, shaking his head, and then stopped, putting a finger on one name. "There's Fran Gallo. He may've been out sick when your boys came by. He's sick a lot."

It was said without rancor, or with a poker player's demeanor. I took the list back. "He here tonight?"

"Yeah. Area five." He pointed toward a large opening in one of the galvanized-steel walls nearby. "Look for a skinny guy, 'bout six feet, lots of pimples, pale face. Always wears a purple cap, even under his hard hat."

I passed into an enormous stacking yard, under the same roof as the rest of the building. It was lit by the same sodium lights, but with chain-link walls on two sides, open to the cold air—presumably a feature allowing both security and flexibility, if not worker comfort. I found Fran Gallo gingerly fitting the blades of a forklift under an enormous stack of lumber laid out on the cement floor. He may have been skinny underneath, but he'd been fattened in appearance by multiple layers of heavily patched quilted clothing. He cut his engine as he saw me approaching and gave me an incongruously affable, off-center grin. I guessed he couldn't have been much over eighteen years old.

"Help you?" he asked, his breath floating before him in a misty cloud.

I showed him my badge and muttered my name as inaudibly as possible, sensitive of the thin ice I was treading. "You know Bob Vogel?"

His eyes grew wide, as befit the publicity Vogel had been getting. "Oh, wow. Sure I do. I mean, who doesn't? Right?"

I looked at him closely, wondering if this was going to be worth the effort. "Do you know him personally? I gather you worked with him."

"Sure I did."

I waited for more, but Fran Gallo's initial exuberance seemed to have abruptly lost wind. He finally raised his eyes to look at me, smiling apologetically. "I didn't get along with him, that's all."

"Why not?"

"He landed on me pretty hard first time we met—called me a douche bag and told me to mind my own business. All I'd done was say hi and ask who he was—just being friendly. We didn't talk much after that."

"Did you ever work side by side?"

"I do with all of them, more or less, at least out here—'cause of this." He patted the steering wheel of the forklift.

"How was he different from the others?"

Gallo pursed his lips thoughtfully. "Is this going to get out?"

"Why?"

"I just don't want people to think I shot my mouth off."

I addressed instead what I thought was the root of his problem. "Bob Vogel is going to jail for a long time, Fran, regardless of how the rape trial turns out. He's never going to know we talked."

He nodded, obviously relieved. "Okay. I thought Bob was a real asshole. He treated everybody like shit, sat on his butt every chance he got, and I smelled liquor on his breath a lot of times. I did everything I could to stay out of the guy's way."

"He had no friends that you know of?"

"Nobody would put up with him."

"He ever talk about women? Or rape?"

"Not with me. I never saw him talk with anybody, except to insult them."

I glanced down at the folder, in which Ron had included a sheet summarizing the questions that had been asked the other workers here. I was beginning to feel this entire outing had been a waste of time.

"Did he seem any different on the night of the rape?"

"Nope," Gallo answered simply.

"Did you see what he was wearing that night—under his overalls?"

Gallo shook his head and opened his mouth to answer, but then paused. "I guess I did—I almost forgot. We were in the men's room at the same time. He came out of one of the stalls and got back into his winter gear near the sinks. We got to wear a lot of stuff to keep warm."

I looked again at Ron's notes. No one else had had this kind of opportunity. "What clothes was he wearing?"

Gallo thought back. "Jeans, work boots, one of those chamois shirts—"

"Anything under the shirt?"

"I don't know—a T-shirt, I guess . . . it was something white."

"What color was the chamois shirt?"

"Blue." He smiled suddenly. "Sort of. He was real dirty, too—smelled awful."

"What else?" I asked, as stimulated by the mention of the blue shirt as I'd been by the oil stain on the road.

"He put on a black insulated vest—one of those quilted things, like this." He unzipped his own overalls to show me a dark-green version of his own. "And then his overalls, cap, and work gloves. I think that's it."

"He wasn't wearing anything red?"

"Nope."

"How about at the end of the shift? Don't you guys generally leave some gear in a locker?"

Gallo nodded. "Most of us do, but not Vogel. He came and left in his work clothes. I heard him tell a guy once he'd sooner give us all blow jobs than leave his stuff where we could rip him off. That's just the way he was."

I returned to the warmth of my car's heater in a thoughtful mood. I'd known already that Vogel came and went to work in his insulated overalls—that much had been gleaned by earlier investigators. It had explained why no one had been found who'd seen what he'd been wearing underneath, until now.

Not that Fran Gallo's testimony did any more to change the case than the oil slick I'd found. No one in his right mind would stealthily enter a woman's house and sneak around wearing work boots and the equivalent of a ski-mobile suit. Vogel could have had the red shirt in the back seat of his car, along with a completely different set of clothes; or he might have even gone home and changed, before going on to Gail's.

But while none of what I'd found would be of any interest to James Dunn, it had made a believer out of me. I was not facing a jury, preparing to paint portraits in black and while only. I was much farther afield, circling like a trespasser seeking entrance to enlightenment. My goal was less to supply answers and more to address questions, and I'd already found more of them than an ironclad case should have.

But I was coming in late in the game, after all the whistles had been blown, and I knew that the news I'd be bearing would not be well received. It was the old story of the messenger better killed than heeded.

Chapter Nineteen

I sat in my darkened apartment, surrounded by the familiar, tangible milestones of my life—books, framed photographs, odds and ends of sentimental value—all barely visible in the gloom, all so anchored in my brain I didn't need to see them to feel their presence.

But despite them, I felt I was in a rowboat adrift offshore, watching impotently as a loved and comforting landscape slipped slowly away to the horizon. It was an estrangement made all the more unsettling because it was intentional and self-motivated. I was willfully pulling away from the status quo I'd worked so hard to create, distancing myself from the people I worked with and the woman I loved, potentially for the sake of a convicted rapist who'd tried to kill me.

I had to wonder why. It wasn't to save a possibly innocent man—at least I didn't think it was. Gail was right about Vogel—he was a bastard, and probably deserved the worst he could get.

But maybe not for this particular crime.

That was the gist of it—regardless of what James Dunn might believe, and a jury decree, I had to know Vogel's guilt or innocence for myself. His history in the courts had already highlighted the system's vagaries, so in this most important investigation of my career, I had to have more than a merely legal conclusion. I had to have the truth.

It was the only way I knew of regaining the shore, my life, and Gail.

*   *   *

The phone by my chair rang in the predawn darkness. I'd fallen asleep, and my startled reaction sent an electric bolt of pain through my stomach. Gail's voice was sharp, on edge, wavering between anger and concern. "Joe, what are you doing here? I just got a call from Leo. You left the hospital without checking out."

"I know. I'm sorry. I meant to call as soon as I got home, but I got sidetracked, and then I just forgot. I nodded off."

"What's wrong?"

I remembered how we'd parted, and wished I had something more concrete to tell her, something that would cool the rage I'd felt then. But I didn't have that yet, and perhaps I never would. "I know you don't want to hear this, but I came back to answer some questions for myself—things I wasn't able to do after I was stabbed."

"The trial's already begun, Joe." Her voice was almost pleading.

"I know that, and I'm not saying it shouldn't be happening. I just never got a chance to finish my job, and I need to do that."

"You don't think he raped me?" She was trying to be more matter-of-fact, forcing her intellect to rule her emotions.

"The evidence says he did. I need to know it's right."

"And if it's not?"

"Then we go from there."

"Damn you," she shouted, "don't you know what that means?"

I started to answer, but then stopped. I only knew what it meant to me. "Tell me," I said instead.

"That whoever it was is still out there—that it's all been a waste of time."

I remembered her sensitivity to sudden noises, her constant checking of locked doors, her insomnia, her apprehension of the outdoors or of being left alone. It was true that much of it had been born from the turbulence surrounding the trauma, and would eventually subside. But what I'd somehow ignored was plain, old-fashioned fear—that what had happened might happen again, especially if we'd caught the wrong guy.

Still, I persisted. "Gail, if he is still out there, then that's what we need to know, right? You don't necessarily want Bob Vogel hung out to dry—you want the guy who raped you."

I could hear her breathing hard, almost panting, trying to harness her agitation. "And you're saying they're not one and the same."

"I'm saying I don't know. Right now, Bob Vogel fits the bill." I rubbed my forehead, wishing I had something else to offer. "I can't tell you more than that, Gail. I'm sorry. I would've liked to have settled all this without troubling you, but I've got to do it— for your sake, too. It won't work any other way."

I paused, waiting, finally wondering if she was still on the line, and then I heard her sobbing—something she'd almost never done in all the years I'd known her. I gripped the receiver tighter, riled by my inability to reach out and lend her comfort.

"I'm not in control of anything anymore," she said after a long pause. "My emotions are all over the place, I'm scared of everything, I can't focus on my work. I tried to turn this into a way to help other women, but I couldn't get over my own fears. I tried taking care of you, but you healed and I felt abandoned. I was hoping to use the trial as a way to get better, and now you tell me you're not sure he's the right man. Even in the news, I'm an 'alleged' victim, as if even that might be taken away. I worry sometimes that I'm just spinning away—that I'll just disappear."

"Can Susan help?" I asked softly.

Gail took a deep, shuddering breath. "She is. She's trying. I'm seeing a therapist again. I've got good support. It's what I should've done from the start. I just thought I could get a handle on it sooner."

"Knowing that must help a little. Would you like me to come over?"

"No—I'm all right. How 'bout you?" she asked, surprising me.

"I'm fine. A little sore. I'm not doing anything strenuous."

There was a moment of silence, during which we contemplated everything we hadn't addressed. "You're pretty sure he didn't do it, aren't you?" she finally asked.

"I honestly don't know. I chased down two ideas last night, and neither one of them proved anything. All I've got are a bunch of little bells ringing in my head, telling me not to let this one go."

She sighed again, and I added, "You're still at Susan's, right?"

"Yes."

"I'll have Tony send someone over today to install some deadbolts and window locks. Maybe they'll help you feel a little more secure."

"Mary Wallis gave me a gun—a nine millimeter."

I didn't like that, but I knew now wasn't the time to say so. "You know how to use it?"

She let out a small, humorless laugh. "Secrets of my hidden past. My dad taught me when I was little. We used to shoot at cans and lightbulbs at my aunt's farm in Connecticut. I got pretty good at it."

"Well, be careful. You want those locks?"

"Thank you . . . Joe?"

"What's up?"

"You're still digging into this because of what you said, right? It's not something else—something you're not telling me?"

How well she knew me. "I just want to make sure the job's been done right."

I sat in my car across from Bob Vogel's derelict trailer, staring in disbelief at what the passage of a few weeks had wrought. The door and several windows were missing; clothing, soiled sheets, magazines, plates, even a few pieces of broken furniture littered the frozen ground. A stained, broken-back sofa lay on the sagging wooden steps leading to the gaping front door, as if it had been shot trying to escape.

I crossed the yard gingerly, noticing the shredded remnants of the plastic yellow "police line" tape we routinely use to seal off a property—obviously to great effect. The vandals, as usual, had been inordinately capricious in their choices, breaking some items of limited value, stealing others that made no sense. Going through the trailer, I worked both from memory and from a copy of one of Ron's files that listed the place's entire contents, complete with "general scene" photographs. Tony Brandt's box was proving to be a gift from heaven.

Nevertheless, I couldn't find the one item I was after.

I stopped short of the doorway before leaving the trailer twenty minutes later, and peered surreptitiously across the yard to the neighboring trailer—the one housing the consumptive scarecrow who'd directed me to the Barrelhead when I'd first visited the neighborhood. A curtain moved slightly as soon as I stepped into the anemic sunlight.

I walked over and pounded on the rattly metal door.

"Who is it?" The voice was as I remembered it—raspy, wet, and ruined.

"You know damn well who it is. Open up."

The door swung back with a rusty complaint and Vogel's bedraggled, bearded, reed-thin neighbor glared out at me with bloodshot eyes, a cigarette dangling from the corner of his mouth. I showed him my badge.

He coughed, as if under attack by the fresh air. "What do you want?"

"Talk. Can I come in?"

He stepped aside and I entered a virtual wall of stench, thick enough to make my eyes water.

"What about?"

I glanced around quickly, and pointed to a mildewed dish rack by his sink. "That, for one thing."

He stared at it in astonishment. I pointed at a cracked oval mirror leaning against the wall near an armchair with three legs. "And that, too."

He swiveled his head like a spectator at a tennis match. "What about 'em?"

"They belong to Bob Vogel. You stole them." I showed him the photographs, placing my finger on each item.

He swallowed hard and glanced at the door, as if contemplating flight. Then he looked at me defiantly. "I didn't start it. I just got what the others left behind."

I didn't believe that for a moment. "I'm sure that's true. So I'll let you off the hook. But I want a favor. I want to see the alarm clock he had by his bed."

He hesitated, weighing whether or not I was setting him up. "Wait a minute."

He disappeared into the gloom to the rear of the trailer, and reemerged moments later with a cracked plastic Baby Ben clock— an old wind-up model dating back thirty years.

I turned it over, pulled the alarm tab up, and moved the hour hand until it touched the alarm sweep. Nothing happened—just as I'd suspected. "Was this broken when you got it?"

"Yeah—piece of shit. Should've known."

"That makes two of us."

I found J. P. Tyler squirreled away in his compact forensics lab. His eyebrows arched when he saw who'd opened the door. "Joe. How're you doing? I didn't know you were back."

"I'm not officially, so don't tell anyone." I handed him the broken clock. "Do me a favor. Find out why the alarm doesn't work in this thing."

He took it from me and smiled. "Sure. You ought to look into buying a new one, though. These aren't too accurate."

"It's not mine. It's part of a case, and it's red-hot priority."

The smile widened. "And you're not back officially."

"Right. Let me know as soon as you can. I'll be in the property room."

The property room was across the hall from Tyler's closet, and about three times larger. A high-security area, it was where we held evidence until it was needed for trial, and therefore was packed to the ceiling with tagged and labeled bags and containers. What I was after, however, was right in the middle of the floor, readily accessible for the case being heard across the street at this very moment. I sat down among the boxes and began sorting through the envelopes within them, being careful not to break any evidence seals.

I hadn't completely closed the door—the stench of stale, confiscated marijuana being reminiscent of old, dirty clothes—but I had dropped the bar that stopped people from inadvertently stepping inside the sacrosanct room. When I heard a movement behind me a quarter of an hour later, therefore, I expected to see J. P. Tyler. Instead, I looked up to find Brandt staring down at me. He didn't look pleased.

"What the fuck're you doing?"

I stood up awkwardly, favoring my wounded gut, and smiled lamely. "I have to put this to rest, Tony. I got too many questions rattling around up here." I touched my temple.

"I'm not so sure you've got anything up there. Hitchcock Hospital called this morning, madder than hell. They'd already contacted our insurance carrier, who in turn called the town manager, who's just finished reaming my butt. I call Harriet and find out you're not laid up at home, feeling sorry for yourself, you're in here, fucking around with state's evidence for the hottest ongoing trial we've had in a decade." His voice had grown in volume and pitch throughout this monologue, but was cut short by Tyler appearing by his elbow. "What the hell do you want, J.P.?" he asked.

Tyler held up the clock between us. "The alarm mechanism's been cut clean through—fresh marks, I'd say probably by a pair of wire cutters."

"It couldn't have just fallen off through wear and tear?"

"No way."

Brandt looked at both of us and took the clock from Tyler. "What are you talking about?"

"Bob Vogel said he missed his meeting with Helen Boisvert the morning after Gail was raped because his alarm didn't go off. It sounded pretty lame then, but lying on my back for three weeks got me wondering. The guy's a total shit—we know he's raped before, and he treats everyone he meets like scum—but he's hanging onto his probation like a drowning man. Look at the effort he takes not to be caught driving that beater of his. Also, since he signed up with New England Wood Products, he's never missed a day, never even been late. I wanted to find out if he'd lied about the alarm clock."

Tony Brandt tugged at his ear, probably wishing he were on vacation. "You're suggesting somebody cut the alarm to set him up?"

"Possibly. The other argument being that he cut it himself to give himself an alibi."

I let Tony fill in the blank on that one. "For missing a meeting with Boisvert? Seems a little elaborate for someone who can barely string two sentences together."

"Plus we didn't find a wire cutter anywhere, in his car or the trailer," J.P. added.

Tony mulled it over for a few moments. "Jesus," he finally muttered, "we're going to have to tell Dunn."

"And he's going to have to tell defense counsel," I added.

I looked down at what I'd been holding when Brandt found me—the photos Vogel had taken of Gail walking around town. They were not sealed but were instead in a brown envelope, tied with a string. I opened the envelope, catching Brandt's attention.

"What's that?"

"Another of the things that bugged me. In that box of files you brought up, I found out we never did find a camera, and that the Green Mountains Lab people who processed the film had no files or recollections linking the film to Vogel."

"And that got you thinking, too," Tony finished morosely.

I didn't answer. As I'd been speaking, I'd also been flipping through the eight pictures, not looking at Gail, as I had previously, but at the backgrounds to each scene. "Yeah, it did," I murmured. "It struck me that since we found them in his trailer, we automatically assumed they were his, especially since we had so much other stuff against him. So we looked at them for who they showed us, and for what fingerprints might be on them, which, conveniently enough, were all smeared. What we never concentrated on was when they were taken."

"Actually, I did," Tyler said, trying not to sound offended. I was finding fault, after all, with his part of the investigation, not something he was used to. "But all I could get was that it was summer. I couldn't find any calendars or clocks in the background store windows, or anything else that would give me a better fix."

I held out one of the pictures to him, of Gail waiting to cross the street at a traffic light opposite the Photo 101 camera store. Next to her was a blue Toyota Corona, its license plate easily readable. On its windshield, barely visible, was a small blob of color. "How about a parking ticket?"

J.P. took the picture from me. "Shit." He quickly copied the plate number and headed off to a computer terminal. All our tickets were issued using a computerized, handheld system, which meant the time, date, parking-meter number, and details about the vehicle would all be in our files.

Brandt let out a sigh. "So what else have you been churning over in that hyperactive brain of yours?"

I told him about the logging-equipment yard near Jamaica, the oil slicks, and of my conversation with Fran Gallo. He absorbed it all quietly, having already adjusted himself to the inevitable meeting with Dunn.

He nodded once I'd finished. "All right. I don't think the oil slicks or the red shirt'll cause much trouble, but this other stuff might." He checked his watch. "They're probably about ready for a lunch break over there. I'll talk to Dunn. You better come along."

Tyler returned and handed him a slip of paper with a date on it. "It's the only ticket that car's had in the last two years. No possibility of confusion. And the owner paid it off personally, here in the building, one hour later, so the picture could only have been taken during about a forty-five-minute time span."

Brandt looked at the slip of paper grimly. "Well, let's hope Vogel doesn't have an alibi."

Chapter Twenty

Robert Vogel did have an alibi for the time the pictures were taken of Gail. He was at a doctor's office, having his cigarette-corrupted lungs examined by special request of New England Wood Products's insurance carrier, who was interested in tacking a waiver onto Vogel's coverage.

We found this out at the end of a long, tense afternoon, spent in the offices of an extremely unhappy James Dunn, who, during the brief times he came out of his office to consult with us in an adjoining conference room, kept giving me looks that he obviously hoped would make me burst into flames.

We never saw Tom Kelly or Bob Vogel—all communications with them were handled either by phone or well out of our sight—but from Dunn's terse reports, both of them were having a pretty good day.

As was the press. On its own merits, this case had already built up enough steam to attract over two-dozen reporters—among them two competing-network correspondents from New York, complete with camera crews—all of whom had been roving about town in packs of various sizes. However, now that something had obviously gone awry—the judge having granted an unexpected continuance in the middle of the state's case, and Dunn sequestering himself in his aerie with all of us—everyone with a tape recorder, a note pad, or a camera was packed into the Municipal Center's third-floor hallway.

The impression of being under siege was further enhanced by

Dunn himself—driven to distraction by the cacophony of ringing phones—who finally ordered all public lines into the office disconnected, leaving only the unlisted ones, which nevertheless stayed busy enough. Outside, the muted rumble of the growing crowd burst into occasional flower whenever one of the staff battled his or her way through the door.

At last, the windows darkened by the coming of night, Dunn called Brandt, me, Todd Lefevre, and Billy Manierre into his office. He arranged himself behind a desk almost as large, polished, and bleak as his ego, and stared at us in theatrical silence.

"This continuance will extend twenty-four hours, at which point the judge will ask both sides if we need further relief. I intend to answer no. That means that you will have totally reviewed this case by then and found it to be as airtight as it should have been when I first received it. I can then present all this as a minor glitch, of no great consequence."

He leaned forward, placing his hands flat on the glistening desk top. "That is what's going to happen—correct, Lieutenant?"

"We'll see," I answered, which caused him to flush. The discovery of that severed alarm had been no minor glitch to me. It had been a crack in a structure perfect in outward appearance, neatly plastered over by a truly malevolent artist. Despite Dunn's wishful thinking, I was sure we'd find more flaws, now that we knew to look for them. Unfortunately, I had no way of proving that to him and thereby sparing him further humiliation.

Dunn glared at me, straightened, and then addressed us all. "Get out. Todd, coordinate with them."

"That arrogant bastard," Brandt muttered as soon as Todd had closed the door behind us.

"Maybe," Todd said, showing an unexpected loyalty. "But he's got a point. He doesn't need his own people pulling fast ones on him in mid-trial."

"If he doesn't like surprises, he ought to give us more than twenty-four hours," I countered. "Now we're going to have to review the evidence selectively. Luck'll have to substitute for thoroughness."

"What do you mean?" Billy asked, leading the way into the empty conference room opposite Dunn's office.

"It means that a few key elements could swing this case one way or the other." I began pacing up and down the length of the room as the others slowly grabbed seats and made themselves comfortable. "Given the down time I've had, I've been able to dissect this one more than most, and what I've found is that the most supposedly concrete evidence—the underwear, the blood on the knife, the knife nicks on the window lock, the red shirt, the Victoria's Secret catalogue, the leaf, and even Vogel's MO—might well be the most circumstantial, the most easily manipulated by someone who wanted to lead us by the nose. After all, it's the kind of evidence we're trained to look for, and that juries can get their teeth into.

"But there are other details—more supportive ones, like the clock and those photos—which were a little harder to manipulate, since they called for more than just planting something in the right place. As a result—if I'm right—those can be traced to the real rapist. It's the window-dressing details that we need to track down."

Tony shook his head and spoke softly. "And all in a single day."

I turned to Todd. "What will Tom Kelly be doing during the continuance? Is twenty-four hours enough?"

He nodded. "No reason why not. He'll probably depose Fran Gallo, the doctor who just alibied his client, Vogel's next-door neighbor, the Green Mountains Lab people for good measure, and maybe even you, so that you can throw the oil-slick and red-shirt angles into question."

"Great," Tony murmured.

" 'Course," Todd continued, "he may not bother, figuring the judge or our newfound zeal will get him off the hook anyway. He's been so cagey up to now, it's hard to tell. But the momentum's going his way all of a sudden. I'd bet he's not going to trust to fate alone."

"What's the judge got to do with it at this point?"

Todd shrugged. "Tom Kelly clerked for the Honorable Gordon Waterston in Burlington way back when, and Waterston's notoriously hard on women in sexual-assault cases."

"Susan Raffner told me that last part," Tony admitted. "So—you're the one who knocked over the apple cart. What's the first step?" he added, looking at me.

"The pubic hairs found in Gail's bed," I answered.

There was a stunned silence.

"That's what I meant by focusing on a few key elements—things we overlooked before. The standard tests on hair don't give us much, especially when the samples don't have roots, and therefore can't be DNA'd. But there are nontraditional tests they can do, including one I thought of when we found out about Vogel's doctor visit.

"One thing you can detect in hair, if you're looking for it, is nicotine. We all have it to a certain extent, because of smoke in the air, but smokers themselves—heavy smokers—have a lot. Since neither Gail nor I smoke, heavy nicotine in the pubic-hair samples will help point to Bob Vogel."

"Unless there is none," Todd pointed out.

I raised my eyebrows. "Either way, it'll point us in some direction."

"All right," Brandt agreed, "I'll send J.P. up to Waterbury with the samples. How long should it take?" he asked me.

"The test shouldn't take more than a couple of hours. Getting it priority attention's something else."

Tony nodded firmly. "I'll handle that. What else?"

"We assumed that some of the minor discrepancies between this rape and the others Vogel committed were because of a learning curve. That was a mistake. What we should have noticed was that there were *too many* similarities between Vogel's third rape and Gail's. Seeing that might've started us thinking of a copycat crime instead of a learning curve.

"I think we need to get the people who investigated those cases on the phone—like Jim Catone from Greenfield—and grill them, point by point.

"We also need to retrace all the physical evidence, from the red fiber on the doorjamb to the Victoria's Secret catalogue, only not for how it lines up against Vogel, but for how it might've been used to frame him. For example, find out where Gail had the catalogue in the house. If it was on a coffee table, Vogel might've grabbed it on the way out. But if Gail had already thrown it out, then why would he have gone through her trash? Or the oil pan on Vogel's car—why did it puncture when it did? Tyler'll be out of town, but Kunkle's pretty good at forensics—have him check it out more closely."

I looked around the room, surprised and pleased at the lack of interruptions. None of them wasted time defending themselves, arguing that the case was sound and that what I was proposing was a waste of time. Not that they were converts—I knew that. But just as one set of evidence had put them on course to one conclusion, they all seemed to accept that another set might result in something different. It was an attitude I didn't expect to be shared by many outside this room, but it was here where it counted.

I took advantage of the silence to make one last proposal: "I also think we need to call in a criminal psychologist, give him or her everything we've got on Gail's case, and see how it matches what we know of Vogel's personality."

"Joe," Tony finally protested, "that's not going to do us any good in court. And if Dunn found out about it, he'd hit the ceiling."

I sat down on the table next to him. "I know, but I want to plan ahead for once. If someone is jerking us around, I want to see if we can get a peek at what makes him tick. It's only going to take a phone call—Megan Goss might be interested. Dunn did say he didn't want any more surprises—this could be a way to grant his wish. Indulge me, okay?"

Tony smiled. "Indulge you? You're not even supposed to be in the building."

"I won't be. I'm going to a bar."

Simply leaving the building proved more difficult than I'd thought. The mob outside the door tightened around us, bristling with questions, microphones, and a battery of camera lights. It was a stupefying assault, and a self-defeating one, the combined noise of all the questions being loud enough to override any response.

Near the top of the main stairwell, where the crowd threatened to stall completely, I muttered, "See ya," into Brandt's ear and cut away in the opposite direction, where resistance was weakest. There was a momentary hesitation on the part of several reporters on the fringe, who were tempted to go after me. I waved them off and walked briskly to the far end of the hallway, hearing one last "Lieutenant Gunther?" clutch at my heels as I made my way down the narrow back stairs.

Two young men followed me. I stopped at the bottom of the stairs, just outside the selectmen's meeting room, and turned to face them. They were from out of town, unfamiliar with the building.

"Lieutenant, why did the judge issue a continuance so abruptly?" one of them asked.

I held up my hand and smiled resignedly. "All right. But it's been a long afternoon. Let me use the men's room first, and then I'll give you what I can." I pretended to look around and then jerked my thumb at the meeting-room door, clearly marked. "They have a private one in here. I'll be right out."

I ducked through the double doors, turned left, and, as quietly as possible, opened the fire-escape door. Below me, the parking lot was empty of people. Keenly feeling the lack of a coat in my weakened and emaciated condition, I slipped outside and went down the broad metal staircase.

Moving in a fast shuffle around the less-frequented front of the building to the parking lot on the south side, I was shivering violently by the time I got to my car. Half bent over, my hand clutched to my stomach, I fumbled for the keys in my pocket, grateful that at least I hadn't locked the doors.

Grateful, that is, until I got inside.

"Hi, Joe. Slip out the back door?"

Stan Katz sat in the passenger seat, looking smug and terribly pleased with himself. Trust him not to run with the pack.

"Get the fuck out of my car, Stan," I said through chattering teeth.

He took the keys from my trembling hand and stuck the appropriate one into the ignition. "At least turn on the heater."

I didn't argue; but overcome by sudden nausea I had difficulty turning the key. The engine caught, and I tried to sit back, fighting the pain that was doubling me up.

Katz's expression and attitude changed abruptly. "Jesus, Joe, are you okay?"

He wrestled out of his overcoat and tucked it around me, its warmth having as immediate an effect as the cold preceding it. "Give the motor more rev," he ordered, sliding the heater control over to high. He watched me carefully. "Should I get some help?"

I shook my head. "I'll be all right. Just give me a few minutes."

"What the hell happened?"

"Nothing—you saw the mob. I guess it was the heat, then the cold, then the running. I'm not in too great shape yet."

He turned the fan on high. The first hints of warmth were

beginning to blow from the dash registers. "So, did you guys come up with something exculpatory on Vogel?"

I closed my eyes briefly, letting the growing warmth sink in. "Give it a rest, Stan."

His voice rose several notches in protest. "Give it a rest? Fuck you. Did I park someone in the hospital hallway after you came out of your coma? Did I have a photographer stake out the farm so we could have shots of you limping around with Gail? No—"

"Fine, I get the point. You're a saint." I returned his coat, feeling much restored now that the heater had fully kicked in. "Look, let's skip this crap. What do you want?"

"Last time we talked, I told you I wanted to turn the paper around—prove to the owners that a tabloid wouldn't cut it in this town, but that I needed some cooperation."

"I remember," I said neutrally.

"Well, I'm not going to let you people read articles about your own department before publication, like you asked, but I can let you and Gail have your privacy and cut down on the titillation."

I shifted my gaze from the darkened parking lot to his dimly lighted face, surprised at the passion in his voice. He had caught my interest.

I made a point not to show that. "So what?"

"So ask around. You've been out of touch the last month or so. The paper's been hosting forums. It's expanded the letter box to two full pages. We've invited guest columns about rape, and women's rights, and sexual whiplash, and half-a-dozen other topics. I know damn well Dunn's going wild up there right now, and that something's about to turn this town inside out. This is my town, the *Reformer*'s town, and I don't want to lose this story to all these fancy bastards from out of town."

"We can't give you an exclusive, Stan. That only happens in the movies. And I'm not going to give you anything right now."

He nodded. "The headlines are common property—I can live with that. I want the inside stuff—the feature material. That's what's going to make my owners realize this tabloid angle is bull-shit."

I smiled in the darkness, constantly impressed by the man's odd combination of energy and ego. Nevertheless, what he'd said had possibilities. "I'll talk to Tony about it."

He opened his door, letting in a wash of cold air. "That's all I ask. So where're you off to now?"

"Good-bye, Stanley."

He laughed and slammed the door, walking toward the other end of the lot. Slightly off to one side, I thought I saw a quick flash of light and the sound of a door slamming, just as I had on the Wardsboro Road. Then as now, I waited for the expected roar of an engine and the ignition of a car's headlights. But nothing happened.

I drove out of the lot, turned right onto Grove Street, and checked my rearview mirror for signs of anyone following. There were none. Of course, Vogel hadn't known Willy and I were following him either, so many nights ago.

The parking lot of the Barrelhead Bar was as still and vacant as the wasteland it resembled. At seven in the evening, it was still far too early for Ray Saint-Jacques's regular crowd. Nevertheless, as implied by the anemic neon beer ads in the window, it was open for business—like some time-frozen, Depression-era snapshot, taken by a long-dead artist with an eye for forlorn irony.

Ray Saint-Jacques had testified this morning as part of Dunn's opening salvo. Never one to start a trial with all the dull, picky, supporting evidence so precious to most prosecutors, James Dunn had an almost Shakespearean flair for presentation. He knew that his jury, like most audiences, would nod off if poorly entertained, and end up giving him bad reviews regardless of how many thrills he provided at the end. Ray's damning description of Bob Vogel's verbal self-incrimination was perfect relief from such doldrums— like the sound of distant drumbeats, it had perked the jury up and made it attentive to whatever might next appear on Dunn's theatrical landscape. From what Todd Lefevre had told me, Ray's had been a muted, low-key, and therefore stellar performance, since everyone in the room knew where it was intended to lead.

It had also been, from the moment Willy and I had first heard it, a crucial turning point in the case against Bob Vogel—the key that had unlocked the search warrant to his trailer, and fully revealed Vogel's guilt. As such, it was also evidence I ranked high among that deserving a second look, and was something I wanted to pursue alone, at my own pace, away from the impatience and expectations of my colleagues. For while I trusted the competence of everyone I worked with, I also knew I was the only one convinced that we'd all made a terrible blunder.

The enormous, nylon-skinned waitress was back on her corner chair; Ray was behind the bar, polishing glasses that probably hadn't seen use all day. The rest of the place was deserted.

I approached the bar unsteadily, a purposely bleary smile on my face. "Hi, Ray."

"What do you want?" His voice was flat, his eyes watchful, taking in my small performance and weighing it against a half-million legitimate ones he'd been privy to over the years.

I raised my eyebrows and parked myself heavily on a stool, getting my hand tangled up in the pocket of my jacket as I did so. "Colder'n a witch's tit out there. Give me a glass of something."

He kept polishing his glass, now gleaming in the television's reflected rainbow of changing colors. "Where's your coat?"

I stared at him a moment, as if wondering what he meant, and then I dropped my eyes to my jacket sleeve. "Shit. Must've forgotten it someplace."

I didn't pursue the point, or ham it up beyond that. I perched on my elbows and lost myself in the eyes of a beautiful woman on the TV screen high above the rows of bottles opposite me.

Ray let a full minute crawl by, waiting for more. I refused to play. "So what'll it be?" he finally asked.

I dreamily returned to him and the present. "I don't know. A beer, I guess."

Ray came back a minute later and put a chipped mug in front of me. "Five bucks."

Barely taking my eyes off the set, I put the money on the counter without protest. He hesitated before removing it, as if allowing me one last chance to drop the playacting.

He became more direct then, blocking my view of the television. "Why're you here?"

I blinked at him a couple of times, surprised by his aggressiveness. Either Ray was using me as a scapegoat for the humiliation he'd suffered from Willy earlier, or he was feeling hot under the collar for some other reason.

I passed my hand over my eyes and rubbed one of my temples as if massaging a headache. "For one thing, I wanted to thank you. Most of all, I guess I just wanted a change of scenery."

"Thank me for what?" The hostility in his voice was slightly tempered by curiosity.

"Testifying the way you did—not that it did much good—but I appreciate it anyway." I picked up the mug and buried my nose in it, wishing it smelled less like old socks.

He stood there for a moment, his interest beginning to gain the upper hand. "I just told them what I told you guys."

I paused to wipe my mouth with my sleeve. Not quite—what he'd said on the stand had been a lot more damning. That, in fact, was why I was here—to find out why he'd fine-tuned his story. "Yeah, well, whatever."

Absentmindedly, he took a couple of swipes at the stained bar top with his rag. "So what happened this afternoon, anyway?"

"Gail got raped twice, that's what . . . I'm not supposed to talk about it."

The rag froze in mid-wipe. "You mean that jerk's going to get off?"

I put the mug back down wearily. "Don't start, okay? I heard enough already. We did the best we could—you did, too. It's just . . . shit, I don't know."

The emotion in his voice was more intense than it should have been, considering that he'd told us earlier he hadn't even known Vogel's last name. "You're shitting me. What about knifing you? He's got to get serious time for that, ain't he?"

I shrugged, and fed his growing anger. "Maybe not. If he's innocent of the rape charge, he can claim we pushed him into a corner and forced him to protect himself. He's got a real good lawyer—he could be in here next month, drinking to your health."

The rag was wadded up in his fist. "Not fucking likely."

I raised my eyes to his. "Why not? This is his favorite watering hole. What do you care?"

He stepped away and threw the rag into the sink in disgust. "You guys. Don't know from shit. That bastard owes me a bundle. He never paid his tab, and he never settled his bets. There's no way that son-of-a-bitch is coming in here again." He walked toward the waitress, muttering, "Fucking deadbeat," and then pointed a nail-bitten finger at her. "Nora, you stupid bitch. There's nobody here. Get your ass out back and do something useful, for Christ's sake."

She slid off her chair as before and vanished without a murmur, Ray glaring at her and shaking his head.

I put the stale beer down, the need for pretense over.

Ray, as if sensing my eyes on the back of his head, slowly turned, his expression an oddly rueful mixture of self-revelation and shock. Seasoned snitch that he was, he knew that he'd just shot himself in the foot.

"You lied to us, Ray," I said in a clear voice.

He made a dismissive gesture and gave me a lopsided grin. "You should talk . . . Christ's sake—you know he did it."

"He never bitched about not having an alibi, did he?"

"He came in that morning in the dumps." His voice was slightly plaintive.

"And you laid it on thick because you had a beef against the guy. You saw a chance to stick it to him."

He scowled at me, taking the higher ground. "I don't believe this. You're her fucking boyfriend. Why're you busting your nuts for this creep? He fucks with everybody he meets, for crying out loud. All I did was help get the right thing done."

"All you did was jeopardize the whole case. We used your testimony to get a search warrant, Ray. If that warrant's ruled invalid now because you lied to us, then everything we got as a result of it is going to be thrown out."

He spread his arms wide and raised his eyebrows, his face incredulous. "Then don't tell anybody. Jesus—are all you guys this stupid?"

I sat in the car outside the bar, torn between elation and dread. My goal from the start had been to find Gail's attacker—for her sake and society's, and perhaps also—in more primeval terms—to prove my worth to her. Now, while my intent was the same, my methods were going to shock a lot more people than just Ray Saint-Jacques.

If what I'd just discovered—and was legally bound to pass through Dunn to Tom Kelly—did contribute to a mistrial, then all I'd really done was destroy our legal case. I hadn't actually proved

Vogel's innocence, much less someone else's guilt. Everything we'd found in Vogel's trailer still stood as damning evidence against him. But as I'd explained to the bartender, they could no longer be used.

There's a whimsical legal phrase covering such a situation; tainted pieces of evidence, secured under what amounts to an illegal search, are termed "fruits of the poisonous tree." Thinking of that now—the ironic duplicity of the image—I felt it applied to much more than just a legal sleight of hand. Its ramifications spilled over to color Gail's and my relationship.

Of course, Ray's story had been but one part of the affidavit used to get that warrant. If the rest held up, Dunn would still have enough to fight off Tom Kelly.

But I wasn't betting on it—and it wasn't going to be long before we all found out.

Chapter Twenty-One

It was close to midnight. The entire detective squad—plus Tony Brandt, Billy Manierre, and Todd Lefevre—was crammed into the conference room. There was none of the usual chatter; everyone's face was a study of apprehension, disappointment, or flat-out disgust. Looking around the table, I could see the emotional toll my news had cost them. Dedicated, underpaid, and generally viewed with skepticism or scorn, police officers tended to be a force unto themselves, self-effacing in public, seeking one another's company when off duty, but finding strength in the conviction that, while they occupied the fringes of "polite society," the very nature of their job helped give them a moral advantage.

They weren't used to having that image tarnished, especially by one of their own.

I had been talking for a half hour, explaining step by step the realities that now faced us, trying to prepare them for what the morning would bring, but I couldn't deny the humiliation they'd soon be suffering at the hands of a probing media and a judgmental public.

It turned out Ray's faulty testimony had not been the only boulder to fall from the pile we'd stacked on top of Bob Vogel. Tyler had returned from the state-police crime lab in Waterbury a few hours earlier with proof that the pubic-hair samples he'd gathered from Gail's bed had no appreciable levels of nicotine, and thus couldn't have belonged to Vogel. Furthermore, he'd reinspected the garbage I'd stolen from Vogel's front curb, as requested, and found that a front-page fragment of an old newspaper, soiled almost beyond legibility, had someone else's address label on it, opening up the possibility that Vogel had collected some of his mail the way we had—from the trash. Scrupulous to a fault now, Tyler had called Gail and asked her where she'd last seen her catalogue. She hadn't been able to swear that she hadn't thrown it out.

All this, combined with the questions I'd already raised about the red shirt and the oil slick, did more than bolster Bob Vogel's prospects—they all but guaranteed that the search warrant that had led to his arrest would be thrown out. The probable cause that had earned us Judge Harrowsmith's signature on that warrant no longer existed.

But now that my official status had been reinstated a few hours earlier to "fully active" by our insurance carrier, I wanted it made clear to everyone in this room that we were finally on the right track, and that the case against Vogel had collapsed for good reason. I used J. P. Tyler's rigorously objective personality to finish that job for me.

He walked to the blackboard at the head of the room, picked up some chalk, and wrote, "Physical Evidence." He then added, on separate lines: "Leaf; Pubic Hair; Red Fiber; Blood Traces; Tool Marks; Catalog; Underwear; Photos; Red Shirt; Oil Pan."

He then turned and addressed us in his bland, almost professorial voice. "These constituted the bulk of the case against Vogel. As the lieutenant's been telling you, some of them don't hold water anymore."

He went back to the board and crossed out "Photos" and "Pubic Hair." "The hair samples and photos you already know about. Of course, *somebody* took those pictures—it just didn't happen to be Vogel. That doesn't mean it wasn't someone working with him."

Ron Klesczewski, tense and defensive, feeling himself targeted for letting things get so fouled up, interrupted, his eyes locked to the tabletop. "Is it a given that rapists always leave hair samples behind?"

"No," J.P. answered after a pause, "it's just generally true." And then he added in a stricly neutral tone, "But to be totally objective, if Vogel did rape her, leaving nothing behind, then the samples we found came from a third party—not Vogel, and not Joe."

Willy let out a short laugh. Sammie, loyal and outraged, glared at him. "You're such an asshole."

"Up yours."

I rose quickly to my feet, alarmed at the sudden spike in tension. "We've got to consider everything," I said loudly and clearly, although I wasn't sure my face was any less red than Sammie's.

Unperturbed, J.P. returned to the blackboard, circled "Oil Pan," and put a question mark next to it. "We have some additional problems the rest of you may not realize yet. The famous oil slick— and where it came from—has been thrown into doubt by now, but the oil *pan* from Vogel's car is another story. According to him, the pan sprung a leak, which he then plugged with a screw. That's exactly what we found. What sidetracked us was trying to figure out how he happened to have the right-sized screw and four quarts of oil in the middle of nowhere.

"Willy took a closer look at the pan this afternoon, and what he discovered—again thanks to one of Joe's suggestions—was a trace of wax around the hole. I've looked at it under the microscope. It's a type of malleable molding wax that melts when heated. Its presence suggests that someone, having created the puncture, then sealed it with wax, knowing that once the engine heated up a few miles down the road, the wax would melt and the oil would leak out."

"That doesn't tell us why Vogel had all the right gear in his car to fix it," Dennis DeFlorio said, receiving an encouraging nod from Ron.

I looked at them all as Tyler continued speaking, pondering their personalities. Despite a few feeble protests, no one could argue with the facts J.P. was detailing, and the impact they would have once they became public knowledge. Sammie, Willy, and J.P., I felt sure, would merely soldier on from here. Ron and Dennis would need temporary protection from the coming limelight—a little time to adjust.

For the next half hour, J.P. addressed each listed item in turn. The bottom line, however, remained as uninspiring as ever—the case was a shambles, and Dunn would soon have to fold his tent. And, never addressed but still lurking in most of our minds, was the bitter possibility that Vogel did rape Gail but had somehow been clever enough to use the system to cut himself loose.

By the time J.P. finally sat back down, I had before me as demoralized a group of people as I could ever remember trying to rally.

I dealt with DeFlorio and Klesczewski first. "Dennis, tomorrow morning I'd like you to hit all the hobby shops and art-supply houses within a fifty-mile radius. We're looking for recent purchases of molding wax. But do it in person, not by phone—it makes it harder for them to brush you off. Also, find out what catalogue outfits handle the stuff and if any recent orders have been made from this area—if so, to whom. That may take some legal paperwork, so coordinate with the SA's office on how to go about it.

"Ron, I want you to continue running the command center. We're going to have to go back to square one on the potential suspects, and you know them better than any of us. One by one, they'll have to be reinterviewed and their alibis rechecked. We may even have to sweat a few of them to see how they react. Make sure we don't step on each other's toes, and flag any discrepancies between new and old stories. It's going to be tougher than before. You won't have as many people helping you, and the press'll probably make you feel you can't even stick your nose out the door."

He nodded without enthusiasm. I turned to Billy. "That's where I'd like you to pitch in as much as you can. More than anything, I need patrol officers in plain clothes to conduct field interviews— people good at getting people to open up."

"You got it."

"One extra note," I told them all. "Earlier, J.P. mentioned those pictures of Gail. Regardless of who took them, he had to have done so at a specific date and time, and from a specific place. Find out if your suspects have alibis for that time period. And J.P.? Maybe you can canvass the area around where they were taken and see if anyone remembers somebody with a camera."

I turned to Tony. "How much interference do you think we're going to be facing?"

Brandt shook his head slowly. "This is the biggest mess we've ever had, and everybody'll have an opinion on how to sort it out. I'll do my best, but to be honest, it's going to be hard to control."

I took J.P.'s spot in front of the blackboard. "That means you're going to have reporters dogging your tracks, maybe getting in your way. They'll want to talk to you, talk to the people you're interviewing. And they won't be alone. Other people are going to make it their business to find out what we're up to. In most cases, they'll be within their rights, just as you'll be within yours by refusing to answer them. Keep that last point in mind. If somebody gets your back up, walk away and report the incident to the chief."

I left my invisible podium and stepped up to the table, leaning on it for emphasis. "On a personal note, I want to thank you for all you've done. We did our jobs as we should have, and it's a credit to the system that, even this late, we can catch a problem and correct it. We still have to find a rapist, and I'm confident we'll do just that. Right now, though, I want you all to go home and get some sleep. We'll reconvene at seven o'clock tomorrow morning to receive specific assignments."

I straightened up and added, "One word of advice: In a town this small, people are bound to find out your phone numbers before long. If you've got 'em, use your answering machines to screen calls. Or unplug your phones and keep your portable radios on so we can reach you. And if the stress starts to get to you, talk to me or Billy or someone you trust. Don't let this get to you."

"Come to my office," Tony said as we left the room, and led the way.

I followed, curiously buoyant. Despite the somber mood of the meeting, I couldn't shake off a certain elation—the sense of having successfully hurdled some half-seen barrier. Bob Vogel was no longer our primary suspect and the real rapist would soon be feeling the heat. I felt back in control, and that my instincts had served me well.

A small, slight, peaceful-looking woman with a benevolent expression and long gray hair tucked back in a neat ponytail was waiting patiently for us in Brandt's office. Megan Goss was a criminal psychologist who'd spent years working with killers, sadists, rapists, and victims of abuse, sorting through the debris of their minds in an effort to understand them, or repair the damage they had suffered. I had known her for years, and the department had used her talents several times in the past. She always brought a thoughtful, measured tone to bear, often shedding light where confusion, politics, or tension had made for impenetrable shadow.

She rose and greeted me warmly. "I hear you have a problem."

The three of us sat in a tight circle of chairs, like conspirators sorting through details. This was the one aspect of our revitalized investigation that I most wanted kept under wraps. Given the bumbling image of us that was about to appear in the headlines, I didn't want Goss's services misconstrued—or even identified. But if my hunch was right, her special knowledge of the criminal mind was going to be of enormous assistance.

"Have you been following the case?" I asked her.

She nodded. "Yes. And I've been working with Susan Raffner in dealing with some of the emotional fallout. An assault of this nature never has just one victim."

"We're now thinking Bob Vogel was framed by someone who copied his MO."

She raised her eyebrows, but otherwise remained silent.

"Would you be willing to review this case from the ground up— to visit the crime scene, study Vogel's style, interview Gail, look at everything we've got—to see what we might have missed?"

Goss sat back in her chair, tapping her lips with the index finger of her right hand. "Yes. But I want to concentrate first on the actual crime. I don't want to see any evidence or any suspect profiles—not yet. If that is how you were led astray, it might be helpful for me to avoid it."

I couldn't repress a grin. "Great. When can you start?"

"The crime took place in the middle of the night, correct?"

"Right."

"Then perhaps we should begin immediately. Can you take me to the scene now?"

The odors that had once given Gail's house life—the smell of fresh food, live plants, clean laundry, and myriad others that arose from her daily routine—had been replaced by a deadened staleness. It reminded me of visits to the homes of the very old, whose tenuous grasp on life saturated the walls around them.

Without a word, I led the way up the familiar set of stairs to the lofty bedroom high overhead, noticing as I went the dead plants, their leaves gray with a fine coat of dust.

I reached for the light switch.

"No. Wait," Megan said quietly, placing her small hand on mine. She stood in the doorway, looking into the darkness ahead of her. "Can we turn off the downstairs lights from here?"

"Sure." I reached back onto the landing and plunged the entire house into obscurity.

"Thank you." We stood there for a minute or two, motionless, before she added, "Does she always leave the drapes open?"

Thinking back, I stared at the disheveled bed, dimly glowing in the indirect moonlight, remembering how we'd enjoyed chatting side by side, gazing up at the night sky. "Damn," I muttered, "the moon was directly overhead that night."

Megan kept her voice very still, as quiet as ours had been on those evenings. "A full moon?"

I furrowed my brow, berating myself for having missed the obvious. "No, not quite, but it was much brighter in here."

I saw her nod thoughtfully in the near gloom. "That's quite the clock."

Surprised, I looked across the bed to where the radio alarm's large glowing numbers were still counting off the minutes on the night table, to the right of the headboard. The clock was the most prominent feature of the room in the half light, apart from the large, pale expanse of the bed. I was beginning to see things the way Megan was—the way Gail's attacker had. It made me grateful we hadn't waited twenty-four hours to do this, when the weather report was calling for a freak, premature snowstorm, straight out of the Canadian north.

"When you two were together, did Gail sleep on the right or the left side?"

"The right. The side nearest the clock."

Megan stepped farther into the room, her eyes fully adjusted to the gloom. She stopped at the foot of the bed. A small shiver went down my spine while I imagined the attack just a few weeks earlier, coming as Gail slept peacefully.

Megan moved silently to the night table on the far side of the bed. She picked up the radio alarm clock and balanced it in her hand. She then replaced it and took one last long look around the room. "All right. You may turn on the lights now."

What leapt up around us was a blinding, chaotic contrast to the sinister, half-seen mystery of seconds earlier. Now it was the crime scene I knew all too well, where one life had ended, and from where a new one would have to be rebuilt.

And yet Megan Goss altered it, even now. She didn't proceed

with Tyler's scientific detachment, with cameras and tweezers and small white evidence envelopes. Instead, she hovered, paused in thought, only rarely touched something, and that usually with just the tip of one finger, as if checking for signs of latent energy.

As she proceeded, she had me read aloud from Gail's statement, made on the morning following the rape. When Gail told of being assaulted, Megan moved to the foot of the bed, staring at it throughout that part of the transcript; when I read of the rapist's rampages around the room, Megan mimicked his movements, pausing before the shards of the broken plate that used to hang on the wall, and running her fingertip across the dusty surface of the expensive, uninjured television set.

Two hours later, we were both back at the door, as I read of Gail listening to her attacker putting his clothes back on, before leaving the house.

I finally stopped, and waited. Megan stood silently, peering into the room, lost in thought. At last, she turned to me. "She didn't smell him?"

I stared at her in astonished embarrassment, remembering Vogel's rank breath in my face, just before he stabbed me. "I . . . it didn't come up."

"Odd, don't you think?" Her smile was kind, conspiratorial, as if together we'd opened the last lock of an intricately closed box.

Chapter Twenty-Two

Susan Raffner's voice was fogged by sleep. "Hello?"

"It's Joe Gunther. I'm sorry to be calling in the middle of the night, but I need to talk to Gail—and to you, too."

"Now?"

"Yes. Is she there?"

Gail's voice, clear and wide awake, came on over an extension. "I'm here."

"Can I come over?"

"Yes."

The porch light was on at Susan's house, and the front door swung back as I reached the top of the porch steps. Susan, her hair tangled, her dressing gown awry, her eyes still at half-mast, stepped back to let me in. "In the kitchen" was all she said.

I knew where to go, down the dark hallway next to the staircase and through a swinging door at the rear. I'd been in the house before—aside from my recent visits—for the occasional politically correct cocktail party, where people like Tony and me usually killed time together, nursing fruit juice from paper cups, our backs to the wall.

The kitchen suited the house—painted wood trim, mottled linoleum, steel-tube furniture from thirty years earlier. It made me feel instantly more at ease. Gail was standing at the stove, her back to the door, fiddling with a tea kettle.

"Hi."

She turned and smiled but stayed put, indicating the reserve remaining from our last encounter.

"How've you been?"

"Better," she answered. "Thanks."

Susan came up behind me and cut straight to the point. "I was fine, too, until 2:45 A.M. What do you want? And what the hell happened in court yesterday? Or is that privileged?"

Even Gail gave her a weary look. "Sit, Susan. Give him a chance."

I smiled at the strength in her voice—the underlying sense of humor. She was improving. I could see it for myself.

I pulled out a chair at the small breakfast table and sat down. "Between these walls, nothing is privileged. What happened yesterday is that the shit hit the fan. Tomorrow, unless Tom Kelly has lost his mind, he's going to move for a mistrial—and get it."

Susan slammed the table with her fist. "You stupid bastards—"

"We have the wrong guy."

They both looked at me in stunned silence. "Gail, what did you smell when you were attacked?"

She froze, and then managed a murmured, "What?"

I let her digest the question. Susan just stared at me.

Gail wrinkled her forehead in thought. She finally admitted, "Nothing."

"Bob Vogel smells like sewer. He smokes, he drinks, his teeth are half green, and he only showers when he's caught in the rain. On the night of the rape, before he left work, one of his co-workers noticed his BO from several feet away. With all his clothes off, he would've stunk like raw garbage."

Susan was at emotional raw ends, muttering angrily to herself, perhaps so wrapped up in the political ramifications of my news that my words were hard to focus on. "She had other things on her mind than body odor," she protested. "She was afraid for her life."

"I remember everything else," Gail tentatively disagreed. "It's not that I didn't smell anything at all—I just don't think there was anything unusual."

I saw the intelligence in her eyes, and knew I'd caught her attention.

"In one of our conversations, you told me the first indication you had that something was wrong was when you felt a weight on your chest—you were having difficulty breathing. You opened your mouth to speak, thinking I'd come back, and that's when he grabbed your face and pushed it to one side. You said it was all a blur."

"Right."

"Which means your eyes were open."

She shook her head, as if arguing with herself. "They must've been—but I didn't see anything. It was too dark."

"I've brought Megan Goss in on this to advise us—that's strictly confidential, by the way. We just came from your place. We were standing in the doorway to your bedroom with the lights off, and I remembered there was a bright moon that night."

"So there was light?" she asked doubtfully, the anger that might have flared a few days ago absent. She pressed her hand against her cheek and looked at the floor between us, thinking hard. "I just don't remember, Joe. I thought it was pitch black."

"That's okay," I said supportively. "That may be good news. Would you be willing to be hypnotized by Megan? To see if you can fill in the gaps? I read her your transcript and she thought hypnosis might help you fill in some of the missing details."

"Joe, for Christ's sake," Susan blew up. "How many times are you going to jerk her around?"

"Susan," Gail answered strongly. "Stop. I'm willing to do it— for my own reasons. He's right—I can use this."

The kettle began to whistle on the stove. Susan rose to tend to it, although Gail was right there and starting to move. "Leave it. I need something to do."

Susan twisted the gas knob, paused as if considering what to do next, and then faced me angrily. "Why the hell wasn't all this done before? Bringing Megan in and asking Gail about the smell? I mean, that sounds pretty basic to me. And what about all the evidence against Vogel? Did you people just make that up?" Her voice rose with emotion. "You come waltzing in here in the middle of the night, full of bright new ideas, casually announcing that you jailed the wrong guy. Do you have any idea what harm you've caused?"

"It's crossed my mind."

She was in no mood for irony. She glared at me, speechless for a moment. "It crossed your mind? Fuck you, Joe Gunther. You see this as some goddamn game—catch the bad guy, put him in jail. Make a little mistake? No big deal. Go after somebody else.

What about all the women who worked so hard to guarantee that, for once, justice would be served. They believed you when you said Vogel was the guy—they let out a collective sigh of relief. And then, in workshops and encounter groups all over this town, they fought their fears that some deal might be cut to set him free, or that Dunn would procrastinate until after the election and piss the case away, or that Judge Waterston would give another rapist a pat on the ass for a job well done. They prayed that for once things would be done right. And now you have the balls to say, 'Oh, sorry—back to square one.' Christ, Joe, it was Gail who was raped—couldn't you have done a slightly better job for her sake?"

My face burning, I rose stiffly to my feet, the anger so caught in my throat I had to focus on my breathing. Bob Vogel had been no mere threat to me—the son-of-a-bitch had tried to kill me. But I was still willing to stick my neck out, risking the enmity of my colleagues, the public, and the best friend I had, because it was the right thing to do.

I knew Susan's outburst stemmed from exhaustion and despair. Those efforts to heighten a society's conscience and change its attitudes had been her own, expended at great emotional cost. But while I understood rationally that no words from me were going to change that, it still took all my self-restraint not to burn the bridges between us and reciprocate with some of her own verbal abuse.

Instead, only barely aware of my own movements, I headed for the door in a stifled blind rage. Gail followed me down the hallway to the main entrance.

I opened the front door and let the cold night air wash across my face. Gail stood beside me quietly, shivering slightly, waiting for me to regain my composure. I was grateful to her for not making excuses for her friend—for trusting me to understand that, despite its appearance, Susan's outburst hadn't been a personal attack.

I finally took a deep breath and asked in a near-normal voice, "How do you feel about this? Are you angry, too?"

"I would've been a few days ago, but Bob Vogel doesn't matter as much anymore. I matter, and you matter, and putting this behind us matters, and that's what I want to work toward. I'm trying to get away from the blame and the fear . . . and the anger."

I gave her the bear hug I'd been saving from the beginning of all this, her words a confirmation that we were both on the mend.

*   *   *

Megan Goss's office was located at the rear of one of a long row of nineteenth-century red-brick buildings that stand along the east side of Brattleboro's Main Street like bluff, Dickensian representatives of a bygone industrial era. In most cases, however, it is more facade than reality, the implications of high-ceilinged, wood-paneled, airy rooms, giving way to a jumble of businesses, offices, and apartments. Some of these had been remodeled into modern, boxlike conformity, and others left dark, poorly ventilated, and reeking of despair. It cannot be said of Brattleboro that its urban poor were forced out of downtown—they are as much a part of the geography as the high-profile stores facing the sidewalks.

The back of this bank of eccentric buildings faces the railroad—parallel to but some thirty feet lower than Main Street—and the broad Connecticut River below that. To walk through the maze of hallways, stairwells, and assorted offices of one of these narrow, deep, brick monstrosities, and reach a window that faces this view, is to make a startling and wonderful discovery—a sylvan scene of impressive beauty lost on the rest of downtown. Apart from the lightly used railroad, the view is of trees, river, islets, and an antique metal bridge, all massively overseen by wooded Mount Wantastiquet, looming high over the neighboring New Hampshire river bank.

In addition to its hidden aesthetic advantages, this rear area provided a sense of isolation from the bustle far to the front. Megan Goss wasn't the only therapist located along this row, and, entering her office with Gail, I understood why. The built-in tranquility was as soothing as the smell of fresh bread in a country kitchen.

Megan Goss greeted us and placed Gail in a soft leather armchair near the window, opposite a comfortable but less regal office chair she took for herself. I sat at her immaculately clean desk, off to one side, and turned on the tape recorder I'd brought with me.

"How are you feeling, Gail?" she asked.

"Fine—a little tired."

"Still not sleeping at night?"

Gail looked sharply at me, but Megan intervened. "It was a guess. I haven't asked Joe anything about you, nor has he volunteered anything beyond the police records concerning your case."

Gail smiled and relaxed. "I don't know why I reacted that way. It's hardly a secret."

Goss waved it away with her hand. "Perfectly understandable. Among other things, your privacy has been violated. You're inclined to hold onto everything more dearly than before." She paused a beat before resuming, "In fact, that could be relevant to what we're about to attempt today. Are you comfortable with the idea of being hypnotized?"

Gail nodded emphatically. "I want all this out in the open."

"All right." From beside her chair, Megan Goss retrieved a thick folder, which she opened on her lap. "What we're going to try is called cooperative hypnosis. It has nothing to do with darkened rooms, or swinging watch fobs, or deep states of unconsciousness. It's more like what happens to you sometimes when you're on a long car trip and your mind wanders. After a while, you realize you're not sure where you are anymore. You haven't been driving dangerously, or been out of control, but you have been in a light hypnotic state. It's what most people call daydreaming, and it's the same thing that gives truth to the phrase, 'time flies.'

"There is a reason we all do this, besides just dealing with the boredom of a long drive. We do it to clean house a little—to occasionally dig a little deeper into our subconscious state and let in some light. That's why these little mental side trips sometimes result in great sadness, or profound self-revelation. In any case, it's a process where a little gentle probing can be used to pursue a specific goal.

"It will take your cooperation, however. Nothing I do can put you into this kind of hypnosis. Listening to my words will help, but only as the hum of the highway and the blurring countryside flying monotonously by helped you when you were traveling on your own."

I blinked my eyes twice and rubbed the back of my neck, realizing that while she was laying out her procedure, Megan Goss had already begun. Her voice had slid into a soft, supportive, sedative tone, and I could see by watching Gail settling more deeply into her chair that it was already having its effect.

For that alone, I was grateful. It was now eleven o'clock in the morning. Two hours earlier, all that we'd anticipated had occurred. James Dunn, stiff with rage, had met with Tom Kelly before Judge Waterston's bench and within seventy-five minutes had been handed a mistrial—the search warrant used to invade Bob Vogel's trailer was invalidated, and all the evidence secured thereby ruled inadmissible. The sole consolation was that Waterston's decision meant no immediate change of address for Vogel. The scars across my stomach were a guarantee of that.

As consolations go, however, it wasn't much, and it did nothing to stem the explosion of anger and outrage we'd all known was going to erupt. Nor had the SA's office and the police department done anything to help cool things off. Falling back on an understandable circle-the-wagons instinct, both offices had barred their doors to all outsiders, and released a joint media communiqué—fatalistically prepared beforehand—stating that a press conference would be held shortly. Whatever deal Brandt might have forged with Stanley Katz was guaranteed to be tested to the limit immediately.

Generally, the communiqué had a predictable effect. Shortly before Gail and I entered Megan Goss's peaceful retreat, the entire Municipal Building had been surrounded by protesters, onlookers, and a small army of newspeople, forcing Brandt and Dunn together to call on the state police and the county sheriff to help secure the place from being completely overrun. Fortunately, I'd already briefed my squad—and the additional personnel lent to me by Billy Manierre—and had put them on the streets, reinterviewing witnesses and potential suspects.

Also, although I hadn't anticipated the extent of the public's fury, I had assumed what its focal point would be, and had placed Gail and myself at a friend's apartment far from the Municipal Building, near Megan's office. When she'd called us to say she was ready to begin, it was a simple matter to walk a couple of blocks without being noticed.

Goss spent the first hour merely laying the groundwork, expanding on her "daydreaming" scenario, getting Gail more and more relaxed until her responses were almost sleeplike murmurs. I, too, became immersed in the exchange, losing track of time, finding myself slipping away from my body's sense of shape and place. But when a train passed underneath the window in a noisy, metallic clatter, I resurfaced with a start. Not so Gail, who remained utterly motionless, her only signs of life being the slight movement of her breathing and the shaping of her lips around an occasional short sentence. Her eyes, not entirely closed, appeared lifeless and dull, the work of an apprentice puppet-maker.

Megan asked her if she was aware of the train's passing. Gail said yes, but only as if from a vast distance. Apparently satisfied, Megan came to the point of the exercise.

"Do you feel like talking about the night of the attack?"

"Yes," Gail answered without hesitation, but without emotion, as if she herself were on that train—a long, long way off.

Megan began by describing the evening—the two of us together, my leaving, Gail's surrendering to sleep. Gail responded in a monotone, without anticipation.

Megan asked her, "Something wakes you up. What is it?"

"A movement—someone moving on the bed. The pillow's gone."

"What do you feel?"

The voice stayed flat. "Surprise. Joe's come back. I feel the covers pull back."

I leaned forward instinctively. We knew she'd thought it was me at first, but these extra details explained why she hadn't woken up more quickly. We'd missed the implication that her sense of security hadn't been disturbed.

"There's a weight on my chest. I feel his skin against mine; his hands on my breasts, pushing them together over his penis."

"Is this something Joe's ever done?"

Gail gave a hint of a shake, and her mouth turned down. "No. It's hard to breathe."

"You're waking up now?"

"Yes. Something's wrong." But the voice doesn't mirror it. The realization that must have blasted her from sleep is passive now, almost bored.

"What do you do?"

"I try to move, but my arms are caught. I can't move them. My wrists hurt. I open my mouth—to breathe—to say something."

"You open your eyes, also?"

"Yes."

"Do you see anything?"

"Yes."

"I want you to keep that picture in your mind, Gail. Fix it in your memory. Take your time."

There was a long pause. "All right."

"Can you describe it to me?"

The words came gradually, but surely. Gail squinted as she spoke, as if the image she was groping for were veiled in mist, and only slowly taking shape. "He's naked . . . not fat, but not skinny either. He's white. His stomach's flat . . . no chest hair."

"Can you see his face?"

"It's too dark."

Megan kept her voice neutral—matter-of-fact. "There's moonlight, Gail, coming through the window above you, lighting his hair, his face."

"I see the moonlight, but the face is dark . . ." Gail frowned in concentration, obviously puzzled. Megan gave her time to think. Suddenly, Gail relaxed, relieved. "It's a mask. He's wearing a mask over his head."

But her satisfaction was my disappointment. Megan didn't react. "Go on."

"His hands leave my breasts as soon as he sees me watching him. He covers my face and pushes it away, so I can't see. He's fumbling with the pillowcase. I can see the clock, remembering the time, to tell Joe later."

I gestured with both my hands to Megan and raised my eyebrows questioningly.

"Which hand did he use to cover your face, Gail?" she asked.

"His right."

I grunted involuntarily at that, caught by surprise.

"And what time is it?" Megan continued.

"Two-thirteen. I'm thinking about that so hard, I can still see the numbers after the pillowcase goes over my head. I'm fighting now to free my hands, feeling the pain in my wrists. I'm kicking up with my knees, but he slips down onto my thighs, stopping me."

"Has he said anything yet?"

"Not yet. Now he does. He laughs a little first, and whispers, 'Simmer down. I'm going to get off your legs now; if you move a muscle, I'll cut your tits off.' Then he pricks me with a knife, and says, 'With this.'"

I held up my hands again to prompt the next question.

"Can you tell which hand he's using when he cuts you?"

Gail knit her brows, and Megan quickly added, "Which breast does he cut first, and on which side?"

I smiled and nodded. Megan Goss knew exactly what I was after. "My left breast, from the outside, then the other, from below." Most likely the right hand again, I thought.

Megan, now fully attuned to the kinds of questions I was after, asked, "Having slid down onto your thighs, how is he positioned now?"

"He's almost lying on me, propped on his left elbow, using the knife."

"His face is close to yours?"

"Yes."

"Can you smell his breath . . . smell him?"

"Yes, but it's not bad . . . It's not anything."

"Okay. Then what?"

Movement by movement, sensation by sensation, Megan Goss had Gail take her on a tour of the rape, the monotone of their voices acting in bizarre contrast to the horror of the description. It took over two hours to complete, and gave me the best sense I'd had to date of what Gail had endured. But it didn't give me anything new.

At the end of the session, Megan told Gail to review everything that had been said, and to retain it, and then asked her if she was ready to reawaken, giving her the option to just drift for a few minutes. But Gail was ready. Slowly, as if inflated by some inner pump, she straightened in her chair, her arms and legs began to move again, and her eyes opened.

She smiled at both of us. "Jesus."

Megan chuckled. "Intense?"

"In a good way, yes. It's the first time I've thought about it without feeling the pain. It's like I finally got it all out in the open, where I can work on it."

Megan was nodding. "Excellent, excellent. That's just the way it should be. This ought to be a big step in your therapy."

But Gail was already looking at me. "You were right about the smell. So it definitely wasn't Vogel."

Chapter Twenty-Three

Gail passed her hand across her forehead lightly, as if making sure it was still attached. Megan Goss watched her carefully.

"So if Vogel wasn't the rapist, who was?"

"Do you accept absolutely that he wasn't?" Megan asked instead.

Gail thought about that for a while, gazing out the broad window at the steel bridge spanning the Connecticut River, lorded over by a gray sky, heavy with the first freak snowstorm of the year. "Yes, I do. It's hard, because it was easier having the man who'd assaulted me in jail, instead of still out there, but I see now it just wasn't him."

Megan nodded, apparently satisfied.

"Which brings up today's second major question," I said, addressing Megan. "Have you been able to come up with a psychological profile of the real rapist?"

She pursed her lips. "I haven't had much time for the kind of reflection I prefer. There is one crucial element here, though, that does help, and that's that whoever did the rape also went to enormous lengths to frame Bob Vogel. That tells me a great deal."

She took the file she'd been holding on her lap for the past few hours and laid it on the floor. "Also, I put great value on several aspects of Gail's account that may have already caught your eye, such as the whispering and the double use of masks—the pillowcase for her, the mask for him—and the almost mechanical methodology of his entire performance. The first two imply a fear of recognition, the third an imitative style. He seems to have forgotten himself only twice—once when he broke the plate that hung on the wall, and said, 'Shit'; and again when he beat Gail at the end and called her a 'snotty goddamn bitch.' That outburst, coupled with his inability to climax, seems to me to have been quite genuine."

"What's the significance of the plate?" Gail asked.

"It connects to the lack of damage to the other expensive items in the room, like the television set. Bob Vogel had an utter contempt for his victims, including everything they owned. This man likes fine, expensive things—things he either cannot afford, or couldn't afford when he was younger. The reference to a snotty bitch reinforces this, since those are words typically used to denigrate someone of a higher social standing than the speaker."

"What about the actual phrasing?" I asked. "Wouldn't Vogel have called her something a little more earthy than a snotty bitch?"

Goss nodded. "I think so. There is an effeminate quality there that Vogel doesn't display anywhere. That could be an important insight."

"God," Gail murmured, half to herself.

"I also think," Megan continued, "that the use of gloves is telling. Joe, you told me you thought the gloves were part of Vogel's learning curve, which could've been very possible. But I'm caught by the fact that the attacker wore them intermittently. He wanted to feel Gail—that's one of the reasons he removed all his clothing—but he didn't want to leave fingerprints or harm his hands when he beat her." She interrupted herself suddenly to consult the file on the floor. "Which reminds me, Gail . . . in the statement you gave Joe and Todd Lefevre, the beating is described as immediately following the snotty-bitch comment. Just now, when we got to that part, you mentioned a pause, during which he put the gloves back on. I think that pause is significant. If administering a beating was a normal part of his MO, it would have spontaneously followed the frustrated outburst—simple cause and effect. The fact that he paused to put on gloves tells me that the verbal outburst marked the end of the emotional spike, and that the beating was imitative again—that he was back under control, framing Vogel."

"So what's all that tell you?" I asked, spurred on by what I felt sure was a breakthrough, and eager for something I could actually use.

"I'd look for someone smart who likes nice things. Also a methodical type—maybe compulsively neat. And a loner."

"You mean he lives alone?"

She shook her head. "Not necessarily. He's a loner in his head, but the more perceptive around him will notice that about him." She seemed to hesitate a moment. When she resumed speaking, her attitude had shifted slightly. She sounded more removed, as if distancing herself a bit from her words. "Look, there is a generalized picture I can see in all this, but I'm worried that if I describe it, you'll take it too literally and perhaps miss the man you're after."

I gave her a slightly helpless expression. "What can I say?"

She let out a frustrated sigh. "All right. From what Gail told us, we know he's white and fairly trim. That would fit his personality, which includes keeping in shape, but in a solitary fashion, as with jogging or weight lifting. I'd say he's aged anywhere from his mid-twenties to his late thirties, but not any younger—his style shows maturity, a control over more youthful impulsiveness. And *control* is the operative word: He's meticulous, even rigid, which also means he presents himself physically that way—no torn jeans, untucked shirts, or weekend stubble. That's also where any effeminate characteristics might be noticed. And he probably collects something to satisfy this need, like stamps or coins, or what-have-you—something tidy and organized.

"All this camouflages a restless, anguished, insecure, and very violent inner man, whose hatred of women dates way back, and whose violence comes out as revenge against a sex for whom he has nothing but contempt." She lifted a cautionary finger at me. "But there again you'll have to watch out, because little or nothing of that will show. This man is a born performer—an actor's actor. He'll date women, woo their socks off, and might even have once been, or still be, married—and not necessarily to a mousy, retiring type. Some of these men go after strong women. Whatever the case there, however, I'll all but guarantee that if you can find out about his youth, you'll find he comes from a family with serious psychological problems."

Megan Goss picked up her thick file and placed it on the desk. I turned off the tape recorder I'd had running from the start of our visit, and rose.

She shook my hand and gave Gail a hug. "I hope you get him soon. Because if I'm right, and you don't, he'll be back—maybe as a killer."

I thought at first that the crowd had dispersed around the Municipal Building, either from boredom or because something had lured it away. But the parking lot was still suspiciously full, forcing me to park illegally on the edge of a grass embankment. Entering the building supplied the explanation—the hallway between the patrol/administration side and the detective squad of the police department was lined with a small army of irritable reporters.

I hadn't made it three feet past the door before a sharp-eyed young woman leapt to her feet from one of the benches. "Lieutenant Gunther, could we ask you a few questions?"

I shook my head at the gathering knot of people she'd stimulated. "Not if you want any answers."

"Where have you been all day? You digging into something new?"

"Rumor has it all this is part of a feud between you and the state's attorney. Any truth to that?"

"None whatsoever," I was stupid enough to answer, adding fuel to the fire. I had planned to retire to my office, but instead I headed directly for Ron Klesczewski's command center.

"You're being credited as the one who undermined Dunn's case in court. Why did you wait till the last second?"

"The case was thrown out because the search warrant was invalidated. Does that mean Bob Vogel is still your number-one suspect?"

Ron Klesczewski looked up at the sudden swell of voices at the door, his face drawn and tired. He smiled at me from behind his long, folder-strewn table, and waited until I'd shut the door firmly behind me. "You're a welcome sight."

"Feeling a little besieged?"

"When I want to use the john, I wait till the last second so I can combine two trips in one. You hear the press conference on the radio?"

I shook my head.

"Not good. It came out sounding like we weren't sure if we had the right guy but blew the evidence, or had the wrong guy and were after somebody else. The chief stood by you. Made you sound like the Lone Ranger, fighting for truth and justice. 'Course, that didn't make Dunn look too good. You could tell the two of them weren't getting along. The press ate it up."

I pulled the tapes I'd made at Megan Goss's out of my pocket. "Harriet around?"

"Yeah—I put her in there." He jerked his thumb at a tiny cubbyhole office that filled one corner of the large room. "All our calls are being transferred in here, too. What's that?"

"More proof that Vogel didn't do it. I want her to transcribe it. What've you heard back from our people?"

"We're supposed to have an update conference at four."

I checked my watch. "Bring 'em in now. Maybe I can cut down on their workload."

The setting was less formal than before. People sat on chairs, on the edges of tables; a few were on the floor with their backs to the wall. In all, there were over a dozen of them—detectives, patrolmen in plain clothes, and, inevitably, Brandt and Lefevre.

I felt an odd combination of skepticism and excitement mingling in the air. "I apologize for yanking you back here on short notice, but I think it'll be worth your while. Harriet's been typing a transcript of a conversation Megan Goss had with Gail Zigman this morning after putting her under hypnosis. As a result of that session, we've been able to get a more detailed description of the man we're after."

I paused for theatrical effect. "He's of medium build, flat stomach, no chest hair—although that could have been shaved off for the occasion—between twenty-five and forty, meticulously neat. He also doesn't smell like a stray dog, which ought to rule out Bob Vogel if nothing else does."

There was a polite ripple of muted laughter. "Based on the fact, therefore, that Vogel was carefully framed, I had Goss draw up a psychological profile of the type of man we're after. I want to use that profile to narrow down our suspects to a revised A-list."

"We throwing out the names that don't fit?" Kunkle asked skeptically.

"Just moving them to the back. Criminal profiling is a good, time-tested tool, but it's not always accurate. However, since we've got one, we might as well use it. If we don't get any hits, we'll go back to knocking on doors."

I looked around, as if inviting debate, but I knew the simplicity of the rationale had already won them over. It would mean a hell of lot less work if it worked—never the worst incentive to a beleaguered, tired, uncertain team.

"All right, let's deal with the solid evidence first—rule out the extremes. Who's got anyone with either a real gut or who's skinny as a rail?"

One of the patrolmen raised his hand tentatively. "I had Barry Gilchrist. He's pretty scrawny—looks like he's starving."

I nodded. "Okay. He gets bumped. Anyone else?"

Encouraged, another one said, "Lonny Sorvin's a porker."

Three more names were added to the pile, for one reason or the other.

"Five down," I said. "Okay. Goss said that, in all likelihood, we're after a loner who's compulsively neat, highly intelligent, likes nice things, and who keeps fit doing a solitary activity, like jogging or weight lifting. She also thinks he probably collects things—stamps, coins, or something similar."

"Well, unless it's empty beer cans, that lets out Harry Murchison," Willy called out. "He and his girlfriend live like pigs, and he's dumb as dirt."

The laughter that followed was accompanied by several more folders being put aside.

"Who do we have left?" I asked.

"There's still Jason Ryan," Sammie spoke up. "He's thin, compulsive, hates women, rides a bike, and doesn't have an alibi."

"He's also nuts," someone added.

J.P. waved a folder in the air. "Philip Duncan fits, and he was on Gail's original list, but he has an alibi. On the night of the assault, he was at that office party until 2:30 A.M.—lots of witnesses, including Mark Sumner. Of course, Sumner's on the list, too, and also fits, but of the two of them, I like Duncan better. The realty office they work at is just a few yards away from where those photos were taken of Gail, but at the time, Sumner was showing a property up near Newfane. Duncan claimed he was working at his desk. Said he didn't see anyone wandering around the sidewalk with a camera." Tyler's skepticism showed in his voice.

I thought of how the buildings were arranged on that street. "You can see the entrance to Gail's building from that office, can't you?"

Tyler raised his eyebrows. "You can see it from Duncan's desk."

There was a slight lull, which Tyler filled reluctantly, forced by his scientific mind to redress some balance. "The downside to Duncan being our man is still his alibi for the night of the rape. That and the fact that whoever put this whole frame together is too smart to be caught taking pictures of his target in broad daylight on a busy street."

"Maybe," I answered. "Maybe not. Concentrate on Duncan. See if he slipped out of the party early. It could be people just assumed he was there when he wasn't."

Tyler wrote a note to himself. I looked around the room. "Who else?"

"Richard Clark," one of Billy's men said. "The alibi's pretty wobbly—the whole family shares a huge bed—'the community bed,' they call it—but that night, it was only his daughter and him, and she can't swear he was there all night."

There was a predictable amount of snickering at that one, followed by Sammie saying, "Johnston Hill was arranging his mother's funeral, but the witnesses he mentioned when we first questioned him are starting to go soft—they either don't want to get involved or they're lying."

"That it?" I asked, checking the list I'd been keeping. "Ryan, Duncan, Sumner, Clark, and Hill. What were Ryan and the last two doing when the photographs were taken?"

Sammie and the patrolman who'd reported on Clark began flipping through their files. Ron answered for them. "I've been keeping track of that. Sumner's the only one who comes out squeaky clean. The rest of them are like Duncan—they were either at work, with no solid alibis, or doing something downtown that could've given them enough time to duck out and take a few shots."

"Which makes Sumner kind of stand out," Willy muttered.

"That's true," I agreed. "He may have an alibi because he knew he'd need it. That would fit a careful planner. Do any of the five of them have priors?"

Ron answered again. "Well . . . Ryan, of course. None of the others do."

"You said the profile calls for a loner. Does that mean he's not married?" Sammie asked.

I shook my head. "Not necessarily. The implication was that he tends to keep to himself more than not, but he could be the ultimate actor, able to play any role he liked."

Kunkle was obviously tiring of all the abstractions. "So what the hell're we supposed to do? Bust the tidiest one with the highest IQ?"

"Goss's recommendation," I answered, "was that since we know this man hates women, we might get lucky using an aggressive woman to punch his buttons."

I bowed slightly to Sammie. "I'd like to send you in to interview each of these men—at their homes, if possible, so you can look around a bit. Really turn the heat up under them—make each one think he's our primary suspect, that we're on the brink of making an arrest. You'll be wearing a wire at each interview, of course, and have a backup team of a detective and a plain-clothes patrol officer that'll remain behind to tail the suspect afterward. Goss thinks those who are innocent will most likely run to their lawyers, the board of selectmen, or whoever, to raise a stink." I turned to Brandt. "Which means you better warn the town manager he might be getting some calls.

"Conversely, she also thinks the one we're after will probably sit tight and bide his time. If it works out that way, it might save us some wear and tear, and allow us to focus on one individual."

"I'll give it a shot," Sammie said without hesitation.

"That may be what you get," Willy countered. "If this man really does have a thing against women, and we convince him he's got nowhere to turn, what's to stop him from blowing your head off?"

There was a moment's silence as we all considered the strong possibility that he could be right.

"We'll just take precautions," Tony finally said softly.

But everyone knew better than to take too much comfort in that.

Chapter Twenty-Four

As promised, it was snowing—large, featherlike flakes, falling so gently, they seemed unsure they wanted to land at all. When they did, however, they stuck, the ground being cold enough to keep them from melting. Not only was this the earliest preseason snowfall I'd ever seen, it had already covered the ground with a good two inches.

I hit the windshield wipers to clear my view of Johnston Hill's elongated split-level Harris Avenue home. I was parked, motor running but lights out, about three houses south. Tyler and one of Billy's patrolmen were north of me in Tyler's personal vehicle. All three of us were listening to Sammie Martens grilling Hill.

Her approach was similar to what she'd used on Philip Duncan an hour earlier, and on Richard Clark and Mark Sumner at the beginning of this process. And Johnston Hill was reacting similarly to Clark and Sumner, too—helpful at first, then apparently stunned into shocked disbelief, and finally flailing in anger and outrage.

She was very good, her voice reeking of suspicion, her theatrical pauses of blatant incredulity. She wielded her pointed, accusatory questions like a stick to keep them off balance. I could picture her dark, intense expression adding to her impassioned fierceness.

And it was working. Each of the men had reacted to the pressure. Even Philip Duncan—the coolest of the three—had finally demanded she leave his house, albeit without fanfare. Richard Clark— he of the community bed—had become hysterical, falling apart when she'd asked him who slept where, what they wore, and—more insinuating—what they didn't. But since their sleeping arrangement had been used as an alibi, he couldn't force her to drop the subject. He'd finally admitted that there were times he was driven—by claustrophobia, by incestuous fantasy, by the futile desire to make love privately to his wife—to seek the solace of the couch downstairs.

On the night in question, he and his thirteen-year-old daughter had been alone—his wife and other child having stayed at his in-laws' house for the night. Sammie had probed and prodded at the man's growing discomfort, until he'd ended up admitting that he'd spent the night alone downstairs, and that in fact he did not have the alibi he'd claimed.

Mark Sumner had been less vulnerable. Not only was his alibi buttressed by other witnesses at the office party, but his trip to Newfane on the day of Gail's surreptitious photo session had been prompted by an unexpected call from prospective clients. Sumner had left his office on the spur of the moment to cater to them—a spontaneous scenario we hadn't been able to discredit, despite working the phones all afternoon. Nevertheless, Sammie had given it her best, going after his being a thirty-year-old bachelor, a solitary drinker, a man who saw Gail as a rival realtor and a success where he was not. Sumner had ended the conversation by calling his lawyer then and there, forcing Sammie to either get on the line and be specific, or leave.

Duncan had been the standout. At first friendly—even charming—he'd quickly become almost robotically aloof, refusing to rise to Sammie's bait. With growing tension, we'd sat in our darkened vehicles, keyed to Sammie's microphone, listening to a floundering interview die against a wall of cold antagonism. By barely saying a word, Duncan had controlled the conversation. When I'd debriefed Sammie immediately afterward, she'd been shaken—even fearful—and very happy to be away from him.

This had not come as a total surprise. All afternoon, Tyler and I had focused on Philip Duncan, running his name through our computer, talking to his colleagues, calling up his friends—all stimulated by the small bell that had gone off in my head when I'd heard he had a view of Gail's office from his desk. What had emerged was a pristine model citizen with a nightmarish child-hood—a man about whom several people told me, "I can't believe he turned out so well."

Unfortunately, that Boston childhood had been routinely brutal. Duncan had been born into a poor family with multiple and tran-sient fathers, an alcoholic mother, in a neighborhood on the ropes. As a youngster, he and one sister had been legally adopted by a domineering and abusive aunt, and gone to live north of the city, where he'd grown up silent, private, and rigidly self-controlled. He'd left home as soon as he'd been legally able, and had never returned since.

The sister, with whom he still kept in touch, lived in Greenfield. She'd moved there just before Robert Vogel had raped Katherine Rawlins.

Shortly before we'd sent Sammie out on her interviews, I'd tele-phoned Gail to ask her again why Duncan's name had appeared on her list. Speaking to Ron weeks earlier, she'd merely said that Duncan gave her the creeps, and, given her state then, we hadn't pushed her for more.

This time, she went into more detail. "I don't know if it'll help, but a few years ago, Ethan Allen Realty had an exclusive listing on a million-dollar estate in Hillwinds. It was Phil Duncan's ac-count, and he couldn't get it to move. He kept urging the owners to lower their price. They eventually got tired of him and came to me, and I sold it within a month. It was a pretty standard deal—no breaches of contract or anything—but I guess Ethan Allen was suffering, so the loss was felt generally. Sumner was pretty unpleas-ant about it—and has been ever since—which is one of the reasons he made it on the list. But Duncan was weird. He confronted me on the street afterward, all smiles and charm, and said he now knew what it felt like to be violated."

"In those exact words?"

"Close enough. But it was the way he said it—kidding around, but cold, too, like it was some private bad joke. I found the comparison offensive. I told him I seriously doubted it, and we parted company. As far as I know, we've never spoken since, and whenever we see each other around town, he makes it a point to avoid me."

I'd questioned her further, but that had been the total gist of it—from Gail, from my own research, and from Sammie after her interview—an accumulation of muted alarms, not one of them loud enough to allow us to do more than we were already doing. I had people back at the station still checking computer files and making phone calls about Duncan, but right now, our current plan seemed as potentially fruitful as any. It also helped us avoid the same trap we'd fallen into with Vogel, of focusing on one man too much and too early.

Still, I had taken the precaution of assigning Klesczewski and Kunkle to watch Duncan's house, instead of the one-detective/one-patrolman teams all the other suspects were assigned.

Now, as I sat in my car listening to Sammie's tinny, metallic voice over the small tape recorder/receiver on the seat beside me, I kept reviewing what we knew of Phil Duncan, hoping to catch a glimpse of some metaphorical chameleon, waiting to be seen . . . Then, as I reached for the receiver's volume control with my left hand, I simultaneously made a grab for my gloves with my right as they slid off the seat.

I froze in mid-motion, my thoughts suddenly crystallized around a similar ungainliness on the night of Gail's attack.

"Which hand did he use to cover your face?" Megan Goss had asked Gail in the depths of her hypnotic state.

"His right," she'd answered, which had surprised me at the time. I mimicked the motion now, using my right hand to push an imaginary face to my right, struck as I had been then by the unnaturalness of the gesture. If I had been the rapist, and had suddenly seen Gail looking at me, I would have pushed her head aside in a crossover movement—moving her face from my right to hers—rather than defeating my own momentum by reversing directions.

Unless I'd *intended* her to see the clock—so that she could become my alibi.

I switched on my headlights, and drove up alongside Tyler's car. Marshall Smith, the patrolman accompanying Tyler, rolled down his window. "What's up?"

I handed him the small case holding the receiver and tape recorder. "I've got to make a phone call. You're on your own."

I pulled out into the Putney Road and turned left, heading

downtown. On my portable radio, I called up Ron Klesczewski. He and Willy were in his car, outside Philip Duncan's house on Allerton Avenue, a middle-class, dead-end street paralleling the interstate. "You had any movement lately?"

"Nothing."

"But he's still there, right?"

"As far as we know."

I pulled into a service station across the intersection from my office, parking opposite a pay phone. I didn't want to risk meeting any reporters at the Municipal Building.

The snow was falling heavily now, making even the nearby phone booth ghostly and ephemeral, drifting in and out of view at the whimsy of the wind.

I dialed Gail's number at the friend's house where she was staying on Lamson Street, far from her own home, her office, or Susan Raffner's, all of which had been besieged by the press.

She answered on the first ring.

"I need to ask you something about the night you were attacked—something we missed at Megan's."

"All right," she answered cautiously, surprised by my urgency.

"Can you think back to before you woke up—before you realized someone was on top of you?"

"What am I looking for?"

I didn't want to suggest the answer I was after. "Sounds."

I heard the phone being put down, and imagined Gail settling into a chair, making herself comfortable, perhaps closing her eyes. There was a silence of several minutes, during which I became covered with snow.

Her voice, when it finally came back on, was hard-edged with excitement. "It's the clock, isn't it?"

"What did you hear?"

"The same sounds I make when I reset it."

I let out a sigh of relief. "He had to change the time to establish his alibi. Then he had to make sure you saw the clock before he pulled the pillowcase over your head. He must have changed it back when he went on the rampage later, making enough noise to hide what he was doing."

She hesitated a moment, before adding, "So who needed that kind of alibi?"

"If my hunch is right, it's Philip Duncan—but we're going to have to dig deep to prove it."

"Here we go again," she murmured.

"You still have Mary Wallis's gun?"

Her melancholy was replaced by surprise. "Yes. Why?"

"We're trying to push a few of the suspects into tipping their hand. Duncan among them. Megan said whoever it was would probably just hunker down under pressure—and that's what he seems to be doing—it just never hurts to be cautious. I'll call you as soon as I know more."

I hung up and got back into my car, dusting off the snow. I was about to leave the filling station to join Ron at Duncan's house when I was abruptly filled with a sense of foreboding, as if the very mixture of warning and solace I'd given Gail had circled back on itself and settled on my chest.

I keyed the radio next to me, foregoing the formalized language we normally used. "Ron, you there?"

Ron's voice came back, mildly surprised. "Yeah. What's up?"

"Knock on Duncan's door—see if he's home."

"What do I say if he is?"

"Just wish him sweet dreams. Let him know you're there."

"10-4."

I got back out of the car and dialed Megan Goss's number, suddenly stimulated by what she'd said earlier. "Besides sitting put," I asked her after she'd picked up, "what might Gail's attacker do under pressure? Sammie's been pushing these guys pretty hard. And she's getting reactions, except from one of them. He just politely lost his sense of humor and showed her the door. Never showed a spark."

Goss considered that for a moment. When she answered, it was with an element of anxiety. "The rape dealt more with power than with sex or violence. That's why I suspected the rapist wouldn't act again until he felt a renewed need to dominate. If properly stimulated, though, he could snap. His repressed violent instincts could overwhelm his cunning, and turn him into a killer with no thought of consequence."

That might've been nice to hear a little earlier, I thought. I hung up the phone angrily, thinking of Gail in a remote house with no police protection. Could Duncan know where she was? I remembered the inconsequential sound I'd heard on the darkened Wardsboro Road, looking for oil stains . . . And another, similarly furtive noise from the far end of the municipal parking lot as Katz and I ended our conversation last night.

I ran for my car, realizing with a cold fear that our man had taken his precautions, following me, following Gail. If Goss was right, and Duncan did snap, wouldn't his target be the very person whose attack had put him in jeopardy?

Driving the slick expanse of Main Street as fast as I could with one hand, I reached for the portable radio next to me. "Ron. Is he there or not?"

What traffic existed was bunching up at the primary intersection of High and Main, cowed by the unexpected conditions. I decided to cut right onto Grove Street and use the residential back streets.

"Joe?" Ron's voice sounded tentative.

"Did you find him?"

I pulled hard on the wheel, and felt the back of the car swing wide on summer tires, sliding into the opposite lane, into the path of an oncoming minivan. I grabbed the wheel with both hands, dropping the radio onto the floor, and managed to fishtail away from a collision, accompanied by the plaintive howl of an offended horn.

Ron's voice eddied up from between my feet. "I tried the door. There's no answer. We're circling the building now, looking for tracks."

I groped around for the radio between my feet, and finally brought it back up to my mouth. As I did so, I noticed its antenna was bent at an extreme angle, the stem connecting it to the frame cracked like a half-broken pencil. "I think he's headed for number twenty, Lamson Street. If he's gone, meet me there. He could be after Gail again."

I put the radio down more carefully and swung onto Oak, gunning the engine to pull out of another skid.

"We found some fresh tracks, Joe, leading from a side window. I guess he flew the coop. Should we do a forceful entry?"

I swore, and tried fumbling with the antenna. It came off in my hand.

I took the next corner haphazardly, this time sideswiping another car waiting at the four-way stop. Spinning away from the sound of crumpled metal and fractured plastic, I sped up the hill to where High becomes Western, and where Union takes a precipitous left-hand plunge into the narrow Whetstone Brook ravine.

I gave the radio one last try. "Ron, goddamn it, get your ass to Lamson Street."

"Joe? You there?"

I threw the radio aside in disgust, cursing a department budget that required personal vehicles for undercover work, and couldn't equip them with dash-mounted mobile radios.

Whetstone Brook cuts through Brattleboro from west to east in a thin, ragged laceration, along an ancient riverbed, the depth and breadth of which are reminders of a far more aggressive ancestor. The ravine walls that line the brook are at points almost sixty feet high and several hundred feet apart, making the town utterly dependent on a few key bridges for easy cross-access. There are enough of these crossings, however, to make the Whetstone as a barrier all but unnoticed by most of the population. I was hoping Philip Duncan, whom I assumed was on foot, had discovered just the opposite.

Union Street is precipitously steep, literally plunging downhill, and with a couple of challenging curves thrown in for good measure. It offers rooftop views of the houses tucked below, presenting a very real threat of some car hurtling through the old wooden guard-rail, and crowning one of the hapless homes like a hellish version of Santa's sleigh. The town's sand trucks usually make Union Street their first stop in a snowstorm.

Except that this one had hit so early, those trucks hadn't even been mounted with plows yet, much less loaded with sand.

As I nosed over the edge off of Western Avenue, I felt the car balancing between the pull of gravity and the resistance of the road. I knew from painful experience how slight this margin was—how one small mishap could cause a momentum to build that only a large, heavy, possibly lethal object could stop. The car's heater began to feel like a sauna as I strained at the wheel, my eyes glued to the swirling funnel of falling snowflakes that swept past the windshield, as if the wind itself was trying to push me back.

Of all the questions assaulting me now, the primary one concerned the size of Duncan's head start. Whetstone Brook was but one of Brattleboro's geographical obstacles; the other was Interstate

91, running on a north-south axis. Between the two of them, they cut the town into quadrants. They'd also turned some neighborhoods into cul-de-sacs, especially near the center where they intersected. Lawson Street was wedged into the southeast corner, far below I-91's embankment, and teetering high above the Whetstone's fast-flowing waters. Thinking only to shield Gail from the public's prying eye, I'd left her alone instead, in a corner pocket with only one easy way out.

Halfway down Union the car slowly sloughed off to the side, coming up against the guardrail. I took advantage of the movement to accelerate rather than brake, and rode along the barrier, tearing at the side of the car, until the rear wheels regained their grip.

I fought to swallow the bitter irony that I might have stimulated Gail's tormentor to show himself, only to incite him to greater violence. That possibility, coupled with the fact that he'd been given a healthy head start, blinded what caution remained in me. Impatient with the snow and the fear it instilled, I finally just gunned the car and sent it hurtling down the rest of the hill, sliding sideways into the five-way intersection at the bottom, rear wheels spinning frantically. I shot across the narrow bridge spanning the river, and used the car's own dead weight to sling myself halfway up the hill on the opposite side, realizing only peripherally how lucky I'd been that no other car had been in my way.

The thick snowflakes were no longer fighting gravity like feathers in an updraft. They formed instead a pale, tattered blanket, and I drove through it like a child running among his mother's windblown laundry, the white sheets wet and clinging, blocking my sight with suffocating efficiency.

The houses to either side of me vanished from my peripheral vision, and the twisting, slippery, snow-clogged streets became a series of interconnected tunnels, as glittering as the headlights they reflected. Staring at the mesmerizing, swirling vortex so hard it hurt my eyes, I began to feel I was falling through the storm, and that the wheel I clenched in my hands was no more functional than the restraining bar on a roller-coaster. Ron's voice, and those of others he was talking to, trying to locate me, faded away into the background.

I circled ever closer to Gail, across the water to the south bank, up Estey Street and around to Chestnut, almost to where it dead-ended against the interstate, and to the right again down Lawson—short, narrow, and pointing like a finger at a precipitous, sixty-foot plunge into the foaming Whetstone, newly thrashed into white water by a brief, stony falls a half mile upstream.

I saw her car first, cloaked peacefully in snow, parked before the old wooden home of mutual friends who were out of town for a few weeks. Windows were glowing along the first floor, the porch light reflecting off the knifelike shards from the front door's shattered right sidelight, the one nearest the deadbolt.

I was out of the car before I knew what I was doing, and stopped halfway to the house, torn between impulse and training—the latter telling me to go next door, to find a phone, to get back-up . . . and to run the risk that in that time, Gail would be made a victim all over again—this time, perhaps of murder. I continued up the steps.

The doorknob turned noiselessly in my hand, and I quietly stepped inside, avoiding the broken glass to my right. Snowy footsteps, barely melting and broadly spaced as if from someone running, led toward the rear of the building, to beyond the closed kitchen door. Standing still and silent, I could hear the murmur of tense, angry voices.

I pulled my gun from its holster and gently went down the hall, constrained by the knowledge that this was the only access to the kitchen from the front of the house. At the thick wooden door, while the two voices were still too muffled to understand, I could tell Duncan's was closer than Gail's, giving me hope that I might be able to come up behind him.

It wasn't much, but it didn't matter in any case. A sudden shout by Gail ended the debate, and sent me flying through the door in a low crouch.

What I saw was later crystallized in my memory as a portrait of matched opponents: Phil Duncan, still in his overcoat dusted with snow, holding a knife, his face set with almost demonic determination, and Gail, in jeans and a turtleneck, armed with a carving knife, facing him with equal aggression. Both stood like combatants, a small table between them, highlighted like prizefighters by the harsh fluorescent panels overhead.

That portrait, however, lasted only a split second. Carried by the momentum of my entrance, I overcompensated bringing my gun around to bear on Duncan and staggered against one of the kitchen chairs.

It was all he needed to drop low and throw his weight against the table, sending one corner of it into the pit of my stomach.

The pain seemed to lift me up like an explosion, blinding me, deafening me, sending my mind reeling back to a dark, dank tunnel far underground. Now as then, I couldn't feel the floor as it came up to catch me, nor could I operate the gun in my hand. I could only watch as Duncan moved to my side, as swift as a cat, and see Gail, who turned and ran to the far side of the room, disappearing from my line of view behind the upended chair now before me.

One foot on my gun hand, the blade of his knife held just under my eye, slanted toward my brain, Duncan pushed the chair aside to reveal Gail standing by the back door, near a row of hanging coats, Mary Wallis's pistol in her hand.

Fighting to overcome the white-hot pain from my reopened stomach, I heard him address her in a careless, mocking voice. "Drop it, or the knife goes in."

Gail shifted slightly, setting her feet better, bringing her other hand up to clasp the gun in a classic shooter's stance. Despite the anxiety on her face, the pistol didn't waver.

"He either dies for your dubious virtue, or I let him live to see you get one last good fuck—right here, on the floor. What do you say?" Arrogant to the end, he slowly reached for the pistol near my immobilized hand.

"I don't think so."

The shot exploded off the walls, instantly matched by Duncan's high-pitched, hysterical scream, filled with agony and outrage. The knife vanished from my cheek as he was spun away from me by the force of the bullet smacking his kneecap, its blood splattering us both.

He rolled on the floor near the corner, both hands trying to contain the devastating damage, covered with blood and splinters of bone. He screamed, over and over, his pale face contorted. "You bitch. You fucking bitch. You think this is going to end it?"

"I hope not," she finally answered, "it's your turn now." And she reached for the phone.

Chapter Twenty-Five

Nurse Elizabeth Pace came into the hospital room, and seeing Gail sitting next to my bed, she checked the catheter in my forearm, closed off the line, and replaced the near-empty bag with a new one. "I heard tell you were unkillable, Lieutenant. You're not trying to test that theory, are you?"

I smiled weakly. "Not willingly."

She filled out something on a clipboard and then fixed us both with a clinical eye. "Good, because you almost flunked this time." She reached over and squeezed Gail's hand. "How about you? Over the worst of it?"

Gail nodded. "Getting there. Thank you."

Pace nodded, smiled, and left us alone.

It was more than a week later—my first day out of ICU. Philip Duncan, crippled and in another part of the same hospital, had confessed to the rape, basking in his cleverness. We'd already located a court clerk in Greenfield, who remembered him spending hours going over the public records there, exhibiting a keen interest in Bob Vogel—a man whose style he could copy, and whose fate he could seal. And now that we knew who to look for, we'd found other evidence of Duncan's stalking of Vogel—a sighting of him near the yard man's garage, at the time of the fire; a screwdriver in the trunk of his car, smeared with the same motor oil Vogel used; a receipt for malleable molding wax. Still, a confession never hurts.

Of course, Duncan's plan had called for Vogel to wind up back in prison, and when our case had begun to unravel, so had Duncan's debatable grasp on reality. By the time Sammie Martens had provoked him in his home, the cold-blooded ruthlessness that had served him so well turned on itself and had sent him raging into the storm.

Goss had been right about the rapist's penchant for collecting. When Tyler had led a team into Duncan's home, they had found not coins or stamps or Early American milk bottles, but keys. Over the years, greatly aided by a profession which gave him access to hundreds of houses and dozens of other realtors, Duncan had copied, labeled, and collected keys. At night, recreationally, as some men go to bars or the movies, he would enter other people's homes—usually those belonging to single women. What he did there still wasn't clear; Megan suspected that he probably masturbated or walked around the places naked, establishing a bizarre, private ascendancy over the owners. But Duncan himself wasn't talking about that yet. What mattered to us was that one of those keys had Gail's name on it.

All of which made Stanley Katz a very happy editor. With the furor following Duncan's arrest dying down, most of the out-of-town media had headed home. Tony Brandt had made a point of giving Katz everything he could on the case, and making the *Reformer* the news conduit to the rest of the world—or that part of it which still showed any interest. The effects of this on the *Reformer*'s future were yet to come, but in the meantime, press/police relations had never been cozier.

Things had not turned out as successfully for James Dunn. On the second Tuesday of a snow-free, balmy November, with the season's first storm a mere freak of nature for future almanacs, Jack Derby had been elected the new state's attorney for Windham County by a considerable margin.

Gail had also made political news. She'd resigned from the board of selectmen and announced her intention to return to law school, resuming an educational path she'd interrupted twenty-five years ago to "drop out," and move to Brattleboro.

She'd been detailing her plans when Elizabeth Pace had come in to check on me. "There's something else," she added, once we were alone. "I think I'll sell the house."

It didn't come as a surprise. Her persistent reluctance to do more than drop by and pick up the odd item or two had warned me of that. But it still caused a cool tremor to run through me. Combined with her school plans, the sale of her home didn't bode well for her staying in the area.

I thought back over the past two months, at the limits to which we'd been pushed, individually and as a couple—at how much I'd come to see her as an integral part of my life.

But apparently those were my feelings alone, and since we'd never made any overt commitments to each other when we could— determinedly living apart and maintaining our "freedom"—I now felt the swelling grief of an opportunity lost forever, sacrificed to selfish notions of independence.

I nodded quietly, suppressing this private turmoil. "Makes sense."

She reached over and took my hand. I felt a hesitancy on her part, and braced myself for the inevitable. "You may not think so in a minute, and maybe this isn't the best time to hit you with this . . ." She paused, searching for the right words.

I squeezed her fingers, spurred on by a sudden impatience. "Go ahead. We can sort it out afterward."

She chuckled, throwing me off guard. "Okay. What do you say we move in together? Get a place of our own?"

I stared at her openmouthed.

She spoke quickly, as if trying to outrun my anticipated rejection. "I'm not talking about marriage, and I'd still have to have my own space—a study or a couple of rooms—so we'd both still have lots of breathing room, like before . . . I realize it would mean giving up your apartment . . ." Her voice trailed off.

I lay my head back on the pillow, slightly giddy at this emotional turnabout.

Gail watched me closely. "Would you be interested?" Her face was a mixture of hopefulness and doubt.

I smiled at her, sharing her feelings, willing to put my trust in the former. "Yes. I would."